Rise

GRACE IRWIN

© 2024 Grace Irwin. All rights reserved.
This book is a work of fiction. Any names, characters, companies, organizations, places, events, locales, and incidents are either used in a fictitious manner or are fictional.

Any resemblance to actual persons, living or dead, actual companies or organizations, or actual events is purely coincidental.

For rights and permissions, please contact:
Grace Irwin
2827 Midway Rd SE, STE 106
PMB 225
Bolivia, 28422

Scripture quotations are taken from the *Holy Bible*, King James Version, originally published 1769. All rights reserved.

ISBN: 979-8-8732702-4-8

Chapter One

EMMALINE SPUN AROUND and around like a dreidel. The music fluttered and crooned in her ears. Mama's fingers leapt across the piano keys. Emmaline danced in a circle, hand-in-hand with her sisters and brother. Mama sang and Papa laughed.

"Spin me, spin me!" her brother James begged her sister Rose.

"All right, all right." Rose smiled and spun little James around.

Emmaline took turns dancing with Kathleen and Charlotte. She danced and danced. The fire crackled in the hearth. The candles flickered in the chandelier. The moonlight stretched across the floor.

Papa snuck a kiss on Mama's cheek as Emmaline

and her siblings joined hands. They skipped in a circle until the room spun around them. Emmaline laughed.

Glass shattered as something soared across the room. Mama cried out, the piano playing ending with a discordant note. Emmaline stood with her sisters and James, huddled together. Papa drew a sword from the wall and stood in front of Mama. No one spoke.

The door fell to the ground with a roaring thud. Like a wave spreading across the shore, dozens of soldiers swarmed into the room. Emmaline held her breath. The Great War had finally snaked into their country, slunk over her family's threshold. They had come, just like they said they would.

One of the men, wearing a short mustache, commanded Papa to drop his sword. The sword clanged against the floor as it fell. Papa scowled at the man.

The mustached man stared at James. He motioned at her brother to come to him. James's mouth hung open, his lips trembling and his eyes large. He glanced at Mama and Papa.

"No, James!" Mama cried.

"Silence, woman!" The mustached man motioned again for James.

Emmaline reached out her hand to keep her brother from obeying the man, but her fingers slipped from James's shoulder as if he couldn't feel them. He walked toward the man, his every step slow and delayed. The man sneered at James. He pulled out a gun from his coat and pressed the barrel to James's forehead. Emmaline froze, unable to join in her sisters' screams.

"You shall be the first to die, boy," the mustached man said. The gun roared. James crumbled to the floor, blood pooling around his head.

Emmaline screamed then, burying her face in Charlotte's shoulder. Mama ran to James's body. His blood soaked her favorite white rug. She pressed his face against her breast and wailed. The mustached man moved toward Mama and cocked his gun. Papa lunged forward but some of the soldiers held him back. Another shot echoed against the ceilings, and Mama fell to the floor.

Papa roared in fury.

The mustached man glanced up from Mama's and James's dead bodies. His eyes roved, setting hungrily on Rose. He ripped her away from her sisters. As Rose screamed and flailed her arms, Papa tore himself away from the soldiers' grip and threw the mustached man to the floor. He wrestled hard with him. The soldiers circled him like a wolf pack and pounced, defending their leader. He glanced up at the girls. "Run, now!"

Emmaline didn't want to leave, but Kathleen snatched her hand and yanked her away from the den. As they made their escape down the hall, another gunshot rang out. Emmaline forced herself not to scream. *Papa.*

Emmaline didn't recognize the halls as she ran through them. The walls shook with gunfire and thundering soldiers. The floors crawled with long shadows. This wasn't the house she grew up in, the house that had kept her safe from the cold and rain. Now, it betrayed her every step, echoed her every move.

She jumped through an open doorway with her sisters. Boots rumbled behind them.

"Go, go, behind the couch!" Kathleen whispered.

Rose and Charlotte whimpered as they all hid. Countless tears rushed down Emmaline's face. She had to calm herself. If she breathed too heavily, they would hear her. They would kill her and her sisters.

Tears were falling down Rose's pretty face. The bodice of her white dress, now soiled and ruined, was torn down the middle. Kathleen held her and spoke soft words. Emmaline and Charlotte stared at each other in stunned silence. *James. Mama. Papa.*

Footsteps pounded down the hall. Several men passed by the door. Emmaline squeezed her eyes shut. *Please, God. Please, don't let one of them come in here.*

The floor creaked. Leather boots whispered on the ground. A man's heavy breathing chilled Emmaline's blood. He breathed like a ravenous wolf. Rose tucked her face against Kathleen's chest. Charlotte reached a trembling hand to Emmaline's.

The boots were closer now. Charlotte squeezed her hand tightly. The clock in the room ticked. *Tick. Tick. Tick. Tick.* The pendulum swung back and forth. Everything else was silent.

Emmaline glanced at the wall next to her. A mirror

hung there, and she caught a glimpse of the man's face: skin like the moon and eyes like the night sky. He had no mustache, like the other man. Everything else was shadow.

The boots stopped moving. Emmaline's heart roared in her ears.

The couch was ripped from the floor and flew across the room. Rose screamed. Emmaline looked up and saw the eyes of death. His smile gnashed at them like a wolverine. He stood over them, tall and ready to sink his teeth into them.

He had a gun. Rose wouldn't stop screaming. He shot her in the leg. She screamed again, then squeezed her bleeding leg and wailed. Kathleen grabbed a bust sculpture and threw it at him. He fell to the ground but quickly stood to his feet.

Emmaline leapt up and kicked the man in the knee. The man howled and snarled curses. She grabbed at the gun but he pulled the trigger over her shoulder. Rose fell over, unmoving.

"*No!*" Emmaline screamed.

Kathleen fell to Rose's side and sobbed over her body. Emmaline wrestled his arms even harder now. Charlotte helped her and tackled him so roughly that he couldn't stand straight. Another shot roared in Emmaline's ears and Charlotte fell to the ground.

Emmaline lost her grip on the man's wrist. Charlotte's blood seeped through her blue gown. The man kicked Emmaline in the knee and she sank to the floor. The man then reached down and grabbed her throat. His fingers burned against her skin. She couldn't breathe. She couldn't see past the tears. She scratched his hand with her nails, but he threw her against the wall. Her vision ebbed away as her head pounded with pain.

Kathleen sprang to her feet, holding a shard of glass. Emmaline wanted to help her, but her whole body rocked like a capsized boat. She could barely see anything. Kathleen's shriek was followed by a slash. The man shouted. Another gunshot shook the small room.

Emmaline sat with her back against the wall, willing her eyes to see. She blinked hard, again and again. She curled her hands into her fists. *I have to see! I have to help Kathleen!*

Then her eyes focused. She stared at her sisters. Kathleen's lifeless eyes gazed at the chandelier, blood draining from the hole in her throat. Charlotte's gown was more red than blue now. Rose's face was tucked against her arm as her body lay sprawled across the floor.

Emmaline wasn't moving. She *couldn't* move. Everything inside her was solid ice. She studied their dead bodies. Tears stained their faces. They were so quiet. Too quiet.

Something burst inside Emmaline and the ice within her started to melt. The more she looked at their paling skin, the hotter her blood became. The ice disappeared, and embers turned into a raging forest fire.

She roared and leapt to her feet. The man was lying on the ground, groaning and cursing and holding his bleeding face. The bust sculpture was heavier than it looked as she swept it up from the floor. Her whole body trembled. She held the stone head over the man as he glared up at her. "You monster!" she screamed.

He aimed the gun at her chest and pulled the trigger back. No sound, no bullet came out. Swearing, he kicked her in the knee again and sent her tumbling down. She tripped over Kathleen, and her head slammed into the brick fireplace. Emmaline was falling, down into darkness, down into silence.

Emmaline sat up in her bed, awake from the nightmare. Though her whole body was cold, she was damp with sweat. She clutched her throat, dry with panting, and swallowed, tasting the bitter tears that fell down her face. She glanced around the room as it spun down in circles. It was the same room she'd fallen asleep in the night before. This wasn't her old home, where hell had shown its ugly face one starless night. This was Tregaron, her hiding place.

Her limbs shook like reeds in the wind. The room had a draft. The window was tiny, and there was no sunlight to kiss her cheek like her mother had every morning.

Someone was pounding on a door. She was surprised there wasn't a hole in the wood yet.

"Git up! Can't 'ave ya sleepin' the day 'way! I got other renters that need yur bed t'night!" It was Bessie, the innkeeper.

Slowly, Emmaline put her feet on the floor. She couldn't stop trembling. She pressed her hands to her eyes and tried to breathe. Bessie beat on the door again. "Git up, 'fore I kick down this door 'n' pour cold water all over ya!"

Emmaline jumped at Bessie's words. The soldiers had kicked the door down. She couldn't bear to hear the groaning of the wood as it collapsed. Not again.

Emmaline forced herself to get up. She straightened her skirts and opened the door. Bessie's bulging body was right in front of her, taking up the entire doorway. Her buxom chest breathed heavily as her glare burned into Emmaline's face. She gnashed her crooked teeth like a dog. "Well, you think yur just so high 'n mighty now, don't ya, ya pretty little princess? If I hadn't waken ya up, you'd still be sleepin'!"

Emmaline couldn't meet her eyes. She hardly ever met anyone's eyes. She tucked her chin into her throat. Bessie's shouting rattled her head.

"Not much of a talker, are ya? Git on outta here 'n don'tcha ever come back!" Bessie's thick hands grabbed Emmaline's shoulders and shoved her into the hallway. Emmaline ran the rest of the way out of the inn and stepped into the unmerciful chill.

She hated the winter. The cold bit into her skin. Clouds hid the sun. The snow sprinkled down upon her uncovered head and fell beneath her clothes. She shivered. There was no color and no life anywhere.

Everything was gray: the sky, the buildings, and sometimes the people, too. The cobblestone streets were unforgiving on her feet enough, without having to dodge puddles of ice water. The wind howled in her ears, like the wolves she'd been running from for so long.

Her hopes of a new start in the kingdom of Tregaron had long been dashed. The peddler woman's words seemed like mockery now. "You'll find safety, food, and warmth there. Go there if you want to live," she'd said.

Emmaline had travelled the long road to Tregaron, the taste of warm bread on her tongue. But in the three years she'd been here, she'd struggled for crumbs. But where else could she go? She knew these streets now, and she was too tired to learn new terrain.

"Watch out, girl!" A brawny man in a brown coat brushed by her.

She pressed her hands against her arms, meeting no one's eyes. She was tired of the dreams, tired of the darkness always chasing her. She lived in shadows. The embers of her past life floated around her and burned her skin. If something didn't change soon, they would engulf her in flames until she was no more.

She was glad she wasn't allowed at Bessie's anymore. The woman was mean and spent most of the money she made on cakes, ale, and furs. She hoarded the nicest things for herself. Staying at her inn was no better than sleeping on the streets. It was just as cold and lonely. And anyway, she did usually sleep on the streets. It wasn't often her begging ventures came to fruition and she had enough for a room. If she had a good day, she stayed at Bessie's or Arthur's. Arthur was the one man she knew who didn't look at her with lecherous eyes, so she stayed there the most.

For nearly three years, she'd been on the streets of Lauderbury. Her nights were cold and dark. Emmaline couldn't see the starry skies past the factory fog and the rooftops of buildings she slept between. An alley was no place for her to sleep. Dogs barked and thieves rushed by. Rats scurried around her, squeaking as they disappeared. Street cars rumbled by, and she hated it when they backfired. It sounded so much like gunfire.

When her eyes finally closed, the ghosts would come alive in her mind, just like they did every night. The guns blasted in her ears, and the screams slashed her insides like knives. Every night she woke up panting and soaked to the skin in sweat. Every night she saw their eyes as if it all had happened yesterday.

When the sun would finally rise and the street sweepers forced her out of the alleys, she wandered the city and tried to ignore the cold. Sometimes she ached for the thick coats of wealthy women passing by. But more than that, she ached with hunger. It was an endless ache, her only companion during these past years.

Even now, her stomach begged for sustenance. She had to find something to eat. She still had a little money left to buy something from a bakery. Perhaps she could persuade the baker to let her buy the stale bread from two days ago. If no one else ate it, she would. She'd eat anything at this point.

She spotted a bakery on the corner of Myrtle Street. She dodged the horse-drawn carriages and throngs of people armed with canes and parasols. The bell jingled as the door closed behind her. It was so warm in here, and it smelled like cinnamon, raisins, and butter. A Christmas tree stood in the corner, strung with popcorn and red satin bows.

Emmaline shuddered as one last shiver racked her body, and then she stepped further into the shop. Her cheeks warmed. *I shouldn't have come here. This is a place for posh people, not people like me.* A woman wearing pearls and a man with freshly shined leather shoes eyed her with repulsion. They stood arm-in-arm, whispering to each other.

Emmaline's face burned as she hung her head. She must look a sight. She had no brush for her hair and no clean water for her face. Her clothing was tattered and torn. She met no one's gaze and stood in the corner by herself.

A woman wearing a striped dress and apron came out of the back room. Her cheeks were pink with warmth as she beamed brightly. "How can I help you ladies and gents this morning?" she asked.

Emmaline watched as the other customers stepped to

the counter and made their orders. She fidgeted with a loose string on her skirt. She hated it when people looked at her. She didn't like all the attention. Someone might recognize her. Someone might know which family she'd belonged to, even if she didn't. It wasn't fair that the predator had such an advantage over its prey.

"Miss? Can I help you as well?" the woman at the counter called.

Emmaline shook herself free of her thoughts and stepped cautiously to the counter. "Yes, please. I don't have much money for anything fresh, but I'd be willing to buy anything else you've got."

To her surprise, the woman didn't look disgusted by Emmaline's appearance like the couple had. She frowned, but her eyes were gentle as if she felt sorry for Emmaline. "Let me see what I can do." The woman disappeared into the back room.

While she was gone, Emmaline took the money she had left in her pocket and counted it. It wasn't much, not much at all. She hated cheating this kind woman out of her profit. She wished she had more to give.

Something shattered in the back room. Again, Emmaline saw James's unmoving eyes staring at the ceiling and a pool of blood foaming around his head. She screamed, dropping her coins.

The couple, still standing there, stifled their snickering beneath gloved hands. Heart drumming in her ears, Emmaline bent and gathered her money.

Tears gathered in her eyes and pelted the coins. She stood to her feet just as the woman returned behind the counter.

"Here you are, Miss. I gave you half a loaf from yesterday's batch and half a loaf from today's." She smiled cheerfully.

Emmaline swallowed the sob bobbing in her throat. "Thank you. Here's all I have." She set the coins down on the counter, then took the bread from the woman. She tried to smile and thanked her once more, then she hurried out of the bakery. The cold swept her away again and almost made her forget the warmth she'd just left behind.

Will life ever change? she wondered as she bit into some bread. *Will life ever be filled with joy and wonder again?* How could it when the nightmares wouldn't end, and—even worse—they had really happened?

Her cheeks stung and she shook her head. That was wrong of her to think like that. She had warm bread. That didn't happen every day. She had more clothes than most of the outcasts living on the streets. She'd had a warm place to sleep last night, warmer than most nights at least. Things could be worse.

This bread, soft and sweet, tasted wonderful. She didn't dare eat it quickly. If anyone knew that good things didn't last for long, it was her. So, she took her time and enjoyed it. It wasn't every day that she was able to get food as good as this.

Shadows billowed on the cobblestones. Emmaline glanced up, watching laundry float in the chill breeze.

A woman leaned out the second-story window, reeling the clothing in and taking it off the line.

The whorehouse door burst open across the street. A man stumbled out, laughing as he straightened his coat. A woman followed him, wearing dark eye paint and undergarments. She laughed and hiccupped as she leaned against the doorframe, watching as the man went away down the street. Two men carrying lumber passed by her and whistled.

Emmaline bit her lip, her eyes stinging. She was grateful she had never lost herself in so deep a pit. Never in her three years of misery had she sacrificed herself on an altar of sin. She'd always kept the name of Jesus on her lips, whispering His name when the nights were long, cold, and dark, when the gunshots rang out in her head and the ghosts wouldn't let her rest. All that time, as she moved on to the next place, His name had been her anthem of hope. She couldn't imagine trading the one possession she'd salvaged from the ruins of her life for something that would strangle her soul.

Something plush squished beneath Emmaline's foot. She glanced down. A crocheted doll lay on the damp cobblestones, staring helplessly at her. The stitch of her red lips had come loose, her pink dress was sooty, and her chestnut brown braids were unraveled. Emmaline bent and picked her up.

How long had she been lying here, separated from her family? What had happened to the little girl that had tied ribbons on her braids, that had sung her lullabies, that had kissed her goodnight? How long had she been lost and alone, away from the love and warmth of her home?

She traced her finger over the doll's torn lip and then put the doll into her pocket. Now they could be wanderers together, and maybe one day, they'd both be mended and loved by a family again.

Someone whistled. Two scruffy men leaned against the barber shop building, their eyes on her as they puffed cigars.

"Have you ever seen anything so sweet, Al?" one said.

"Not since I went to the candy shop, Eddie."

Eddie laughed, a hungry snarl. "That's a good one, Al."

Emmaline walked on, moving quickly down the street.

"Where ya going, my lovely?"

"Come on, we gents know how to have a good time. We'll show ya!"

Her breath rushed in her lungs. She walked faster.

"Come back!"

Footsteps pounded behind her.

Emmaline's heart panged painfully against her chest. She dropped the remainder of her bread, picked up her skirts, and dashed through the streets. The men barked at her like dogs snapping at her heels. When could she stop running? How much longer could she run? She didn't have a choice. If she stopped, they'd sink their teeth into her and drag her away.

She bumped into people, slicing right through their groups. They flung insults at her as she flew down the street. Their clothing was nicer than most people she encountered daily. They wore furs and suits and satins instead of soiled rags and cotton. She was getting closer to the palace. Perhaps one of the guards would see the men chasing her and help her. Surely someone would rescue her.

How long had it been since other men had chased her? How long had it been since her heart hammered like a hunted hare? Would there always be someone following her? Would there be no escape?

Jesus, help me!

Emmaline leapt through a crowd of aristocrats and ran right in front of a pair of white horses. They shrieked in response, jerking back. The driver of the coach scowled at her. "Watch where you're going, you filthy rat!"

Emmaline took what little breath she had left and darted away. A group of women gasped as she ran past them, then screamed as Al and Eddie plowed through them.

Plenty of people were around her. The two men shouted vulgarities. Didn't anyone see? Didn't anyone hear? Would they all ignore her and let her be attacked? Tears choked her. *Jesus, I need you!*

She dove into an alley and flew around a corner. A wall of brick stood in her way. Panic filled her lungs. There was no way out, save for the way she'd come.

She turned around. The two men prowled toward her like two young lions on their first hunt. *I'm trapped.*

She looked around for something to ward them off. A forsaken broom stood against the wall. She grabbed it and jabbed it at Eddie. "Stay back!" she shrieked.

"Spirited, are we?" Eddie laughed.

"We like the spirited ones. They're so much fun to break." Al walked closer to her.

Grunting, she swung the broom, but he caught it. "Let go!" Her voice ripped from her throat painfully.

Al chortled, his chest heaving with jubilation.

She wrestled his strong grip but lost and fell to the ground. Al tossed the broom aside. Both men laughed, stepping closer and closer. She put her arms over her head and screamed.

A gun roared at the end of the alley. She screamed again, burying her head in her knees.

"Get out of here, you dirt-encrusted pigs!" a man bellowed.

Two sets of footsteps retreated, and then another pair headed straight for her. "It's all right. They're gone now." It was the same voice that had shouted, but it was gentler this time.

She didn't dare move. Her heart pounded as her head throbbed with memories of gunshots all too familiar. A few muffled sobs managed to escape her throat.

Fingers lifted her chin and forced her face out of hiding. As she met the man's gaze, his eyes widened with shock. He quickly recovered and cleared his throat. "You're safe now."

Safe. The word was a stranger to her. Could it be true? Had she finally found peace?

Unlike Al and Eddie, this man was clean and well-kempt. His brown eyes were as hard as his angular jawline, and his golden curls caught the sunlight. He wore the red uniform of a palace guard.

"Thank you," she whispered.

He stood to his feet, and then helped her to her own. "My name is Captain Ross. I serve her Majesty the Queen."

"I'm Emmaline. I live on the streets." She bit the inside of her cheek, shame coiling inside her. How had she fallen so low in just three years?

Ross smiled sadly. "I gathered as much." He looked her up and down. "I saw you drop your bread. Can I buy you more?" When she hesitated, he said, "Please?"

She didn't think she wanted to go through that again. She'd had enough of whispers and laughter behind her back for one day. But he didn't seem like the kind of man that would accept the word "no." Slowly, she nodded.

He took the reins of his black horse and walked down the street with Emmaline. She watched his tall form in front of her, his steely eyes unwavering. He was quite stony.

She stepped closer to him. "Thank you again for saving my life."

He glanced at her, then faced forward again. The traces of a dimple pulled at his left cheek. "It was nothing," he said.

When they reached the bakery, he gave her the reins to hold and told her to wait there. He disappeared inside and she stood with his horse, watching the people come and go.

She must look strange. A girl like her standing next to a huge stallion with a shiny black coat and a fine leather saddle. People stared at her, and some were even bold enough to glare. She could see the accusation in their eyes. *What's she doing with such a fine beast? Does she spend all her money on him and simply not care about the state of her clothes? Perhaps she stole him. Look at her, a girl like that. She could never afford him, much less his saddle!*

Her toes wiggled nervously in her shoes as she waited for Captain Ross to return. Other guards like him stood at the palace gates several feet from here. What if someone told them what she was doing, and they came to arrest her?

She took a deep breath and forced such anxious thoughts away. If she were arrested, Captain Ross would explain the situation before she was put into prison. She had to calm herself before she became hysterical. That would help no one.

She turned her gaze to the magnificent palace in the distance. The flags whipped in the wind and clouds drifted over the towers. It stood tall and secure, guarded by highly-trained men, completely safe against all threats.

What would it be like to live in the palace? To dance at balls, to wear glittering gowns, to listen as the music swelled in your ears? To feel seen, beautiful, and carefree?

Her life before had been similar. She'd lived in a house as grand as a palace as a child, skipping beneath crystal chandeliers and attending lavish tea parties. Sometimes she wondered if it had been real or just her imagination. How could she, with ashes on her face and patches on her skirt, have lived such a rich, wonderful dream? But the memories were too real. She really had lived such a life once before she'd lost it all in a baptism of blood and death.

No matter how much she longed to return to her life of warmth, to have a family like the one she'd once had, it would never happen. She was a different girl now. Marble halls and glittering gowns were no longer for her.

The bell rang, and Captain Ross emerged from the bakery. He carried three paper bags. Her blood turned to ice. She hadn't meant for him to spend so much money on her.

"Captain, you needn't have spent so much money on a stranger," she told him.

His dimple came back. "I wanted to. I know you've got to be starving, so take your pick. I've got banana bread, danishes with jam, and hot buns."

Her tongue tingled. She hadn't had jam in three years. She remembered sitting in a white room at a table with fresh bouquets. Her father would read the newspapers as she and her siblings would lather the scones with jam. Her brother, when he was very young, would often get it all over his face. Mama would fuss while Papa laughed.

"I'll take the jam danish."

He handed it to her. It smelled wonderful. The crust was flaky on her fingers, and it was filled with cheese and jam. "Thank you, Captain," she said.

"Please, call me Ross."

She smiled at him, then took a bite out of the danish. Warmth spread throughout her body. She closed her eyes in pleasure.

Ross put the rest of the bread into the big satchel hanging from his horse's saddle and took the reins. "Come on, let's take a walk."

She nodded and kept eating as he headed toward the palace. The crowds swelled in waves, feeding into and out of the shops. Groups of women walked by, carrying gift boxes under their arms, their cheeks pink with cold. Some people ate as they walked, just like her. A newspaper boy called out the latest headlines and gave his price.

"How long have you been on the streets?" Ross suddenly asked.

Emmaline swallowed. "Three years."

"An awful long time for a girl like you." He glanced at her from the corner of his eye.

"An awful long time for anyone, I'm afraid."

"Yes, you're right." He turned his face toward hers

for a moment but kept walking. "Why aren't you with your family? Did you run away?"

Her heart fell from her chest and into her middle, splashing and creating waves of upset. Her hunger seemed to leave her. "No, they're dead."

"Oh, I see." He furrowed his brows and frowned. "What happened to them?"

Why was he asking her all these questions? "They were killed. I survived. I don't know why. I don't even know who they were." She forced herself to eat again.

He didn't meet her eyes again. "Oh. I'm sorry."

"It's not your doing."

Ross paused before speaking again, as if he were thinking deeply about something. Then he asked, "Have you heard the queen's latest proclamation?"

She shook her head. "I'm afraid not."

"She has proclaimed that for six months, six girls will learn how to live in the palace and will get to know the prince. They will each have the opportunity to win the prince's heart, and at the end of the six months, one of them will be engaged to him. The unsuccessful ones will become the future queen's maids of honor."

"That sounds wonderful," Emmaline said distantly.

"But the queen has a problem. So far, she has only found five candidates for her son."

"I see."

"And I think that you are the destined number six."

She turned to meet his gaze, her eyes wide. "I beg

your pardon?"

"You're very beautiful, you know." His dimple was tugging at his face again.

She blushed, unused to the compliment. She shook her head. "But I can't possibly woo the prince. Look at me; I'm covered in ash, and my rags have rags."

"That can all be fixed. A person does not cast aside a diamond simply because it is covered in dirt. Emmaline, I think you'd fit right in." His curls were in his eyes as he looked down at her. "Besides, anything would be better than living on the streets, wouldn't it? Even if you don't marry the prince, you would live in the palace as the future queen's maid of honor."

She bit her lip, trembling. Live in the palace? Could it be true? Could her one longing, to return to the golden world in which she'd lived once, come true?

Ross was right. Anything would be better than living on the streets with the rats and the drunks. But could she do it? Could she fit in this world of carriages and ballrooms? She'd long forgotten the steps of every dance she'd learned. The world she once knew was gone, and so were the people that had made it worth living in. "I don't know, Ross."

Ross lifted her chin, as he had when they first met. Her heart thumped against her chest at this familiar gesture. He was acting as if he already knew her, yet she wasn't afraid of him. He wouldn't hurt her, not after he'd protected her so fiercely.

His eyes pleaded with her. "Please, Emmaline. I won't be able to protect you forever from men like that. I can't leave you out here."

Did he really care about her so much? No one else she'd met in the past three years had ever cared before, so why did he? She bit her lip again, harder. Her hands fidgeted like uneven puzzle pieces. "Do you really think I can do this?"

His gaze didn't waver. "I know you can."

She turned her gaze to the palace. The palace flags waved in the wind, as if beckoning her inside. It was such a big place. It stretched for miles, covered with dozens of windows and barricaded by colossal gates. Something about it frightened her, but a strange calm also filled her. She had to find somewhere safe to live before the girl she'd been once was gone forever. She turned back to Ross. "I'll do it."

He smiled. "Good." He mounted her on his horse, then mounted behind her. As he urged his horse into a gallop, she closed her eyes, trying to calm her pounding heart, trying to breathe.

Chapter Two

NICHOLAS STOOD ON the solar balcony, overlooking the city below him. Huddled houses with tiled roofing stretched as far as the eye could see. Chimneys exhaled puffs of smoke into the gray sky. A cathedral in the distance stood over the shorter buildings, like a shepherd guarding sheep.

Someday, this city would be his. This kingdom of Tregaron would be his.

But first, he needed a queen.

His fingers tapped impatiently on the railing. And

when would this queen arrive? When would she pass through the palace gates? When would he hear her voice floating through the halls?

Perhaps he was being impatient. But could he be blamed if he was? The other five candidates had arrived nearly two months ago, and his mother wanted Nicholas married by the summer. If he wasn't, she'd force him to marry some stuffy countess or duchess.

Nicholas shook his head and pressed his lips together. He'd rather live alone than live out his days at odds with a stranger. Arranged marriage was a fate far too many shared, a fate he'd determined years ago he would not suffer.

Besides, his father had married for love, and Nicholas knew love had made his father a good ruler, a good man. Nicholas wanted to live the way his father had, and marrying for love would allow him to.

But the contest couldn't begin until the sixth candidate arrived. All of Tregaron's queens had five lady's maids, and so the next one should, too. So, since the five remaining candidates would become lady's maids for Nicholas's chosen bride, he had to wait.

He did not understand why God was being so slow about it. The other five candidates had arrived so quickly, all within a week of each other. Each of them had come only days after the proclamation had gone out. Excitement grew in the palace with each carriage that had appeared. But after the fifth girl had arrived and time had crept by, the excitement had faded.

So where was she? What was she doing? When would she find him?

His mother didn't understand his need for love. She didn't think it was necessary to become a good ruler. But if he hadn't needed love, it wouldn't have saved his life, pulled him from the depths, brought air back into his lungs.

Only a year ago, he'd returned from his service in the army. After losing his whole platoon, watching them die while the world seemed to burn, Nicholas couldn't imagine losing anyone else to death. He had isolated himself, but the emptiness tormented him. He had found, much to his disliking, that ghosts were especially audible in the silence. He had nearly gone mad with the grief, but nothing had haunted him more than his unkept promise to Tom.

The enemy had found their hiding place and were getting ready to pounce.

"The world's gonna burn anyway, Prince," Tom said, wiping the dirt from his face. "Way I see it, it's better to have someone watch it burn with you." He looked at Nicholas. "Don't you?"

Nicholas agreed and finished setting the bomb. Tom told him to run and said he was right behind him. Nicholas sprang from their hiding place and ran several feet away. He turned just as their bomb roared and shattered everything around him. When Nicholas's lungs recovered and the dust settled, the enemy were gone—and so was Tom. When the rest of

Rise

his platoon found him, they dragged him away from the rubble before Nicholas could find Tom's remains.

Tom had been the first, then George, Benny, and Conor. Soon they were all gone. A little platoon, and somehow Nicholas had been the only one left standing.

Tom's words had haunted his days and his nights. His mother had prayed for him continually. Then, one night, after a terrorizing dream, God had whispered Tom's words to him. The darkness had broken. Tom's words no longer tormented him. They healed him. They were his weapon. He had to go on living. He had to rise for the fallen. He had to find love.

The cross crowning the cathedral's tallest tower caught Nicholas's eye. Perhaps he was being impatient. The Scriptures were full of stories of men and women of old watching the skies, waiting for salvation. And they'd waited far longer than he had.

Forgive me, God. I should not try to rush your plans. If you have put something on my heart, it will not go unfinished.

Nicholas's gaze swept the streets of the city. This sixth candidate was out there somewhere. She did exist. He just had to wait for her.

And perhaps, she would be the one worth waiting for.

The palace swallowed Emmaline whole—heart, body, and soul. Everywhere she turned, the painted eyes of portraits watched her walk down the halls with Ross. Cherubs in the ceiling mural played harps and danced in the clouds. Garland cascaded down the doorframes and Christmas trees stood guard in the hallways. The smell of chestnuts and oranges overwhelmed her senses.

She wrung her hands, twisting them around in an anxious dance. She didn't belong here. Her reflection in the marble floors was proof of that. She shouldn't have come. The queen would never let *her* live here.

Ross kept walking, completely unaware of the frantic voices screaming in her head. "Just a little farther," he said. "Genevieve will be in the stateroom."

Emmaline raised an eyebrow. "Genevieve? You call the queen by her first name?"

"Sometimes. She and I have a history together. We get along well, but"—He stopped her right there in the hallway—"I must warn you: You must say nothing out of bounds. She can be stubborn and irritable, and first impressions are extremely important to her."

Her heart pounded in her throat. Could Ross see it?

He shook his head. "But don't worry too much. I know she'll warm to you—in time."

In time? How long would it take? How much more would she have to endure?

As he walked on, her feet stuck to the floor. She couldn't move for a moment. So many doubts and memories and fears were whirling through her head.

Her breath hitched in her throat. Would all this be worth it?

"Come on!" Ross called a few feet away.

She ignored the voice inside her and followed him.

When they arrived at a doorway, Ross turned and said, "Wait here. I must announce your presence." He disappeared through the door.

Emmaline glanced behind her, down the series of halls they'd just come through. Giggling and playful screams broke through the silence. Two children in servant attire appeared, chasing each other. They noticed her and gasped, then ran away. Their laughter sounded just like her sisters' when they used to run through their house. How different it had been to run through those same halls with Mama's blood on her skirt.

A mirror hung on a wall a few feet away. She could see her reflection clearly now. It had been some time since she'd seen herself. She was older now, eighteen if she remembered correctly. Her eyes weren't as bright as they once had been. Her dark brown hair was long and tangled, no longer ringlets tied back with ribbon. A filthy, tattered dress took the place of the silks and linens she used to wear. Dirt smudged her face. Mama had always insisted on cleanliness.

She couldn't present herself to the queen like this. Emmaline would be thrown out before she even opened her mouth. The girl in white with ribbons in her hair was gone, and in her place stood a street rat, dressed in rags, and caked with dirt. She turned to leave.

Stay, Emmaline.

She glanced up at the ceiling. Cherubs played with God's hair above her.

The door opened. Ross appeared with a smile as if trying to encourage her. "She's ready for you now."

Emmaline didn't breathe as she passed over the threshold. The whole room was yellow and white and filled with sofas and tables and chairs. Two chandeliers hung from the ceiling. A fireplace brought warmth to her face from the distant side of the room. The biggest Christmas tree she'd ever seen sat in the corner of the room, hungrily taking up the little space it had.

"*This* is the girl, Ross?" a cutting voice groaned behind her.

Emmaline spun around, startled by the voice.

A handsome woman sat in an elaborate chair, wearing a disdained look on her face. Her ruby red dress shimmered in the light from the windows. A crown of jewels sat on her head. Her cheeks and lips were pink, and her eyes were sharp and blue. She pressed a hand to her forehead and propped her elbow on the chair arm. "Oh, Great Jehoshaphat, Ross. You've brought me a street rat!"

A hard punch slammed into Emmaline's stomach. She trembled and didn't meet the queen's eyes. Her face burned and tears brimmed at the surface. She knew it. She had been right. She didn't fit in here. The queen could smell a rat, and she wouldn't allow it in her palace.

Ross stepped forward. He looked like a lion with his golden hair and confident swagger. "Your Majesty, I have good reason to believe she is the destined last candidate for your son's heart. She is not like other commoners. She carries herself with grace, and her voice is cultured. She can learn whatever she must."

The queen leaned forward, squinting her eyes in irritation. "And how do you know this? You've only just met her."

"Didn't you give me my position as captain because you trusted my judgement?"

The room held its breath in silence. Emmaline glanced at Ross, her heart quickening. She had never heard of someone being so frank with nobility. What did the queen think of his bold choice in words? She chanced a glance up at the queen but found her staring at Emmaline like a bug. Emmaline looked back down, playing with the string on her skirt again.

"Come closer, girl."

Ice spread through Emmaline's veins. She looked up. The queen's cheeks were pinched as she glared at her. Emmaline glanced at Ross again, and he nodded at her. She swallowed and moved closer, trembling before the queen. She tried not to breathe too heavily.

"Look up at me," the queen snarled. "Do not hide like a tortoise. Be bold and look me in the eyes."

Would her heart burst here in this room? She met

the queen's gaze and melted beneath it.

"What is your name?"

"Emmaline."

"How old are you?"

"Eighteen."

"Are you in love with anyone? Have you ever been with a man?"

She blushed. "No, Your Majesty, on both accounts." Her voice shook.

"Where are you from?"

She stammered. "I—I don't know, Your Majesty."

"Who is your family?"

"I don't know that, either."

The queen shot Ross a venomous glare. "Who on *God's green earth* have you brought me, Ross? For all we know, she could be a common prostitute!"

The ice in Emmaline's veins cracked. She curled her hands into fists. "I've told you that I've never been with a man, Your Majesty. You have my word, and my word is my bond."

The blue in the queen's eyes turned to fuming seas. "Speak only when spoken to, girl! I am your queen. Did I tell you that you could speak?"

Emmaline looked down and did not look up again for a few moments.

The queen was silent. The whole room was. Only the clock ticked. The sound nearly drove Emmaline mad.

"Are you strong?" the queen suddenly asked.

Emmaline trembled. For three whole years, she'd

never been able to stop shaking, either from the cold or from fear. She cried almost every night. She screamed at every loud noise. "I don't know, my queen."

"I asked you a question. Are you strong?"

Emmaline was determined to show this queen that she wasn't a coward. She took a deep breath and pressed her shoulders back. The motion seemed familiar to her. She forced her voice to be clear. "I can be."

The queen stared at her, hard. Ages passed before the queen said, "Good. My son will not marry a weak girl. I'll make sure of that."

Ross winked at her, then stepped toward the queen. "So what say you, Your Majesty? Will Emmaline compete for your son's hand?"

The queen stared at Ross for a moment. "Yes, she will. Might as well so that Nicholas can end this whole charade as soon as possible." She waved her hand at Emmaline. "Go, go, then. The candidate suite is on the third floor, and the door is the third one on the right."

Emmaline's insides quaked. Had she really convinced the queen to let her compete for the prince's hand? Not that she wanted to marry him. If she could only get a job and live somewhere besides the streets, she'd be happy.

Emmaline bowed but wobbled as she tried to stand. The queen moaned in dismay. Emmaline's face turned crimson. "Thank you, Your Majesty, for this wonderful opportunity."

The queen motioned her away. "Yes, yes. Now go."

Emmaline hurried from the room and the door closed behind her. She'd never felt so relieved to leave such a beautiful room. She wanted to collapse and catch her breath but decided against it.

Now. The rooms. The queen had said they were on the third floor and that it was the third door on the right. She set off down the hall, trying to find a staircase.

The corridors were eerily silent. Only her footsteps clicked against the smooth floors. A servant here and there passed her, but she saw no one else.

Would she come to like living in a castle? Of course, it'd be much better than living on the streets. Anything would.

But what would happen if the prince did fall in love with her? Would she want to marry him? Could she risk her heart again? She shook her head. She wouldn't worry about that. Why would the prince fall in love with her? Surely the other candidates would be far more beautiful and more deserving of a crown.

A piano in a room she passed caught her eye. She wanted to walk by it, to forget about it, but it'd been ages since her fingers had danced along ivory keys. She wanted to create music, to melt into it again. She glanced over her shoulder. No one was there. She turned inside.

The windows were open and the curtains flapped in the breeze. The piano shone in the dim light. She sat down and lifted the lid. The keys smiled back like white teeth. She pressed a finger on one key, and the sound thrilled her ears. She placed her fingers on the keys and began their dance.

Emmaline smiled as the melodies sang their familiar song. Closing her eyes, she let the music take her away. She was soaring, untouchable, unreachable, unseen.

"Play 'Lavender's Blue,' Emmaline," her sister Rose said. Emmaline felt Rose's phantom hand on her shoulder.

"All right," she whispered into the silence. She played the song as best as she could remember. Every note brought back the years to her.

"Dance with us, James!" she heard Charlotte exclaim.

As Emmaline glanced over her shoulder, her fingers still tapping away, she could see her brother and sisters all holding hands, dancing in a circle, spinning round and round. Papa spun Mama around in his arms. They both laughed like two young lovers.

But every song comes to an end. The memories faded, and the room fell silent again. She stared at the keys, numb. Their voices, Rose's hand on her shoulder—it had all felt so real. Would they always live inside her?

"That old piano hasn't been played in years." A man's voice came from the doorway.

Emmaline jumped and her fingers played a discordant note. She sprang from the seat and turned.

A young man stood there, leaning against the doorframe, his blue eyes twinkling at her. His dimples were deep, and his jawline was nicely sculpted. Dark curls fell over his forehead. Her heart drummed in her throat.

She moved away from the piano. "I—Forgive me. I shouldn't have come in here."

He stood up straight and held his hands up, as if to stop her from leaving. "No, please, don't apologize. It was a pleasure to hear it come back to life. You play beautifully."

Emmaline blushed. "Thank you." She glanced at her shoes. Her shoes were so dirty and old. He must think she snuck inside. He'd call the guards in at any moment. And the queen would know she'd played her piano. Emmaline would be tossed back into the streets for sure. *Oh, what have I done?*

"I'm sure the whole palace would love to hear it played again," the man said. "It hasn't been used since the queen's husband died, and when he died, all music and life went with him."

Perhaps that was why the queen had been so bitter and angry toward her. Ross had said it was hard to get close to her. She glanced at the man. "That's awful."

"Yes." His Adam's apple bobbed as he grinned.

She brushed her fingertips over the piano. "It's a wonderful piano." She glanced back at the man. "I didn't mean any harm. It's been so long since I played that I couldn't restrain myself."

He shook his head. "No harm done, Miss. I hope to

hear you play it again."

She smiled. "Perhaps I will." She glanced at the clock. "But I must go now. Good-bye."

"Good-bye."

Emmaline felt his gaze even as she turned down the hall and found the stairs. He'd seemed kind. Perhaps one day she could grant his wish and play the piano for him again.

"Third door on the right," Emmaline whispered to herself as she entered the third floor. She'd been walking for so long, she had begun to wonder if she was in the right place. Not that she didn't enjoy wandering in a palace. All this beauty was preferable to the sewage in the streets.

She turned to the right and stopped at the door. Giggling and lively conversation greeted her from the other side. Her hand froze over the knob. What if they didn't like her? What if they were all snobby?

I've come this far. I can't stop now. She inhaled and knocked on the door.

The laughter and conversation paused. The door opened. A lovely young woman with striking green eyes and soft red curls looked back at her. Her dress was a pretty shade of lavender, with lace gathered at the collar and the hem of the sleeves. Emmaline's face heated at her own attire, but to her surprise, the girl didn't seem to notice her raggedy dress.

"Is this the candidate suite?" Emmaline asked.

The girl smiled. "Yes, it is. Are you the last one?"

"I am. I'm number six," Emmaline said.

The girl smiled and motioned for her to enter the room. "Come in, please."

Emmaline followed her inside. The enormous room was filled with side tables, chairs, sofas, and bouquets of exotic flowers. Soft carpet blanketed the floor. A hearth danced with flames in the corner. The velvet curtains were pulled back and let the dim afternoon light inside.

Emmaline turned and met the other girls' gazes. They all wore fine laces, silks, pearls, and gemstones. With their coiffed hair and flawless faces, Emmaline must have looked pitiful to them.

"Even in those rags, you're beautiful!" a blonde-haired girl with big blue eyes exclaimed.

"Julia!" a light-brown-haired girl hissed.

Emmaline smiled at the blonde-haired girl, touched. "Thank you. But you are too kind."

"What is your name?" a girl with golden brown hair asked, lifting her chin.

"Emmaline."

"Where do you come from?" A dark-haired girl looked curiously at her.

"The streets," Emmaline answered. "Before that, I don't know."

Julia, the blonde, cocked her head. "How did you get here, then? The queen would never approve of a commoner marrying the prince."

"Julia!" the light-brown-haired girl hissed again.

Emmaline bit her lip. "She did approve it. Captain Ross had to convince her, but she—"

"Captain Ross?" Julia asked, leaning forward in her chair. Her eyes, to Emmaline's surprise, had gotten even larger. "You know him?"

Emmaline nodded. "Yes, as of today. What of it?"

"Didn't you notice how handsome he is?" Julia sighed. Some of the other girls giggled.

Emmaline blushed, taken aback by the question. "Well, I suppose."

"But we are here for the prince, are we not?" the golden-brown-haired girl asked.

"Yes, of course," the light-brown-haired girl said, blushing. "But he is handsome."

The dark-haired girl giggled.

The red-haired girl took Emmaline's arm. "Now that we know your name, you need to know ours." She motioned around the room. "You already know Julia Quinn. We have found that she often lets her tongue get away with her."

Everyone laughed.

The girl continued her introductions. "That's Eleanor Montgomery, the light brown-haired girl. The one beside her with the golden hair is Diana Foster, and the brunette is Lydia Lee. And I'm Anna Edwards."

Emmaline smiled. "It's very nice to meet you all." She sat down next to Eleanor and tried to arrange her skirts in a certain way so the mud wouldn't be so noticeable.

"Are you frightened?" Anna asked. "It's all right if you are. All of us are, too."

Emmaline nodded slowly. "Yes, I suppose I am."

"Just think, in a few months, one of us could be married to the prince!" Julia gasped, cupping her hands between her legs. "To be a princess must be wonderful."

"I won't marry him unless he loves me, and I love him," Lydia said. "That's what all the girls in the stories are doing now."

Eleanor nodded. "I think that's wise. And I won't marry him unless he wants a big family. I've had my heart set on children since I started my monthlies, and I won't give up my dreams for him, even if he is a prince."

"I care not for love or children. I came here to secure my father's wealth. It's a girl's duty, anyway." Diana lifted her chin once more. "And of course, the luxury and fine dresses attract me."

"And what about you, Emmaline?" Julia asked.

Emmaline thought about it for a moment, staring down at her skirts. "Well, I suppose that luxury and fine dresses are nice to have. But someday, the luxury will become everyday trivialities and the fine dresses will waste away. I'd rather feel safe and secure, surrounded by love."

She glanced up and all the girls stared at her in amazement. Diana slit her eyes in annoyance. Emmaline shifted uncomfortably at the attention before continuing. "I don't need to marry the prince.

I've lived on the streets so long, it's enough to simply live in the palace and serve the future queen."

"But," Julia said, "don't you want to marry the prince?"

Emmaline fiddled with the string on her skirt. "Well, I don't know. I don't even know him, after all."

Another door in the room opened. A man entered, walking toward them as he studied a pile of papers in his hands. "Get into a single-file line. I want to study each of you one by one." His voice was distant and distracted.

Who is he? The man was well-kempt, his beard neatly trimmed and his hair brushed to perfection. His clothing was so clean, she could smell the soap that was used to wash his suit, and his shoes shined so much that they reflected the light in the room.

The girls lined up in a single row, starting with Diana, then Anna, Eleanor, Lydia, Julia, and Emmaline. Emmaline's heart chimed like a heavy bell in her chest. She tried to remember to use her best posture.

The man stared down at his papers for a few minutes more, then glanced up. He studied Diana, lifting her chin and touching her hair. He seemed satisfied. Emmaline was not surprised. It appeared to her that Diana had no flaws.

"Good, very good," the man said, moving on from Diana to Anna. He furrowed his brows at Anna. "Don't tremble so much, Miss Edwards. I won't hurt you. I'm only testing the texture of your hair." He studied her a little longer, then whispered, "Lovely."

As he studied the other girls, Emmaline stared at the wall. A painting of the biblical account of the ascension hung in front of her. *God, I know You've brought me here. Please give me the strength to do this. I can't do this alone.*

The man appeared in front of her. He stared at her face, studying her. She resisted the urge to blush or look away. Instead, she met his gaze.

He touched her hair. "Knotted, but it's a lovely color and an even better texture. Very thick." He held her chin up and studied her face again. "The eyes are beautiful."

Her heart fluttered in her chest. When the man was finished, he stepped back and looked at her dress. His eyes grew large as he gasped, "What is this?"

"It's rags." Diana snickered.

"Diana!" Eleanor gasped.

Emmaline bowed her head in shame.

"Poor girl," the man said. He pressed a finger to his chin. "A star like you should be dressed in silk. Lavender or blue, I think. Don't worry. Once I am finished, baths will be drawn, and new gowns will be given to all of you."

"Thank you," Emmaline whispered.

"Now, my name is Mr. Harrison. By decree of Her Majesty the Queen, I am in charge of teaching you the proper manners that befit a lady of the court. This will include how to dress, how to dance, how to speak, and how to curtsy. With my help, one of you lucky ladies will become the prince's bride."

Julia squealed.

Mr. Harrison glanced at her, annoyed, then went on. "And the rest of you will become her lady's maids. I need to know your names and where you come from."

"Anna Edwards from Bloomsdale."

"Lydia Lee from Boburn."

"Eleanor Montgomery from Hatsfield."

"Diana Foster from Thornchester. My father is the duke." She puffed her chest.

"Julia Quinn from Portsmouth."

Emmaline blushed. "Emmaline from the streets."

Mr. Harrison blinked at her. "Forgive me, but even with those rags, you don't strike me as a girl who comes from the streets."

Emmaline bit her lip. "I've lived on the streets for three years. Before that, I don't know."

He stared at her and glanced down at his papers. "Hmm. Right." He met their gazes. "Well, now that we've all met, it's time for you to go and freshen up. Dinner is at six, so don't be late. We won't be dining with the prince or the queen for three months. I need to teach you all how to behave before you embarrass me in front of the monarchy."

Emmaline sighed silently in relief. She was glad he wouldn't give her the chance to humiliate herself.

"Wait here, and I'll order a maid to draw your baths." He gave a curt nod. "I shall see you all soon."

When he closed the door, the girls dropped their shoulders and sighed in relief.

"Well, I'm glad that's over," Julia said, flopping down on the couch rather tomboyishly.

"But it's not over yet, Julia," Diana said. "It's only beginning."

For the first time since she'd met her, Emmaline agreed with Diana.

Chapter Three

EMMALINE STARED AT her reflection in the mirror. A girl with porcelain skin stared back at her, eyes wide and shining. Surely this couldn't be her. Did she really look like that? Was it wrong to feel . . . beautiful? She looked like the silky-haired, red-lipped girls she had passed when she lived on the street. A smile tugged at her lips. *I'm beautiful.*

The new blue gown fit her perfectly, as if it'd been tailor-made for her. Her hair, now washed, hung in chestnut curls down her back. Diamonds hung from her ears and silk shoes covered her feet.

For so long, she'd been hidden beneath grime and tangled hair and rags. Now, she was out in the open, visible to all. And she would be far more noticeable now dressed like this. She fidgeted her hands, trembling at the thought.

"Oh, Emmaline!" Lydia gasped as she walked into the suite's sitting room. Her forget-me-not blue eyes were wide with surprise.

Emmaline turned, blushing. "I'm trying to convince myself that it's really my reflection I'm seeing in the mirror."

Lydia opened and closed her mouth a few times before speaking. "Emmaline," she said again. "You look stunning."

Emmaline was just about to tell Lydia how lovely she looked when the other girls burst into the room, a flock of lace, tulle, big hairstyles, and perfume. Julia straightened her pearl necklace, then turned to Emmaline and gasped. "Oh, saints above!"

The others followed Julia's gaze, their gowns shifting crisply as they moved. Julia's mouth still hung open as Anna blinked rapidly.

"Emmaline..." Eleanor held a hand to her chest.

"You look beautiful in that dress." Anna gasped.

Diana's face flushed pink as she frowned anxiously.

Heat flew up Emmaline's back. "I don't know what the big fuss is about, girls. I look no better than the rest of you." Her insides quaked at being gawked at so. There was nothing special about her. Why were they giving her so much attention?

"I'm not entirely sure that's true, Emmaline," Lydia said.

Mr. Harrison came into the room before Emmaline could protest further. He glanced around the room, studying the other girls. He nodded approvingly. "You all look wonderful. The queen would be pleased to have you sit at her table."

"Mr. Harrison, look behind you." Anna nodded toward Emmaline.

Mr. Harrison lowered his brows. "Look behind me? Whatever for? I—" He turned and stared at Emmaline. He cleared his throat as if something was suddenly caught in it. He walked toward her, beaming. "Oh, Emmaline. You look marvelous."

Emmaline fidgeted with her skirt. She hated all this attention. She preferred being in a dark corner all by herself, away from everyone's eyes.

His fingers came under her chin and lifted her face toward his. He smiled gently down at her. "Don't look down," he said. "Hold your chin up and look me in the eye. You may be queen one day."

"Especially looking like that," Julia whispered to Anna.

Emmaline did as she was told, despite the twisting in her stomach.

Mr. Harrison clapped his hands together. "All right, girls. Come, come. It's time to teach you all the art of table etiquette."

As the girls left with Mr. Harrison, Emmaline stole one last glance at herself in the mirror. The reflection didn't lie after all. *This is me.* She allowed herself a smile, then hurried down the hall.

Emmaline hadn't seen so much food in one place since she had sat at the dinner table with her family. Her mouth watered. She hoped the others didn't notice her eagerness to eat. No doubt they took one look at her thin body and thought she would be delighted to see so much food.

Julia's eyes lit up as she saw the sweets. "Oh, tea cakes are my favorite!"

They did look delicious, but Emmaline cared more about the meat and the fruit dishes. The ham's glaze dripped down the side and glowed in the candlelight. Colorful jellies and meringues, baked pears and apples with cinnamon, and savory cakes lined the entire table.

Tears of joy rose in Emmaline's eyes. In one day, God had given her so much. Last night, she'd gone to bed with no luck in her hunt for food, but tonight, a feast lay before her. It took every ounce of self-control to stop herself from reaching across the table and snatching a roll.

Mr. Harrison wasn't sitting with them yet. After

the girls had sat at the table, Mr. Harrison had disappeared into the kitchen. While they waited, the girls spoke one over the other, like a flock of birds all chirping at once. Emmaline was quiet, watching their brows move in conversation and the candlelight flicker over their faces.

Papa would hypnotize them all with stories about the battles he'd won. Emmaline's older sisters loved it when Mama described all the balls she'd attended. After a day's playtime with James, Emmaline and her brother would recite their tales of climbing trees and beating the male servants in sprinting races. She liked tables that bubbled with conversation. Sitting there with the girls, she was back in the white hall, sitting between Rose and Kathleen, watching Mama sip her tea and James tease Kathleen.

"So, Emmaline," Eleanor crooned. "Tell us the story of how you met Captain Ross."

Julia giggled.

Emmaline blushed. "He saw me being chased by two men."

"How horrible." Lydia gasped behind her.

"Did they hurt you?" Anna asked, eyes wide with concern.

"No, thanks be to God." Emmaline closed her eyes, her breath rushed and her shoulders tight. They'd chased her so hard. They'd almost caught her. But it was over now. She swallowed and went on. "Captain Ross scared them off before they could hurt me. Then he brought me here."

"Oh, how wonderful," Julia breathed. "I hope one day a man will rescue me."

"Really, Julia, life isn't a fairytale," Diana snapped, her blue eyes flashing.

"But it could be," Anna said.

"Yes, it certainly could." Emmaline remembered the dances her family once held at their house. So many women had floated past her in silks and tulle. The music had fluttered in her ears. Papa had spun her across the slick floors, beneath the chandeliers, between the waltzing crowd. She'd felt lost in that dream world, the kind of lost where one wants to never leave. But now she felt a different kind of lost in this land of horrors, this land of sweat-soaked, sleepless nights, this land of phantom screams—and she couldn't leave.

The dining hall doors roared open. Emmaline jumped a little, stirred out of her thoughts.

Mr. Harrison's shoes clicked on the floor. "All right, shoulders back and hands in your laps." He put his pocket watch into his suit jacket as he walked to the table.

Emmaline shook herself from her trance. Mr. Harrison sat himself at the head of the table.

"I've arranged for a series of courses to be made for us tonight. Our first lesson is in table manners. The queen will not condone barbarians at her table, and neither will I. It is important that the prince's future wife be taught the art of etiquette properly."

"I am far from a barbarian, Mr. Harrison." Diana

sniffed and held her chin high. "I have been taught the art of etiquette my whole life by the very best teachers."

Mr. Harrison chewed the inside of his cheek. "That may be, but perhaps not all of the girls were as fortunate as you. Perhaps you need to be instructed in the art of humility." He clapped his hands.

Instantly, a little army of servants appeared from the same entrance Mr. Harrison had. They carried pitchers and platters and stood at attention behind the girls' chairs.

"Now, the meal will be served to the right of you." Mr. Harrison motioned to the servants. "Come, come."

The servants spooned a bubbling, brown liquid into their bowls. Carrots and chunks of beef floated in the soup.

"First comes the soup. Obviously, we will be using a spoon to eat this." Mr. Harrison held up a spoon. "What you must remember is that spoons must only be used when you cannot use your fork. The fork must become your friend, and the spoon shall be your distant enemy that you only call upon during desperate times."

Emmaline glanced at the other girls. All of them seemed alert. She hoped this wouldn't take too long. If it did, she knew her resolve would come crashing down, and she wouldn't be able to help herself. She'd starved for so long; she couldn't bear it for much longer.

"Now, when selecting your silverware, start from

the outside and work your way in."

What does that mean? Emmaline studied the silverware in front of her and selected her best guess. Lydia pressed her fingers to Emmaline's wrist and shook her head. Emmaline's cheeks heated as she bit her lip. *Oh, that wasn't the right one.*

Mr. Harrison cleared his throat. "Lydia, while I appreciate your helpfulness and believe it is an attractive quality in someone who might be queen, Emmaline must learn to stand on her own."

Lydia blushed. "Forgive me."

Emmaline bit her lip. Hadn't she learnt to stand on her own already? But something told her the lesson was only beginning.

Emmaline watched as Julia spun around to her own music, waltzing in between the beds. She lifted her silk nightgown, as if it were a grand ballgown, pretending to be watched by an adoring crowd.

Julia laughed, apparently unembarrassed by her childlike behavior. Emmaline liked to watch her. Julia wasn't unlike Emmaline and her sisters when they were young, when the world seemed so innocent and magical.

Lydia stared at Julia, watching her over the book she was holding in her lap. "You dance so gracefully, I have no doubt that you'll best us all when Mr. Harrison teaches us how to dance."

Julia kept dancing, swaying and lifting her arms

dramatically. "I love to dance. Especially in silk. These nightgowns feel divine! I could get used to living in a palace."

"I don't know," Eleanor chimed in, braiding her hair down her back. "I prefer manors and cottages. If a house is too big, it starts to feel empty."

"Then why are you here, competing for the prince's hand?" Diana wrinkled her nose. Julia stopped dancing, waiting for Eleanor's answer.

Eleanor inhaled, pausing her plaiting. "My father sent me here. He believes that it will serve me well to marry the prince. And even if I don't marry him, he still thinks a position as the future queen's maid of honor will be advantageous." She continued the braid.

"But love is a choice." Lydia closed her book with a sharp *snap!* "Your father shouldn't have sent you away if that's not what you want."

Eleanor tied off the braid, then straightened her nightgown's skirt. "He gave me no choice. He told me about it, and then the next morning, he sent me on my way here. Boys are bred to defeat kings in battle, and girls are bred to tame kings to bring about peace."

Emmaline couldn't imagine her father ever forcing her to marry a stranger. Her father had had her best interests at heart, not his own. What was it like to grow up with a father like Eleanor's?

"But if men write romance novels in which the heroine decides who to give her heart to, can't they see that's how real life ought to be?" Lydia stared intently at Eleanor.

Someone sniffled in the corner of the room. Everyone turned to look. Anna sat on the edge of her bed, her hands folded in her lap and her head bowed.

"Anna, what's the matter?" Eleanor rushed toward her.

Anna sniffled again. "My mother sent me away, too. She thinks I spend too much time picking flowers and counting clouds for my age. She said I would either come here, or I would be sent to a convent." She pressed her hands to her face, her shoulders shaking. "She's never loved me. I know that's the real reason why she sent me away."

Emmaline wanted to say something but wasn't sure what. Diana opened a drawer and pulled out a hanky. She gave it to Eleanor, who lifted Anna's face and dabbed at her cheeks.

"It's all right, Anna," Lydia said, sitting on the other side of the young red-haired girl. "I'm sorry that happened to you."

Emmaline glanced down at her folded hands. Her heart ached. These girls were brave enough to share their pain and comfort each other. Could she tell them what had happened to her? Would they understand?

She had hidden her past away for so long. Surely it would sting when she opened the wound again to let other people see she'd been hurt.

"Well, all that matters is that we're here now, and I believe we're all here for a purpose." Julia suddenly sounded much older than her age.

"Julia's right." Lydia brushed her hand over

Anna's back. "We're here for a reason. We just have to be patient to discover what that reason is."

Emmaline wondered why she had ended up here. Surely God had not brought here simply to give her food and shelter. After all, this was a palace, not a poorhouse.

"Thank you." Anna attempted a smile. "At least I'm not as lonely here as I was at home."

"And we'll make certain that you never shall be again," Eleanor declared.

Anna sniffled and looked up. "Why did you come here to the palace, Lydia?"

Lydia sighed and sank down on her bed. "Well, ever since I was a child, I've always loved books. Fairytales and romances are my favorite. When my parents informed me of the queen's proclamation, I wanted to try my hand at it. If I don't marry the prince, living in the palace and meeting someone here shall be just as romantic."

Julia giggled and plopped down on an ottoman. "I came here because I've always wanted to be a princess, ever since I was a little girl. I can just imagine the balls and the gowns and the tiaras. My father wasn't sure that was a good enough reason for marrying Nicholas, but I convinced him eventually. Speaking of, I've heard that the prince is simply divine. While Lydia is reading fairytales, I shall be living one!"

Lydia scoffed good-naturedly and hit Julia with a pillow. Julia shrieked and then laughed. She retrieved her own pillow and hit Lydia back. Eleanor and Anna joined in. Emmaline giggled, then picked up her pillow and hit Eleanor. Eleanor cackled with laughter, holding her middle. Diana scoffed, shook her head, and went to bed.

The girls soon sat back down, laughing.

"Emmaline," Julia said. "We've all talked about our families and what brought us here. While we know why you're here, we don't know anything about your family. What happened to them?"

Emmaline's heart panged inside her. **Tell them**, a small voice whispered. **It helps to talk about it.** She retreated from their faces, walking to the window to try to muster up some courage. The glass was cold and chilled her skin as she stood close to it. "I don't remember much. But what I do is very precious to me."

"What do you mean?" Julia asked. All the other girls had gone quiet. Emmaline barely even heard them breathing.

She turned from the window. "My family is dead." The blade re-entered her chest. She caught her breath. "My sisters, my little brother, my parents. They're all dead." The blade twisted deep, slashing away at her insides.

No one said anything as they stared at her.

She couldn't bear the looks on their faces so she turned back to the window. "My life before was a fairytale. My sisters and I wore white lace and played croquet. My father held balls in our house for my mother. She was the most beautiful woman I'd ever seen. My brother and I chased each other through the house and climbed trees. Then in one sickening night, it all vanished. They were all gone."

She glanced around the room. Lydia wiped her face with her small hand as the other girls frowned deeply. Emmaline looked past them, staring at the crucifix on the wall. Small, whispered words tickled her ear. **Look to me for strength.**

"Oh, Emmaline. How awful," Julia whispered.

"Yes," Eleanor chimed in.

Emmaline's mouth trembled as her eyes burned. "Thank you." She wasn't sure what else to say. She walked toward her bed and climbed into it. "I suppose we should get some sleep now. I'm sure Mr. Harrison will have us quite busy tomorrow."

After a moment's silence, Eleanor nodded. "Yes, I suppose you're right." She crawled into the bed next to Emmaline's, her braid swishing behind her.

The rest of the girls got into bed, the playful energy in the room now dead. Emmaline bit her lip. She hadn't meant to kill the mood. Perhaps she shouldn't have said so much. She should have known better. Death followed her around everywhere, so why wouldn't it follow her here?

As the girls slept, Emmaline stared at the ceiling, trying to think about anything but her family's murder.

She felt so full for the first time in years. That ham had tasted like heaven. She couldn't remember the last time she'd had meat. Bread and rotten apples had barely kept her alive while she was on the streets. Sometimes she had been able to find a chunk of cheese or maybe even an orange. But tonight, she'd dined like royalty.

Even so, dinner had been far from perfect. She'd managed to spill a jelly on her skirt and knock over a cup of tea. Could she really learn all these things? She didn't know, but she wanted to learn. Ross had been kind enough to give her a place to stay. Besides, she'd learned how to live on the streets. If she could do that, she could learn how to live here, too.

She closed her eyes and buried herself beneath the covers. She hoped that tonight the ghosts would stay far away from her and finally let her sleep.

"Emmaline!" someone hissed. "Emmaline. Wake up!"

Emmaline opened her eyes to the darkness. Moonlight filtered in from the windows and illuminated her sisters' faces. Rose giggled and put her hand over her mouth. "Come on! Let's go see the stars!"

"*Please, Emmaline?*" Kathleen pleaded.

Emmaline sat up, smiling. "All right, all right!" She tossed away the covers and draped her robe over her shoulders.

"Wait, wait! You mustn't forget your crown." Charlotte placed the crown of flowers they'd made earlier that day on Emmaline's head. Emmaline breathed in its pleasant aroma.

"Now, come on!" Kathleen took her hand and pulled her out of the room.

They skipped down the halls and leapt across the moonbeams stretching along the floor. The stars twinkled down on them through the windows. Emmaline and her sisters held their arms out like wings and spun across the floor, flying through the house.

Rose giggled, a little too loudly.

"Shh! We mustn't wake anyone!" Charlotte whispered.

Rose caught onto Emmaline, holding onto her for support as she laughed uncontrollably. Emmaline couldn't help but join her. Her bubbling laughter was contagious.

Charlotte screamed and froze in the hall. Blood spurted from her middle and stained her dress.

Emmaline stared in disbelief. "Charlotte!"

Kathleen cried out now, blood flowing down her throat. She wrapped her hands around the wound, her eyes bulging with fear. She choked and fell to her knees. Emmaline trembled, tears burning her eyes.

Rose's grip on her loosened. Emmaline looked down and saw blood dripping down Rose's leg. Rose gasped and groaned, falling to the floor. As the ruby-red liquid pooled around her, Rose put her hand on her chest and lay on the ground.

Emmaline's heart roared in her ears. "No, no. This isn't happening." She glanced over her body. Where was the blood flowing out of her? Why wasn't she dying?

She fell beside Rose. Gasping, Rose wrapped her blood-stained hand around Emmaline's. Her skin was like ice in Emmaline's palm. Rose bored her blue eyes into her. "Don't forget us."

The moonlight fell upon the three bodies spilled across the hall. Against the knot in her throat, Emmaline raised her head and wailed.

Someone squeezed Emmaline's arm, over and over. "Emmaline, Emmaline. Wake up!"

She opened her eyes to Lydia standing in front of her. Julia, Eleanor, and Anna stood around her. Julia yawned and looked ready to fall over on the floor.

"What is it?" Emmaline sat up, her heart roaring in her ears.

"You were screaming," Lydia whispered.

Emmaline blinked. "What?"

"You were screaming. We've been trying to wake you, but you wouldn't until now."

"Are you all right?" Eleanor asked.

Emmaline glanced up, then out the window. The moon peeked into the room, like an eye watching her. Her whole body trembled. She could still feel the iciness of Rose's hand. "I suppose. Forgive me for waking you all."

"It's all right," Anna said. "You didn't mean—"

A large, growling noise came from the corner of the room. Diana moaned, then turned over in bed.

Julia glanced back in Diana's direction, then rolled her eyes. "Some queen she'll be. She'll keep the prince up all night!"

Eleanor laughed. Emmaline's eyes burned with tears. She could still hear her sisters' laughter echoing down the halls and smell the blood staining their clothes.

Lydia put her hand on her shoulder. "Try to dream of good things this time." She smiled, then walked back to bed with the other girls.

Emmaline laid her head back down on her pillow. *If only it were that easy.*

"*Don't forget us.*"

How could she forget when the ghosts wouldn't let her rest?

Chapter Four

EMMALINE COULDN'T WAIT to stop spinning around. What was the use of learning to dance if she didn't want to be queen, anyway?

"Keep your shoulders back!" Mr. Harrison said. "Don't look at your feet, Emmaline. Look at your partner's face, for pity's sake. Slow down a bit! The waltz must be done with poise and grace. You're not a hummingbird, you're a swan."

Emmaline danced with Lydia, her cheeks burning. She'd danced many times with her sisters and brother, but knowing how to dance was one of the many things she'd forgotten. She did remember that dancing with James, as her mother played fast melodies on the piano, had been fun and carefree. But these dance lessons were not.

"I don't even want to marry the prince, Lydia," Emmaline whispered. "And I most certainly don't want to dance in front of a ballroom full of people."

"I think it would be wonderfully romantic," Lydia sighed. She spun Emmaline for the tenth time, and for the tenth time, Emmaline's foot caught on her skirt, and she nearly tumbled into Lydia.

Mr. Harrison sighed. Emmaline's cheeks prickled with heat again.

Emmaline regained her position. "It might be, but I don't belong in such a world," she replied to Lydia.

"Really?" Lydia arched a brow. "Then why are you in the palace now?"

"I wish I knew."

"Beautiful form, Diana. Good work, Eleanor!" Mr. Harrison shouted over the music. A quartet played instruments in the corner, meeting none of the girls' gazes. Still, there were too many pairs of eyes in this tiny room for Emmaline's taste.

Emmaline glanced at Diana, whose movements glided across the marble floors like a swan floating over a lake. Diana closed her eyes and craned her neck as she spun, her skirts fluttering around her like flower petals. Diana was born for this world of shimmering gowns and swelling music. Unlike Emmaline, whose world had burned to the ground and would never rise again.

The music ended and Mr. Harrison clapped, signaling the end of their dance lesson. "Well, ladies, most of you did very well in today's lesson. I am proud of each of you, but some of you need to devote yourselves to your practices a bit more." He glanced at Emmaline, and her cheeks burned with embarrassment. "I've an idea," he said suddenly. "Why don't you all join me on a walk? You need to practice your enunciation, and singing is the best way to do that."

The girls murmured their approval and headed for the door.

Emmaline started to follow Lydia but Mr. Harrison called after her. "Emmaline, I'd like to speak with you for a moment."

She muffled a moan, instead turning to face him. "Of course, Mr. Harrison."

His dark eyes held her gaze gently. "Emmaline, you must apply yourself in these dance lessons. Dance is an important part of what may be your future life."

She hung her head. "I know, Mr. Harrison. And I try—I do. It's just hard."

"I know you do. That's why I'm stricter with you than the other girls. I see your potential, your drive to learn. You're special, Emmaline." His eyes shone back at her.

She tried to smile, but her mouth fell. "I'm not entirely sure of that."

His expression was hard, as if he meant what he said. "I am. None of the other girls are like you."

She smiled then. "Thank you, Mr. Harrison."

His eyes softened. "I believe you can do it. Keep practicing, and you'll soon be the most beautiful dancer in the ballroom." He motioned toward the door. "Let's go."

Mr. Harrison was right. It was time for Emmaline to learn to dance again. It was time to make a new life for herself. She couldn't help that the old one had turned to ashes, but it would be her fault if she let her new world crumble, too.

"You two, go to the eastern quarter. There are reports of robberies there." Ross pointed in the direction he'd given, then watched two of his men stride down the palace yard for the stables. Satisfied, he nodded to himself. He liked his position of protecting the crown, her castle, and all who dwelt inside its walls. It kept him busy, kept his mind's eye trained on anything else but his past.

Distant singing caught his attention. A small group of people were coming down the staircase, heading for the garden. He looked closer. Mr. Harrison led the flock of girls outside as they sang a song. Emmaline was in the back, her chin held high. Even from here, he could see the pink in her cheeks from the chill in the air. The girls' soft voices were lovely, like the promise of spring. Ross's heart skipped.

He could scarcely believe he'd found her, after all this time. He'd searched and searched for her, hoping the rumors had been true. After three years had passed, he'd been forced to give up. But now, she was here, safe inside the palace walls, singing only a few yards away.

"She's lovely, isn't she, Cap'n?" William asked.

Ross jerked his gaze from Emmaline, startled. "Who?"

"The brunette in the back. I see the way you're looking at her." William stood with John, who was grinning at Ross with his eyebrows raised.

Ross smiled, shaking his head. "Get on back to work, both of you."

William and John laughed as they walked to the stables.

They were right. And Ross was glad they'd caught him. If they hadn't, he might not have realized he was falling. He needed to stop while he was ahead.

Ross strode through the palace, his boots thudding in the empty halls. The portraits of past rulers stared at him as he passed, their necks stiff and their eyes emotionless.

"Come on, get it right already!" a girl huffed somewhere.

Ross slowed his steps and stopped in an open doorway. Emmaline stood in the middle of the room, with one arm raised and the other holding her skirts up. She stepped around in a circle, as if dancing, but tripped over her hem. "No!" she cried.

Moaning, she wiped her face and turned around. Her eyes widened as her cheeks turned as pink as roses. "Ross!" she gasped. "How long have you been standing there?"

He grinned apologetically, leaning against the doorframe. "Not long but long enough to see that you are in distress." He stepped into the room. A clock ticked above the fireplace mantle while frost glittered along the windows like diamonds. An Indian rug lay spread across the mahogany floor, and a dozen satin couches were sprawled across the room.

Emmaline huffed again and plopped down on an ottoman. "I've been practicing for hours. Dance is the one hoop I can't seem to jump through."

Ross smiled. "It's more difficult for some than for others. You'll get it."

She glanced up, pushing her shoulders back. "I know. It's more difficult than I imagined it would be. But I have to get it right." She straightened her skirts, then met his gaze again. "I can't dishonor my family any more by not living when I have the chance. They would not want me to wallow in the shadows. I've been dead for so long that I have to learn how to live all over again."

Her eyes held the power of mountains, and delicate curls hung over her marble forehead. She was the loveliest thing he'd ever seen. His heart sped up and his lungs tried to keep up. "I'm glad to see you so full of spirit now."

She smiled. "I am, too."

His chest tightened. What if she were still living on the streets? What would have happened if he hadn't stopped those ruffians from touching her? No doubt, she would have been ruined, or even dead. She wouldn't be alive now, smiling at him, regaining the courage to dance again, even if the music in her ears had long been discordant. He wanted to help her, to teach her how to dance, to teach her how to live again.

Ross stood to his feet and extended his hand down to her.

Emmaline furrowed her brows. "What are you doing?"

"Teaching you to dance."

Her mouth fell open. "What? You can dance?"

He shrugged. "Perhaps not as well as the prince, but yes, I can." He tilted his head in pleading. "It's not every day someone is resurrected."

She smiled and stood to her feet. "Well, then, I accept."

Ross held out his left arm and offered her his right hand. She took his right hand, then extended her arm and took his left hand. Her lashes cast shadows over her bold cheekbones. Heat spread over him like a warm fire over icy skin.

What was happening to him? He was captain of the queen's guard, trained to handle any disaster that may befall the Crown. But this young woman disarmed him with just one glance.

He cleared his throat. "Good, you've got that part down. Now, let's get on to the next part. Ready?"

She nodded.

With his heart stuck in his throat, Ross took the first step and she followed him. They danced across the Indian rug, their feet turning over the blue and red kaleidoscope-like shapes.

"One, two, three, one, two, three . . ." He counted their movements, counted the seconds he spent with her hands in his, every moment more precious than the last.

"Keep your head up," Ross said. "I know you're afraid, but you have to look at me. Pretend I'm someone you admire."

Her head shot up. "Oh, but you are, Ross!"

The breath in his lungs escaped for a moment but he shoved away the hope rising inside him. She was here to impress the prince, and he knew she would. He was behaving childishly.

"Not everyone would have shown the same kindness you've shown me. You are a good friend." She smiled warmly.

Friend. A metallic taste coated his tongue. *That's good of her to keep her mind focused on what really matters, on what she came here for. If only I could do the same.*

They kept dancing. Her feet moved rapidly and stumbled over the rug.

"Try to slow down a bit," Ross said. "You're not a hummingbird, you're a swan."

Emmaline bit her lip and cast her gaze away. "Mr. Harrison said the same, and I'm still not certain of that."

"That's all right. I am, and one day you will be, too."

Emmaline grinned. "I hope so."

He flexed his jaw in an effort to ignore the warmth shooting through him again.

As she spun, Emmaline tripped over her skirt. Gasping, she fell into his chest and then glanced up at him. His heart nearly barreled out of his chest. The clock in the room stopped ticking. Flecks of gold were scattered like stars in her brown eyes. He wanted to chart the constellations in them.

Emmaline moved away quickly, her cheeks red as blood. "Forgive me. I'm so dreadfully clumsy sometimes."

Ross shook his head, trying to shake away the desire that she was still there against his heart, her soft cheek against his chest. "No apology necessary. Let's start again."

When they had finished, Ross pulled his hands away and clapped. Emmaline giggled, beaming proudly ear to ear.

"That was wonderful, Emmaline." His hands were still warm, even after he'd let go of her hands.

"Do you really think so?" Her eyes glowed.

He nodded. "You were made for marble ballroom floors and golden halls."

She furrowed her brows again. "How do you know that?"

He swallowed. He'd said too much. "I just know it.

I can see it inside you. Soon, it'll be as if you've lived in a palace your entire life."

Emmaline smiled again. "I hope so. And with your help, I'm one step closer. I've been praying for strength." She cocked her head to the side. "Are you a praying man, Ross? I hope you don't mind my asking."

Ross chewed on the inside of his cheek for a minute, the warmth of moments before leaving him. "I used to be. Then I lost my home and lost interest."

She glanced toward the window. "I see. If I had done that, I don't think I would be here right now. I'd be dead in an unmarked grave."

His heart skipped a beat. Her words made the hair on the back of his neck stand up. "You really believe that? Even after you've lost everything?"

"No one's ever truly lost everything until they lose their faith." She gazed back at him like a fortress of strength.

He had no reply. What she said sounded true, but was it true for him?

She took his hand between hers. "Thank you, Ross, for helping me." She glanced at the clock. "I'd better go now. Mr. Harrison will be teaching us more table etiquette in a little while."

"Until next time, then."

She nodded. "Yes, of course. Goodbye for now." She turned toward the door.

"Goodbye." He watched Emmaline leave the room. Such grace in her walk. She may not have known it, but she was born for this life. She was born to live within grand halls and wear beautiful gowns.

She had smiled back at him. He'd never felt so alive in his life. Did she know she put breath in his lungs? Did she know that she was on his mind every hour of the day?

He knew he shouldn't feel this way. She wasn't ever his to begin with. He brought her here for a better life, and that life might exist with the prince. It was dangerous for him to feel this way. If he let her overtake him, heart and soul, he would bleed to death when she was ripped away from him. As lovely as she was, there was a fair chance Nicholas would fall in love with her.

After all, who wouldn't?

Snowflakes fell like diamonds outside the window. They clinked against the frost-covered glass as Emmaline watched from her bed.

Sheets rustled a few feet away from Emmaline. Julia sat up, rubbed her eyes, and announced, "It's Christmas morning!"

A knock came at the door, and the rest of the girls awakened. A maid appeared, a smile stretching her pretty face. "Mr. Harrison has instructed me to tell you all to get ready. There's a surprise waiting for each of you in the red room."

The girls glanced at each other, giggling with excitement. Nearly in unison, they leapt out of bed and scrambled around the room, as if the surprise would disappear if they did not hurry.

When their corsets were tied and their hair curled, the girls scurried down the staircases, whispering their ideas of what would be waiting for them. Emmaline floated away to a time in the past, when she had run down the stairs with her sisters in their nightgowns, James cutting in front of them to get to the presents first.

Julia was the first to reach the red room. Emmaline could hear her gasping even from several feet away. "Oh, it's so beautiful!"

The girls poured into the room. Emmaline gasped. A fire roared in the hearth, the flames leaping merrily. A tree stood in the center of the room, so tall Emmaline had to crane her neck to see the star on top. Red satin bows were tied to the tree limbs while popcorn lay strung along its body. Presents lay at the bottom of the tree, glittering in the sunlight filtering in through the windows.

Mr. Harrison appeared from behind the tree, looking dapper in his suit. "Happy Christmas, girls." He smiled.

"Happy Christmas, Mr. Harrison," they said in unison. Julia giggled, twirling the skirt of her nightgown around.

"Who did all this, Mr. Harrison?" Eleanor asked, stepping further into the room and staring at the garland hanging from the ceiling.

Mr. Harrison grinned, his hands behind his back. "I'm afraid I cannot give you his identity. He has asked that I keep that a secret." He winked at them.

Lydia sank to the floor in front of the tree, her skirts puddling around her. "Oh, I wish he hadn't. I'd like to kiss his cheek in thanks for all this!"

"It really is too generous." Emmaline glanced around the room as if something would give a hint as to who the man was.

"Can we open our presents now, Mr. Harrison?" Julia asked, her eyes like two big sapphires as she bit her lip in wait.

"Go right ahead. But don't dilly-dally. He's also arranged for us to have a Christmas breakfast."

"Oh, how wonderful!" Anna cried. Even Diana looked excited.

As the gifts were opened, wrapping paper flew through the air and piled up on the floor.

Julia ripped open her boxes and gasped. "Oh, it's pearls! I have pearls! Aren't they pretty, Eleanor?" She held out her new necklace for everyone to see.

Eleanor chuckled as she lifted the lid on her box. She gasped and slipped two white gloves out of the box. "Oh, they're lovely. I've always wanted a pair like this."

"Mr. Harrison, there's something here for you!" Diana announced. She sat up from her sitting position and handed him the box.

"Thank you, Diana." He opened the box, his face brightening. He held out the contents of his box. "It's a pocket watch. I've been needing a new one."

Emmaline smiled, then glanced down at the

present in her lap. She smoothed her thumb over the tag that bore her name, admiring the handwriting. She untied the ribbon and lifted the lid, then pulled out a book.

"*The Melodies of Mikhailov*," Emmaline whispered. She brushed her fingers over the words, their smooth texture cascading over her skin.

"What did you get, Emmaline?" Lydia asked, her cheeks flushed with joy.

Emmaline beamed, her heart thrumming to a quicker rhythm. "It's a piano book. *The Melodies of Mikhailov.*"

She knew exactly who had done all this. She knew who had decorated the red room, who had bought each of these gifts, who had arranged for the Christmas breakfast. *It has to be him. Who else could have known that I love to play the piano?* It was the boy from the piano room, the one who had listened to her play the day she arrived.

Emmaline flipped through the pages. One of them had something written on it: *"Nightingale's Soliloquy" is my favorite.*

She smiled, hoping she could play it for him one day. Even though she'd uncovered the mystery, she wouldn't tell anyone else. She'd keep it a secret like he wanted.

But who was he? And why had he done all this?

Chapter Five

TWO MONTHS PASSED. Emmaline had forgotten how quickly time could fly by. During the past three years of walking from place to place, time had seemed to drip slowly away. Now it spun away like Julia whisking by her.

Emmaline spent her days in the palace, sitting with the girls around their bedchamber hearth and watching the snow fall. When they weren't huddled together in front of the fire, reading and crocheting, the girls were fitted for new gowns and practiced their dancing, curtsying, walking, and speaking skills. Each night at supper, Mr. Harrison taught them how to eat like the refined ladies they were all becoming. Emmaline would have never guessed she could learn so much and do it so well.

She loved the girls. Every night they braided each other's hair and danced around the bedchamber. Sometimes they sparred with each other with their pillows, and when they were all drunk with hysterical laughter, they would fantasize about the prince. Emmaline drank in every moment with them, and the more she drank, the more alive she felt.

When she wasn't with the girls, Emmaline talked with Ross when he wasn't making his rounds or solving a crisis. She often found him at the stables, brushing down his horse. Sometimes, she would bring his stallion, Felix, an apple. She liked to talk to Ross about her lessons and to hear about his day.

As the months passed by, Emmaline knew in her heart that becoming the future queen's maid would keep her content. After all, she lived in a beautiful palace, she wore lovely gowns, and she had wonderful friends all around her. The prince might be a good young man, but she had all she wanted. What more could she need?

Golden sunlight streamed into the windows and into Emmaline's heart. She breathed it in and tasted it on her tongue. The last two months had been wonderful. Every day was filled with conversing over tea with the girls and learning how to live as a young lady again. It hadn't been easy, but Emmaline was learning her way.

Emmaline stood in her undergarments with the other girls. Three maids went back and forth between each girl to tighten their corsets. Emmaline raised her arms as the maid draped the petticoat over her.

Julia spun around, holding her petticoat between her fingers as if it were the skirt of a grand ball gown. She waltzed between the beds as gracefully as a flittering butterfly.

Eleanor gasped as her corset was tightened. "Julia! Not so close to the window! You'll expose yourself to everyone outside!"

Emmaline couldn't bite back her amusement, giggling as Julia moved her dancing away from the window. A maid carrying an elaborate pink gown tried to get her attention, but Julia was in her own little world. The maid sighed in frustration.

"Julia!" Anna called. "She's trying to dress you."

Julia turned and bit her lip. "Oh, sorry."

Emmaline shook her head and smiled to herself. She wasn't quite sure why they were being dressed so exquisitely today. There was no ball or other social event happening of which she was aware. For all she knew, it was just another day at the palace.

Emmaline's own maid walked toward the couch, where dozens of gowns lay for the girls to choose from. "Which one would you like to wear, my lady?"

Emmaline pressed her finger to her lip. "Hmm." Her eyes roamed over the choices. Silk, tulle, taffeta, and lace. Sunshine yellow, delicate lavender, shy pink and green, and ocean blue. Mr. Harrison had suggested that she wear either lavender or blue. The lavender gown was lovely, with a square neckline, a fitted bodice, and a shimmery skirt overlay. "I'll wear the lavender one, please."

The maid smiled. "I hoped you would pick that one. It would look just lovely with your hair if you don't mind my saying so."

Emmaline returned her grin. "Oh, I don't mind. Thank you."

When everyone was dressed, Mr. Harrison came into the room and gave his approval. He looked Emmaline over and smiled. "I see you took my advice."

Emmaline nodded. "Of course."

He grinned, then glanced at the maid. "Bring me the jewelry box." When she brought it, he opened it and placed a golden bracelet on her wrist. She'd had her ears pierced a few weeks ago, and now pearls dangled from them. When he was finished, he smiled again. "Beautiful and lovely."

She smiled. "Because of you."

He shook his head. "I haven't done anything. I've only accentuated your natural beauty."

She blushed and didn't say anything more.

He gathered the girls together and sat them down on the couch. "Now, I know you're all wondering what you will be doing today since you've been dressed so finely." He paused, looking each of them in the eye. "Eight weeks have passed, and I've never been so pleased. You've all excelled in your lessons. All of you belong in the palace. You've all transformed into lovely, graceful swans that will fit with the nobility. And now, today, you will meet the queen and her son, Prince Nicholas."

Julia squealed, then remembered to be well-mannered and shushed herself.

Emmaline's insides twisted. So this was what the dressing up was for? She had to see the queen again–already? Her palms dampened with sweat. The queen hadn't liked her. What if the prince was the same way? What if the queen had told him about her? What if Emmaline forgot everything she learned and embarrassed herself in front of the monarchy?

Mr. Harrison continued. "We will meet them in the blue room in ten minutes, so we must leave now."

The girls sprang from the couch, but Emmaline stood up slowly. She followed Mr. Harrison and the girls down the hall. Perhaps there was no need to worry. If she embarrassed herself or if the prince had already made up his mind about her, then her role as queen was not to be—which was what she wanted. Besides, who would honor her as the leader of a whole country once they found out she was an orphaned street rat, anyway?

Still, her heart pulsed in her throat. Her legs trembled. She tried to pray for peace, but the words wouldn't come. Only—*Please, God. Please.*

Nicholas watched himself in the mirror as he straightened

his tie. He smoothed down his clothes and ran his hand through his hair. He preferred to dress himself. Underneath the crown, he was just a man, a man like any other. And someday, he hoped his subjects would know that.

Something crashed in the distance. He jumped a little, then rubbed his forehead. He blocked out the memories of the flames and the screams. He was getting better, and he didn't want to fall into the same pit again.

He had to remind himself that he'd had better luck than his friends. None of them had made it out, but he had. He was alive, wasn't he? And today, he was going to meet the girl of his dreams.

A knock came to the door. "Nicholas! We must hurry."

"Coming, Mother." He smiled at his reflection.

Mother's face was pinched when he met her outside his bedchamber. "I want to get this over with," she snapped. "I have other important tasks at hand, and they cannot wait so you can find love."

Nicholas sighed as he walked with his mother and a few guards. "Mother, you know I cannot marry someone I don't love."

She frowned sardonically. "So you've told me."

He thrust out his arms in exasperation. "Even you married for love!"

Mother stopped in her tracks. Her face was stone but her blue eyes glimmered fiercely. "And my whole world crumbled when your father died. A monarch doesn't have time to mourn for the loss of their spouse. It's better that we don't marry for love so that we can pick up the pieces more easily when they die."

"I can't go my whole life without knowing what love is." He didn't know why she was upset with him. For a while, she had been the one that wanted him to marry. Now it seemed he and his mother had switched places. Now she was the bitter one. He wasn't sure why or how she had changed so quickly. Perhaps it was growing more and more difficult for her to live without his father. He hoped she would heal one day and return to her old self. He hoped that she would see that he wanted to be like his father, a good man in love with a good woman.

He'd prayed for weeks that out of these six girls, he'd find the one. Something told him she was here. It was almost like he could feel her here, wandering down the halls, waiting for him.

Nicholas and his mother entered the blue room, their names announced as they came in. Nicholas glanced toward the group of girls but couldn't make out all their faces. They were all lovely, dressed in elaborate gowns and jewels. One with blonde hair smiled eagerly at him.

Mr. Harrison moved down the line and introduced him to each girl. The blonde one was first. "Your Highness, this is Julia Quinn from Manchester."

Julia curtsied, grinning from ear to ear. "It's a pleasure to meet you, Your Highness."

He gave her a smile. "Likewise."

"This is Anna Edwards from Bloomsdale."

The fetching red-haired girl had a sprinkle of freckles across her nose. "I'm honored, Your Highness," she said gently. She couldn't quite meet his gaze.

She's nervous, poor girl. He smiled again in an effort to dissolve her nerves. "As am I."

Mr. Harrison introduced him to three other girls: Lydia Lee, Eleanor Montgomery, and Diana Foster. All of them were beautiful and seemed like the kind of girl his mother would like. Soft. Quiet. Reserved.

"And the last girl is Emmaline," Edwin said. "I'm afraid she doesn't know her last name. Captain Ross found her living on the streets before she was brought here. But, as you can see, she is just as cultured and lovely as the other girls."

He did see. All he could do was see and look. His heart melted like a candle in his chest. The breath in his lungs fluttered like a bird testing out its wings. The more he looked, the more she stole what little breath he could muster up. Her deep brown eyes held a story he wanted to read again and again. Curls hung around her forehead, in front of her ears, and down her back. She was pale as ivory but her lips were red as a rose. This was the girl he met in the piano hall. Only he hadn't found out her name, and she hadn't known who he was.

She gasped, as if shocked. "You. You're the man I met in the piano hall."

He smiled. "Yes. I remember you, too."

Her chest heaved. "But, but . . . *you're the prince!*

And you gave me the piano book."

The one named Julia gasped loudly. Nicholas's mother shot her a look, and she blushed, looking down at the ground.

"Yes, I'm afraid so," he said. "And yes, I did." He liked her voice, cultured and smooth.

The girl's chest rose and fell rapidly. He reached out and caught her hand, steadying her. A jolt of pleasure went up his arm and through his whole body. "Are you all right?"

She nodded, dazed. Her eyes were wide and her skin was white as a ghost. "Yes. Forgive me for my outburst, Your Highness."

"No apology necessary." He smiled at her. "It's nice to meet you again."

She blushed. "And you."

He wanted to paint her and leave no detail unmentioned. The pink of her cheeks. Her full brows. Her long lashes. Those deep, dark eyes. The flutter of curls gathered around her ears.

"You know this girl, Nicholas?" Mother's eyes flashed.

"Yes. We met in the piano room. She plays quite well." He smiled as Emmaline blushed again. He liked it when she did that.

"Where would a girl like her learn to play piano?" Mother pursed her lips.

Nicholas waited for Emmaline to offer an answer. She opened her mouth as if to speak, but no words came. She frowned and gazed down, her brow knit

Rise

together in worry.

Nicholas glanced up at his mother. "I don't know, but what I do know is that she plays like an angel."

Her head rose then. "You speak too highly of me, Your Highness."

"Oh, I could never do that."

They met each other's eyes. Nicholas wasn't breathing for quite some time, and he didn't even care.

The other girls watched them. He hoped they wouldn't be jealous of the attention he'd given to this girl. Then he realized he was still holding her hand. He let go, his tie suddenly too tight.

"Nicholas, I believe you have something to tell everyone," Mother said.

He cleared his throat. "Oh, yes." He stood where he would be visible to all. "Each of you will spend individual time with me so that I can get to know you personally. Then when I've made my decision, and when you've made yours, one of you will be my wife."

He glanced at all the girls. Emmaline wasn't meeting his eyes. She was looking at her feet. Did he make her so nervous?

"Well, Your Highness, we have all been delighted to stand in your presence," Mr. Harrison stepped forward. "I hope we haven't taken too much of your time."

He held out his hand as if dusting away Mr. Harrison's apology. "Oh, no. It's no trouble."

"Good." Mr. Harrison grinned. "We must be on our

way, then."

"I look forward to seeing you all again," Nicholas said. Emmaline was still staring at her feet.

As Mr. Harrison led the line of girls out of the room, Nicholas watched them go. *Look back. Look back at me.*

Emmaline stole a glance over her shoulder, met his gaze, and quickly turned back.

His heart sang in his chest as he glanced at the ceiling. *Oh, God, she's wonderful.*

When the door clicked behind the girls, and Nicholas and his mother were alone in the room, she turned her flashing eyes on him. "What was that?" she snapped.

He blinked. "What was what?"

"That—that display with that girl just now! As if you know her!"

"Well, we did meet on one occasion. She was playing the piano, and I happened to hear her playing. She didn't know who I was then. That was why she was surprised just now."

Mother's lips were red from her pressing them together. "And what is this that I hear about your giving her a piano book?"

Nicholas sighed, smiling as he ran a hand through his hair. "That was at Christmas, Mother. I gave each of them a gift, but none of them knew that it was I who had done it. I asked Mr. Harrison to keep it a secret. Emmaline must have figured it out." *Clever girl.*

Dimples appeared in Mother's pinched cheeks

and her eyes shot irritated darts at him. "Well, she may be clever, son, but she is not for you. So you had better get rid of that blush of yours and put her out of your mind. I will not allow such goings-on to continue." With a snap of her skirts, Mother left the room, obviously not interested in waiting for his reply.

He didn't care what his mother said. She was bitter and biased. No matter what, he had to see Emmaline again.

"How did it feel to hold his hand?"

"Was it warm?"

"Was it soft?"

Emmaline lay in bed, remembering every question the girls had peppered her with. Her hands were spread over her middle as she stared at the ceiling. *It felt wonderful. It was as warm as the sun on my face. It was as soft as silk.*

Something new spread through her veins. It pulsed through her. It stored itself inside her lungs like oxygen.

His eyes flashed in her mind, over and over again. She'd seen the ocean before, but it had never been so blue as his eyes. His hair was dark and swept over his forehead. It was slightly wavy. He was tall, but not too tall. His shoulders were firm, hidden beneath his suit jacket.

And his name. Oh, his name. *Nicholas.* She breathed

it in like spring air after a long and cold winter. She felt its sweet rhythm as she whispered it to herself as she lay in bed. "Nicholas. Nicholas." Her thumbs rubbed over one another. "Nicholas. Nicholas."

She kept whispering his name. It became her anthem of hope. Was this her dry path through the sea, leading her to a new life? She kept whispering, kept hoping, until her eyes closed and she dreamed a new dream.

Chapter Six

"COME BACK HERE!" Emmaline shouted.

Anna giggled, running across the white plain of the palace yard. Gray clouds billowed over them, but the sun peeked out like a shy child peering out from behind its mother's skirts.

"You'll never catch me!" Anna shrieked.

Emmaline's throat burned with the icy air as she laughed. "Oh, yes, I will!" She wound her legs into a fast gallop and chased Anna, the snow crunching beneath her feet.

She must look like a child, playing a game of tag, but she hadn't felt so free, so light in years. She liked running. It felt like flying, flying over a world of storms, flying in the sky where everything was safe and bright. When she ran, she could escape the shadows hounding her.

Her sides ached. She came to a stop, trying to catch her breath. She glanced back toward the other girls, all gathered in the courtyard. Julia sat in front of her easel, and Eleanor sat on a bench, holding her position so that Julia could paint her. Diana shivered and hugged herself while Lydia built a snowman. Mr. Harrison had given them the day off from lessons, and the decision to play in the snow had been nearly unanimous.

Emmaline turned away, eyes roving over her surroundings. The trees were bare and covered with icicles. White powdery snow blanketed the grass. The palace grounds had been turned into a shimmering world of white.

Anna walked back, panting hard. "I thought . . . you were . . . chasing me."

"I had to stop. I was missing so much by running past it."

"I see what you mean." Anna's freckled nose wrinkled as she grinned. "I love being outside. There's always something new to discover."

Emmaline smiled back. She sank into the snow and laid down. *The world looks much different down here.* The sky was misty and white, like a bride's veil in the wind. Anna followed Emmaline onto the ground.

Emmaline sighed. "This feels wonderful."

"Yes, it does," Anna said. She turned toward Emmaline. "Watch this." She spread her arms and legs out and waved them across the snow.

Emmaline laughed, her breath turning to fog.

"My governess taught me that," Anna chirped. "She called it a snow angel. Mother didn't like her very much after that, so I didn't have her for very long."

"Your governess sounds like a lovely woman." Emmaline waved her arms and legs in the same motion. Something melted in her chest, and a weight lifted. She laughed again.

"What on earth are you doing?" Diana towered above them, her brows furrowed and her hands on her hips.

"Making snow angels," Anna said innocently.

"You're welcome to join us," Emmaline added.

Diana scoffed. "I would die before I would lay down in the snow and do something so childish."

"It's quite fun, Diana." Anna sat up.

Diana pursed her lips. "We aren't here to have fun. We're here to learn how to become proper ladies of the court, and *ladies* would never do this. What if the prince walked by?"

"Then he would see us as we really are. Two fun-loving girls who aren't afraid of life." Emmaline rose from the ground.

"More like two—" A snowball flew in front of

Diana's face and she screamed. "What was that?"

Emmaline craned her neck and searched for the source of the snowball. Lydia stood several feet away, bent over with laughter. Diana followed Emmaline's gaze and huffed.

Anna laughed, rolling a snowball of her own into her hands.

Emmaline laughed, too, when she saw the horrified look on Diana's face. Diana backed away and ran across the yard, screaming.

"Come on," Anna giggled. "Let's get her. Someone has to teach her to have fun."

Emmaline rolled more snowballs and carried them in her arm. She leapt to her feet and, together with Anna, chased Diana across the snow.

Diana shrieked and flailed her arms. "Help! Help me! They're insane!"

Moments later, Lydia, Eleanor, and Julia joined the chase.

Emmaline was surprised by how fast Diana ran. She didn't look like someone who enjoyed the exercise but looked more like someone who'd rather spend their days reclining on a marble couch. Diana finally stopped, panting, her hands on her knees. When the girls neared, she glanced up with a dark scowl in her eyes. "Don't you *dare* hit me with those things! I'll report you to the prince—and to the queen! She'll have you thrown out for behaving like barbarians!"

As the girls' snowballs whistled through the air,

Diana squealed and shielded herself. She jumped around like a frog, trying to dodge the balls but failing.

Emmaline laughed until her sides hurt. Snow hit her neck and slid down her back. She shrieked and whipped around, trying to find the culprit. Julia giggled.

Emmaline scoffed. "I'm going to get you, Julia Quinn!"

She chased Julia over the plain. Julia was much better at dodging the balls than Diana was, but finally, Emmaline hit her. Julia squealed, cackling with laughter.

"I thought I'd never get you!" Emmaline shouted.

"I play this with my brothers," Julia said, gulping big breaths of air. "They're older and bigger than me, and I had to learn to be as good as them to defend myself."

Emmaline laughed. As Julia walked toward Emmaline, wiping her eyes with her fingers, a snowball flew toward Julia.

Julia gasped. "Did you do that?"

"No." Emmaline looked around until her eyes landed on the source. Her heart dove down to her toes, nearly knocking her off-balance.

Nicholas stood a few feet away, laughing. "Mind if I join you all?"

"No," Emmaline smiled, though she was terrified she would accidentally hit him. He was the prince, after all. The queen already hated her, and she would be furious if she knew Emmaline hit her son with a snowball.

"I couldn't resist coming down." He smiled at Emmaline and Julia. "I saw you all playing together, having fun."

"Oh, yes, we are having fun," Julia said. When Nicholas was out of earshot, she grabbed Emmaline's arm and whispered in her ear. "Even more now that he's here." She giggled.

"*Julia!*" Emmaline gasped, laughing.

Emmaline liked to watch Nicholas play. His dimples were the biggest she'd ever seen, and his blue eyes lit up like stars. Warmth spread in her cheeks and almost made her forget the cold.

Diana didn't seem very happy, even with the prince here. She shrieked every time someone hit her. Finally, she curled her hands into fists and stomped away toward the palace. "This is a game for children!"

Emmaline watched her go, then blinked as something light and cold fell on her eyelashes. White flakes cascaded from the sky and dusted the ground. "It's snowing again!" She opened her mouth and let a few flakes melt on her tongue.

A snowball hit Emmaline in the back. She spun around. "Julia!"

Julia cackled, holding her sides. Emmaline bent and rolled snow into a ball. "I'm going to get you!" She pushed her arm back and threw it toward the giggling blonde. Julia dodged it, and the snowball hit Nicholas square in the chest.

Emmaline gasped, covering her mouth with her

wet gloves. Her heart pulsed in her throat. "Oh, forgive me, Your Highness! I was aiming for Julia."

Nicholas grinned at her. "It's quite all right, Miss Emmaline." He bent and made a snowball. "Now it gives me a chance to have . . . my . . . *revenge!*"

Emmaline laughed, hitched up her skirts, and ran.

"I'm right behind you!" he yelled.

"Not for long!" she yelled back.

She headed deeper into the palace yard, right toward the trees. Her chest rose and fell in rapid succession as her feet sped through the snow. Emmaline spread her arms out and closed her eyes. She couldn't hear the snow crunching beneath her feet anymore. *I must be flying, then.* She ran and didn't stop. Her feet were surely pounding the ground but she couldn't hear them. She was high in the clouds now.

"Watch out, the pond's froze over!" Nicholas shouted.

A crack roared in her ears, a phantom gunshot in the distance. She glanced down and fell into the water, screaming.

She was drowning in blood. It was cold and ruby red all around her. Shrieks sliced her eardrums. Rose, Charlotte, and Kathleen fell through the water beside her, their skin pale and their gowns stained with blood. "Help us, Emmaline!" they cried before disappearing into the depths.

"I'm going to get you!" a voice said from beneath

her. The voice pounded in her ears, so deep it consumed her. Emmaline glanced down. A man swam toward her, reaching for her legs with jagged, claw-like nails. He gnashed his teeth at her. And worst of all, where his eyes should have been were black holes.

Emmaline's heart panged like church bells. She flailed her arms and kicked her legs. She had to escape. She gasped for air and a flurry of bubbles flew above her. Her throat was dry with the chill swallowing her whole. She kicked as fast as she could and swam toward the surface.

She screamed when her face broke through the water. The cold blasted through her. The wind howled in her ears and she heard Rose screaming. A hand wrapped around her foot and pulled. She screamed again and kicked the surface of the water. "He's got me! He's trying to pull me under!"

Screams of a faraway night deafened her. She sobbed and choked on the water splashing in her face. The hand on her foot tugged harder, digging its claws into her skin. Dark eyes flashed in her mind, teeth bared and ready to consume her.

"Emmaline, grab the branch!"

She opened her eyes. Nicholas was lying about a foot away from her, extending a branch toward her. His blue eyes were like wild seas, his forehead creased with worry.

She kicked her legs again and wrapped her hand around the branch. "Don't let go!"

"I won't. I promise." Gently, he pulled the branch,

and, as he did, she was lifted from the water and onto the bank of the pond.

She gasped over and over again. Her chest ached and her throat burned. Tears gathered in her eyes but she didn't feel them rolling down her cheeks.

Nicholas held her shoulders. "Are you all right?"

"I'm so cold." She wrapped her arms around herself.

The girls gathered around her. "Her lips are purple," Julia gasped.

Emmaline's vision spun. Arms wrapped around her and lifted her. Something solid and warm pressed against her.

"Will she be all right?" Anna whimpered.

"*Yes*, if I can help it," Nicholas grunted.

Emmaline heard herself sigh as the darkness closed in on every side. She couldn't help falling into it again without coming up for air.

Nicholas ran towards the palace, Emmaline limp in his arms.

"I need help!" he shouted. With five steps up the garden staircase, he was inside. "*Hurry now! I need help!*"

Captain Ross appeared from a side room. "What happened?" He walked quickly toward him. He stared at Emmaline, his stony face unusually soft. Emmaline hung in Nicholas's arms, water dripping from her icy body and onto the floor.

Nicholas struggled for words, his rushed breath stealing his voice. "She fell through the ice and into the pond. She didn't know. Go and find Dr. Reid."

"Yes, Your Highness." Ross glanced at Emmaline one last time, then ran off.

The rest of the girls were behind him, clustered together and white as sheets. "Show me to her bedchambers," Nicholas ordered.

As they showed him the way, Nicholas's footsteps pounded down the hall like battle drums. Emmaline moaned softly. His heart constricted inside his chest. Her skin was whiter than the snow blanketing the ground outside.

"In here," Lydia opened the door for him and he rushed inside.

He strode toward a bed and laid Emmaline across it. Echoes of Emmaline's cries in the pond consumed him as he gazed down at her unmoving face. "You will all need to remove her wet clothing and dress her in something else. I will wait outside." He stepped out and closed the door behind him.

He paced up and down the hall until the door opened again. He rushed to her bedside again and sank to his knees. He took one of her hands, kneading her skin gently but firmly.

Lydia and Anna scurried through the bedchamber, ripping the blankets from the beds and stuffing them into their arms. Eleanor and Julia sank down at the hearth and started a fire.

Nicholas pressed his forehead against the

mattress as he rubbed her fingers, whispering prayers. *Please, God. Let her wake up. Warm her body. Let me help her.*

Still asleep, Emmaline shook her head across the pillow. "No. Leave them alone. Don't hurt them. *No!*" Her face was twisted with fear.

Nicholas brushed her cheek, the way a matronly nurse had done to him when he'd been injured in battle, his leg screaming with pain and the ground rocking with explosions. As Nicholas's fingers brushed her skin, the lines on Emmaline's face ebbed away, and she relaxed.

She had screamed so shrilly when she was in the pond. She'd said that a man had a hold of her. Something had happened to her before she came here. He didn't know what, but she was definitely haunted by ghosts of some kind. He knew the signs. He knew them all too well.

This was all his fault. Why hadn't he warned her earlier? What if she died? It would be his fault, just like Céline. He should never have asked Céline to spy on her husband. Nicholas had underestimated General De Witte's cunning. He should have known that the general would find out about his wife's spying. Now, because of him, a woman was dead. And it would be his fault again that another woman would die.

What would his father, the very man he had mimicked as a child, think? Would he say he was a reckless boy unworthy of the crown? His father, watchful and disciplined, would never allow oversight to cause an incident involving a frozen pond and an unsuspecting girl. He should have remembered the pond. He should have warned her earlier.

He pressed the heel of his palm against his forehead. *God, forgive me for my recklessness. Let her wake. Fill her body with warmth.*

He glanced at the door. *Where in the blazes is Dr. Reid?* Nicholas swallowed his frustration. It wouldn't help Emmaline to be filled with anger.

Julia, still sniffling, buried Emmaline with more blankets and stirred the fire. Lydia rubbed Emmaline's other hand, while Eleanor did her feet.

"She was crying out in her sleep." Nicholas looked up at the girls. "Has she ever done this before?"

Lydia bit her lip. "Her first night here, she woke up, screaming. Just screaming. No names. We had to calm her. I've never seen anything like it before."

"She told us her family was killed," Eleanor added. "We don't know anything more than that. It's like she's haunted." Her eyes were large but solemn.

It wasn't unusual to meet someone whose family had been killed. Ever since the war had begun, so many families had been slaughtered like pigs. Nicholas could not imagine losing his parents in such a way. *Poor girl*, he thought as Emmaline's chest rose peacefully.

"But she has changed quite a bit since she's been here," Anna said, taking one of Emmaline's feet from Eleanor's grasp.

Julia nodded, no longer crying. "Yes. When she was first here, she seemed afraid of everything, but now she's smiling more. She seems like a very lovely girl. She just needed a friend."

"I'm grateful that she has you all, then." He did his best to smile.

Nicholas had longed for someone who could understand what he had gone through after the war. If Father had been alive, it would have been easier to put the ghosts of the past to rest. Father had been in several battles himself, and Nicholas had never understood why the broad-shouldered man had jumped at the shattering of a jar until Nicholas had returned from battle himself. But Father had died when Nicholas was fifteen years old, several years before Nicholas had joined the military. And with his father gone, Nicholas had been alone when he'd returned from the battlefield, the bombs still roaring in his head.

It had been a long year, but with his mother's prayers, Nicholas had overcome many of the ghosts howling in his ears. But something inside him still longed for someone who understood what it was like to make it out of hell alive. Could Emmaline become that person?

Captain Ross burst into the bedchamber with Dr. Reid, the doors roaring as they opened. Dr. Reid hurried toward the bed, examining Emmaline.

"How long has she been unconscious?" the doctor asked.

"About five minutes."

"And how long was she in the water?"

"Not long. Perhaps two minutes. I saw her fall in and got her out as soon as it happened."

Dr. Reid looked her over. "I see her wet clothing has been removed and that you are warming her slowly. You must have experience with this emergency. Well done, Your Highness."

He almost smiled. Dr. Reid was right. Thank Heaven above he knew how to handle this emergency. If he hadn't, Emmaline could have lost limbs—or worse.

Ross began to bend on one knee but then stopped himself. As Nicholas watched, Ross fidgeted with his hands, glanced at him nervously, and then clasped his hands together behind his back. *Why is he acting so odd?*

Ross cleared his throat. "So how is she?"

Dr. Reid kept his gaze on Emmaline. "I believe she will make a full recovery. Her body is merely reacting to the cold. The fear of the situation and the shock of the cold made her lose consciousness. She could not hope for a better rescuer, Your Highness." He fiddled through his bags. "It seems I used the last of my smelling salts. I will go and get more."

Once Dr. Reid left, Ross stepped toward Nicholas. "Good work, Your Highness."

"Yes, I'm glad the doctor gave us such positive news. Though my nerves are still unsettled. She was crying out a moment ago." Nicholas moved on from her hand, now warm, and to her arm.

Ross frowned. "Crying out?"

"Yes, she was calling for help. She was frantic in the water, too. She said a man had a hold of her."

"Hmm." Ross stared at Emmaline strangely but turned away. He took over stirring the fire. He gazed at the dancing flames and flickering embers.

A knock on the door was followed by an entering servant. "Your Highness, Her Majesty the Queen has requested your presence urgently," he said.

Nicholas didn't look away from Emmaline. Her chest rose and fell steadily. Drying curls fell over her forehead. "Tell her I'm occupied with something else."

"I'm afraid I can't. She said urgently."

Heat burst inside him and spread through his blood veins.

"Tell her I can't come and that if it's so urgent, she can come to me."

Silence swallowed the room and its inhabitants. The servant bowed. "As you wish." He turned away and closed the door.

"Will she ever awaken?" Anna sighed.

"If she doesn't, Dr. Reid is coming with salts," Nicholas said. "But she's getting warmer. I can feel it." *God, please. Let her wake up.*

The door opened, and Mother appeared, her blue eyes glinting like the sapphires hanging around her neck. Her hands were curled into fists. "What do you think you're doing?"

"I'm helping Emmaline," he snapped.

Her eyes would have turned anyone to ash, but he knew how to withstand her flames. "After I asked you to appear before me? I said my business was urgent, and you should have come."

Nicholas stood to his feet. "Emmaline's life was hanging in the balance just a few moments ago, Mother. Tell me, which business is more urgent: yours or mine?"

She stared at him, and he could see her resolve slipping away. She glanced at Emmaline. "What happened to her?"

"She fell through the ice and into the pond." He still couldn't believe it had happened. If only it had never happened.

"Perhaps she should have been watching where she was going."

He could feel his patience peeling away. "It wasn't her fault. It was mine. I didn't tell her until it was too late. I should have thought about it, but I didn't. Don't blame her."

Her eyes burned into his. "Fine." She glanced around the room.

"Ross, what in the blazes are you doing in here?"

Ross poked the fire and embers erupted from the flames. "I'm helping, too, Your Majesty. I was there when Nicholas brought her inside."

She frowned sardonically. "I see this girl has you all wrapped around her little finger."

Nicholas glanced back at Emmaline. Shadows fell beneath her long lashes. Dimples rested next to her lips. *She does.*

His mother scoffed, shook her head, and left with a snap of her skirts. Nicholas's heart sank. Why was she always so angry with him?

A few moments later, Diana walked inside. She glanced at everyone, her brows raised and her mouth open. "What's going in here? What are you all doing?" She walked toward the bed and saw Emmaline. She gasped. "What happened to her?"

"She almost drowned, not long after you left," Eleanor said.

Diana put a hand to her hip. "I knew nothing good comes from playing in the snow."

Emmaline moaned again, and all eyes turned toward her. Her eyes snapped open as she sprang upwards. She grabbed her ankle, breathing hard. "He had a hold of me! His nails went into me!"

Nicholas grabbed her arm and looked into her eyes. "Emmaline, you're safe now. No one is going to hurt you."

Emmaline glanced at him, biting her lip, then looked down at her ankle. "There's nothing there," she breathed.

"It was just a dream," Lydia soothed, coming to the bedside and helping Emmaline lay back down.

Emmaline lay there for a few moments, her eyes closed. Her breathing slowed. A few moments later, her eyes fluttered open. Nicholas's chest ached with their beauty.

"Where am I?" she whispered.

He moved toward her. "In your bedchamber. You're safe now."

She turned her head and looked at him. The light filtering in from the windows glowed on her cheekbones and played in her eyes. She gave him a small smile and the breath in his lungs all but disappeared. "Thank you," she whispered.

Dr. Reid's smelling salts weren't needed now. Nicholas was relieved she'd awakened on her own. He wanted to ask her about the man she'd said had a hold of her, but he didn't want to frighten her. He'd ask her another time. Once he knew who these ghosts were, he'd make sure they'd never return to hurt her again.

Chapter Seven

EMMALINE STARED OUT the window as she sat in the library. The skies were blue, and the snow was melting. It had been a few days since she had almost drowned in the pond. Sometimes she could still feel the phantom hand wrapped around her ankle, pulling her down, down, down. She didn't like to think about that. It made her shiver uncontrollably again. She'd uttered countless thanks to Jesus for saving her life.

The skies were so blue beyond the glass. Like Nicholas's eyes. She remembered the look of fear he'd had in his eyes when he pulled her from the water. As if he were afraid to let her go. As if he were afraid to lose her.

Her heart warmed as she thought about the relief on his face when she awoke. Why did he care so much? He barely knew her.

Emmaline bit her lip and pressed her nail into her palm. *Foolish girl. He's a prince. He doesn't care about you. He was only rescuing you because he's good and chivalrous.*

"There you are."

Emmaline turned at the familiar voice. "Ross."

He stepped closer to her. "You weren't in your chambers, and Lydia told me you were here." He glanced around, taking in the room around him. "Are you doing well?"

"I am. Especially in here." Emmaline liked the quiet of the library and how the bookshelves towered around her. She especially liked it in the evening when the light from the window caught the dust floating in the air. There had to be thousands of books in here, surely. Sometimes servants would come in, climbing the ladders to the second floor to get a book the queen had requested. Emmaline breathed in the musty air, pleasure filling her senses.

A dimple sprang up next to Ross's mouth. "I didn't know you had an affinity for books."

She smiled. "I must confess, I haven't been doing much reading in here. I've mostly been looking out the window. The sky is so beautiful today, I can't help but stare."

He slid the chair back and sat across from her at the table. "I must admit, I'm glad winter is nearly over. I've had enough of it." He sighed, his eyes solemn. "It's good to see you sitting up. You gave us all a scare a few days ago."

"I know. The girls told me the very same thing." They had all paid a visit to her, bringing Emmaline her meals, reading to her, and stoking the fire in the hearth. "I'm glad that I'm not dead." Emmaline rested her chin in her hand and grinned.

"Me, too." He smiled back.

She cast her gaze around the library, her eyes roving over the walls lined with books. She took a deep breath. "There have been times when I thought it would be better that way, but I've come to know that isn't true. God has been merciful."

Ross glanced down at his lap, something severe in his expression. His jawline hardened, as if he was buckling from an invisible load on his back.

Emmaline shifted in her seat. "Ross, what's the matter?"

He jerked his head up, eyes wide. "Nothing. Nothing's wrong."

She studied his eyes. Her brother James had had that same look in his eyes when he'd been bullied by their cousins. She leaned forward. "No. You want to say something. Go on, tell me."

A few moments passed before he spoke. He swallowed and took a breath. "Forgive me, but how could God be merciful? Why did He let you fall in the pond in the first place? You could have died."

Emmaline bit her lip, the shards of the past flying toward her. Heat spread in her cheeks as her heart quickened. *God, give me the words to answer him.* "Ross, we live in a fallen world. There will be hard times. But hard times give me strength and remind me to remember that someday, I'll live in a better world. A perfect world. A world where I'm with my family, and where they're whole again. A world where I'm whole again."

Pain flickered in Ross's eyes. "But you were whole once. Why did God break you?"

Something gnawed at her chest, desperate to eat at her soul. Rose's screams and visions of her mother on that blood-stained rug sliced through her. But that was the past. She had to move on to survive. "People don't question why storms come, bringing thunder and lightning and pouring rain down on them. They know without rain, flowers wouldn't grow."

Emmaline could tell Ross wasn't ready to raise the white flag. He shook his head. "It's rained for three years, and I haven't seen any flowers growing anywhere, Emmaline."

She pressed her lips together. "Maybe you haven't been looking for them."

She could see the arrow tip of her words had struck true in Ross. He took a deep breath, looking down. He was like that for several moments. Then he looked up at her. "Where do I find these flowers?"

Rise

Emmaline smiled gently at him. "You can start by going to the chapel. It seems to me you and God have a lot to talk about."

He tried to smile, but she could still see the fear in his eyes. He stood up, thanked her, then left.

Emmaline glanced at the crucifix on the wall and smiled. A prodigal was returning home.

Nicholas straightened his tie and tugged at his collar. He could swear his shirt was trying to choke him. He glanced up at the staircase, and when no one appeared, he tapped his finger against the banister.

Would the outings with all six girls feel like this? Like he was going to run out of breath and collapse? Like his head was spinning out of control? He'd fought battles less worrisome than this.

"I hope I haven't kept you waiting, Your Highness," a smooth voice crooned above him.

Diana stood on the landing, dressed in a fur coat and a pink evening gown. A pair of white gloves hung in her hand, and the diamonds hanging in her ears caught the light and nearly blinded him. She smiled gently at him, every bit the lady his mother had dreamed of him marrying one day.

"Not at all." He forced a friendly smile.

She came down the stairs, slowly and gently, her shoulders pressed back and her head held high. "Which ballet are you taking me to on this beautiful night?"

"Swan Lake. I hear it's very good."

Diana stood in front of him now, straightening the fingers in her gloves. "Oh, it is, Your Highness. I've seen it twice, and I simply adore it." She looked at him, her red lips stretched into a smile. "You must be the only nobleman who hasn't seen it yet. Why is that?"

He chuckled nervously. "I was away in Germany for many months. I'm afraid battles don't fight themselves." He swallowed, a bitter taste on his tongue. "It's been almost four years since the murder of the archduke of Austria, and I'm beginning to wonder when this war will ever end."

"Oh, and why have you returned? If you don't mind my asking, that is."

He scratched his head, even more uneasy. He didn't usually like talking about it, especially with people he hardly knew. "I have shrapnel in my leg. It flares up every now and then, and I was sent home several months ago because I could no longer fight."

Diana folded her hands in front of her. "Well, that's well and all. My sympathies go to you and your wounded leg, but I am glad you are back home, and I am sure your mother is glad to have you home, too."

He straightened his suit jacket. "She is." Although she didn't show it that often. He knew she loved him, but she was so unrecognizable now. Bitter and hostile, determined to not let anyone through her barricade. He wished he could help her heal, but if she kept resisting him . . .

Rise

Diana took his arm and knocked him out of his thoughts. "We don't want to be late for the ballet. Let's go before Odette and Siegfried take their watery death, shall we?"

He linked his arm under hers and led her outside. Snowflakes dusted his hair and coat, falling gently from the sky and blanketing the cobblestones. He helped Diana into the carriage, and then watched the palace fade as the carriage rolled away. The horses' hooves clicked through the city, and the streetlamps glowed in the darkness.

When they arrived at the ballet, Nicholas led Diana up the stairs and to their booth. They weaved their way through the throng of people. Only a few people seemed to notice who he was. Most were otherwise preoccupied to see that he was walking among them. He was glad. Like his father, he did not enjoy being stared at.

"It's so wonderful to be a part of such a beautiful crowd," Diana breathed, her eyes large and bright. "I always feel at home among the elite."

He frowned. He hoped that wasn't all she cared about. "I suppose, but we're not here for them. We're here for the swans." He glanced at her again and smiled.

She swallowed. "Yes, of course."

As they sat down and waited for the curtain to rise, Nicholas turned toward Diana. "So, I must ask, how is Emmaline? Is she doing better? My mother has kept me busy with other tasks, so I haven't been able to see her." He hated the way that excuse sounded, but it was the truth.

Diana frowned, a little spark of jealousy in her eyes. It wasn't much, and it vanished as quickly as a shooting star, but he had seen it. She straightened herself and pressed her shoulders back. "Well, I've been there to see her every day, and she has improved greatly under my care. The girls and I always make sure she has enough blankets and that there's a fire burning in the hearth. She is doing quite well, Your Highness."

He smiled, his heart lifting. "I'm happy to hear that. Thank you for your excellent care of her, Diana."

"It is my Christian duty, after all." Diana glanced toward the stage and gasped. "Oh, the curtain is rising! The show is about to begin."

Nicholas faced forward and turned his attention to the stage. The music swelled but he could only think of the girl back at home. Emmaline was doing better. What more could he ask for?

After the ballet was over, Nicholas and Diana stood outside waiting for their carriage. The snow had ceased falling, and now he could see the stars hanging in the sky. Diana held herself, shivering in the cold.

"The carriage should be here soon. I apologize for the wait," he said.

"Oh, it's quite all right—" She shrieked as two children bumped into her and flew down the street, running as fast as they could. "What dirty children! What on earth are they doing in this part of the city?"

He glanced at her, frowning. How could she say such things? Those children would grow up knowing only the streets and nothing else unless someone had compassion for them. Had she no pity?

A police officer ran through the crowds, his face scarlet and perspiring. Just as he was about to pass by, Nicholas grabbed his arm and stopped him.

The officer scowled at him, his expression dark as lines webbed over his face. "Let me go! Those children need to be taught a lesson!"

Nicholas swallowed down his fury. Did this officer not see they were children? "Excuse me, officer, but can't you just let them go?"

The officer struggled in his grasp, staring down the street where the children had disappeared. "They stole from an honest man! Thieves must be punished, whatever their age."

"I will pay whatever must be paid, officer. In fact, you may tell the baker that I will pay him for however many loaves the children ask him for."

"And just what makes you care so much?" The officer finally looked at Nicholas full in the face. He turned pale as his eyes grew twice their size. "Forgive me, Your Highness. I didn't know it was you."

Nicholas shook his head. "Please, let them be. They need that bread more than you know." He slipped his hand into his pocket and paid the amount owed by the children.

The officer still seemed dumbfounded. "Thank you, Your Highness."

The carriage arrived, and Nicholas helped Diana inside. He stood on the carriage step and looked at the officer. "Remember this night from now on and be kinder to those who aren't as fortunate as you." When the officer nodded, Nicholas bent and entered the carriage.

Snow fell in quiet hushes again, and the wheels rattled against the street as they made their way back to the palace.

Diana barely spoke on the ride back. She fidgeted with her gloved hands and glanced at him several times. She opened her mouth as if to speak, but it was several moments before the words came. "I think, perhaps, I was in error when I spoke about those children. I apologize, Your Highness."

He shook his head. "No matter." But it was. He didn't want to marry someone who only cared about the wealthy people in his kingdom. And he didn't want to marry someone who only regretted what she said because of how it made her look. His father would not have chosen such a wife for himself or his son. His mind was already made up, just from one night. He hoped none of the other girls would be like Diana.

Especially one in particular.

Chapter Eight

THOUGH THE PARTING clouds melted the snow across the castle grounds, winter had not completely disappeared. Ice still shimmered on the windowpanes and the girls' bedchamber had been close to freezing until Eleanor lit a fire in the hearth.

Diana had returned from the ballet with Nicholas late that night. Emmaline had been the only one awake when Diana had tiptoed into bed. She wanted to know everything—what the prince had said, if he had enjoyed Diana's company, and how the ballet had been. Instead, she let her mind fill with questions as Diana snored, until she herself fell asleep.

Now it was morning, and the girls spoke over one another in excitement.

"Did you have a nice night, Diana?" Anna asked.

"Did the prince say anything about your gown?" Julia looked ready to burst.

"Did you hold his hand, and if you did, how did it feel?" Lydia squealed.

Emmaline watched Diana's face. She didn't seem as excited as the other girls. Her lips were tight as she stared at the floor with a glare. The girls continued to pepper her with questions.

Diana waved her hands around. "Girls, girls!"

The girls stopped fluttering around her, their eyes wide.

Diana huffed and sat in the bay window. "The night couldn't have gone worse. He was kind to me, and the ballet was beautiful, but I believe I offended him when I spoke of the upper class's attire. And he seemed more interested in helping a couple of ragamuffin orphans escape with their stolen bread." She bit her lip. "I don't believe I pleased him at all."

No one spoke for quite some time. Emmaline's insides twisted like the raging waves of the sea. She hadn't known it would be so hard to win his heart. But that was a good thing, wasn't it? That he knew what he was looking for? That he wouldn't marry just anyone? That he wasn't interested in girls that only cared for his money?

Emmaline shook her head. What did she care? It wasn't as if Nicholas would choose her.

She watched the clouds parting and searched herself. She knew what it was like to be both rich and poor. And while she had been happier when she had been rich, her contentment didn't come from the money. It had been her family. She cared nothing for money, or what it could buy her. She only wanted to be surrounded by love, as she once had been. And now that she had found so many friends here in the palace, she knew their love was enough. Would have to be enough.

Julia shifted her skirts up and sat on the bay window next to Diana. She took Diana's hand and put it in her lap. "It's all right, Diana. There'll be other chances to win his heart. He's got to get to know you more. He can't possibly do that in one night. He'll see what we all see, trust me."

Diana turned from the window and met Julia's soft eyes. "Do you really think so?"

Julia nodded. "Of course. Any prince would be lucky to have you."

The other girls gave their approval. Emmaline forced a nod, her mind drifting to the way Nicholas's hand had felt in hers. She waved her thumb over her palm, warmth dripping into her like honey. It had been years since she'd had memories she could cherish, and her night with the prince would be a happy memory to keep for herself as she served the future queen.

And that would be enough. Would have to be enough.

Ross brushed down Felix, the smell of new grass and fresh hay in his lungs. He needed to finish quickly. His men would be waiting for their instructions for the day, and he couldn't keep them waiting. Late arrivals looked poorly for any captain of the royal guard, but especially for ones who were only twenty-two years old. As it was, some of the guards—younger and older than him—resented him for his position at such a young age. He realized that he was privileged to have such a high rank, but he was also unsure why the queen had given it to him.

Well, perhaps he was not *entirely* unsure. She had made it quite clear that she was impressed by his discovery of the former captain's scandal, especially after serving in her guard for only one year.

Still, sometimes even he wondered if his age would affect his ability to fully carry out his job. After all, he had not trained for this position for many years as most of his men had. Even this country was new to him.

But those factors were just obstacles, and Ross had dodged those all his life. He could overcome these, too.

He glanced toward the west wing, where the candidates stayed in the palace.

Last night the prince had had his first outing with

one of the girls. He wondered if it had been Emmaline. If it had been her, had her night gone well? Had she enjoyed the prince's company? He wasn't concerned about the prince's behavior toward her. He'd known Nicholas for two years, and he knew what a good man he was. Emmaline was safe with Nicholas; Ross was sure of it.

Still, something inside him ached. He almost wished she'd had a horrible time, and that she had no desire to marry the prince. He wanted to kick himself for feeling this way. What had Emmaline ever done to him? Didn't she deserve the happiness the prince could give her?

"It looks as if spring might finally be arriving," a girl said behind him. He knew the voice at once. He turned and saw Emmaline standing there. A grin pulled at her dimples.

"Yes, I think so," Ross said, continuing to inspect Felix's hooves.

"I'm glad to see winter go away. I prefer spring and summer. I like hearing the birds sing and watching the flowers bloom." She leaned against the wall of the stable.

He caught a glance at her naturally pink cheeks and grinned to himself. If he wasn't mistaken, a few flowers had already bloomed.

He grunted and dusted himself off. "So, were you the girl that went with the prince last night, or was it another?" He hoped that nothing gave his feelings away. He was usually good at keeping his emotions hidden, but Emmaline had a way of unmasking him. He reached for his bridle and slipped it over Felix's head.

"No, I didn't go with him," Emmaline said softly. "Diana went."

He couldn't help feeling a little happy, even though it made his cheeks sting with guilt. "Oh." He didn't know what else to say. He was certain that if he did speak before collecting himself, he would give himself away. He tightened Felix's bridle, and then turned and noticed Emmaline's fidgeting hands. "Is something wrong?"

"Not really." She cleared her throat. "It's nothing."

She was hiding something. He'd questioned thieves and other criminals before, and he could see that she was still finding it difficult to say whatever needed to be said. He walked toward her. "Emmaline, you do know you can talk to me."

She hesitated, then said, "Yes, I know."

"Then what is it? You seem nervous about something."

Finally, she met his eyes. "Do you think the prince would pick me?"

He couldn't breathe for a moment. He blinked at her, dumbfounded. How could she ask that, as if she were so insignificant that she wouldn't be noticed by the prince? Even the prince had eyes to see her beauty and ears to hear her soft voice.

How could he answer, when his heart pounded for her and all the breath rushed out of him whenever he saw her? But he could tell by the look in her eyes that she needed to know she was capable of being loved. She didn't know how capable. He spoke past the arrows digging into his flesh. "I think the prince would be foolish not to."

Emmaline blushed deeply. "You flatter me, Ross."

He shook his head. "No, I speak the truth. You're beautiful. Your smile is contagious, and you're kind and compassionate." Every word drove the knife deeper. He couldn't believe he was finally saying this to her. These are the words he'd wanted to tell her for weeks, words meant to tell her how he felt about her, not to reassure her that she could win the prince's affection.

She shook her head, brows pressed. "But he knows I'm haunted. I must have seemed so strange screaming like I did that day. He's sure to think me mad."

Ross held himself up against the beam in the stable, his legs weak. "He doesn't think you mad, Emmaline. I've been to see the queen a few times, and he was there expressing concern for you." Every word took more and more strength from him. He sank further against the pole. For weeks, he had wanted to confess his love to her, and now here he was, reassuring her that someone else shared his affections. "He asked his mother to let him see you, but she simply gave him more obligations."

Emmaline gazed at him, and the hope coming to life in her eyes killed the hope that had been growing inside him. "He's concerned about me?"

He swallowed. "Yes."

She turned her gaze to the ground and smiled. "I know it sounds silly since I barely know him, but I can't help feeling this way. I haven't hoped or dreamed like this in forever, and I finally feel alive again."

Ross swallowed, curling his hand into a fist and tucking it against his thigh. "So, you feel something for him, then?"

She glanced down at the ground, her long lashes casting shadows over her cheekbones. "I think so." She looked back up at him.

He ignored the burning pain engulfing him and forced himself to smile. "I see. Well, I'm glad. Glad that you have the courage to feel again."

"Thank you, Ross, though I'm not sure I have the courage you speak of." She smiled. "But I am glad I have a friend like you."

He nodded. "Of course. I'm glad I could have the honor of being called your friend." He tried to smile but his lips wouldn't stretch as far as he wanted. The ache in his chest burned him alive. A friend? That was all?

Emmaline looked over her shoulder and then back at him. "Well, I must leave. Mr. Harrison has new lessons to teach us, and I mustn't be late."

Ross waved and watched as she ran off and disappeared. How quickly she had faded from him. *You should be happy. After all she's been through, doesn't she deserve someone like Nicholas and all that he could give her?*

Still, Ross couldn't help thinking of all that he had just lost.

"Just a little color for her cheeks, Anna," Lydia said, sticking pins into Julia's hair.

Emmaline hooked a pearl necklace around Julia's throat, while Julia wriggled her gloved fingers around each other. A week had passed, and now it was Julia's turn to spend time with the prince.

"Try and settle down, Julia," Emmaline said. "Just think about what a wonderful time you'll have with the prince tonight. You're going to the art gallery, after all, and you paint nearly every day. You'll have a wonderful time."

"Oh, I am excited," Julia breathed as Anna brushed some color onto her cheeks. "But I'm still terrified. What if I make a mistake? What if I say or do something humiliating? What if it's nothing like I imagined it?"

"Put it out of your mind, Julia," Eleanor crooned, fluffing Julia's skirts. "If you don't think about it as much, it won't happen."

"And most certainly don't talk about fashion or money as I did," Diana retorted.

Julia laughed nervously. She bit her lip, as if to keep control of herself.

"There." Lydia moved away, and Emmaline and the other girls followed her. Julia stood in front of the mirror, wide-eyed as she stared back at her reflection.

"Well? What do you think?" Anna asked.

Julia fidgeted with the fingers of her gloves anxiously. "It doesn't matter what I think. I must dress to impress."

"No, that's not true." Emmaline shook her head. "If you feel beautiful, then you are. It doesn't matter what anyone else thinks of you, only what you think of yourself."

Julia stared at herself in the mirror again. Her hands stopped trembling. "Well," she said softly. "I think you all did a fantastic job. I feel beautiful."

"Good." Eleanor smiled. "And like Emmaline said, that's all that matters."

Julia turned, beaming. "Thank you." She opened her arms and embraced them all.

A few minutes later, after Julia had left the bedchamber, Emmaline sat on the cushioned window seat and pressed her face against the chill glass. Two figures emerged down the palace staircase outside, and the man opened the door for the girl. *Nicholas.* He helped Julia into the carriage, and then got in and shut the door. As the driver slapped the reins, the horses pulled the carriage away from view.

Emmaline closed her eyes. She could still hear Nicholas's voice and see his face from the day he'd rescued her from the icy waters. He had held her in his arms and carried her into the castle. He had been the first person she'd seen when she'd awakened.

She wished she was going to the art gallery with

Nicholas. She wanted to ask him about the paintings and walk down the long halls with him.

Perhaps she was being foolish. She barely knew him. Was she so willing to give her heart away? Didn't she remember the pain of heartbreak? What would happen to her if he didn't choose her? Or what would happen if he did choose her, and she lost him the way she'd lost her family? She couldn't give her heart away to a man she hardly knew. Not when he would most certainly reject it for another. Not when she remembered the price that love demanded.

"I wasn't aware I was in the presence of such a learned artist," Nicholas said as he and Julia walked down the halls of the art gallery.

Julia blushed. "I wouldn't go that far, Your Highness. My father simply provided me with a tutor when I was thirteen, and I haven't stopped spraying color onto a canvas since."

"It seems to me that you are passionate about it." Nicholas cupped his hands behind his back, glancing at all the artwork.

The hall was long and lined with large vases of flowers. Paintings lined the walls, and the middle of the hall was filled with sculptures of every size and design. Chandeliers hung from above and shimmered on the marble floors.

"Oh, I am," Julia said. "I like to study things I see and then reflect them in my art. There are so many moments that deserve to be remembered, and I like to think I'm doing that when I paint." She glanced at him. "You know, many men think it's silly that I, a woman, want to paint. But you're different."

She was right. Nicholas had heard a few lords say such things about women, that they had no place in the world of art. But he'd met French nurses who had quite an eye for color and sketching, perhaps more so than male artists that had painted his portrait before.

"Well, you have eyes, don't you?" he asked her. "And a soul?"

Julia blinked. "Of course, Your Highness."

"And you use those things to observe the world around you, to draw meaning from it, and to give meaning back to it, right?"

She nodded. "Yes."

He shrugged. "Then why wouldn't you be able to paint?"

Julia smiled. "I wish all men could be like you." She turned her gaze to another painting, and gasped. "Oh, it's the *Nebuchadnezzar* painting by William Blake! My, he doesn't look too happy, does he?"

Nicholas glanced at Julia, who was smiling as if she was under an enchantment spell. "I imagine living in the fields and becoming like a beast wouldn't leave anyone very happy. Especially a man who was king."

"What an awful thing to be put through." Julia fidgeted with her gloves.

"Yes, it is." He studied her as she stared at the painting. He liked Julia. She had a lovely smile and a contagious curiosity about the world, but he couldn't think of her as a wife. She seemed a little . . . young. Mr. Harrison had told him all the girls' ages, and Julia was the youngest at only sixteen years old. While it was only two years younger than most of the other girls, sixteen seemed far too young for marriage. Julia should be free to live her life a little before settling down with a husband. If she married him, she would have to grow up far too fast with all the expectations required of a royal wife.

Julia walked on and pointed at another painting. "This one is new. It was finished last year. The artist is John Nash, and he calls it *Over the Top*. It's very fascinating, isn't it?"

Nicholas could only stare. In the painting, young men wearing metal helmets and carrying guns climbed out of the trenches and staggered across the snow. His heart thundered. He could feel the rush of memories coming back, all at once, pulling at him and dragging him away.

"Come on, over the top, boys!" Cap bellowed.

Nicholas climbed up the shaking ladder, the ground trembling as blasts roared in his ears. Clumps of dirt flew over his head. Smoke billowed in the sky like dragon's breath. He made it to the top.

A shot rang out. His bones shattered against the roaring of the bombs as a searing pain sliced into his leg. With a cry of agony, he fell back into the trench. His Irish friend Conor fell beside him, the side of his face covered in what looked like red jam.

Conor clutched Nicholas's wrist. "Tell my Talulla that I love her, won't you, Prince?"

Nicholas nodded, panting. "I will. I swear to you, I will."

The familiar pain burned in his leg. Nicholas inhaled and leaned against the wall, unable to stand upright.

Julia grabbed his arm, her eyes wide. "Are you all right, Your Highness?"

He tried to breathe. "Yes, yes, of course." He closed his eyes and shoved the memories away. His heart pounded with the amount of effort it took. He forced a smile and gazed down at Julia. "Forgive me for frightening you."

"It's all right, but something has obviously frightened *you*."

He ran a trembling hand through his hair. He didn't want to talk about it, but Julia deserved an explanation after he'd made a scene in front of her. "Oh, it's just . . . looking at this painting. Brings back memories."

Julia glanced from him to the painting. She gasped. "Oh, what a fool I am! I completely forgot that you—please forgive me, Your Highness."

He waved her apology away. "That isn't necessary. It was an accident."

"Does it happen often?" She gazed into his eyes, her face pale.

"It used to when I first returned. I've gotten better, though."

Julia clutched her heart. "I can't imagine what that must feel like. To remember something as terrifying as that so vividly."

No, he didn't suppose she could. Not many others could, either. It was like one of her paintings, a memory preserved onto a canvas that not even the wettest rag could remove. None of his friends had survived, and he didn't have anyone to talk to about it. He wished he did, so he would know that someone understood.

"I'm such an idiot!" Julia sniffled, struggling to breathe past her emotion and dabbing at her eyes with Anna's handkerchief. "Why did I point out that painting to him? He probably thinks I'm the most senseless girl in the kingdom!"

Eleanor stroked Julia's golden hair, frowning sympathetically. Anna sat at Julia's skirts, her eyes glimmering with shared sadness.

Emmaline couldn't help but pity the poor girl, too. Julia had burst into the room and broken into tears within moments. Between sobs, she had told the girls that she had caused Nicholas to have an episode when she pointed out a painting of a battle scene. She had been berating herself for the past half hour now, despite the girls' desperate attempts to console her. They had tried everything: ordering a fire to be started in the hearth, asking for tea and biscuits to be brought up, and covering her with a blanket. Nothing had helped.

Lydia shook her head. "It's not your fault, Julia. It was an accident. He's a good man. He knows your intentions well enough."

Julia blew her nose loudly, and Diana wrinkled hers in disgust. "It's no matter," Julia said softly, closing her eyes.

Diana blinked, eyes wide. "What do you mean, Julia?"

"I'm not even sure I want to marry the prince." She stood to her feet and walked toward the hearth.

Emmaline could scarcely believe her ears. For months, Julia had hardly talked of anything else other than marrying such a handsome prince and becoming a princess. But now she had changed her mind?

Julia took a deep breath in front of the hearth, her gown glowing golden against the flames. "I was a spoiled child, girls. I was not a brat, mind you, but I was spoiled. I was raised to love gold and diamonds and pearls. Gowns and balls. Parties and grand orchestras. My parents spared no expense. I was given everything I ever wanted. Marrying into another world not so very different from my own seemed like my purpose. It was my one desire." She turned as her mouth wobbled. She swallowed and took back her composure. "Until I came to live here. I don't think I want to live so extravagantly any longer, girls. I believe I will be quite content with a quiet life. What I have here in this room is worth more than any gold. And after tonight, after the compassion you have shown me, I know that this is what I want now. The kind of love you have all shown me."

The girls smiled back at Julia. Tears fell down Anna's freckled cheeks. Eleanor strode toward Julia and embraced her. Within moments, they had all wrapped their arms around this brave new girl, their Julia, so transformed from the one they had first met.

Emmaline blinked back tears. How had Julia grown up so much since she'd first met her? She was such a wonderful young woman. She knew what she wanted.

Unlike Emmaline. She was so torn between her longing for love and her desperate need to protect herself, she was not sure she would ever be whole again. Would she ever know what she wanted?

Or, better yet, would she admit to herself what she knew what she wanted and chase after it? Doubtless she would stay in the shadows. Nothing could hurt her there.

Chapter Nine

EMMALINE'S STOMACH CRAMPED with nerves. She fidgeted with the strand of pearls hanging around her neck, certain the pearls were growing tighter and making it harder for her to breathe. Tonight, she and the girls would be dining for the first time with the prince and the queen. Emmaline would rather have starved than face the queen at the dinner table.

"Don't play with your pearls, Emmaline!" Eleanor fussed. "If you pull at them too much, the necklace will break and there'll be a million little pearls all over the room."

Emmaline bit her lip. "Sorry."

"There's no reason to be nervous," Diana said, smiling genuinely. Ever since her return from her night with Nicholas, Diana had been scowling less and smiling more. She no longer frowned at Julia's antics or Anna's humming. Now, she joined in.

"There isn't?" Anna asked, brows raised.

Diana's smile faltered. "It's what I keep telling myself. I'm hoping I'll convince myself sooner or later."

"Whatever happens, we can't let our nerves be on display," Julia said smoothly. She thrust her head back in a ladylike fashion and walked across the room, her movements like a swan. "We are dining with Her Majesty the Queen, and we must be at our best."

What if we're not feeling our best? Emmaline wondered as her head thundered.

"Does anyone have a necklace I can borrow?" Anna sighed. "None of mine will work with this dress." She huffed anxiously and pushed a hair behind her ear.

Diana bent over her jewelry box and pulled out a sapphire necklace. She bit her lip. "You can have mine, Anna. You'll look lovely with it."

The room fell silent, and the girls stopped primping. Diana hadn't ever displayed such kindness. Emmaline held her breath, wondering what had gotten into her.

Diana looked around the room and met everyone's gaze. "I know I haven't been very nice to any of you, and I know it was undeserved. I want to change. Please, forgive me, and allow me to begin again."

Emmaline glanced at the others, who seemed just as surprised as she did. Emmaline nodded. "Of course, Diana. I would love nothing more."

The other girls voiced their approval, bringing tears to Diana's eyes. She sniffled. "Right. Enough with this emotional display," she said, smiling. "My eye paint will be ruined."

A knock came at the door, and Anna answered it. Mr. Harrison walked in and lifted his chin with pride. "You're all looking especially lovely tonight, girls. Well done."

Emmaline gave him a wobbly smile.

He glanced at each of them. "I'm detecting a room full of nerves. There isn't any call for that. You all know what to do. I've taught you well. Do you honestly think I'd let you dine with the queen before you're ready? She'd have my head on a platter! Simply remember your lessons, and this night will go well." He clapped his hands together. "Let's be going." He led them out of the room and down the corridors.

Anna linked her arm into Emmaline's. "You needn't worry yourself, Emmaline. You'll do fine. Heads will turn as soon as you enter the room, and everyone will be hypnotized by you."

Emmaline chuckled. "You exaggerate, Anna."

Anna shook her head. "I merely say what I know."

Emmaline swallowed. Even if someone was hypnotized by her, she would not be surprised if she did something foolish to break the spell.

The queen's table was much like Emmaline's family's had been. Three candleabras stood atop the table, one on the far left, one on the far right, and one in the middle. Their flames shimmered in the silver dinnerware, adding to the dishes' shine. A crystal goblet sat at each spot, ready to be filled with wine. A quartet played a whirling melody nearby, the conductor raising his arms in intervals. Emmaline wished the music weren't so loud; her temples were aching. This table was all too familiar to her. Her family's chirping breakfast conversations echoed in her mind.

The table moaned with the weight of the feast: roast chicken, filet mignon, stuffed crab, fruits and cheeses, vegetables, cakes coated with cream and raspberries, plum pudding, and chocolate vanilla eclairs. Emmaline noticed Julia staring at the eclairs, a childish hunger in her eyes. Emmaline bit back a smile. She was so much like James, who'd always snuck sweets into his bedchamber and shared the spoils with his sisters.

Two red velvet chairs remained unoccupied, waiting for the queen and the prince to grace their cushions. Several men and women she didn't recognize sat across from the girls. Their clothes were lavish, and the women's jewelry sparkled like the diamond chandeliers. She wondered who these people were.

A man in a pressed suit entered the room. He cleared his throat. "Her Majesty, Queen Genevieve, and her son, His Royal Highness Prince Nicholas."

Emmaline shifted in her seat and pressed her shoulders back. *It's time to look alive.* Her heart was racing so fast, she was sure she would die of an attack of the heart.

The queen entered first, wearing a golden crown studded with sapphires and a blue silk gown with a skirt that filled the room. She made no eye contact but smiled tightly as she glided toward the table.

Nicholas followed, dashing as ever in his suit. His black curls were brushed to the side. He greeted his guests with a bow, then sat beside his mother on the right. He glanced at each of the girls on the opposite side of the table, then winked at them. Lydia and Julia giggled while Emmaline blushed, glanced down, and played with her fingers in her lap.

Queen Genevieve stood, her skirts swishing. "I would like to thank you all for dining with me tonight. I'm afraid most of you have not dined with me since Nicholas left for battle, and it has lifted my spirits greatly to see familiar faces sitting at my table." She glanced at the girls. "Ladies, these are some of my closest friends: Lord and Lady Wheaton, Lord and Lady Byron, and Lord and Lady Midsummer." She nodded to the girls and turned her gaze to the nobility. "And these are Nicholas's prospective brides: Lydia, Julia, Anna, Eleanor, Diana, and Emmaline. They have stayed in the palace for three months,

Rise

learning how to become a lady of the court. This will be their first time dining with my son and me." The queen glanced at Emmaline. "Let's hope they have paid attention during their lessons."

Emmaline swallowed the bile coming up her throat. Why did the queen insist on singling her out? What had she done to make the queen hate her so?

The lords and ladies greeted the girls as the queen sat in her chair. With a clap from the queen, servants appeared and dished out potato soup into their china bowls. It smelled hearty, and the steam rising from it warmed Emmaline's cheeks. She said a quiet thanks to God.

Spoons clattered as the guests ate their soup.

"So, Your Highness," Lord Byron, a man with kind eyes and a head full of gray hair, began. "I understand that you returned from Europe last summer. From your personal opinion, do you see this war ending any time soon?"

Nicholas cleared his throat and met Lord Byron's gaze. "I think so. I have remained in contact with a few lieutenants, and they all believe the war is coming to an end. One of them has even suggested the end may come this year."

"Let us hope so," Lady Wheaton sighed, her thick hair pulled into a beautiful updo. "This war has gone on for four years, and that is much too long. Too many young men are dying before their lives can really begin." Her voice lowered. "Two of my own nephews have been lost to this awful war."

"Forgive me for speaking out of turn, Your Highness, but how did your company fare?" Lord Midsummer asked, his mustache drooping as he waited for the prince's reply.

Nicholas paled a little as his eyes fell. He swallowed and set down his spoon. A familiar shadow came over his face. Emmaline knew that shadow all too well. Was he haunted by his memories too? "They did not fare well at all, Lord Midsummer. I'm afraid I was the only survivor. I survived because I was sent home early for a leg wound that put me out of action. I was lucky to have made it out with all my limbs intact, but I could no longer fight. If I could have, I don't believe I would be sitting here with you all."

The scraping of spoons stopped. Lord Midsummer pulled at his collar and cleared his throat. Emmaline's heart sank at Nicholas's words. *Poor Nicholas.* She knew what it was like to be the only survivor, to spend silent hours wondering why she had been chosen to live, to ask herself if it was all a mistake.

Lady Midsummer touched her husband's arm and smiled gently. "Let us move on to happier subjects. Perhaps you can introduce us all to these pretty girls sitting across from us. Surely you have gotten to know more than their names."

Nicholas instantly lit up. "Of course. Lydia Lee is from Boburn. She is as well-spoken as she is well-read. Julia Quinn is from Portsmouth, and she is constantly hidden behind an artist's canvas. One day her artwork shall be in a gallery." Nicholas grinned at

Julia, and she blushed, giggling.

Was Nicholas in love with her? Emmaline's stomach cramped at the thought, and then she scolded herself. She ought to be happy for her friend, not jealous, especially when Emmaline was not willing to give away her wounded heart.

"Eleanor Montgomery comes from Hatsfield. She has a way with children, and she knits clothing for the orphanage here in Lauderbury. Diana Foster hails from Thornchester, and her father is the duke there. She loves ballets. Anna Edwards came here from Bloomsdale, and when she's not taking part in lessons, she's picking flowers in the field behind the palace." Nicholas took a deep breath, his Adam's apple bobbing as he swallowed. He looked at Emmaline from across the table, but she could not hold his gaze. "Emmaline lived in Lauderbury before she came here. She plays the piano far better than any of the greats. No one deserves to hear such lovely music."

Emmaline's heartbeat skipped. Nicholas hadn't revealed that she had lived on the streets. He'd saved her the embarrassment. Her cheeks warmed.

"Goodness!" Lady Wheaton exclaimed. "You certainly have gotten to know all of them well. My Edward can't even remember our anniversary." She laughed as her husband turned scarlet.

Nicholas laughed and everyone else joined in—except, of course, for Lord Wheaton.

The queen cleared her throat and pasted on a smile. "Yes, out of all the girls learning how to become a lady of the court, Emmaline impresses me the most."

Emmaline glanced at the queen, her heart lifting. Was the queen finally raising her white flag? Could they finally start off on a new path?

Queen Genevieve sniffed, her face darkening. "After all, she probably found her lessons the hardest, since she lived on the streets for three years."

Emmaline's hope dropped to the floor and shattered like delicate china. What would the lords and ladies think of her now?

"Mother," Nicholas said sharply, his eyes like arrows.

Queen Genevieve glanced at her son, brows raised as if she were innocent. "It's true, Nicholas. She doesn't know where she comes from, and she has no family to speak of. She's simply a lost girl that found her way into my palace."

Emmaline sounded no better than a rat with the way the queen was speaking about her. Her heart came up her throat as her cheeks burned. She bowed her head over her bowl.

"What happened to your family?" Lord Byron asked. His eyes flashed with shock.

"*Arthur!*" his wife hissed hastily.

Emmaline swallowed, not looking up. "They were killed three years ago."

Lady Byron gasped. "Oh, dear. This war has taken so many civilian casualties. I am sorry."

Emmaline nodded. She glanced at the queen, who gripped her spoon hard and glared at Emmaline.

Nicholas still frowned at his mother. "Yes. For three years, all on her own, Emmaline braved the streets and managed to survive. Few ladies have that strength and courage."

Emmaline shared a smile with him. Her heart began to lift again.

The queen whispered in the butler's ear, and he clapped. "Time for the second course!"

The soup bowls were whisked away and replaced with plates. As the servants carried the bowls away, a dish fell to the floor with a sharp *crash!*

The windows of Emmaline's house shatter, and Mama's piano playing comes to a discordant halt.

Papa throws himself in front of them all, shielding them from the shards that shower the room like rain.

James falls to the ground, his head leaking blood.

Rose screams as a hairy man with a hungry grin tears the front of her dress.

A gunshot roars as Emmaline and her sisters leave Papa behind.

The couch is thrown across the room, and Kathleen is tossed to the floor.

Blood and glass crown Charlotte's head as Emmaline's head pounds with pain against the wall.

Emmaline screamed in her chair and covered her burning ears with her hands, the cries of her sisters growing louder, louder, louder . . .

The servants' pitchers hung in the air. The servers' tongs were poised over a platter. The forks of the lords and ladies hovered by their open mouths.

Everyone stared at her.

Emmaline lowered her hands, her chest still heaving from adrenaline, her throat still burning from the smoke of gunpowder. No, there wasn't gunpowder. She was in Queen Genevieve's dining room, not in her families' shattered living room.

But she wished she were. Anywhere would be better than this place at this moment.

Lord and Lady Wheaton glanced at each other, then back at her. Lord Byron coughed, looking everywhere but at Emmaline, while Lady Byron stared only at Emmaline, her ruby lips agape. Lord Midsummer glared at her, and Lady Midsummer glanced from the queen to her husband and back to the queen again.

The girls glanced pitifully at her. Nicholas stared at her, too. Was that pity or shame in his eyes? The queen smirked at her, her eyebrows raised in victory.

I've known you didn't belong here since the moment you stepped foot in my palace, Emmaline could almost hear the queen say. *And now everyone else knows it, too.*

Emmaline panted, realizing what she'd just done. Her chair scraped the floor as she sprang from it and bolted toward the entrance. She had to get out of here. She didn't belong here, and she never would.

"Emmaline, wait!" Nicholas called. "Emmaline!"

She kept running and didn't stop. Her heart pounded in tune with her feet. Tears blinded her. She'd never been so embarrassed in her life. She had to get away.

As long as she was far away from the queen and all the lords and ladies, she didn't care where she went. And she knew the queen didn't care, either.

Windows shattered and sent shimmering glass across the battlefield. Fires feasted on the civilian houses at Somme. Nicholas grabbed Conor's arm and pulled him beneath the rubble. They had to hide. Germans were coming around the corner. The enemy was coming. The enemy was—

Nicholas rubbed his head, forcing the ghosts away as he sat at his mother's table. It was just a bowl that a servant had dropped. He was safe here, far away from the German battlefields—

A girl screamed across the table. Nicholas knew the tortured sound, the sound of someone who had worn the blood of loved ones. He glanced up, his chest seizing by the panicked look on Emmaline's face. She pressed her hands against her ears and breathed heavily. Nicholas's heart skipped several beats. He remembered her screaming in the water when she'd nearly drowned. He remembered her begging for help and saying that someone had ahold of her foot. And now, the ghosts from her past were back, making her seem mad to everyone in the room.

But not to him.

She glanced up and looked around the table. Her eyes settled on him, and something broke in her face. He knew her family had been killed, but there was more to the story, something that haunted Emmaline. What had happened to her that could be so terrible?

His mother chuckled beside him, and Nicholas glanced at her. She was smirking at Emmaline, even as the poor girl's lip trembled. His heartbeat roared like a steam engine as his blood heated. Why was his mother so cruel to her? What had Emmaline ever done to her?

Emmaline leapt from her chair and ran toward the entrance. Nicholas slid back his chair and stood. "Emmaline, wait! Emmaline!"

She kept running and disappeared out the door. His heart sank. What was so horrible that she had to run away? Was it what his mother had done, or something far worse? Or both?

He glanced at his mother, who was biting her lip and sneering at the doorway where Emmaline had fled. He fisted his hands and walked away from the table.

"Where are you going, Nicholas?" Mother demanded.

"I'm going to see if Emmaline is all right," he said, forcing his voice to remain steady.

Mother scoffed. "Don't concern yourself with that girl's affairs. You are the prince, and she is a street orphan. She is nothing."

Nicholas turned and glared at his mother. "That's right, Mother. I am the prince, but I am also the future king. And as that girl's future king, I owe it to her to care about her. As a king, I will pledge my life to help those who need me, and I see no reason to wait to help 'street orphans' like her until I am crowned."

The lords and their wives were staring at him, eyes wide with shock. *Let them think whatever they want. Mother should be ashamed of herself. Even Father would be outraged to hear her speak such words.*

Mother sprang from her chair, her face scarlet. "I won't let you leave, Nicholas. We have guests here more important than she."

He spoke past his heart pounding in his throat. "Do you think this is what being a monarch is all about? Hosting dinners that only people like us can attend? Lavishing yourself in jewels and other riches? Father was not so seduced by the luxuries of royalty that he forgot to treat *all* of his subjects with compassion. He did not forget that the throne is God-given, and God forgive me if I ever forget as you have. I swear before God that I'll fill my palace with paupers who need my help rather than princes who have been born to privilege." He spun on his heel and stormed out of the room.

He ran through the corridors. *Where would she go to be alone?* "Emmaline! Emmaline!" *Where is she? God, help me find her.*

He slowed to a walk and passed the marble staircase. Someone sniffled. He hurried into the staircase and saw Emmaline sitting there, her blue gown flowing over the steps.

He approached her slowly, hoping she wouldn't

run from him like a frightened fawn. "Emmaline," he said softly. "Are you all right?"

She glanced back at him, her eyes wide as if she were startled. Her face was stained with tears. "Why did you come after me?"

"I was concerned about your well-being."

She bit her lip. "It wasn't necessary for you to come and find me, Your Highness. Don't concern yourself about me."

He stepped down next to her. "It's my duty and privilege, Emmaline. I came here because I wanted to." He swallowed. "I must ask you to forgive my mother. She wasn't always so cold. She used to be kind and compassionate."

"We all wear masks, I'm afraid." Emmaline did not meet his gaze but stared at the marble pillar in front of her. "Some are more obvious than others."

Nicholas did not speak for several moments. She was right. His mother did seem to be wearing a mask, and a rather unflattering one at that. She needed healing just as much as Nicholas had upon his return from battle. She needed healing just as much as this girl sitting at his feet did, silent while her soul bled.

"Are you all right?" He waited for her reply, the silence deafening.

She swallowed. "I haven't told anyone about it."

He sat beside her. "You can tell me." He glanced at her, then sighed. "I know what you're going through. When I returned from battle, I was different. All my friends were dead, and I had seen much I wished I had not. I had nightmares, and certain things brought back vivid memories. God helped me before it became irreparable. I still see things I lived through sometimes, but I'm getting better." He glanced at her again. "Is that what happened when the bowl shattered?"

She shuddered and swallowed, closing her eyes. "Yes, it was." She pressed her fingers into her knees and took a deep breath. "I was fifteen. My mother was playing the piano, and my siblings and I were dancing. The window shattered, and the door came crashing down. Soldiers marched inside, and the man in charge told my brother James to step forward. He shot him."

Dear God. Nicholas swallowed.

She went on, squeezing her skirts between her fingers. "My mother was crying over his body when they killed her. Papa told us to run." Her knuckles whitened. "I heard them kill my father as we escaped down the hallway. My sisters and I hid in a room, but one of the men found us. He killed my sisters." She pressed her lips together. "He thought he killed me, too, but he threw me against the fireplace, and I fell unconscious. I don't remember anymore after that."

Nicholas's heart throbbed in his chest. To have seen all that when she was only fifteen. So young. At least he'd been a man when he'd seen the horrors of war. She'd only been a child. What could he say to her? What would be sufficient? He struggled for words. Slowly, he put his hand over hers. Her skin felt like ice.

"I'm sorry," he whispered. "I'm sorry that happened." He hated the taste of these words. They seemed so useless, especially after they'd never helped him. He had to do something else, say something else, something more than "I'm sorry." It just wasn't enough, for her or him.

She caught a tear on her lip. "Thank you."

"I know how it feels, to be haunted by the past and to feel trapped and alone in it. With God as my witness, I'll help you." *Help me to help her, God.*

Emmaline nodded. "Thank you, Your Highness."

He smiled. "Please, call me Nicholas. I prefer it much more."

She smiled and nodded again.

He stood to his feet and took her hand, helping her up. "I know you don't want to return to the dining hall, so how about we go to the kitchen together? There'll be plenty of servants to act as chaperones, so it'll be perfectly appropriate." He smiled at her, hoping she would accept his offer. He didn't want her to go hungry tonight. "Please?"

Her dimples spread as her eyes lit up. "Yes, I'll go."

He grinned and led the way to the kitchen. All the way, he prayed. *God, help me to help her. She needs me, God, but more than that, she needs you. Help her.*

"And when he saw my artillery of snowballs, he ran so fast he slipped on the ice." Nicholas laughed, cutting into his roast beef. "He wasn't hurt, thankfully, but I must say, I'd never seen him run quite so fast."

Emmaline laughed, picturing Nicholas's young friend Tommy slipping on the ice. "You're making my cheeks ache, Your Highness."

"I told you, I much prefer to be called Nicholas. Your Highness takes much too long to say. Besides, it doesn't quite fit my charming personality." He winked.

She laughed again. "Well, all right, then, *Nicholas*. I shall call you that, for the sake of your pride."

He smiled at her, and her heart skipped a beat. Truly, he was the most magnificent man she'd ever seen, with the shine in his eyes and the dimples in his cheeks.

She curled her toes in her shoes, forcing her eyes away from his handsome face. She only wanted to be his friend, and doubtless, he only wanted the same of her. Anything more and the fortress she'd been slowly rebuilding would come crashing down in flames.

"I was quite the troublemaker as a child, too," Emmaline admitted, biting back a smile.

Nicholas lifted his eyebrows. "Really? I can't picture you as a troublemaker. Enlighten me."

She smiled. "Once, when I was six years old, I stole my Aunt Ida's clothes while she was bathing. She was nasty to me, always saying it wasn't good for a girl to climb trees or snag her dress. So I stole her clothing and hid them in the sitting room. She screamed in the bathroom for a good while until someone had found the clothes and given them to her. She promised never to return for another visit."

Nicholas roared with laughter, his head bobbing. "And what did your parents say?" he managed to say.

"Mama was furious and told me I was to go to bed without sweets for a week. Papa, however, was pleased, as he had never enjoyed Aunt Ida's company."

"You sound like a delightful child."

"Oh, I was. When I was being good." She smiled at him, then realized she might be flirting with him. She couldn't deny that it felt good, even with the warnings she'd given herself lurking just below the surface in her mind.

He grinned at her and took another bite.

She studied the shadows his lowered eyelashes made in the dim candlelight, the dimple in his chin, the way his thick, dark hair fell over his forehead. Her heart beat slowly as she drank him in, drank in every detail.

Stop it. You must stop, Emmaline. This isn't good. She pressed a fingernail into her hand and shook herself awake from her daydreaming.

"Nicholas?" she said, trying to shoo the butterflies away from her stomach.

He glanced up.

"Thank you. For your kindness. For coming after me when I ran away."

He shook his head. "I should be the one thanking you. You rescued me from a night of boredom. I quite like sitting in this kitchen with you."

Her heart pounded in her throat. "Me, too." Did he really mean it, or was he just saying it to be nice to her?

He smiled at her again. Something inside her wanted to believe that he was being honest. Something inside her forced her to believe that he was only extending an offer of friendship.

"Sorry to interrupt, Your Highness," Edna, the palace cook, said as she hurried over with two plates, "but I thought you and this charming young lady might want some of my marble cake to go along with your roast."

Nicholas looked up at the cook. "That's perfectly all right, Edna. I make it a point to excuse offense when cake is involved." He winked at her.

Edna laughed. "So much like your father, you are." She set the plates in front of them.

"I hope to be."

Emmaline forced herself not to lick her lips. Cake had been a favorite of hers since childhood–or rather, sweets in general had been a favorite of hers since childhood. She remembered a birthday cake she'd had once, with cream and raspberries. James had blown out the candles with her. It'd tasted like a dream.

"Enjoy, you two," Edna said as she walked away.

Nicholas grinned at her. "Who needs an orchestra and a fancy table to eat, anyway? This has been far better than having Lord Byron drag war stories out of me." He laughed.

He was right. Who needed an orchestra when the

best music in the world was the prince's melodious laughter?

"Will there be anything else, Your Majesty?" Polly asked.

Genevieve didn't turn from the window. She gazed at the moon and stars and shook her head. "No, Polly. That will be all."

Polly's skirts swished as she bowed behind Genevieve. "Of course, Your Majesty." The girl's shoes clicked against the floor as she left Genevieve's bedchambers.

Genevieve twisted the doorknobs and walked onto her balcony. The nights were growing warmer. Lights flickered on and off in the houses of Lauderbury. The moon hung in the sky, like a protective eye watching over the city.

Dinner had not gone as planned. She should have known it wouldn't with that Emmaline girl attending. She was different than the other girls. It was clear that she had known privilege at one time, but surely that had to be forgotten after three years of street life.

Perhaps she had been wrong to treat Emmaline in such a harsh fashion. The girl could not help that she'd found herself orphaned and alone at just fifteen, with memories that burned in her mind like stray embers floating around a fire. She could not help that she'd been forced to live on the streets. It was a miracle she'd kept her virtue intact, and it spoke of her character. Perhaps she had judged the girl too quickly.

But perhaps Genevieve wasn't entirely to blame. Emmaline was partly responsible. Genevieve had seen how she'd bewitched her son already, and she knew that the girl would eventually steal her Nicholas away. Every time she looked at the girl's lovely face, she saw the happiness she would bring to Nicholas, the days she would spend with him, and the children she would give him.

And she couldn't bear for that to happen. She didn't want Nicholas to be happy. She knew first-hand that happiness leads to expectations, and when those expectations are ripped away, they shatter a person. Just as she had been shattered, the moment when Henry's hand went limp and cold in hers.

If her son went through the same heartbreak, she couldn't bear it. It was better for him to be unhappy than broken beyond repair. She'd seen him broken once when he'd returned from the war, and she'd rather die than see him wounded again. And Genevieve would do everything in her power to make sure that never happened.

"Oh, it was so awful. I can't believe I screamed like that, right in front of the queen!" Emmaline flopped backwards onto the bed, staring at the alabaster ceiling but seeing nothing except the same scene playing again and again in her head. She wiped her face with her hands, as if that would make the memory disappear.

"You can't help it, Emmaline. It was simply a reaction to a sudden noise. It might've happened to anyone." Lydia sat on the floor and put her books back into proper order. She stroked the cover of one, then set it lovingly into her trunk with the others.

"But it happened to me," Emmaline moaned. "I don't know how I'll bear the embarrassment. The queen is sure to hate me now."

"Come, come, Emmaline," Eleanor hushed, carrying a brush. "I've heard that the queen is very hard to get to know. She has thick walls that she's spent over a decade building, and it'll take a special person to knock them all down." She motioned with her hands for Emmaline to sit up. "Let me brush your hair. It'll make you feel better."

Emmaline sighed and sat up. Eleanor sat behind her on the bed, running the soft brush through Emmaline's hair. "I made a complete fool of myself. What should I do?"

"Laugh it off," Eleanor said.

"What?"

"Laugh it off. Everyone makes mistakes and embarrasses themselves in front of others. Even the queen."

Julia piped up, raising her head from her sketchbook. "I heard that during her coronation dinner, she accidentally drank a bit too much wine and belched as the prime minister was giving a speech."

Emmaline laughed breathlessly. "Oh, that's awful!"

Diana smiled, her eyes twinkling. "My father fell asleep during the opening of a very esteemed play, and his snoring was so loud, it interrupted one of the scenes. Mother had to elbow him in order to awake him."

Anna leaned back against her bed, laughing and clutching her stomach.

"And remember, your night wasn't completely terrible," Julia chimed in. "You ate dinner with the prince—alone!"

The girls squealed in delight, sounding more like a clowder of alley cats than well-groomed and refined ladies.

Emmaline's cheeks heated. "We weren't alone. There were servants all around us."

"Well, I suppose," Julia admitted.

As Eleanor finished brushing Emmaline's hair, Emmaline gripped the banister of the bed and pressed her chin against it. "But he was very kind. I haven't ever known a man like him, except my father."

He was a very good prince. *And an even better friend,* she was quick to remind herself. And someday, he'd be a great king. She just knew it.

A knock came at the door. The conversation fizzled as Anna hurried to the door and opened it. Anna gasped and curtsied. "Your Majesty."

Queen Genevieve strode into the bedchamber, still wearing her dinner attire. "I must speak with Emmaline." She roved her eyes across the room until they settled on their target. She frowned.

Emmaline felt naked in her nightgown as she stood a mere few feet away from the queen. She curtsied, trembling. "Your Majesty."

The queen still stared at Emmaline with eyes like knives poised to cut her to ribbons. "I heard that you dined in the kitchen with my son."

Emmaline nodded. "I did, Your Majesty."

Queen Genevieve raised her chin and stepped toward Emmaline, circling her like a vulture preparing to devour its prey. "I don't know what it is about you that has my son so hypnotized."

Emmaline prepared herself for the sharp talons.

"Yes, you are very beautiful. Yes, your nature is sweet." The queen stopped and looked at Emmaline fully in the eyes. "But there is something else about you I do not understand, something that doesn't belong in my palace."

The queen's words cut deep but Emmaline did not dare reveal that she was bleeding.

"Stay away from my son," the queen snarled. "He is not for you."

Little did the queen know that Emmaline did not want to give her heart away to the prince, as charming and compassionate as he was. But she could not say so. If Emmaline told the queen she merely wanted to be the future queen's lady's maid, the queen might be insulted that she didn't want to marry her son. She might throw Emmaline out of the palace, and then where would she be? Back on the streets, prey for the predators stalking the alleyways.

Rise

God, let my words be soft. Emmaline steadied her breath. "I know I am not the likeliest of candidates for your son. I've never dared to claim that I am. But at the very least, I deserve your respect. Even though you see me as an insect to be swatted away, I am still a human being, just like you and just like your dinner guests are. I deserve your respect as a human, however low I am. I will not beg for your pity as an orphan, nor ask for your kindness, but I do demand your respect."

Emmaline could feel the girls holding their breath behind her. Her own heart pulsed in her throat, so rapidly it felt like it was trying to claw its way out.

Queen Genevieve's cheeks were scarlet. Clearly, she hadn't expected Emmaline to fight back against her attacks. "Well, if you want my respect, then you must earn it."

Emmaline did not falter in meeting the queen's gaze. "I shall try my hardest."

The queen stared at her for a few moments, then shook her head, spun around, and left the room.

Emmaline stood where she was, putting her icy hands over her roasting cheeks. Had she really said what she'd said? Had those words, bold and strong, come out of her? Directed at the queen?

"You stood up to her," Anna said, her voice soft and shocked. "You stood up to the queen."

Emmaline released the breath she'd been holding back. "I did." *How?*

It is the Lord your God who goes with you, a

small voice in the corners of her mind whispered. ***He will not leave you or forsake you.***

The girl who'd arrived here only months before was beginning to fade. The girl who awoke from nightmares, her throat burning from her screams. She was leaving. *Finally.*

Chapter Ten

LESSONS GREW EASIER and easier as the days passed. Emmaline spent nearly every waking hour learning how to sip tea with a graceful air, how to arrange her hair like a lady-in-waiting, how to walk with her shoulders straight and her chin high, how to speak meekly yet forcefully, and how to dance with beauty and grace at the many balls she would attend. Every day, she thanked God for her new life. Every day, she wondered how she'd gone from the streets and to the palace—and why.

On cloudless days, she broke away from the sipping and spinning and retreated to the gardens. It was quiet and peaceful there, with no one watching her but the buds of blooming flowers. She was just ordinary Emmaline in the gardens, and she could breathe for half an hour or so there.

Today was one such day. Emmaline walked down the staircase leading into the gardens, the robins swooping through the air and chirping little notes. The sun cast its rays onto the flowers, bringing them to life beneath the blue sky. Emmaline straightened her straw hat and readjusted the ribbon tied beneath her loose curls before trailing down the cobblestone path.

An arch covered in ivy appeared, encased by walls on either side. Emmaline stepped through the arch and smiled at the familiar sight. Hummingbirds zipped by her, drinking their fill of nectar. Butterflies fluttered lazily through the flowers. Shrubs stood guard around the gardens, where an abundance of flowers made their home. Emmaline hadn't known so many colors existed until she'd visited the gardens for the first time.

She walked down the path, gazing at the topiaries and fir trees lining the garden walls. She turned left, eager to see how many rose buds had opened their faces.

She, like all these flowers, had been doing growing of her own. She never dreamed, in her three years on the streets, that she would make such leaps and bounds in becoming a lady of the court. She never thought she could do it. But her new friends had believed in her. Someday, Emmaline would show the queen just how far she had come from the day she'd first met her.

The smell of roses trickled down the path. At the end of the path, another stone arch framed a doorway through the wall, but instead of ivy, the walls were covered with flowers. The flowers trickled down from the wall and lined the pathway. Thanks to Anna, Emmaline could name almost all of them: lilies, violets, lilacs, bugles, sweet peas, and orchids.

Emmaline smiled at all the beauty. Bees buzzed around her, on their way to gather pollen from the hundreds of flowers engulfing her. A gathering of daisies reminded her of her mother. As a child, she'd picked daisies nearly every day to give to her mother. She'd smell the tiny bouquet with a smile and put one of the flowers in Emmaline's hair. "A flower for my flower," she would say.

Emmaline kept going down the path and closed the distance between her and the roses. Her heart skipped a beat when she saw how big the rose petals had gotten. She cupped a bud in her fingers and breathed in its scent, closing her eyes in pleasure.

A whimper made her jump. Someone sniffled. Emmaline turned toward the noise, suddenly seeing a little girl among the daffodils. Her knees were drawn up to her chin, her loose dress dirty and tears running down her soot-covered cheeks.

What was she doing here? Was she a servant girl, or the daughter of a servant perhaps? If she was, why was she so dirty? All the servants Emmaline had seen were clean and properly clothed. But this little girl was dressed in rags and had rather angular cheekbones. Emmaline pressed a hand to her heart and stepped carefully toward her. She didn't want to frighten her and make her run away. "Why are you crying?"

The little girl glanced up at Emmaline, her blue eyes enormous and terrified. She jerked as if to turn, but Emmaline blocked her path and knelt before hr. "You don't have to leave. I won't hurt you. I want to help you." She smiled gently. "What's your name?"

The little girl sniffled, wiping her arm across her nose. "Minnie," she whimpered.

"Well, Minnie, my name is Emmaline. Can you tell me why you're crying?"

Another tear rolled down her cheek. She was awfully skinny. "They hit me again."

A whoosh of shock rattled her. "Who hit you? Your parents?"

Minnie shook her head. "No. Mama and Papa are dead. Frank and Opal hit me." She drew forth her arm and peeled back her tattered sleeve. A red mark stretched across her wrist, and several purple and green bruises freckled her skin.

Emmaline gasped, pressing her hand against her mouth. Her heart ached as more tears fell down Minnie's cheeks. "Oh, I'm so sorry, Minnie." She

Rise

glanced back down the path where she'd come from, her mind spinning. "You've got to be hungry. Why don't I take you to the kitchen and find you something to eat?"

Minnie glanced at her, her eyes suddenly lighting up. Slowly, Minnie nodded and wiped the tears from her face. Emmaline took Minnie's hand and helped her to her feet. Minnie's shoes were so worn, her toes poked through. Emmaline grimaced at the sight and led the little girl down the path and out of the gardens.

How could someone treat a child so harshly? How had her parents died? Were these people she lived with related to her, or had they taken her in as a servant? How long had she been living with them and suffering this abuse? Minnie had said their names were Frank and Opal. If Emmaline told Ross about it, perhaps he could find the couple and arrest them for their crimes.

Emmaline helped Minnie climb the staircase leading out of the gardens and into the palace. "Watch your feet there, Minnie. There you go." As Emmaline held her by the hand, she could feel callouses on the girl's palm. Her blood burned.

They stepped into the palace together. Their shoes clicked against the marble floor as Emmaline led Minnie to the kitchen.

"Do you have any strawberry jam?" Minnie asked, her wide blue eyes taking in every wonder the palace held.

Emmaline smiled. "Do you like strawberry jam?"

She nodded.

Emmaline squeezed her hand affectionately. "Then strawberry jam you shall have."

Minnie grinned, walking a bit faster now.

They came into the kitchen, where Edna, the palace cook, and her maids were preparing tea and the delicacies that went with it. When they saw Minnie, a few of the maids clustered together and whispered.

Edna stirred something in a pot. "Lizzie, get me some more honey! The queen is adamant about her honey."

Emmaline cleared her throat. "Excuse me, Edna, may I speak with you?"

Edna turned. Her round, pink cheeks spread as she smiled. She was a pretty older woman, though her dark hair was disarrayed, and sweat glittered above her lip. Emmaline had befriended Edna over the last few months. When she had nothing else to do, sometimes she would come downstairs to the kitchen and shell peas or roll bread. She enjoyed the comradery she had with a few of the kitchen girls.

Edna brushed her hands over her apron. "Of course, Emmaline. Go right ahead."

Emmaline glanced at Minnie. "I found this little girl in the gardens. Her name is Minnie, and she was wondering if she could have some strawberry jam."

Edna looked at Minnie and smiled sadly. "Minnie can have all the strawberry jam she wants." She turned to one of her maids. "Ruby, will you get this little girl some scones with strawberry jam? And I expect she'll be wanting warm milk as well."

Minnie grinned, her dimples the largest Emmaline had ever seen.

Emmaline laughed. "I think she likes the sound of that."

Ruby took Minnie by the hand and helped her sit at the table in the kitchen. Moments later, she brought her a cup of milk and a plate full of scones glistening with jam. Minnie licked her lips.

As Minnie ate, Emmaline told Edna what Minnie had told her and about the red mark on her arm. The whispering maids gathered around, their eyes sullen as Emmaline relayed Minnie's story.

She had to tell Ross what had happened to Minnie. After Ross had rescued Emmaline from the streets, he had told her that he had arrested the two men who had attacked her. "Ever since I became captain, I've been working to clean criminals off the streets," he'd told her. "I only wish I would have discovered that scum before they discovered you." He would want to know about this couple that had beaten an innocent child.

"I have to find Captain Ross and tell him so that he can arrest Frank and Opal." Emmaline told Edna. "Can Minnie stay here while I go find him?"

Edna nodded quickly. "Yes, of course she can. Go now and find the captain. Those people must be found and stopped."

Emmaline hurried down the halls, hoping to catch Ross walking through the palace. Instead, she found him in the stables, giving two guards instructions.

When the guards left, Ross turned around and smiled. "Emmaline! I didn't notice you come in." His smile faded as he looked into her face. "Is there something you need?"

She swallowed. "Yes, I need to speak with you. It's important."

He stepped closer to her. "Go on."

"I found an orphan girl named Minnie in the gardens. She ran away from the people she's living with."

"Why did she run away?" Ross asked.

Her breath hitched. "She said they've been hitting her. She has a red mark and bruises on her arm. She's the skinniest little girl I've ever seen, and her clothes and shoes are in tatters. They must be treating her like a servant and abusing her when she doesn't do what they want."

Ross swallowed, a muscle flexing in his jaw. "How old is she?"

Emmaline spoke past the emotion welling up inside her. "About five, perhaps six."

Ross cleared his throat, his brown eyes blazing as he glanced to the side. "My men and I will find those people. Did Minnie tell you their names?"

Emmaline nodded. "Yes. Their names are Frank and Opal." She bit her lip. "You have to stop them, Ross."

Ross gazed at her and placed his hand on her arm. "I promise they will be. They won't hurt Minnie or any other children ever again."

Emmaline breathed a sigh of relief. "Thank you, Ross. I knew you would help."

Ross retrieved his stallion Felix and began saddling him. "I'll go at once."

Emmaline smiled, then said her goodbyes and hurried back to the palace. As she was returning to the kitchen, she remembered something she kept in her chest at the foot of her bed. She turned around and hurried toward her bedchamber.

When she'd retrieved it, she ran back down to the kitchen. Minnie sat at the table sipping milk, the plate of scones now empty. Her hair was wet and braided, and the green ribbons in her hair matched her new dress. Minnie turned around, exposing a mustache of milk glistening above her lips. "I had a bath!" she announced cheerfully.

Emmaline giggled, putting her hand against her mouth. "And I see your lip is already dirty again." She walked toward her, holding her hands behind her back.

Minnie frowned, leaning sideways for a glimpse behind Emmaline's back. "What have you got?"

"A surprise for you." She brought her hands forward and held out a doll. It was the doll Emmaline had found the day Ross rescued her, the doll with the torn dress and the misplaced eyes. Emmaline had restored the doll to its former glory, mending the dress and the eyes and cleaning the dirt from the doll's white face. And now that the pieces of Emmaline's life were mending, it was time for the doll's life to begin anew, too.

Minnie gasped and wiped her hands clean. "Oh, a doll! Can I hold her?"

"Of course! She belongs to you now. I saved her for someone who would love her again."

Minnie took the doll from Emmaline gently and brushed her skinny little fingers over the doll's face, cradling the doll against her. The doll stared up at Minnie's face, her stitched smile somehow seeming bigger. Tears tickled Emmaline's eyes.

Edna cleared her throat and motioned for Emmaline to come. Emmaline patted Minnie on the shoulder and left her side.

"What is it?" Emmaline asked.

Edna's wide eyes twinkled with joy. "While you were gone, one of my maids pulled me aside to ask me something important concerning Minnie."

"Yes, go on."

"This maid has been married for four years, and there's been no sign of pregnancy in all that time. She believes she is barren, so she has just gone to ask her husband if they can take in Minnie, seeing how she needs a new home."

Emmaline bit her lip, glancing at Minnie as she whispered to the doll. After all Minnie had suffered through, she deserved to go to the best home Emmaline could give her. A home filled with warmth, safety, and love. Would this maid and her husband give her such a home, or would they hurt her like Frank and Opal?

She looked back at Edna. "I don't know, Edna. I can't let her go with just anyone."

Edna nodded. "I understand your hesitation, Miss, but I can promise you that Daisy and Peter will give her the home every child ought to have. She has wanted a child for some time, and she believes God left Minnie in the garden for you to find and bring to her."

Emmaline glanced at Minnie again, and then back at Edna. "She's a good woman, and her husband is a good man?"

Edna smiled. "The very picture of good people. Good Christians, too."

Emmaline fiddled with her fingers. Daisy hadn't worked in the kitchen very long, so Emmaline didn't know her very well yet. What if Minnie was hurt again? What if Minnie had to endure more heartbreak and pain?

I have brought her to this place, Emmaline. She will be safe. If she is hurt, I will bind up her wounds and heal her, just as I have healed you.

Emmaline breathed in the warmth of God's voice as she nodded. "Then yes. I think it's best that Minnie goes with Peter and Daisy."

A few minutes later, a young couple stepped into the kitchen, pale as ghosts with eyes full of hope. They approached Minnie slowly and spoke to her in soft tones. They asked if they could sit with her, and she nodded. As the man and woman introduced themselves to the girl, Emmaline smiled, tears gathering in her eyes.

Minnie deserved so much, and the greatest gift Emmaline could give her was the gift of family. Minnie would be safe and loved. Emmaline just knew it.

Ross glanced over east Lauderbury as Felix trotted across the cobblestone square. Men loaded timber into the back of a wagon, their beards unkempt and their clothes patched. A mother scurried through the streets, her bags on her arms and her children staying close to her skirts. A cat bathed itself on someone's front porch. A shopkeeper threw his trash into the alley.

This wasn't the first time he'd had to exact justice against those who would dare to hurt an innocent child, and this wouldn't be the last. In this world, children weren't much better than rats, and because they had no authority, they could be forced into doing anyone's bidding. Ross bit the inside of his cheek as heat burned the back of his neck.

Thank God Emmaline had found Minnie. What would have happened if Minnie had been frightened away from the palace and found by her abusers? Frank and Opal. Those were their names. The people who could dare to hurt a child. The people who believed there would be no consequences.

There was a boy who had hit Maria, his little

sister, when she was just eight years old. Ross had never wanted to hurt anyone more than he'd wanted to then. He'd given the boy a proper thrashing. Ross would never forget the way Maria had smiled at him and embraced him.

And now, her body was reduced to ash scattered over his homeland.

When would he tell Emmaline the truth? When would he tell her that he knew the secret of her past, the mystery of who she was? Was he being cruel by holding the truth back from her? Surely it wasn't the mark of a good friend.

Are you concerned with being a good friend, or are you only concerned about winning her heart?

It wouldn't be fair to confuse her. Surely, she would only develop an attachment to him because of their shared identities. And she already had feelings for Nicholas, feelings she was trying to fight off and hide from herself. But winning the prince's heart would heal hers. Nicholas had been through hell like her, and he would give her the life of luxury she deserved. The life she used to have.

Ross cleared his throat and swallowed. He couldn't tell her. Not until his wager in this game of romance was disqualified. Not until he had lost her for good.

A stout man carried a newspaper under his arm and strolled in the same direction as Ross. Ross ordered his stallion Felix to stop. "Excuse me, sir. I need your assistance."

The man turned around, his eyes wide before

relaxing. "Oh, Captain. What is it?"

"I'm trying to locate the house of a couple called Frank and Opal. Do you know it?"

The man rubbed his chin as his eyes wandered over the ground. "Hmm. Frank and Opal." His head sprang up. "Ah, yes, Frank and Opal! They live right around the corner, next to the bridge over the pond. Their door is painted red." He raised an eyebrow. "What business do you have with them?"

"They were abusing a little girl. I'm going there to arrest them." He started to urge Felix on.

The man held his hands up, his eyes wide again. "Wait, Captain, wait. Do you mean . . . Minnie? Is she all right?"

Ross glanced the man over, puzzled as to why the man was so concerned. "Yes. She is well. She was found in the palace gardens, and she's in good hands now."

The man scratched his head. "I always meant to say something, but I never did." A scarlet hue shot up his neck and spread into his cheeks.

Ross nodded. "I hope this has taught you something, then. Don't wait."

The man didn't look back up.

"Thank you for your help." Ross clicked his tongue and urged Felix on.

Nicholas moved his feet across the checkered floor, raising his arm and lowering it as Ross parried

Nicholas's sword. Their swords clashed together, the slicing sounds echoing off the high ceilings. Nicholas panted, his heart thumping in excitement.

Ross was a good friend of his and his mother's. He'd served Nicholas's mother well, even before his mother had instated him as Captain of the Royal Guard. He was quiet, clever, and violent with a sword. He'd helped Nicholas build his strength back in his leg and release his pent-up emotions after Nicholas had returned from battle. It had been good to gain a brother of sorts after the loss of his father.

Nicholas parried Ross's blows quickly, keeping the blade from his face.

"Something on your mind, Your Highness?" Ross asked, a teasing grin on his face.

Nicholas drew in a breath. "Oh, it's Mother. She's got me busy with preparations for my birthday ball. I think I'll be glad to see my birthday over and done with."

"I've been wondering what has been keeping you from our fencing time. I was beginning to think you were afraid of being beaten." Ross raised his blade over Nicholas's head.

Nicholas slammed his blade into Ross's, pushing the sword away from his head. He grunted, his arms flexing. He laughed breathlessly. "You know I could have you imprisoned for saying such things." With a final blow of strength, he pushed Ross's blade away and knocked it from his hands. The blade clattered to the floor several feet away.

Ross laughed, his chest rising and falling as he breathed hard. "Shall we call it even?"

Nicholas raised a brow. "Quitting so soon?"

"It wouldn't be right to embarrass the future king."

Nicholas chuckled, and then walked across the room and put away his sword. Ross followed him and did the same. "So, what have you been doing while I've been preoccupied?" Nicholas asked.

"I tracked down a man and woman in the city and arrested them. That took about a day."

Nicholas raised his eyebrows. "What did you arrest them for?"

"They had been beating an orphan girl and treating her like their servant. She was found in the palace gardens, hiding in the flowers. Emmaline was the one who made the discovery, actually. She brought her to the kitchen to eat something, then told me about it."

She did that? His heart quickened. "And what of the girl? What happened to her?"

Ross grinned. "She went to stay with a childless couple who work in the palace. They all seem happy together." He turned to the window and looked out. "If Emmaline hadn't acted, Frank and Opal might have taken her back and hurt her again–or worse. Emmaline's a remarkable girl."

Nicholas smiled to himself, imagining Emmaline helping the girl into the kitchen. "Yes, she is." *And she bears the mark of a true queen.*

Perhaps that was a sign.

Chapter Eleven

TWO WEEKS HAD gone by, and as more days passed, more flowers grew and bloomed. Their scents filled Emmaline's lungs as she breathed in new air. Now that it wasn't cold, she often went to the fields behind the palace and stretched in the grass, burying herself in the flowers and watching the bees gather their pollen.

It had been three weeks since the girls began to

spend time alone with the prince, and so far, Diana, Julia, and Lydia had had their turns. Lydia had just spent time with the prince last night. This morning, she had said her night had gone differently than she'd imagined. She and Nicholas had gone to his private libraries, and he'd shown her all the books she wanted to see. She said the prince was a good and kind man, but she wasn't sure if he was the one.

"I like him, but I can't imagine living the rest of my life with him. I'm not entirely sure I want to share my husband with the kingdom," Lydia had said while brushing her hair. "Don't feel sorry for me, girls. I'll find love one day with another man. I know it.

While the other girls practiced their dancing in the palace courtyard, Anna took her flower book and went with Emmaline to the meadow. As they walked through the grass, Anna read and mumbled the words to herself. Blue birds swept through the trees. Butterflies kissed Emmaline's dress and drank the sweetness from the flowers. The sunlight caressed Emmaline's face. *Thank You, God, for this meadow.*

Anna glanced up at Emmaline, clutching the open book to her chest. "Would you like me to tell you all the names of each of these flowers?"

Emmaline smiled. "Of course I would."

Anna smiled back. "Good. I believe that one cannot appreciate something fully until they know its name." She pointed at each flower swaying in the breeze. "Those are sweet peas. And there's ramsons, cornflowers, lady's bedstraw, field poppies, sweet violets, and delphinium."

"How do you remember all their names?" Emmaline asked, lips parted in amazement.

Anna frowned a little. "Well, until I met you and the rest of the girls, flowers were my only friends. I remembered their names and spoke to them as if they were people. They were there every spring and summer to listen to whatever I said."

"I suppose you were rather lonely in the winter, then."

"Yes, I was." Anna frowned, burying her face in her book.

Emmaline wrapped her hand around Anna's wrist. "But not anymore." She smiled at her.

Anna beamed, closing the book and sinking into the grass. She lay down, her red hair collecting around her head. "Flowers are so lucky."

"How so?"

"They're always out here, soaking in the sun, tasting the rain, drinking in the moonlight. They live every second of every day of their lives without stopping."

Emmaline smiled. She slipped off her straw hat and sank down into the grasses with Anna. The bright blue sky swallowed her vision.

She sighed. "This feels wonderful."

"Yes, it does." Anna agreed.

A ladybug flashed by. Emmaline pointed her finger upwards and watched the ladybug crawl across her skin. It went around and around her finger, and then flew away again.

"Are you nervous?" Anna asked.

"About what?"

"Spending time with the prince."

"Oh, that. And yes, I am. A bit." The truth was, sometimes Emmaline lay awake in bed thinking of it. How would she compose herself that night when it came? Would she enjoy Nicholas's company? Would he enjoy hers, or find her odd? How would she react if he took her hand? What could she say to tell him she wasn't interested in marrying anyone?

Emmaline shifted on the ground, suddenly uncomfortable. She turned her head toward Anna. "Are you?"

Anna huffed, her green eyes staring at the sky. "Yes. Actually, I'm a bit jealous."

Emmaline's heart began to pound. She couldn't imagine good-natured Anna holding any ill will against anyone, so Anna's words surprised her. "Who of?"

"You."

Emmaline sat up. "Me? Why?"

Anna put her hands over her middle. "You're just so beautiful, and you have this spirit about you that is so gentle and graceful and lovely. The prince is sure to pick you."

Emmaline blinked. Was that how she saw her? Beautiful and gentle, graceful and lovely? Anna might feel that way, but Emmaline felt like a great big buffoon in a silk gown sometimes. She hadn't realized that her reflection could look so different to someone else. "Is that what you think?"

"I don't think—*I know*."

"But I'm not so sure. I don't think I'm worthy of the prince's love, so how can I possibly attract him?" She laid back down. "Besides, I don't want to marry him. I can't marry him. I've been shattered once, and I'm fairly certain that the pieces won't be mendable next time." Her cheeks heated. "Forgive me. I said too much."

"No, you didn't. I'm glad to have someone to talk to. The flowers are notorious for their listening abilities, but their speaking capabilities leave much to be desired." She turned her head toward Emmaline. "Were you talking about your family? When you said you had been shattered?"

Emmaline swallowed. "Yes."

"I'm sorry about what happened to them. No one should go through what you have had to." She turned her head again. "And I thought I had troubles with my family."

Emmaline had always felt there was more to Anna than she had revealed, but she hadn't felt it was the right time to press her for answers. The last thing she wanted was for Anna's petals to shrivel up. "What happened to your family?"

Anna rubbed the blades of grass between her fingertips. "My mother doesn't care for me. She and my father were in love at one point, but something happened early in the marriage that made them hate each other. I came nine months after the vows were made. They were never happy with each other, and so I never had siblings. Mother has always tried to make me into something she can be proud of. I suppose she does it so that her life isn't a total waste. I've known she doesn't love me for most of my life."

Tears pricked Emmaline's eyes. How could anyone not love Anna? Anna, the girl who had memorized all the flowers, whose smile was warmer than spring, who sang sweet songs and hummed like a bee as she brushed her red hair? "Oh, Anna. How terrible."

"It isn't so terrible. I suppose others could have it worse. Like you."

Emmaline pressed her lips together. "You needn't tidy away your pain because of my own. Pain is pain and hurts no matter what has happened or to whom it has happened."

Anna smiled sadly. "I suppose you're right." She looked up at the clouds. "You know, I came here because of my mother's wishes, but if I'm truthful, I was glad to have a chance to find love. I'm simply not sure that I want it with the prince. I don't need the future king to love me, just *someone*. I don't want to be alone again."

"Even if the prince doesn't choose you, you won't be alone. Another man will see your red hair and your green eyes and will sweep you into his arms and carry you away."

Anna laughed. "It sounds as if you've been spending a great deal of time with Lydia lately." Her smile faded as she gazed up at the sky. "I don't think being the king's wife is my calling. I'd rather have a small sort of life."

Emmaline turned her face toward Anna. "That sounds wonderful." She swatted away the thought of what it might be like to be queen as if it were a pesky fly. Would she ever have rest from these daydreams? They would do nothing but re-open old wounds.

"Anna!" Julia called. "Come over here! I want to paint you."

Anna sat up, her hair falling over her shoulder. "I thought you were painting the flowers."

"I was, and now I want to paint you. Please, Anna?"

Anna shook her head and smiled. "Yes, I'm coming." She waved at Emmaline, then stood to her feet and left.

Emmaline closed her eyes and moaned pleasurably. It felt so good to lay here in the grass. The smell of wildflowers wafted in her nose. Birds flew by overhead. They looked as if they were soaring to other worlds from down on the ground.

After a day of skipping in the pasture, she and her sisters had done this very thing. They'd eaten almost a whole bushel of strawberries that day. Kathleen had told them about a boy she was in love with, and Rose had pointed out the shapes in the clouds. Then James had snuck up on them and scared them all. He was no match for four girls. Emmaline and her sisters had soon caught him hiding behind a tree and attacked him with tickling. James's giggling rang in her ears, even now as she lay in the grass behind the palace.

Emmaline hadn't realized those days in the sun would end so quickly. She'd grown up, and now she had to think about her future. Emmaline bit her lip. She hoped Anna's future would be brighter. She could not imagine a life without ever being loved. It almost seemed worse than losing love in a shower of bullets and blood.

"I was wondering where you were," a man's voice said. The sun blazed on his face so brightly, Emmaline couldn't tell who it was. Until he bent down.

"Your Highness!" she gasped. She sat up, so quickly her neck ached.

Nicholas smiled, as if impressed. "I was just on my walk and saw the others, but I didn't see you. I must say, I wasn't expecting to see one of you lying in the grass."

She smiled sheepishly. "Well, I was just admiring the meadow. I admit, it isn't very ladylike to lay in the grass, but—"

He waved her words away, still smiling. "Never mind that. I like seeing people connect so deeply to nature."

Her heart slowed. "Oh."

He lowered his hand and helped her to her feet. "I apologize for startling you again. I've got to stop doing that."

She brushed herself off and tied her hat's ribbon beneath her hair. "Oh, it's quite all right, Your Highness.

You didn't startle me much."

"Good." He gazed into her eyes for a minute, as if lost in thought. "You know, I think I might know of something you'd find interesting. It's in the palace gardens. I can show you if you'd like."

She nodded. "I'd love to see it."

He smiled, his teeth white as pearls. "Come on, then."

Together, the two of them walked through the field of flowers. Butterflies fluttered in the tall grass and pollen floated down around them like the sprinkling of snow.

Nicholas turned to her. "I heard what you did for that little girl. It's very remarkable."

Emmaline blushed. "Oh, it's nothing, really. I simply found her and brought her to the kitchen. I hadn't planned for Peter and Daisy to take her in, but I'm so glad they did. Edna has told me that Minnie is happy."

Nicholas glanced at her. "You gave her the gift of family, and that's one of the best gifts a child could ever receive."

How does he know about Minnie? Who could have told him? She knew that word travelled quickly in the palace, but it had already made its way to the prince's ears?

Swells of purple rose like ocean waves as they came closer to the gardens. Bushes brimming with lilacs took Emmaline's breath away. She put a hand over her chest. "Oh, lilacs!"

Nicholas chuckled. "You like them?"

"They're one of my favorite things, next to a night sky full of stars. They're so lovely, aren't they?"

"Yes, they are beautiful this year." He gazed thoughtfully at the bushes.

She quickened her pace. "What about you? What's one of your favorite things?"

A dimple jumped in his cheek. "Horses. When I was stationed in Belgium, my company was camping on the edge of a field. We woke up one morning to this thundering noise. We thought it was the enemy, but it was a herd of wild horses, running across the field. It was one of the most beautiful things I've ever seen. They looked so free."

"That sounds wonderful."

"It was."

His grin warmed her chest with a heat that burned her cheeks and forced her eyes to look at the ground, away from his blue irises.

Nicholas pointed to a tree in the distance. "Over there by that oak was where I had my first—"

"Stop! There's a snake!"

Emmaline snatched Nicholas's hand and jerked him backwards.

Nicholas stumbled but regained his footing, putting his arm before Emmaline, waiting for any sign of movement from the snake.

"It's an adder," Nicholas said breathlessly, keeping his eye on the snake as he took Emmaline's hand. Certain it wouldn't awaken, he slowly pulled her away from the sleeping creature. He looked at Emmaline. "I could've been bitten if I stepped on him."

She felt faint. She'd never grabbed a man like that before. It wasn't ladylike, but what else could she have done? "Forgive me if I frightened you."

"Frightened me? Don't you think it was time for you to frighten me, after all the times I've frightened you?" He winked.

She blushed. "I suppose."

His expression softened. "Thank you, for saving my life."

"It—it was nothing, Your Highness."

Nicholas shook his head. "It wasn't nothing." As he gazed at her, Emmaline felt the seas swelling in his eyes crash against her soul. She was so warm that she was certain the sun was shining directly on her.

She shook herself from her trance and felt the warmth fade from her skin.

Nicholas snatched his gaze away and turned toward the palace. "Let's go, before he wakes up."

Nicholas took his hand away from hers. She hadn't realized he had still been holding it. As they walked side-by-side, Emmaline studied her hand when he wasn't looking at her. There was nothing new about her hand. It looked the same as it always had. But now that she had touched Nicholas's hand again, she was sure that her hand was on fire. And a small part of her didn't mind one bit.

Nicholas sat in his mother's study, taking in the large room. Fresh flowers had been brought in from the gardens and filled the room with the aroma of spring. His mother loved flowers. She'd kept one from each bouquet his father had ever given her. Sometimes he caught her looking at the flowers Father had given her, wiping her eyes.

The door opened, and Mother appeared. He rose as she glided toward her desk. "Hello, Mother."

"Do you need something, Nicholas?" She sifted through the pile of papers on her desk and sat down.

He ignored her hard tone and moved toward her. "Actually, yes. It's about Emmaline."

"What about her? Have you finally decided to ship her away?"

He raised his eyebrows. Was she in one of her moods again? "What? No, Mother. I've come here to tell you something that she's done."

Mother looked up at him, a dark scowl in her eyes. "She's broken something of mine, hasn't she? And she's sent you in here to calm the seas."

Nicholas sighed. "Why must you always assume the worst about her, Mother? She's a lovely girl and she doesn't deserve your unfair opinion."

Mother bit the inside of her cheek. "Fine. Perhaps that was childish of me. Go on, son."

He put his hands in his pockets. "I was walking in the gardens today with Emmaline. I didn't notice there was an adder snake in the grass, but Emmaline did. She stopped me before I stepped on it. She saved my life."

Mother played with the feather on the end of her pen. "Well, that's very good, but what do you want me to do? Call the nobility to court and knight her?"

Nicholas's blood heated. Why was she so against Emmaline? What had the girl ever done to build up such walls against her? Was it because of Emmaline's past? Was it because she was not nobility? Where had the mother he'd known as a child gone? His father had been a man to judge a person on their character, not their status, and his mother had been such a woman too. But not now.

He put his hands on the desk and leaned forward. "No. My intentions for coming here were to tell you what she did. You're wrong about her. She's the most remarkable girl I've ever met. Besides saving me, she also helped a little orphan girl find a family."

Mother pressed her fingers to her forehead. "Don't tell me you've fallen for her."

"What if I have?" He shook his head and scoffed. "I thought the fact that she saved me, your son, would change your mind, but I see now you're far too stubborn for that to happen." He turned to leave.

His mother stood up. "Nicholas, I am grateful that your life was spared."

He held her gaze. What had happened to his mother? When would this stranger leave and his mother return? "Then why don't you thank the one responsible for that?" He shook his head and left the room.

"Now, tell me why it is important for rulers to respect their thrones," Ross said as he stood with Emmaline in the garden lawn.

Emmaline took a deep breath, thinking about the answer she would give. Ross's work had come to a brief pause, so he had agreed to help her with her lessons. Right now, he was helping her practice speech-making.

She cupped her hands in front of her and raised her head. "Scripture says that the throne is given to certain people by God. They are chosen to sit upon the throne and rule from their palaces over their kingdoms. A king or queen's subjects are like the sheep belonging to a shepherd. It is their responsibility to protect their sheep from wolves and other such enemies. If a king or a queen does not respect their role, they do not respect the gift God has given them. If He has privileged them with such responsibility, they should step up to the task willingly and passionately."

Ross smiled, clapping enthusiastically.

Emmaline laughed, curtsying in jest.

"Very good." He stepped toward her. "I remember the passage you mentioned. My mother loved the letters of Paul, so I heard that verse quite often."

She smiled. "Paul's letters are some of my favorite books in Scripture. Perhaps you should read them again." She raised a brow suggestively. She hoped Ross would return to his faith one day.

He gazed at the woods in the distance, his golden curls blowing in the evening wind. "Perhaps I should." He looked back at her and grinned.

She laid her hand across his arm, and he quickly turned his gaze back at her. She blushed. Had she made him uncomfortable? She removed her hand just in case. "Thank you, Ross, for all your help. And for bringing me to the palace."

He shook his head and raised his hand. "There's no need to thank me. I did it because you belonged here."

Emmaline smiled. Even though her feelings for Nicholas and her desire to protect her heart often left her in confused knots, she did feel as if she belonged here. As if God Himself had put her on Ross's horse and led her through the gates to live in this palace among so many friends and the queen.

"I'm glad I could help you with your lesson." Ross stood, his tall figure looming above her. "But I must be getting back to my work now. Perhaps I'll see you tomorrow."

She nodded and watched him leave.

Her gaze shifted to the skies. The sun was beginning to set, melting through the trees like gold dripping from the sky. Strokes of orange and pink glowed against the clouds. Emmaline wanted a better view of it, so she ran up the staircase leading to the palace and grasped the railing.

Birds flittered through the air toward the woods. The clouds drifted lazily through the colorful sky. The smell of flowers intoxicated her. She quite liked this view.

"I heard that you saved my son," a familiar, hard voice said.

Emmaline turned, and her heart sank to her stomach. "Your Majesty." She started to bow.

The queen waved her hand. "That's not necessary." She stared at Emmaline for a moment. "Not after the way I've treated you."

Emmaline blinked. "I don't know what you mean."

"I misjudged you too quickly, I'm afraid. You'll have to forgive me. My husband took the best part of me away with him when he died." She chuckled sardonically, and Emmaline thought she saw a flicker of tears. "I apologize for the way I've treated you. My son Nicholas is a much better person than I am. You've done nothing to deserve my accusations and harsh words."

Emmaline could hardly believe what she was hearing. The queen, apologizing to an orphan girl like her? "An apology is not necessary, Your Majesty. I—"

"It is more than necessary." The queen swallowed. "My son told me how you saved him from the snake earlier. I cannot begin to thank you enough for that. I don't know what I'd do without my son." She sniffed as if willing the tears away.

Emmaline's breath quickened. Had the feud between herself and the queen finally come to an end? Was the queen finally waving the white flag and stepping out of her lonely fortress? "It was my

Rise

pleasure, My Queen."

She stared at Emmaline again, clasping her hands in front of her. "You've earned my trust and respect. That is difficult to do these days. And I know you will continue to prove yourself worthy of it."

Emmaline couldn't help but smile. "Thank you."

Queen Genevieve smiled back, and peace was born between them.

A manservant appeared. "Your Majesty, I have here a telegram from your cousin. He says he will be arriving in a few months for a visit."

The queen wiped away her tears, sniffling. "Ah, good news! He is due for a visit." She turned to Emmaline, a shine Emmaline had never seen entering her eyes. "Please, excuse me, Emmaline."

Emmaline curtsied. "Yes, of course, Your Majesty."

After the queen was gone, Emmaline turned back to the sunset, her heart dancing. *What just happened?*

Victor pulled the cigar from his lips, the smoke billowing from the tobacco. It had been a boring day here in this grand house with three floors and a chandelier in each of its lavish rooms. His manservants tended to his horses while his maids scurried about, some of them bold enough to wink at him and others too pure to even meet his gaze. Ah, but the pure ones were extra sweet. They were like ripe fruit, beautiful and ready for him to enjoy.

But even his mousy maids could not keep his

attention for long. Small prey was not enough to satisfy a lion. Victor missed the days he spent on horseback, riding from country to country, doing his bidding in whichever way he liked.

He looked at his shiny leather shoes, propped up on his mahogany desk as he reclined in his chair. They were far too shiny for his liking. He wanted to go out and get them dirty. He wanted the thrill of running and being run away from.

A knock came at the door.

"Who is it?" Victor huffed more smoke.

"Nigel, sir. It's a message from the queen. She says she would be delighted to have you."

A grin curved his mouth. "Ah, thank you, Nigel. That is good news."

"Of course, sir." Nigel's footsteps drifted away as he left the cracked doorway.

Very good news, indeed. It had been quite a long time since he had seen his dear cousin. In fact, it had been quite a long time since he had felt the coolness of the Tregaron fog. He'd grown up there, in Lauderbury, and had lived in a place some might deem unattractive. A whorehouse, no less. But he almost preferred the whorehouse to the manor. Victor had certain tastes, and the whorehouse was more to his liking.

Of course, he didn't always appreciate the company there. The drunks that came to play with the women had nearly pounded him to smithereens.

Until he met Captain Polov, a man who had seen

his potential. And then the hell those men put Victor through became their reality. That was his first taste of revenge. And with a past like his, he had plenty of opportunity to quench his thirst. Now that he had the queen's blessing, he could finally have his fill.

In just a few months, Victor would trade this cigar for a golden cup. And from it, he would drink the sweet nectar of victory over anyone who had dared stand against him.

Now, what shall I bring?

Chapter Twelve

ROSS STRODE ON horseback through Lauderbury's thick crowds, looking over the hustle and bustle of the city. Every once in a while, he liked to see how the city was faring, whether he and his men were doing a good job of protecting the city and keeping the peace between travelers and inhabitants alike. With the war still raging on battlefields in countries so close to his own, emotions still ran high. He could understand the tension, but he would not stand for it.

Shouting rose in the distance, growing and growing, as if more people were joining in. Ross craned his neck over the crowds of merchants and customers, of servants scurrying about, of paper boys shouting the latest news. There, several feet away, a crowd was swelling in front of the apothecary. The shouts grew louder and louder amidst pounding and thudding.

Ross clicked his tongue, kicked his feet against Felix's sides, and stirred him into a gallop toward the cacophonous crowd.

Men jeered, punching the air with raised fists. "Fight, fight, fight, fight!" they roared. Two men fought in the center of the crowd, one of them much thinner than the other and taking the brunt of the brawl.

Ross dismounted his horse without stopping Felix and pushed his way through the crowd. "The captain of the Queen's Royal Guard has arrived. That's enough, men! Move, or you'll all be spending the night in the dungeon!"

Once the men surrounding the brawlers saw his uniform, they quickly stepped back. Some even hurried away from the scene.

Ross shoved through the remaining audience and leapt at the two fighting men. The bigger man had the smaller one on the ground, pinned with nowhere to escape the continuous punching.

"Get off him!" Ross kicked the bully off the skinny

man. "Why do you treat this man like an animal?" He scowled at the broad-shouldered man scrambling to his feet. Ross glanced at the smaller man on the ground and winced. His lip was bloodied, his face was red and scratched, and his eye was already bruised. He glared at the other man. "Do you see how you've hurt him?"

The broad-shouldered man wiped his lip, his bald head trickling with sweat. "He deserved it, Cap'n! Stole my merchandise, he did!"

"And do you think starting a brawl is justice?" Ross couldn't keep the growl from his voice.

"So you would have him get away with it?" the man snarled.

"No. But I am interested in hearing what he has to say, if he is still able to speak." Ross bent and helped the man to his feet. He wheezed for a moment, leaning over and pressing his hands against his knees. Blood dripped from his lip and onto the cobblestone ground. Shattered glass from a bottle was sprinkled over the ground a few feet away.

Ross winced again as the man stood to his full height. "Please, tell me what happened."

The man kept his bruised eye closed, his face tense with pain. "I didn't come to steal the medicine, Cap'n. Honest, I didn't. My Freddy is always poorly, and he needs his medicine. I came here like I do every two or three weeks, and the druggist says he won't give the medicine to me on credit. Any other day, he'd say yes. But today, he says no."

Ross glanced at the broad-shouldered man. "And why is that?"

"Because he found out I'm Konovian, that's why!" the skinny man shouted.

Ross whirled around as if a ghost had called his name. A Konovian. There were many made-up stories about Konovians constantly flowing through the kingdom. They were a people rarely spoken of in Tregaron, until recently, when a group of men had begun stirring a pot. Was this man right? Had he been denied medicine because of prejudice?

If God loved everyone as Emmaline said he did, why did He allow such persecution to go on? Why didn't He punish those who stood atop the throats of the innocent? Why didn't He send fire from heaven on those who cast the helpless into hell?

"Is this true?" Ross asked the druggist.

The man scoffed, indignant. "No. It's because I refuse to keep giving medicine away to men who haven't paid me back! When I told him he couldn't have it, he just ran out of the store with it."

"I told you I would pay you back when I could!" The skinny man barked and fisted his hands. His mouth trembled as tears came to the surface. "Things have been tight for the past few months, with the new baby and the leaking roof."

Ross crossed his arms, shaking his head. "You were both wrong." He turned to the thief. "It was wrong of you to steal. Had you pled your case to the authorities, the issue would have been dealt with in a proper manner." He turned to the other man. "And you were wrong to deny a struggling man medicine for his son. If you will not give him medicine, I will."

"Rewarding the sinner, are we?" the druggist asked, nostrils flared.

Ross scowled. "No. And I'll thank you for not questioning the Queen's captain."

The broad-shouldered man paled, unable to meet Ross's gaze any longer.

Once Ross had bought the medicine for the man and enough bread to last the man's family for a month, he helped the man carry it all home. The man was quiet for almost the entire walk, until they entered the Konovian quarter.

"I'd like to thank you, Cap'n," he said in a small voice. "I know I don't deserve this."

"Perhaps not, but your family does."

He turned to Ross, one eye almost completely purple. "I'm prepared to accept any punishment you deem necessary."

"I think your face has endured enough punishment." Ross tried to smile in jest.

He smiled back. "Oh, Cap'n. You are too gracious for a man like me."

"I know what it is like to struggle."

They walked a little further, then the man led Ross into the entrance of his house. It wasn't much to look at, by any means. A wooden board closed up a window, and the front door looked as if it had suffered much abuse.

How could God allow families to live like this if He

Rise

was so loving? Did He not see? Or did He simply not care?

If I didn't care, would I have allowed you to find this man and help him?

Chills spread over Ross's body. It had been some time since he'd heard that voice. But it was still unmistakable.

Perhaps the voice was right. Ross had been led to help this man when he'd needed it most. Surely that was no coincidence.

Ross carried the goods inside, finding sleeping children and a knitting woman inside. When the woman looked up and after her husband had explained Ross's presence, she dropped her needles and gasped.

"Oh, sir!" she exclaimed softly, careful not to awaken the children.

"It is nothing, ma'am." Ross smiled. "I was just glad I was able to help you and your husband, Mr.—?"

"Little. Harry Little." He put his arm around his wife. "My Sarah and I thank you."

Ross nodded. "Of course." He said his goodbyes and then mounted Felix and left.

Harry Little. He'd remember that name and pray for him every night. If God cared, certainly he'd help this man. Surely He wouldn't forget another family.

Emmaline could barely stand; she rocked like a ship sailing across raging seas. She'd spent weeks preparing and learning how to become a proper lady. She'd learned how to dance, how to curtsy, how to behave at a table, how to dress, how to stand, how to walk, and how to speak. And now, this was her night. This was her night with the prince.

It was dark inside the bedchamber, so more candles were brought in to help the girls prepare Emmaline for her night. Lydia brushed and curled Emmaline's hair, while Julia powdered her face and colored her lips. Eleanor, who had been on a carriage ride with Nicholas the week before, tightened Emmaline's corset and helped her into her dress.

Emmaline's heart pounded like a thousand battle drums. Her hands fidgeted in her lap. How could she resist her feelings for the prince if she had to spend an evening alone with him? What if she tripped when she curtsied? What if she said something wrong? What if the prince decided he didn't like her company? What if he—

"Worrying does nothing for the knots in your stomach," Anna said, pinning her hair.

"I can't stop thinking about what could go wrong."

"Why don't you try to think about what could go right? The daughters of commoners dream of the way they could meet the prince. Try to dream about what it will be like."

She closed her eyes. What would it be like? Would he be breathless when he saw her in her gown? Would holding his hand burn her own again? Would he smile at her and gaze at her when she wasn't looking? Would she be able to pull herself away before the tide of his ocean blue eyes swept her into their depths?

One of the girls cleared her throat. When Emmaline opened her eyes, Diana and Julia stood there, smiling. They each held something in their hands.

Julia stepped forward. "I brought about a hundred different hair combs to wear at the palace, and I thought this one went best with your dress." She opened her hands and revealed a hair comb, encrusted with dozens of tiny little diamonds and four bigger-sized sapphires.

Diana came closer. "And I brought my necklaces. When I saw Julia was giving you her diamond hair comb, I knew my diamond necklace would look wonderful with it." She opened her hands, revealing a strand of diamonds coiled in her palms.

Emmaline gasped, blinking back the tears. "Thank you, both of you."

"Don't go and ruin my powder with your tears now," Julia said, smiling.

Emmaline smiled back at her. Anna took Julia's comb and pinned it into Emmaline's hair, and then took Diana's necklace and put it around her neck.

Anna came around the chair and put her hands on her hips, studying Emmaline. "Right. You're all finished."

"Go look in the mirror," Julia squealed.

Emmaline drew back her skirts and walked to the mirror. She stared at her reflection, stunned. The dress shone like a night sky, glittering like a galaxy.

Her hair was pinned in a loose bun, with little curls falling around her face. Julia and Diana's gifts worked perfectly with her dress.

She turned back to the girls, who were all smiling at her. "I can't ever thank you enough." Emmaline forced the tears away.

"You can thank us by enjoying yourself, no matter what happens," Eleanor said.

Emmaline nodded. She glanced at the clock. The servant had told her that the prince would meet her at the western staircase at eight o'clock. She had ten minutes to spare. She hurried to the door, said goodbye to the girls, and then left.

She flew through the castle, hoping she wouldn't faint from the lack of oxygen in her lungs. A few servants gawked at her as she ran past them. Her dress swished as she ran, her shoes clicking on the marble floor.

What if I'm running toward my destiny? she wondered. *What if this is the night where the past fades into the past, and I can look on toward the future?* She ran faster. *What if that terrified girl on the streets is gone? What if this is the night where I become someone new?*

She passed corridor after corridor, hall after hall. She'd run through halls like this before, but she wasn't running from death tonight. Perhaps she was running toward life.

But what if this new life ended with death again? The next time she lost someone else, she would be tidied away into a grave. She couldn't survive another loss.

You can't think like that right now. You must go to Nicholas tonight. You can't hurt his feelings, after everything he's done and been for you. Just do your best to resist everything.

Finally, she came to the western staircase. It was styled after an imperial staircase, with divided flights. The banisters were made from white marble and encrusted with gold designs. Chandeliers aglow with candlelight hung from the ceiling, where a painting of cherubs playing in the clouds stretched above her.

A man stood on the flight of stairs on the right side, and she was on the left. Even from here, she could tell who it was. The man was dressed in a sharp suit, and his dark hair was brushed to perfection. His hands were in his pockets, and his head was held low. *Nicholas.*

Her hands were clammy as her breath stilled in her chest. Perhaps she should go back. Perhaps she should run away from the palace. What if she was only sealing her fate? What if she was stepping right into enemy territory, where all her defenses were down?

She called his name before knowing what she had done. "Nicholas?" Her voice trembled, and she wondered if he had heard her. Part of her hoped he hadn't.

He turned and stared at her as if he had lived in darkness and she were the rising sun. He didn't speak for what seemed like an eternity. She didn't mind. She drank in the sight of him, drank in the gaze in his eyes. And in that moment, she knew she would never be the same again.

"Nicholas?" a girl called softly. Nicholas could hear the trembling in her voice.

He turned and nearly lost his balance. The world he'd known came tumbling off its axis as everything spun around him. There, on the flight of stairs across from him, stood Emmaline, glittering like a galaxy of stars. Diamonds sparkled in her dark hair and along her marble neck. She gazed at him, fear written in her eyes.

He was certain that, together, their pounding hearts could have created a symphony. He was breathless. This was the first time he'd ever had something stolen from him, and he wasn't sure he'd ever get his breath back.

She smiled at him and a bolt of energy struck him. He hurried down the stairs and came toward her. "You look stunning." He gulped in a breath.

She blushed. "Thank you."

He looked at her again, as if it were painful to look away. He wasn't used to being so helpless, but this beautiful creature tore down all his defenses. "Forgive me." He winced. "It appears words fail me tonight."

She chuckled. "I'm rather speechless myself." She raised her brows. "Where are you taking me?"

He smiled, flustered. "Oh, yes. Well, that is a

surprise." He held out his arm. "I'll take you there and show you."

She took his offered arm, stepping closer to him. She smelled like violets and vanilla.

"I have to admit, I have been nervous about tonight," Nicholas said suddenly. He wasn't sure why he was admitting this. But he was certain he could trust her.

She glanced at him, the corner of her mouth springing up. "Why?"

"I wanted this night to be perfect, I suppose."

"I know it will be." She smiled at him as if she were trying to ease his nerves.

They went up another set of stairs, and then entered a spiraling staircase leading up to the top of the palace. When they reached the top, Nicholas let go of her arm, opened a door, and led her inside. Emmaline gasped as she went into the room.

Windows covered both walls, and the domed ceiling was painted with the moon, the sun, the stars, and the planets. A mahogany desk stood in the corner, littered with parchments, books, quills, and vials of ink. The balcony door stood in the back of the room.

"What is this room?" Emmaline asked, glancing all around her.

He smiled at the childlike wonder on her face. "The solar. This is where astronomical events are studied and predicted in the palace. I remembered how you said you loved the stars. I must have asked Arthur, the astronomer, a hundred times, but I made certain with him that it would happen tonight."

"That what would happen tonight?" She raised a brow.

"I'll show you." He led her toward the door and stepped outside.

They stood on a balcony, high above everything else. The stars twinkled like a million diamonds above them. The city was below them, candlelight streaming from the windows.

"The astronomer swore it would be a clear night tonight. I hope you're not afraid of heights." Nicholas took her arm.

She shook her head. "No. It makes me feel unreachable." She gazed at the moon, hanging like a pearl amidst the darkness. The clouds of dusk unfurled themselves and disappeared, making way for the stars. They glittered like silver.

"They're so beautiful," Emmaline whispered. She turned toward him. "I'll treasure this night for the rest of my life, Your Highness."

"As will I." He gazed into her eyes. She looked away, the moonlight illuminating her face. He cleared his throat and leaned against the railing. "What makes you love the stars so much?"

She took a deep breath, and he wondered for a moment if he had re-opened a wound of hers. "The stars remind me that there's still light in the darkness," she said softly. "Sometimes the starlight is faint, and sometimes they're hidden behind the clouds, but I can remember that they're still there, twinkling in the night."

Nicholas wished he could have her outlook. She was so pure, so hopeful.

She turned toward him with a smile. "If I look hard enough, I can see my brother James smiling and making silly faces at me."

He grinned. "So your brother was mischievous, was he?"

Emmaline laughed, a sound like bells. "Yes. Very much. He learned from me, I must confess. James and I enjoyed terrorizing the cook the most. It was fun to watch her face get so red so quickly."

Nicholas chuckled and waited for her to go on. She was silent for a long time.

Finally, she spoke. "Sometimes I wish I could live those days over and over."

"And I wish I could live the days with my father over and over. My mother was happier then. But I suppose if we were stuck living the past over and over again, we wouldn't be here looking at the stars."

She moved a hair from her eyes. "Yes, I suppose you're right."

He fidgeted with his hands. "So. You like being high up, then?"

"Yes. It feels safe somehow. When I was younger, I used to climb trees to avoid lessons. I would pretend I was stuck so that my lessons would be delayed."

He laughed. "You were quite the troublemaker, weren't you?"

"I tried to tell you."

"I believe you now."

She gazed at the sky, the reflection of the stars playing in her eyes. "They really are beautiful, aren't they?"

He studied every detail of her face in the moonlight. "Yes, but they cannot compare to you."

She glanced back at him, blushing. She turned away, but not before he'd caught the smile on her face.

"Emmaline?"

She turned, her dark eyes round. "Yes?"

His heart skipped like young rabbits. He had to swallow to regain his voice. "I had the piano brought up for you tonight. It would be my honor to hear you play it again."

She smiled, and not a star in the sky shined brighter. "Oh, how wonderful. Thank you!" She hurried inside.

He followed her into the room. Straightening her skirts, she sat down at the piano. She smiled up at him and then set her gaze upon the keys.

From the very first note, Nicholas was whisked away into another world. He closed his eyes, savoring every note as if they were breath and he were breathless. The melodies washed over him, baptizing him in a way he'd never felt before. Emmaline was playing *Nightingale's Soliloquy*, his favorite. He'd never heard it played so beautifully, so purely.

Emmaline's fingers danced over the keys as she played, her arms moving with grace as she spun melodies into music. It was as if she were performing some kind of magic, her and the piano together. A peaceful wistfulness was on her face, her hair gathered around her ears. How was it that she was so lovely without even trying?

She played and played at his behest. "Are you sure you want me to keep playing?" she asked after she'd played for several minutes. "I'm sure you're getting tired of it."

"If I was, I'd be a fool," he answered. "I could never tire of hearing such beauty."

She smiled. "All right, then. I'll keep playing."

She played everything that had ever been written. Tchaikovsky, Beethoven, and even a few hymns they played in the cathedrals. She played it all, and his heart played along with her. He'd never felt so alive. Something new pulsed through him.

Finally, she finished. He applauded as she laughed, blushing. "You could be one of the greats, Emmaline. Truly." He leaned against the piano.

She shrugged. "Perhaps. But I think my path has led me here."

He felt his dimple pop up. "I'm glad it has."

She met his gaze, her cheeks bright pink.

An hour had passed, and the night had grown late. It was time for them both to leave. He didn't want to soil her reputation.

He walked her back down the spiraling stairs. When they came to the staircase where they had met earlier that night, she gazed softly at him. "Thank you,

Your Highness, for the night you gave me."

He smiled. "It was my honor."

"Good night."

"Good night."

He watched her peel away from him and then disappear from view. He wasn't sure he wanted to see anyone else. No one could compare to the starry-eyed orphan girl. No one at all.

Chapter Thirteen

"FORWARD, MEN!" ROSS shouted across the castle plain. Four dozen soldiers stomped in a straight line, their faces set in firm lines as straight as their glistening bayonets. "March!" Ross bellowed.

Their legs moved in formation. Ross had spent months training this newer, younger batch of men who'd dared to lay down their lives for God and country. While Emmaline learned to dance, wave a fan, and speak eloquently, his men had learned to march in formation, wield sabers and fire muskets, and gain courage, even in the face of death.

And as the soldiers had progressed in the school of war, Emmaline had progressed in the school of royalty. The strides she'd made were so wide, he couldn't believe she'd been on the streets for three years. She was a regular lady now, with white gloves and curtsies. If he didn't know better, he would never guess all that she'd been through. All her secrets and shadows had been swept away now.

"Ross!" a girl's voice cried out.

He searched the courtyard, alarmed by the urgency in the voice. A girl in a violet gown raced down the stairs, her dark hair flying behind her. Emmaline. "Ross!" she cried again.

He glanced at the guards, still marching across the grass, then bolted toward her. Was she in trouble? If she was, the source of her danger would regret ever threatening her. He met her halfway. "What is it? Are you all right?"

To his surprise, Emmaline was smiling, as if she'd seen the sun for the first time. "Yes, of course, I'm all right. I've never felt so wonderful in my entire life." She laughed airily.

Ross breathed a silent breath of relief. "Oh, and why is that?"

She gulped in a breath, then swallowed. "I had the most wonderful night last night. I was with the prince." She closed her eyes, as if willing herself to go back in time.

He glanced down at his chest, certain that a bayonet had just struck him and that it was now lodged between his ribs. He grappled for his next breath. "Oh, I see."

She smiled. "He took me to the solar. He showed me the stars. He remembered how I'd said before that I loved the stars. I could see the city from where I stood. It was the most beautiful thing I'd ever seen."

Ross forced a smile and tried to be sincere. "That sounds wonderful."

"Oh, it was, Ross." Her smile faded. "But I'm still afraid."

He lifted a brow, ignoring the bayonet twisting around inside him. "Afraid of what?"

"Afraid to love again. The last time I did, I lost my family and nearly myself. I don't know if I ever want to put myself through that again. But then I think about Nicholas, and I'm not sure."

The bayonet plunged deeper into his flesh, but no blood drained from the wound. His hopes were dashed before his eyes, and the taste of iron on his tongue overwhelmed him. Before he had even taken her hand, she was pulled away from him, in a very different direction. But he couldn't run after her now, not when she was finding happiness with Nicholas. It was too late. "Emmaline, you can't let the past scare you away from the future, especially one as wonderful as this one would be."

She bit her lip, looking down. "I suppose. I just

don't know." She glanced at the marching men and paled. "Oh, forgive me. I've interrupted your routine."

He waved his hand. "It's quite all right. You didn't know." He smiled softly at her. "And I'm glad to hear you had a wonderful night. You deserve it."

Emmaline returned his smile, and then glanced back at the palace. She lifted her skirts. "Well, I've got to go now. Mr. Harrison wants us to refresh our dancing skills. The prince's ball is in a fortnight, and he wants us to show us off to the queen again." She waved at him hurrying off.

And just like that, she disappeared. He'd always known she was a bird and that she would find her wings again. He just never guessed that when she did find them, she'd fly away from him and never return.

How foolish he had been to hope. Nicholas had given her the stars. How easy, how simple to win her heart when Nicholas had not just the world but the very sky at his fingertips. Ross had nothing to give that compared to Nicholas's gifts, but he would have fought for them, would have died to give Emmaline something worthy.

Emmaline was confused at the moment, and with good reason. But it wouldn't be long before she came to her senses and changed her mind about loving again. Ross would prepare for when that time came, and he would help her in any way he could. If she wanted stars, then he would make sure she would have them. He'd give her a whole galaxy, even if it killed him.

Emmaline was sure a brood of young rabbits was inside her, hopping around to the music she could hear from downstairs. She pressed a hand against her heart as Eleanor tightened her corset.

"Is anything the matter?" Eleanor said.

Emmaline smiled. "How could anything be wrong? It's my first ball, and I'm terribly excited." She could hardly wait to get there, though she secretly hoped she wouldn't make a mistake and look like a fool.

Eleanor chuckled. "And you have every reason to be. You're a fine young lady." She drew closer to Emmaline's ear. "And just between us, I think Mr. Harrison favors you above the rest of us."

Emmaline frowned, searching for words. Surely Eleanor's estimation was wrong. She couldn't think of anything more preposterous. "I don't know why he would," she said. "It's not as if I'm any better than the rest of you."

"Perhaps he's noticed the makings of a queen inside you." Eleanor lifted her brow suggestively.

Emmaline bit her lip. Even if Mr. Harrison did see the makings of a queen inside her, did Nicholas? And more importantly, did Emmaline see it in herself? She might know which spoon to use and how to walk across a marble courtyard, but could she be queen? Could she rule and govern hundreds of thousands of people? Could she gain their loyalty and love by showing them the same qualities in return?

She shook her head. She was concerning herself with a future that was not hers. She glanced over her shoulder. Anna laughed gaily and fluttered about the room in her yellow gown, the picture of beauty and spring. Perhaps Nicholas would choose her. Or perhaps he would choose Lydia, or Julia, or any of them.

Eleanor helped Emmaline into her dress, a lovely shade of lilac with a flowy skirt and sleeves that dropped off the shoulders. Emmaline looked in the mirror, admiring the gown. Mr. Harrison was right—Emmaline looked best in blue or purple. She smiled at her reflection.

Julia waved her fan in front of her face, her delicate golden curls swaying in the small breeze her fan created. "I hear that the queen has wasted no expense for her son's ball. There'll be flowers from India and glistening crystalware and a French composer."

"And here we are, like six wildflowers brought in from the field and into someone's lavish home." Anna frowned.

"We shall stick out amongst all the ladies that are sure to be here." Lydia wrung her gloved hands.

"We have as much a right to be here as they do," Emmaline said stoutly, surprising herself. She had all of the girls' attention, so she went on, lifting her chin. "We have learned to dance, learned to dine, and learned to govern ourselves. We are ladies in our own right, and we don't need anyone else's approval."

Rise

Diana beamed. "Here, here!"

Eleanor lifted her brows. "And that is why you were the best at expressing yourself when Mr. Harrison asked us difficult questions about governing a kingdom."

Emmaline smiled, blushing. She hadn't known it would feel good to be the stronger one. She'd spent so much time living like a ghost, drifting in and out of the walls, unseen and unheard. And now she remembered that she had a body and a soul, and she knew she was becoming whole again.

The clock chimed nine o'clock. The girls squealed together. "Let's go!" Lydia exclaimed.

All six of them dashed into the hall toward the ballroom, a flurry of silks, taffetas, and jewels. Servants appeared, and the girls slowed down, determined to behave like the ladies they'd become.

Emmaline glanced to the side and saw a wall of portraits. She stopped for a moment to look at them. The paintings were all different styles, all from past centuries and artistic movements. Pale-faced kings and queens stared back at her, adorned with pearls and rubies and crowns. She wanted to make them proud. She wanted to live up to the expectations of all who had passed through these halls before her.

Don't give yourself a mountain you can't climb, a small voice whispered. ***You please me with who you are to me, and that's enough.***

Emmaline released a small breath and felt the burden fall from her shoulders. She peeled her gaze away from the portraits.

The girls weren't there. She swept up her skirts and ran after them. She didn't care who saw her. If she was late, Mr. Harrison would be mortified, and so would she.

The swelling music grew louder and louder. Relief began to bubble up inside her, like water spurting from the ground. She followed the sound until the music could not be denied. A pair of doors stood before her, tall and elaborate. She saw the girls gathered there, chattering quietly.

Lydia glanced behind her, eyes widening as Emmaline ran toward her. "There you are!"

"Sorry, I was distracted." Emmaline winced.

"It's all right. We haven't been called in yet." Lydia squeezed her hand. "Calm down, Emmaline. You're more than ready for tonight."

Emmaline bit her lip. "Thank you."

She stared up at the doors and trembled. What if these doors led to her destiny? What if this was the night the prince fell in love with her?

She closed her eyes and shook her head. *And what if he falls in love with one of the other girls?* If that happened, Emmaline would be the future queen's maid of honor. That would be better for her. She could not bear to lose someone else she loved the way she had lost her family. She could not rip open old wounds. How many times would she have to remind herself of that?

Still, she could feel her resolve weakening like a

house built on the sand. How would she be able to resist when she danced with Nicholas tonight, when she would be under his soft gaze and held close against him?

You have to dance with him tonight. You've no choice in that, Emmaline, not with all these guests. It will simply be a happy memory to remember one day, when you're serving his future wife as her maid.

A booming voice broke through her thoughts. "Announcing the arrival of the prince's most advantageous suitresses: Lydia, Eleanor, Anna, Julia, Diana, and Emmaline."

"That's our cue," Julia whispered as the doors opened.

The music roared in Emmaline's ears, an angelic symphony that stole her breath. Golden chandeliers glittered as they hung from the ceiling. Tall candelabras stood like guards next to the glass doors lining the front and side walls. Multitudes of finely-dressed guests stood on what little floor Emmaline could make out between the ladies' gowns.

The guests craned their necks to see their prince's suitresses and gasped as the girls stepped forward. Emmaline's heart bobbed in her throat like a buoy bouncing on the surface of the sea. Would she ever get used to such attention?

Eleanor led the way down the staircase and onto the ballroom floor. Emmaline wanted to reach for Anna's hand, knowing she was as nervous as she was, but remembered herself. With her head held high, she followed the others down the stairs.

Once they were at the bottom, the girls stood in a line in the middle of the heavily-perfumed crowd. Emmaline wished her corset wasn't so tight. Her upper lip trickled with sweat.

Trumpets blared, and the same booming voice that had announced the girls called out, "Announcing the arrival of His Royal Highness, Nicholas Edward II, Duke of Tredan Bay."

Several feet away from Emmaline, on the opposite end of the room, a man appeared from behind velvet curtains. The crowd gasped and cheered in unison. Emmaline's heart swelled. *Nicholas.*

His suit was navy blue, bringing out his dark curls and the hue of his eyes. Medals were scattered across his chest, and his golden epaulettes glittered in the candlelight as he bowed curtly towards his guests. He glanced over the crowd, caught her eye, and smiled. Her heart fluttered as she smiled back, all the warnings she'd given herself fading away.

"The prince shall take turns dancing with each of the six ladies," the man with the loud voice said. "He will go down the line until the very end. Let the dancing begin!"

Nicholas stepped toward Eleanor, the first in line. She smiled and curtsied as he bowed before her, his arm behind his back. He offered her his hand, and she took it, letting him lead her to the center of the dance floor.

A tapping sound caught Emmaline's attention. On

a platform, an older man with wild hair waved his baton at his army-like orchestra. The musicians, buried behind their instruments, began to play a quick, swelling melody.

Eleanor moved like a butterfly on the floor. Nicholas smiled at her, and she at him.

"Look at her, making us all proud," Diana said, fluttering her fan at her face.

"Let us hope we can do as well as she is," Julia whispered, biting her lip.

As Nicholas moved on from Eleanor to Lydia, the laces of Emmaline's corset squeezed her even more, wringing all the breath from her. She fanned her face quickly, struggling to find air while making sure her movements were delicate. So many people stared at her and the other girls, whispering as they sparkled in their gemstones or shone in their silken suits. What did they think of her? What were they saying about her?

After Diana danced with Nicholas, earning the applause of the crowd, it was Anna's turn. Emmaline watched with increasing anxiety as Anna's dance with Nicholas came to an end. Anna held Nicholas's hand, then curtsied. The room thundered with the crowd's applause.

Anna joined the girls back in line. Now it was Emmaline's turn. She took a deep breath, her vision spinning. Would she faint before she could dance?

As if in slow motion, Nicholas walked toward her without a trace of uneasiness on his face. *Of course he's not nervous. This world of nobility is all new to you, Emmaline, not to him.*

She took his offered hand and felt the earth move beneath her. He smiled at her before leading her to the center of the ballroom.

A slower, sweeping melody began to play. Nicholas must have noticed how hard she was breathing, because he leaned close and whispered in her ear, "Don't be afraid. I'm here."

Warmth spread over her body as he pulled away. Had he really said that, or had she imagined it? Surely, she had. She hoped she had misheard him. If she hadn't, she wouldn't be the only one who was wounded when she resisted him.

He took her hands and led her into a dance. Her heartbeat slowed, in tune with the music. She closed her eyes for a moment. She wanted to remember every step of the dance, the way the marble floor felt beneath her feet, the way Nicholas's hands felt in hers. He smelled like peppermint. The candlelight from the chandeliers above glittered like golden stars on the floor. Colors whirled around as she caught sight of the gowns and suits the crowd wore.

Nicholas smiled at her again. She felt like a swan, stretching her wings as she came down on the lake. Nicholas raised his arm as she took his hand, stepping in a circle. He gazed at her the way she gazed at the stars. She spun, then joined hands with him again.

Emmaline breathed deeply, her hands still in Nicholas's. It seemed as if they had always been there, her fingers intertwined with his. Her hands fit perfectly in his, like a key inside a lock. Like any key, it had opened up the door to a whole new world. But soon, the time would come when she would have to leave this new world behind and remember it fondly as the years went on. This door was not hers to open.

Genevieve, with her full skirts shifting as she craned her neck, watched Nicholas and Emmaline dance. The music ebbed in her mind, like one's reflection on the surface of a river. It was both familiar and new, the same waltz she'd first danced to with her Henry.

The girl was indeed lovely. Anyone could see that. And Nicholas certainly had. She knew her son well enough to know that he was lost in the girl's dark eyes, that he could barely hear the music swelling in the room.

But Emmaline was just as lovely on the inside as she was on the outside. There was a quietness yet a boldness in her spirit, like a wild mustang, unbroken by all the heartache she'd faced. It was a spirit that bespoke of a future queen.

Emmaline spun in her son's arms. He hadn't smiled like that in years. She saw the way they both danced, with stars in their eyes, as if their worlds were uniting.

Genevieve might be growing old, but she wasn't blind yet, and her memory was still intact. She knew what it was like to be young and in love. And though she was queen and had troves of gold and jewels, she knew it was time to give her son the one precious diamond he desired, the one star she did not possess.

The crowd rumbled with applause as the music faded away.

Nicholas smiled, his chest heaving. "You danced beautifully."

"Thank you, Your Highness. You did as well." His praise was something Emmaline hadn't expected. Surely her dancing had been as clumsy as her attempts to ignore his soft touch.

With a smile, she returned to the girls' line. She wished she could dance with him again, forgetting where she was, even who she was, weightless as if floating in a dream. She wanted to be in his arms again, forever a part of that weightless dream.

But all dreams come to an end sooner or later, and Emmaline knew that all too well.

Nicholas escorted Julia to the dance floor. Music swelled again, and Julia and Nicholas began to dance.

Someone tapped Emmaline's shoulder. A young man wearing servant's attire stood next to her. "Her Majesty the Queen has requested your presence."

Emmaline blinked. "*My* presence?"

He nodded stoutly. "Yes, Miss."

She bit her lip, then nodded. "All right, then."

What could the queen want with her? The queen may have apologized for her actions toward Emmaline, but the two hadn't spoken since. Of course, there wasn't much call for a girl like Emmaline to come into the company of the queen, but still. What if the queen had changed her mind and still didn't like Emmaline?

The servant led her through the thick crowds and to a raised dais where the queen sat on a throne. Dressed in layers of lavender silk and sporting an elaborate hairstyle, the queen looked as if she bore a heavy weight upon her shoulders. Emmaline wondered how her neck did not bow from the tiara, but the queen did not seem to notice. Perhaps the weight of an entire kingdom and the weight of her husband's death were so burdensome that heavy curls and a crown of diamonds weighed nothing. She stared at Emmaline, but not in the same way she had before. Now she seemed to respect Emmaline, to admire her, though Emmaline could not think of any attributes she possessed worthy of royal admiration.

"I have brought Emmaline to you, Your Majesty," the servant said.

"Yes, I see that, Clarence." The queen bit the inside of her cheek, then smiled. Clarence blushed from his neck up. "I was just joking, Clarence. Do not worry." She waved him away. "You may go. I wish to speak to her alone."

Clarence nodded and headed for the refreshment tables.

Emmaline bowed low before the queen but, while doing so, could not believe her ears. Was the queen truly jesting with a servant? The queen had hardly even smiled at Emmaline, and now she was teasing a servant?

"Rise, Emmaline." The queen's voice cut through her thoughts.

Emmaline picked herself off the ground and meekly met the queen's eyes.

"Don't be afraid, girl. I don't bite. I simply want to speak with you." She motioned for Emmaline to draw nearer. "Come closer."

Emmaline stepped toward the queen, catching a whiff of her rosy perfume.

Queen Genevieve smiled, sending waves of shock through Emmaline. "I saw the way you danced with my son," the queen said. "I want to thank you for treating him as you have. He may be a prince, but he has struggled much for someone as young as he is. You have helped him greatly. You have helped him to forget the past and look to the future. Even I haven't been able to do that."

Emmaline blinked. "I've helped him?" She struggled with her own past, and now the queen was giving her credit for helping Nicholas with his?

Queen Genevieve's eyes glittered. "You have, Emmaline. You've helped him more than words can express. I know that he cares for you."

Emmaline's breath faltered. "He does?"

She smiled as if she was amused at Emmaline's disbelief. "I am the queen. I do not tell lies."

Heat shot through Emmaline's body. "Of course, Your Majesty. I would not accuse you of doing so. It's

Rise

just that I—"

"Have wanted him to care for you, too?" The queen leaned forward, lowering her voice. "Believe it or not, I was once a young girl like you with a heart as soft as yours. I know what it's like to wish for love."

Emmaline bit her lip. "But what about the other girls?"

"He speaks only of you. And your stars."

Emmaline smiled, unable to keep it from forming. "You've given me hope, Your Majesty. Perhaps too much."

The queen smiled and leaned back. "I have been known to be overly generous. Among other faults." She winked.

Emmaline chuckled.

"You may return to the ball and your friends." The queen waved her away.

Emmaline pressed through the crowds, careful not to get her hem caught. As she passed the refreshment tables, she overheard two dukes in a heated conversation.

"The Konovian riff-raff are polluting our cities," one of them said. "They should have stayed in their country."

"They have no country any longer," the other snapped. "Their country was destroyed. They are living as homeless orphans. Have you no compassion?"

Konovia? That name sounded awfully familiar.

Still, Emmaline was far too distracted by everything the queen had said to remember how she knew the name

"Konovia."

Nicholas cared for her. For her. A street rat. An orphan. Why did his eyes stray to her when he could have any girl he wanted? Any girl would give up her heart for him, but he wanted hers. Could it really be true? Or was she trapped in a cruel dream from which she would one day awaken?

When Emmaline had returned to the spot where she'd stood with the girls, she found they were all gone. They each danced with a man, laughing as the music swung happily. Nicholas was surrounded by girls she'd never seen. They fanned their glowing faces as they giggled.

Could she really belong in this world? She wasn't like those girls who knew how to flirt and carry a conversation with the prince. They were much bolder than she. She still felt awful about hurling a snowball right into him all those months ago.

But somehow, something felt right as she stood between the glittering chandeliers and the iridescent floors. Something had felt right when Nicholas's hand was in hers. Did he truly feel the same way?

Emmaline stood in the garden courtyard, watching the flowers glow in moonlight. The moon hung like a pearl in the sky, shrouded by hazy clouds. The water in the fountain glimmered in the dim light. She held on to the railing, breathing in the scent of the flowers gathered at the garden staircase.

The doors opened. Emmaline glanced back and saw Nicholas holding two glasses.

He grinned. "I thought you might like some punch."

"Thank you, Nicholas. You're too kind." She smiled and sat on the railing, her skirts draping onto the ground. He handed her the glass, their fingers brushing. Sparks danced across her fingertips as he sat beside her.

He wiped his upper lip. "It's sweltering in there with all those people."

"But it feels wonderful out here in the cool air," Emmaline sighed. She took a sip of her punch. It tasted like cherries.

"Yes, it does." He glanced around before grinning at her. "Perhaps I should suggest a garden party for next year's birthday party."

Emmaline grinned, then glanced down at her lap, lost in thought. She turned to him. "Do you ever grow tired of it?"

He lifted a brow. "What do you mean?"

"All the parties. The ceremonies. All the people expecting you to behave a certain way. The rules, the rhythms."

He glanced down, his jaw jerking. "No one's ever asked me that."

Heat crawled up her back and shot up her neck. "Oh, I apologize. I didn't mean to be forward."

He shook his head. "No, no. I'm glad you asked." He turned to her, a relieved smile on his face. "Thank you."

She smiled, waiting for him to go on.

"And yes. Yes, I do grow tired of it, putting on a show. That night when the bowl broke at my mother's dinner party, for example, I was exhausted by all the questions and ceremony. But I'm convinced that if I find someone to share this life with . . ." He swallowed, his Adam's apple bobbing. "Someone to help me carry the burden . . ." His hand blanketed hers, his thumb waving over her knuckles as his voice lowered. "I think I might grow to bear it." He gazed into her eyes.

Her breath stilled. Suddenly, the garden's fragrance overwhelmed her until her lungs could no longer take the aroma of the roses. Every brush of Nicholas's thumb against her skin stole the air, spurred a wave of heat that crashed on the shores of her heart. She swallowed. "I hope you do find someone, Your Highness."

"I think I already have."

She wondered if he could hear her heart beating. It was certainly louder than the music swelling inside the ballroom. Her ears ached from the cacophony of her wild heart.

He lifted her hand to his face, his breath falling over her skin like gentle whispers, and kissed her knuckles. Butterfly wings could not have been lighter, and no wings of any size would have lifted her any higher off the ground.

Emmaline studied Nicholas's lashes as his eyes lowered over her hand. She studied the dimple in his lip and his cheeks, the shape of his nose, his jawline. He was beautiful, the work of an artist.

A gunshot fired. Soldiers' boots thundered. "James!" Mama cried. "Run!" Papa roared. The couch soared across the room. Charlotte fell to the ground, her lungs filling with blood.

Emmaline gasped. The ghosts slowly faded, returning to Nicholas's crystal eyes. His concerned, loving eyes.

"Emmaline?"

She'd had the world once. And in one moment, blood had spilled and death had consumed everything she'd ever loved. What if that were to happen again? What if Nicholas's hand grew cold in hers and his blood stained her dress? Her fortress had fallen once, and though God had been rebuilding it, she could not allow its defenses to become vulnerable again. She'd barely survived the heartbreak before. It would kill her the next time.

What had she done? She'd told herself time and time again that she mustn't let herself fall for Nicholas, that pain was far too big a price to pay for love. But ever since the queen had told her about Nicholas's feelings, all her vows had vanished like misty clouds.

Nicholas was not the fire which stoked her heart. He was the fire that would consume it. Emmaline jerked her hand from his and lowered herself from the railing. She struggled to regain her breath. "You mustn't allow yourself to give in to this behavior, Your Highness."

He jumped down from the railing, his eyes soft but his brows raised. "What do you mean?" He stepped toward her.

"I know you care for me." She forced the words out, the flowers heavy in her lungs. "But it cannot be so. You must pursue one of the other girls." She swallowed again and tried to hold her head high. She had to convince him that she meant what she said. She had to convince herself.

He took both of her hands, firmly but gently, as if he were holding the most expensive china in the world. "I more than care for you, Emmaline. I love you. Do you not feel the same?" Lines were etched into his face, such pain-filled lines that did not belong on the face of a prince. On the face of such a wonderful man.

She looked into his eyes and saw that she was hurting him now. Better now for a moment than later for a lifetime. She bit her lip. "I cannot."

He stared into her eyes intensely. "Why?"

"I-I cannot lose you as I lost my family." Her voice dropped. "It nearly killed me, Nicholas. And I know it shall if I lose you."

"You can't think like that, Emmaline. You can't let the past determine what you do in the present." He reached out for her hand and waved his thumb over her knuckles. Her heart fluttered. She wanted to slap herself, to dunk her face in a bucket of water until she was sober from this feeling.

She shook her head. "The past is there for a reason,

to keep us from further pain." Though she couldn't imagine how anything could hurt worse than this.

Nicholas tightened his grip. His jaw was set, but his eyes glistened with softness and fear. "Listen to me, Emmaline. I don't want a single day to pass without you there to share it with me. Hearts are made to be broken and healed again and again. It's the only way we know we're human, that we're alive. I'm terrified of losing you, too, after all the people I've lost. But I've never lost anyone who was as special as you are to me. And if my heart does break, then I'll know my heart had something worth breaking for." He cupped her cheek in his hand. "You."

Tears burned her eyes. How could he say such things?

The doors opened again and a portly man in a suit appeared. Emmaline jumped, trembling like a tree caught in a storm.

"Your Highness," the man said. "Her Majesty the Queen has requested your presence."

This was her chance. Emmaline ripped her hands from his. "I must go!" Without another glance at him, she picked up her skirts and retreated inside.

"Emmaline!" Nicholas called.

She didn't stop running, not through the ballroom, not up the staircase, and not in the halls. When she'd made it to her room, she pressed her back against the door, tears falling from her chin. A sense of guilt sliced through her, but what other option had she had but to run? She raised her tear-filled eyes to the ceiling, seeing nothing. *Forgive me, God, but I can't do this. I've already broken once, and I can't break again.*

She waited for the guilt to pass, for God's acceptance of what she'd confessed to fill her, but there was nothing between her and the ceiling but silence.

Nicholas clenched his lips together and shook his head. He should have gone after her. He should have run after her. He shouldn't have let her leave.

Had he moved too quickly? Had he been too bold? He knew all too well the trials of giving away a heart that was already maimed. He'd scared her off. He'd been too forceful. But he could not help it. Whatever resolve he had was stripped away any time he caught sight of her. She had captivated him completely. The way little curls were always falling into her eyes. The way she blushed. The way she walked, like an angel floating by. The way she spoke in soft, lilting tones. The way she looked at him. He was weak, and all his defenses were destroyed with just one glance.

She loved him. He knew she did. And the ghosts of her past had been losing their grip over the past few months; he could tell. Love was healing her.

But she was still frightened. The gunshots were still too familiar a sound to her. The terror of her past was still too deep a cut. Would she live in such agony all her life? Would she be so afraid forever?

If she continued to run, she would find herself all alone. And no heartache could ever be cured by isolation. She would never heal. She would never know his love and how real it was.

Nicholas gazed at the sky and swallowed his emotion. Not one star glittered down on him. *Dear God, she needs help. Let me be the one to help her. Let me love her.*

He could not give up now. He had to catch up with her now before she disappeared from view. His night sky would be barren without her.

Chapter Fourteen

BLACK CLOUDS MARCHED across the sky like soldiers preparing for battle as the grass swished in the quick wind. Thunder rumpled a distant song of battle drums. A storm was coming.

Emmaline stood in the garden, hugging herself tightly. Loose curls danced in her face.

"And if my heart does break, then I'll know my heart had something worth breaking for. You."

Emmaline bit her lip. Why was she so afraid of

having the one thing she'd dreamed of having again? Why was she so terrified of taking hold of the one hope that had kept her alive during those three long years?

I can't lose it again. That is why.

Soft thunder groaned in the distance. Emmaline glanced up at the sky, the smell of rain filling her senses.

Don't You understand, God? Don't You understand why this is hard for me? You know everything. Why aren't You giving me peace about it? Why?

Rolling clouds blocked the sun, dimming the light in the garden. Her chest tightened, like a stone rolling across an entrance, blocking out any rays of the sun.

It hurts too much, God. There's not a day that goes by that I don't hear their screams or see their blood. I'm not angry with You. I never have been. I've just accepted it and kept walking. Then You brought me to this place. I loved learning how to be a lady of the court. I was content with my future as the queen's maid. If I was content with that, why aren't You?

Because I have more for you.

Emmaline balled her hands into fists. She fell to her knees, yanking at the grass. *I don't want more! I have all that I need.* She threw the blades into the wind. Tears scorched her cheeks. *I have You. You're enough for me.* She ripped up more grass and sent them flying away. *You're the one thing I have that will never be taken from me.* She gripped more blades in her hand.

"Emmaline."

She turned. The grass stood tall around her, swallowing her as if she was a ship flailing about in monstrous waves. But Nicholas stood there like a lighthouse, shining his rays toward her and beckoning her back to the shore.

She wiped her face, flicking the hot tears away. "Nicholas, I–"

"Let me speak," he said, his voice deflated.

She bit her lip. He wasn't wearing his usual smile. His eyes drooped from lack of sleep. She'd broken his heart. He had every right to be angry. She was being selfish. In an effort to protect herself from further pain, she was wounding him. She was despicable. What crime had he committed that would deserve such treatment from her? None, and she could never imagine him being guilty of anything.

Nicholas smoothed his fingers through his hair, his chest rising and falling as if he were trying to catch his breath. Emmaline half-heartedly played with the strands of grass, sorry she'd been so violent to the emerald blades.

"I want you to know . . ." His sudden voice made her jump. "I want you to know that I don't hold anything against you. I know how much pain you carry, how afraid you are." He swallowed. "I know, because I've felt the same way, too."

She looked up at him, her heart like a drumbeat in her ears. He wasn't angry with her? She'd made a fool of him last night by running away. She'd broken his heart. She'd earned his trust and then slammed the door in his face. But he wasn't angry? "You have?"

He nodded. "Yes." He held out his hand. "I'd like to show you something if you'll allow me. Please, come with me."

She stared at his hand as if choosing her fate. But he simply wanted to show her something. She was not signing her life away.

With a deep breath, she took his hand, and he helped her to her feet. He didn't look at her when she removed her hand from his, but she knew it hurt him just as much as it hurt her. Surely losing a limb couldn't be more painful.

As they walked side-by-side, Nicholas's knuckles brushed hers. A shiver shot up her back. She glanced at him. He kept his gaze trained toward the path.

She followed him across the cobblestones in the garden and through the hedges. They came to a small pond enclosed in the garden. The water shimmered in the dim light as frogs croaked softly.

"When I came back from the war, I was destroyed," Nicholas said before he paused.

Emmaline glanced at him, surprised at his sudden confession. *What is he doing?*

"I was not the same boy that left home to fight for God and country. I struggled for sleep. Some nights were so bad, I didn't want to sleep. I was angry. I'd lost all the friends I'd made. Not one of them survived. Only me. I was plagued with questions. Their ghosts haunted me."

Tears stung her eyes. Hadn't she struggled with this very thing? She bit her lip, trying to find courage amid all her tangled emotions.

"When I came home, my mother wanted me to marry before I became king. I didn't want to. I was afraid of losing someone I fell in love with the way I'd lost all my friends. I wrestled with it for months. Then I realized . . ." He swallowed and looked at her again. "I realized that love is what we're made for. Yes, God is enough for me, but He wants us to be brave enough to find love in another human, too. In a mother or father. In a child. In a friend . . ." He turned his gaze toward her. "In a spouse."

Emmaline bit her lip, willing the tears to stop burning her eyes.

"So, to make peace with the past, I had to put my friends to rest, before the pain killed me. I came here and laid flowers along the water's surface. I dedicated every flower to each of my friends. I spoke their names, then I let them drift away."

She wiped her face, every muscle screaming at her to run away.

Nicholas turned toward a rose bush and plucked six buds. He took her hands and placed them in her palms. Looking into her eyes, he said, "I went through hell after I came back from the war. And if I have to, I'll go through hell again to pull you out." He swallowed. "I want you to be healed like I was. Say your family's names, then lay the roses on the water. Let them go."

A sob nearly choked her. "I can't say goodbye to

them. I don't want them to leave."

"They are more than ghosts, Emmaline." Nicholas's warm hands pressed against her cold skin. "They did not haunt you at night only to slip away when the sun comes. You've told me about your family. They don't deserve your fear. They deserve to be memories, wonderful memories that you have. Memories that you'll always have. Memories that no one can take away."

Despite his warm hands, a chill shook her shoulders. She tasted salt on her tongue. "Yes, I know that the memories will always be with me. Always with me to remind me of who they once were . . ." A rock lodged in her throat. She hung her head, tears falling down her neck. "Who I lost."

He held her wrist. "Emmaline, I had to learn to hold onto their best moments, not their last. You'll learn, too." He waved his thumb over her skin. "Their best moments are the moments that will keep you going. Those are the moments you have to remember. Remember the sun, not the darkness."

Emmaline stared at the water. Could she finally let the ghosts rest? Did she want to let them go, even after all the nightmares and the memories they brought unbidden to her mind?

Nicholas stroked her knuckles before moving away. "I'll step back and give you a moment to yourself, but I'm here with you. You won't be alone."

How many nights after the attack had she felt alone? How many days had she believed she was the only one walking the path of grief? And now, here was another vagabond. He'd made it out of the fire, made it past the shadows, made it to the shore. Could she do the same?

She wanted to be healed. She was weary from walking through life with an open wound. But she was afraid. The healing would hurt. But wasn't it worth it? What would she lose that was worth sacrificing all she could gain? Pain? Doubt? Sorrow? Did she really intend to live alone all her life in her fortress and lock everyone else out of it? That was no way to live.

It was time to shed her old skin for good. She'd been given wings, and now it was time to learn how to fly, no matter how hard it was. She couldn't risk the view she would have, the horizon she would share with Nicholas.

Nicholas's soft but steady gaze was on her as he stood a small distance away. This boy had been wounded like her. He carried scars around just like she did. But his past did not rule over him as hers had for so long. She wanted to drink from the same healing water as he had.

God, I'm ready to drink. Let this water wash me from the inside out.

Emmaline took a deep breath, readying herself for the blow. It was time to shake the ashes from her head. She stepped toward the water and knelt down. She lifted a single rose bud to her lips and kissed it.

"Papa," she whispered.

Papa had chased her through the halls when she

was a small child. He'd let her stand on his shoes when they'd danced at balls. He'd picked her up when she scraped her knee and held her when she awoke with nightmares.

Her fingers dipped into the water as she set the next bud on the surface.

"Mama," she said softly.

Mama had kissed her cheeks at night before bed and sat through tea parties with Emmaline's stuffed animals. She'd read stories to her and plaited her hair. She'd tickled Emmaline until she was vibrating with giggles and tucked her into bed.

Tears fell onto the petals as she kept whispering their names. "Rose."

Emmaline could still see Rose's smile, the way her eyes had often stared into nothing, full of thought, full of dreams. They'd called her the blue-eyed angel. She used to pick flowers for Mama. She used to read stories to Emmaline when they were small. She used to imagine what it would be like to fall in love and have children.

"Charlotte."

Charlotte had always been next to Mama, sewing or reading the latest newspapers. She used to pretend she was a nursemaid, running around to her siblings' beds and giving them each a spoonful of jam instead of medicine. She'd cared for any stray kittens that wandered around their house.

"Kathleen."

Kathleen had been the eldest, the leader. She'd

been trusted with the many secrets her siblings had told her. She and Papa had often played tennis together. She'd negotiated peace between warring siblings like a queen. Emmaline's fingers were numb and cold as she laid the rose into the water.

Emmaline took the last rose. It fit perfectly in her palm. "James."

James had been the littlest, the baby. He and Emmaline had often stolen chocolates from the kitchen when Mama wasn't looking. He'd climbed trees with her and rode a horse as if he'd been doing it his whole life. He'd come into Emmaline's bed once when he had a nightmare. She'd kept him safe and warm all night.

Emmaline bent and put the last rose into the water. When she was finished, she stood and watched them drift along the surface.

Nicholas stepped toward her again and took her hand. She bit her lip and tried to force the tears away, wrestling hard with the emotion rising in her like the tide.

"Emmaline," Nicholas said.

She turned to face him and instantly regretted it. Her resolve crumbled to the ground with that look he was giving her.

"You don't have to be brave. Not for me."

A disobedient tear slipped down her cheek, then another. Was the ground shaking? She could no longer keep her balance. Nicholas must have seen, because his arms came around her, catching her before she fell into the grass below. She held tightly to him, her arms around his neck and her head resting on his shoulder. Tears rose and fell, dampening his shirt. He twisted his fingers around her loose curls with one hand and smoothed his fingers over her shoulder blade with the other.

How foolish had she been last night? All those times she denied herself what she wanted? She'd longed for love and safety for three years, and when it finally arrived with blue eyes and a beautiful smile, she'd turned away. No, she'd *run* away. God had led her right to the well, but she'd been too afraid to drink.

Emmaline pulled away, her eyes burning. She wiped her face. "Forgive me, Nicholas. I shouldn't have run away last night. I broke your heart."

He smiled gently. "There's nothing to forgive."

"I was so afraid. I still am. But I know now that I can't let that stop me."

He cupped her head in his hands and smiled as if she'd given him back the hope she'd stolen last night. "Emmaline." He spoke her name softly, like a small evening breeze, and pressed his forehead against hers.

She breathed in the new hope she had. *This was what You meant, God, wasn't it? This is my more that You have for me.*

Thunder rumbled as the sky opened. Rain bucketed down on them. Nicholas leapt back and laughed. Emmaline shrieked, laughing with him as the cold drops pelted her skin.

"Come on, let's get inside!" He took her hand and pulled her through the garden. Raindrops fell like stars all around them.

Inside, puddles gathered on the tiled floor from their dripping clothes. Nicholas laughed, water dripping from his jawline. "Oh, you're soaked!"

"So are you!" Emmaline chuckled.

A maid bustled into the hall. She turned, catching sight of them. Her eyes widened as she turned white. "Oh, Your Highness! I'll find some towels for you both right away." She hurried off.

Emmaline giggled behind her hand as Nicholas called out, "Thank you!"

Nicholas turned to her, grasping her arms. "Look at you! Your sleeves are soaked through!" His laugh could chase away the darkness. And it did. The memories of fire were still there, but their embers could no longer burn her.

She looked into his eyes, surer than ever. *I've got to step out of my fortress, don't I, God? I've trusted You so much already, it's time I trust You with everything.*

She took Nicholas's cold hands in her own as she filled her lungs with new breath. She waved her thumbs over his knuckles. He watched her with a soft glaze in his eyes. His heart raced; she could feel it. She lifted one of his hands to her face and closed her eyes. Here's my heart, God. You can have it. She pressed her lips against his knuckles, a shower of stars bursting inside her. He was still gazing at her when she looked up. "I love you, Nicholas. With all my heart."

His face broke into a smile as he drew nearer to her. His hand came over her cheek. "And I love you,

Emmaline. With all my heart."

She laughed, the shackles dropping and the tears falling.

A woman cleared her throat a few feet away. The maid had returned with towels, now with very scarlet cheeks.

She nodded at them both. "Apologies, sire, miss."

"No apologies needed, Hattie." Nicholas held his arm out for the towels. "Thank you."

Hattie smiled, somewhat awkwardly, and scurried off quickly.

Emmaline closed her hand over her mouth, muffling her giggles. Nicholas wrapped a towel around her shoulders, and warmth flooded her body.

"I'll see you at supper, then?" Nicholas asked.

She nodded. "Yes. Goodbye." She ran off toward the stairs, clutching the towel around her arms and embracing the new feeling growing inside her.

Chapter Fifteen

NICHOLAS'S HEART THUMPED in a new way that was quickly becoming familiar. It thumped this way every time he caught a glimpse of Emmaline's face. It thumped when he saw her smile, when she looked up at him from beneath heavy eyelashes, when he heard her fairy laughter.

He couldn't stop thinking of her. Out of all the girls, she thrilled him the most, but not just because of her beauty. While she was more beautiful to him than all the others, her spirit was what had captured his mind, body, and soul. She was like an abused horse who had escaped its captors and now ran wild among the mustangs on the Tredan Bay shore. He wanted to run alongside her for the rest of his life, to run until they fell into each other's arms.

Nicholas stepped into the chapel, the sunlight filtering through the ruby and emerald mosaic and falling across his face. He dropped to his knees at the altar, gazing at the crucifix above him.

The time had come. The six months had ended, the girls had learned to become ladies of the court, and now it was time for him to choose a wife. He'd spent the whole night praying, searching his heart. One name echoed over and over in his mind as he'd prayed. He could hardly keep quiet when God had told him Emmaline was the one.

And now, he would keep quiet no longer. "Thank you, God, for Emmaline. She is more wonderful than I could have ever imagined or hoped. I know she is a gift from You. I don't deserve her, but You have still given her to me. I only hope I can be the man she deserves and the love she needs. I swear to You, before I am king to this country, I will be a husband to her. Give me the strength to keep my word. Show me how to love in a way I never have. Let me love as You do."

He bowed his head, his arms lifted in worship.

The world stopped when the girls' bedchamber door opened. From the moment Mr. Harrison walked into the room, time crawled by. Or at least, it felt that way to Emmaline.

"The prince has stated that he is ready to propose," Mr. Harrison said.

Some of the girls gasped. Some of them made no sound at all. Lydia glanced at Emmaline. Emmaline did not move or speak. She wasn't even sure her heart was beating. Or perhaps it was beating so fast, she couldn't feel it.

"He will propose tonight to one of you. You will all be given letters."

"Letters?" Julia asked, blinking.

"Yes, these letters are addressed to each of you. When you read their contents, you must not share them with anyone. That is between you and the prince. The letters will give you directions on where to go." Mr. Harrison put his hand inside his suit jacket and pulled out a bundle of envelopes. He stepped toward them and handed them each a letter. "Remember, keep it to yourselves."

Emmaline ripped hers open, a sound in her ears like the thrumming of a hummingbird's wings. When it was open, she pressed the piece of parchment to her chest and closed her eyes. It smelled like Nicholas—pine trees and mint. She breathed in his scent and was filled with warmth.

She opened her eyes and quickly read Nicholas's handwriting:

Dear Emmaline,

Meet me in the gardens. When you arrive, there's another letter.

-Nicholas

The time had come. She would become the future queen. She would have a whole new life in Tregaron. She would be the one Nicholas would love for the rest of their lives.

Mr. Harrison cleared his throat. "It's time for your journeys to begin."

Tears of gratitude nearly spilled from her eyes. She folded the letter back into the envelope, then headed out of the bedchamber.

Like Mr. Harrison had said, she was going on a journey. She'd been on those before. This journey would lead her into Nicholas's arms, where he would offer his heart to her. This journey would lead her to the altar, where she would pledge herself to him. This journey would one day lead her to carry a child, a gift to her and Nicholas and an heir to the throne. This journey would lead to a life of love and joy and adventure, the kind of life she used to have, the kind of life she'd always wanted to get back.

The walk through the halls was silent. Emmaline trembled like a ship at sea. *Oh, God, I can't begin to fathom how terrified I am. Prepare me for this moment, and for whatever moments that lead on from this one. Give me strength.*

Meet me in the gardens. The gardens would lead her to her destiny. God had planned it all, and if He had planned it, it would certainly be something good.

Emmaline wished she could walk faster. She wished she could fly to Nicholas. Every step she took seemed slow. She wanted to see him now.

She watched as the girls scattered, each following her own path, each going to her own destiny. She walked alone down the halls and stepped toward the doors leading to the garden.

The night air was cool and smelled of roses as she stepped outside. The water in the fountain sounded like whispers in the distance.

Emmaline looked around for the other letter and saw it resting on the stone pillar. She opened it and held it to the moonlight.

Follow the rose petals.

Her heart screeched to a halt. *Rose petals?* She glanced down and gave a small cry. Rose petals were scattered across the ground, trickling down the stairs and along one of the paths through the gardens.

Her heart pounded like soldiers marching into battle. Tears gathered in her eyes as joy came alive inside her. Nicholas had healed her with roses, and now their petals sang of his love for her. *He shouldn't have gone to so much trouble for me.*

This was it. Her dream was coming true. She felt so undeserving. Perhaps she should run away and save Nicholas from what must surely be the biggest mistake of his life. But even as she considered it, her feet wouldn't turn from the path. She kept going. This *was* her path to walk, and nothing would deter her from reaching the end.

The smell of roses would forever fill her memory. She'd have this night to remember for the rest of her life. She only hoped she wouldn't be drowning in tears by the time she reached Nicholas.

She journeyed through the maze of hedges, her only light coming from the moon. The petals grew in amount, the aroma nearly hypnotizing her. At last, she came to the end of the maze and there, standing in a heap of petals, was Nicholas.

He looked more handsome than he ever had. He was dressed sharply in a black suit, and his hair was brushed to perfection. Only a few curls had managed to escape and fell down his forehead.

Sobs threatened to shake her like a snow globe. Nicholas must have seen her rising emotion because he came to her and took her hands.

"Don't cry." He removed one of his hands from hers and wiped her tears with his thumb. She shook beneath his touch.

"I can't help it." She smiled at him, more tears rising to the surface. "After everything I've been through . . . I've never been so happy."

"Neither have I." He grinned. "How did you like your journey through the rose petals?"

"I don't think I've seen so many petals in one place," she breathed, half laughing. "It was the most beautiful thing I've ever seen."

He held both her hands again. "Strange, I thought the same thing when I saw you come around the corner." His face was seized by a thousand emotions that flickered in his eyes, like fireworks bursting through the sky. "Emmaline, I brought you here to tell you something."

She swallowed, feeling as though she'd just swallowed her heart. "And what is that?"

His breath hitched. "I used to hear my friend Conor talk about his wife Talulla all the time. He prayed for her before every battle, and he wrote letters to her constantly. His eyes always lit up when he talked about her, like a dying man dreaming of heaven. I knew that if I made it off the battlefield alive, I would search until I had the kind of love he'd had." He lowered his eyes, his voice dropping to a whisper. "I lost my way for a while, but I found her." He lifted his eyes again, gazing into her own, his irises twinkling like the stars. "I found my Talulla." His thumb brushed the top of her hand. "Both of our worlds have crashed around us. Both of us have lost our way in life. But somehow, we survived. Somehow, we found our way to each other. I think we're both just falling stars, destined to fall together." He fell to his knee, gazing softly at her. "And I want to fall with you for the rest of my life, Emmaline . . . Will you marry me?"

Emmaline bit her lip, her eyes burning with tears as she savored his words to her. They washed over her like the waves, cleansing her soul, pulling her toward him like the tide. She was going to be his wife. She had a whole new life in Tregaron now. No longer did she have to tread on endless roads, relying on scraps and old hymns to keep her alive. She'd be safe and warm and loved. God had provided. She uttered another cry, strangled and dry. "Yes! Oh, yes."

Nicholas's face broke into a smile as tears shone in his eyes. He sprang to his feet and threw his arms around her. She clung to him as he weaved his fingers through her hair, their foreheads pressed together. He pressed his lips to her own. The ground beneath her turned to clouds as gravity fell away.

When he released her, the warmth of his kiss still on her lips, he rummaged through his suit jacket. "I have a ring. It's here somewhere," he breathed. She noticed his blush and giggled.

"Ah, here it is!" He brought out a tiny, black satin box and opened it. The ring inside looked as if he'd plucked a star from the sky to put on her finger. The diamond shimmered in the moonlight, nearly blinding her tear-filled eyes.

Emmaline gasped. "Oh, Nicholas."

He smiled and slid it down her finger. As Emmaline's tears came, Nicholas cupped her hands in his. "I prayed every night it would be you. I prayed that you would be the one. And I thank God that He heard me."

Emmaline shook her head. "I still don't understand. You had so many wonderful girls to choose from, and you chose me?"

Nicholas stroked her cheekbone with his thumb. "There is none other so wonderful as you, Emmaline."

"But there has to be a reason why you chose me."

He smiled. "Because you showed me the stars."

Nicholas held Emmaline's hand, running up the garden steps and into the palace. She laughed all the way. A new kind of energy pulsed inside him, like a new stream bubbling with life.

He jumped in mid-air, clicking his feet together, and shouted joyfully. Emmaline squealed and then laughed again.

"We're getting married!" he shouted.

A few maids and servants passed them, cheering and applauding at their news. Nicholas glanced at Emmaline, his future bride. She would look lovely, all dressed in white. He would seal their destiny together with a kiss. He hoped that day would come quickly.

Ross appeared in the distance, and Nicholas waved at him like an excited little boy. "Ross! Ross! We're getting married–Emmaline and I! I asked, and she said yes!"

Ross smiled. "Congratulations, both of you. You'll both do well together." He glanced to the side, still smiling. "If you excuse me, I have somewhere to be."

Nicholas waved at him again and turned to Emmaline. "I can scarcely believe it."

"Neither can I." She gazed into his eyes. "If this is a dream, don't wake me up."

Nicholas wrapped his arms around her waist and pressed his forehead against hers again. "Never."

He kissed her lips, but it was a kiss that would seal, not waken, their blissful dream.

Rise

Ross concentrated on each step and each breath, his feet pounding through the halls. Or was that his heart? He couldn't tell. It didn't matter. Nothing mattered now.

Emmaline was engaged. He'd known it would happen; he just hadn't known when. And now that it had, he could scarcely believe it.

Her barriers had finally collapsed. She'd finally surrendered to love's pleas. Both she and Nicholas were glowing with joy. This was a miracle. So why did an invisible blade impale his lungs? Why was he eager to escape everyone's eyes?

He stumbled through countless corridors until his shallow breath forced him to stop. He leaned against the doorframe, gathering his thoughts. If he felt this way, he didn't deserve Emmaline. She was free to make her own choices. Even if she didn't choose him. Even if he had never been an option.

He glanced up, noticing where he was for the first time. The chapel doors were cracked, as if they were inviting him in.

Dare he step inside? Could he, after the news he'd received tonight?

But could God be blamed when He deserved thanks instead? Emmaline was engaged to Nicholas, a good, strong man who would rule with a kind, steady hand and protect his wife all his days. Wasn't that a good thing? Did God really deserve Ross's anger?

Perhaps God wasn't to blame. Emmaline had said

God was loving, and what better proof was there than this? An orphan girl had found love and a new life in a palace. So what if Ross was crushed by Nicholas's cheerful announcement? Was his happiness more important than Emmaline's?

"*My ways are not your ways* . . .'" The old Scripture floated through his head, like a voice he remembered from long ago.

God's ways were certainly not his ways. And it was time Ross remembered that.

Trembling, he stepped into the chapel. The candles, still burning brightly, stung his eyes.

It had been too long since he'd prayed. For three years, he had lived in the darkness. For three years, the past had haunted his every step, his every moment. It whispered in his ears and deafened him with its screams. Its touch on his skin turned him to ice.

He had been taught to pray as a child. His mother and father had knelt at his bedside with him and taught him to say the words. He had sung praise songs with the villagers. He had read the Bible from cover to cover. He knew every promise God had ever spoken, but he'd quickly forgotten them when everything he'd known was ripped away in a night of blood and fire.

Was he angry with God? Was he furious with Him because of what He had done, because of what He had taken away, because of the scars He allowed him to have? Or was he afraid of Him? Was he terrified of what He would do again, should Ross slip back into the old trust he'd had in Him?

He didn't know. He didn't know what had kept him away from God for three years. But there was a barrier, a ravine dividing them. All those cold nights, he'd forgotten His warmth. All those screams in his ears, he'd forgotten His tender whispers.

Ross still saw it all. The whole night. Gunshots ripping through the houses and through everyone he'd ever known. Women wailing and children screaming.

"Come on, children! We have to run!" Mama cried.

Mama snatched Ross's arm in her hand, her grip hard despite her trembling body. Tears stained her face and a look he'd never seen before haunted her eyes. "Ross, I need you to help your siblings. Help me, please!"

The roof creaked as cannons roared. He grabbed Maria and Matthew from the corner, their wails deafening him. He ran out of the house. The palace burned, and the smoke rose in the sky like a dragon's breath. His heart stopped, and so did his feet.

A cannon screamed again. The house next to theirs crumbled to the ground. Ross reached out. "Mama!" Something crashed into his head, and he fell, fell to the ground, fell into the darkness.

Ross trembled as he crept down the aisle. It was a small chapel. The only light came from the candles and the mosaics spraying colorful light on the floor. A mosaic of Jesus hung in the window, staring back at him with glassy black eyes.

His heart drummed within him. He'd abandoned

God. Somewhere, deep inside him, he'd blamed God for what had happened to his mother, his brother and sister, and his home. But hadn't He been the one to sustain him all these years? Hadn't He protected him from death? Hadn't He sent him to the palace and given him a position? Ross had cut God's heart through and through with his accusations, but He had never turned away.

A dampness spread on his forehead. Ross made it to the end of the aisle and stared at the crucifix. Hadn't He always loved him, no matter the pain he caused Him? Nails were drummed into His hands and crushed His bones, yet He still embraced him. Thorns were shoved into His head and blood dripped down His face, yet He still called him "son." He was mangled, ripped open, and beaten. Still, He whispered, "I love you."

His ways were higher than Ross's ways. And if God had allowed Emmaline to become engaged to Nicholas, then it must be for a reason. It must be for the best. Not only for Emmaline, but for Ross, too.

He closed his eyes as tears fell down his cheeks. He lifted his hands, palms open, and fell to his knees before the crucifix. His breath was shallow as he bowed his head. His heartbeat echoed in the small room; he was sure of it.

"Oh, God . . . forgive me. I have blamed You. I have abandoned You. But no more. I want this barrier between us to be gone. I want to step over this ravine and cross over to You. You have a reason for everything.

Rise

Whatever You have in mind for me, let it be accomplished. I give myself to You again, mind, body, spirit, and soul."

His tears fell onto the marble floors. When he found his courage, he looked up at the Jesus mosaic again. Such deep, black eyes. Perhaps they weren't as dark as he had thought before.

Chapter Sixteen

WHITE. IT WAS a familiar shade to Emmaline. She'd never lived anywhere that wasn't caked with snow in the winter. The beaches her family had visited on holidays had rolled with white sands. She and her sisters' wardrobes were filled with silks and lace, all made of brilliant white. Mama had urged purity of clothing and of spirit from her girls. Sometimes she called them her little snowflakes.

Today, Emmaline was once more buried in a cloud of

white. Pearl buttons trickled down her back as Lydia closed each of them. The sleeves were puffed at the top, stopping at her elbow, and the rest of the sleeves were made of flowery lace. The full skirt practically filled the room with its long train.

Today was her wedding day. The girls would accompany her down the aisle, holding her veil and train. Ross would escort her down the aisle. With Mr. Harrison gone caring for his sick mother, and with their close friendship, Ross had seemed the obvious choice. She knew no other man at the palace half as well, so two weeks ago, she had asked him and to her delight, he had accepted.

Emmaline glanced at the clock. In just a few short hours, she and Nicholas would pledge themselves to each other for eternity. And she would be happier than she'd ever been.

"Anna, you must stop your crying," Diana fussed, her voice thick. She sat on the floor, adjusting Emmaline's skirts, and swiped at her eyes. "You'll get tears all over Emmaline's flowers!"

Anna sniffled, a vision in her yellow gown and braided hairstyle. "Sorry," she whispered. "She's just so beautiful."

Lydia stood back from her, finished with the buttons. She clasped her hands together and bit her lip. "She is."

Anna wiped fresh tears away. Eleanor smiled like a proud mother. Emmaline blinked rapidly and swallowed the rising emotion. Did she really mean so much to all of them?

"Now for the veil and tiara," Julia said. She brought the veil toward Emmaline and pinned it to her hair. The girls voiced their opinions on how to straighten it.

Next, Julia took the tiara from the satin pillow and placed it on Emmaline's head. The tiara's weight felt strange but somehow familiar. It was heavy to hold upon her head, but she managed.

"The tiara looks made for you," Eleanor gasped.

Anna stepped forward and held out the bouquet to Emmaline. Anna's lip trembled and her eyes glittered, but she still managed to smile. "Flowers for you, Emmaline. I thought these would look beautiful in your hands."

Emmaline smiled, slowly taking them from Anna and bringing them to her nose to smell. She filled her senses with their fragrance. The bouquet was the most beautiful she'd seen, filled with white roses, forget-me-nots, violets, and baby breath. "Thank you, Anna. It's lovely."

The girls stared at Emmaline, smiling sadly.

Emmaline fidgeted with her hands, her voice shaking. "You're going to make me cry with all of you staring like that."

Julia smiled sadly, a tear straying down her cheek. "You'll have to forgive us. It's just that–well–it feels as if we've all become sisters."

"Julia! Don't remind her of that today of all days." Diana hissed. Julia turned white as a sheet, then blushed

Rise

and glanced down.

Emmaline shook her head. "She said nothing out of turn. I feel the same way. And while no one can replace my sisters, my parents, or my brother, my family can certainly grow. And it has. I've got all of you and Ross and now Nicholas." She couldn't help but smile. She held her arms out. "Come here, I want to hold all of you."

The girls wrapped their arms around her. Emmaline was so warm inside, she wondered if sunlight had somehow found a way into her body. "I love you all."

A knock came at the door, and the servant announced it was time to make the trip to St. Sidus Abbey. The girls turned to Emmaline, eyes widening as they exploded with squealing. Emmaline laughed at their joy, her cheeks already sore from smiling so much.

The air was unusually cool for a summer day as the carriage drove through the streets. People dressed in their Sunday best cheered and hailed her as she passed. Children ran alongside the carriage and threw flower petals into the air. Some girls wearing wreaths of flowers spun ribbons and danced as she passed by them. Emmaline smiled, waving back.

If her family were here, the carriage would be full of giggles from her sisters and misty eyes from her mother. Rose would wear a ribbon in her light brown hair and sit next to Emmaline. Charlotte would stroke Mama's hand, and Kathleen would wave to the children like the lady she was. Papa would be waiting at the mouth of the abbey, tears running into his beard, and

James would pretend to be brave while holding back sadness of his own.

She ached inside, though she couldn't seem to stop smiling. She wanted them here, more than anything. But in the blueness of the sky and the warmth of the sun, Emmaline knew they were here, in some small way.

The driver turned a corner. Emmaline took a deep breath. It was time to leave one chapter of her life and step into the next one. And she was more than ready.

A black carriage pulled along the sidewalk, stopping in front of St. Sidus Abbey. The driver shouted something at the horses, but Ross couldn't hear him over the crowds' cheering.

Emmaline's friends stepped out of the carriage. Ross hurried down the stairs and offered his hand to Emmaline. Her ivory fingers closed around his as she made her way out of the carriage. Ross glanced up, his breath faltering.

Emmaline glowed like the sun filtering through diamonds. He could tell, even with her face covered with a veil. She smiled at him, then stepped down from the carriage.

It was her wedding day, the day she'd pledge her heart to someone else, the day when she would forever fly away from his grasp. He ached inside, as if someone had pummeled him over and over, without ceasing, without mercy, without hope of respite.

Rise

He swallowed past the pain as he looked at her. She was gazing at the cathedral clerestories stabbing the sky, beaming beneath her lacy veil. She looked like a star that had fallen from the galaxy, shimmering like she was. And as quickly as she had come, she was fading away.

He had to stop. Hadn't he already decided that this was for the best? But was it wrong to still feel this way? Wouldn't God understand this kind of disappointment?

"You're a vision, my lady." Ross beamed at her despite the knife in his chest.

She wore a crown on her head. She was a princess now, no longer just Emmaline. *But has she ever been just Emmaline to you?*

Emmaline lifted her brows. "There's no need for all that, Ross. We were friends before Nicholas chose me, and we shall remain friends hereafter. Call me Emmaline, as if nothing has changed, because nothing has."

He offered his arm and forced a smile. "Then Emmaline it shall be."

Ross felt himself stiffen as he walked Emmaline toward the abbey's entrance. The girls stepped behind Emmaline, holding her train as they traveled up the staircase.

He'd known this would be a possibility from the very beginning, that she might win the prince's heart. He'd been foolish to let himself fall so deeply, knowing she was never his to claim, never his to lose. It wasn't fair to

Emmaline. He should be happy for her, after her hellish past. He should be happy that she was marrying a man like Nicholas, a man who loved her, who would keep her safe, who would make her happy. He should be happy for Nicholas, too. After all, they were friends, and he'd had hardships of his own. Ross never knew he could be so selfish. *God, forgive me.*

The crowd roared even louder as they neared the doors. Why couldn't he rejoice as much as the people did? They had no idea who Emmaline was, yet they shouted praise to her simply because she was marrying their prince. But Ross knew who she was and where she'd come from, yet all he felt inside was something like broken glass. One day, he would have to tell her who she was. But not now. Not when he was still licking his wounds.

"Does something pain you, Ross?" Emmaline asked.

He glanced at her, startled. "I'm sure I don't know what you mean."

"Is something the matter? You seem . . ."

"Seem what?"

"I don't know. Unhappy, I suppose."

He forced the words to come and made himself mean them. "Unhappy? Why on earth would I be unhappy? You're no longer living on the streets, you've found a new family now, and you're getting married to a man you love and who loves you. How could I be anything but happy?"

She smiled, laughing. "Well, all right, then." She glanced at him and tightened her soft hands in his. His

Rise

whole body burned. "And let's not forget: I've got you as a friend."

He smiled back, the glass inside him ripping through his body. "I shall never forget that."

Nicholas clasped his hands together, feigning a calm he didn't feel. He could hear the excited, cheerful whispers of the guests behind him, even as the choir boys sang a soft melody.

Any moment now, the doors would open, and Emmaline would walk down to him. He turned around and glanced at the doors, making sure they hadn't opened while he'd been daydreaming.

Arthur, the priest, laughed. "My dear boy, you aren't supposed to turn around. It's tradition," he whispered.

Nicholas smiled sheepishly. "Sorry, Father. I simply can't wait any longer."

"Your bride will come sooner than you think. She may be behind those very doors as we speak."

Was her heart pounding as quickly as his was? It wasn't only the marriage she'd have to grow into. She was entering the world of royalty. She wasn't used to this life—the formalities, the diplomacy, the rituals, the invasion of privacy. But he would make certain that it would never become too hard for her.

Trumpets sang, and the doors opened. Nicholas's heart rattled like military drums.

"Here she comes now," Arthur said with a smile.

Nicholas did not turn around but kept his eyes on

the crucifix on the wall facing him. He bit his lip, anticipation and impatience twisting him inside out. Gasps and quick whispers rose from the crowd behind him. The guests had seen Emmaline.

Nicholas clenched his hands together, his resolve shredding away with each passing moment. *Oh, away with tradition!*

Nicholas turned and did not regret it. His breath hitched in his throat, and he wasn't sure if he'd ever get it back. Emmaline floated toward him on a cloud of white, and though her face was hidden behind a veil, he recognized that starry smile.

His eyes burned as his heart galloped to a steady, hard beat. She stood in front of him at the altar, her eyes never leaving his. She was his. This beautiful creature, this saintly angel, this smooth-voiced, starry-eyed girl was his. A skyful of diamonds could not compare to her. What had he ever done to deserve her?

The priest cleared his throat, and the ceremony began. A while later, the priest looked at Nicholas, Emmaline, and Ross. "Who gives this woman to this man?"

Ross smiled. "I do."

The priest nodded. "Very well. You may be seated."

Ross let go of Emmaline's arm and sat on a nearby bench. The ceremony continued.

Emmaline vowed to love Nicholas for all their days together, to sacrifice for him, to care for him, and to remain by his side. He did the same. The people in the abbey sang a hymn along with the choir boys. Their voices rang off the ceiling. Nicholas caressed Emmaline's knuckles and smiled at her.

When the hymn was over, the priest said the words Nicholas had been waiting for all day. Nicholas lifted the veil away from her face. The abbey's candles flickered in her eyes. As if she were made of mist and might suddenly disappear, he pressed his lips to hers and melted at her touch.

When he drew away, a cheer echoed throughout the building. The people applauded as the priest chuckled.

"We're married," Emmaline whispered, her breath caressing his face like a sea breeze.

"Yes, my love." He held her cheek in his hand, then dove in for another kiss.

The crowd roared even louder.

When he released her again, they faced their guests, holding hands as they stood above the crowd. He glanced at Emmaline, the angel in white with her fingers entwined in his. With her, he had a new chapter to write. And he'd savor every word.

Hand-in-hand, Emmaline and Nicholas ran down the hall, laughing like mischievous children. Before they'd turned the last corner, she'd lost both her shoes, and before that, her veil had flown off her head. Her sides ached from running and laughing at the same time. Nicholas pulled her along through the castle, his boyish smiles giving her the strength to keep running.

"Here it is!" Nicholas announced. She couldn't stop laughing and put a hand over her mouth. Nicholas opened the door and pulled her inside.

Emmaline's breath, coming in quick, passed against her lips. She held her hands behind her back and pressed herself against the door. Nicholas stood in front of her, smiling, gazing at her in the quiet of his bedchamber. They were alone, away from the guests and all the curious eyes. It was only them, as if they lived in a whole new world together.

He gazed at her as one gazes at a painting. Taking in every detail. Marveling at each color and shimmer. Her heart raced like a herd of wild mustangs, finally free to run across new pastures, seeking a new horizon.

She took in a deep breath, the anticipation and silence tightening her chest like a corset. "I'm so glad to be away from everyone." Did she sound as breathless as she felt?

He smiled. "Me, too." He moved a hair from her eye. Many curls had tumbled out of her hairstyle as she and Nicholas had run through the halls, as if they were two children who had escaped a stifling party to go exploring.

Sensations like falling stars shot through her as his fingertips brushed her hair away. "I hope you don't misunderstand. I'm glad they were all there for our wedding day. I appreciate their well-wishing, but I feel so relieved to be away from all their staring. I know they were watching my every move."

He grinned, and the appearance of his dimples made her legs tremble. "How could they not? You made hundreds of people today believe in angels." He took her hands in his and stepped closer to her. His warm breath brushed her cheeks.

Tears burned her eyes. "I don't know how I deserve you."

"Nor I you." His blue eyes glistened like the sea as he leaned closer. "I believe that we will wonder about that all our lives." Nicholas pressed his lips to hers and kissed her. A whole galaxy of stars shot through her. Her heart quickened as her body relaxed against the door. She moved her hands up his chest and put her arms around his neck.

He pulled away from her lips, then wrapped his hands around her waist, lifted her, and spun her around the room like a dreidel. All her worries peeled away, one-by-one. She laughed, holding her head back and letting her whole body drink in the joy she felt.

When he stopped, he held her against his chest. Her feet weren't on the ground. She was floating, weightless, like a cloud. He moved his lips against her ear. "You sound like heaven when you laugh."

How did she deserve him? He was the most magnificent man she'd ever known, save for her father. And now he belonged to her.

He put her down and they embraced in the middle of the room. Closing her eyes, she breathed in his scent. Peppermint swelled in her nostrils and in her chest. She liked being this close to him, dizzy with his scent, melting beneath his warmth.

She breathed him in again and pressed her ear against his heartbeat. "You smell like heaven."

He pulled away, smiling down at her. He was the sun, and she was a flower, budding beneath his light and blooming under his warmth.

"Ready for our honeymoon?" Nicholas asked.

She nodded, glancing at the suitcases already packed for them and sitting against his wall. "I'm ready to begin life with you."

He chuckled and smoothed his thumb down her cheek. "My love, it has already begun." He kissed her on the mouth again, warmly and deeply.

In just a few months, her whole world had changed. She'd gone from dark street alleys to candlelit halls. From the cold of the night to the warmth of her new husband's arms. In those lonely nights, she'd never dreamed of ballroom waltzes or a prince's love. But now, she couldn't imagine her life any differently.

Chapter Seventeen

"EMMALINE, WAKE UP. We're here."

Emmaline opened her eyes and raised her head from Nicholas's shoulder. She had not expected to fall asleep with the rattling of the carriage and the clamor of the horses' hooves.

She scooted toward the carriage window. Her breath stilled in her chest as crying seabirds dove through the misty white clouds. Grassy plains stretched out in front of her, and a little farther north, the sea shimmered beneath the golden light of early morning.

Tredan Bay.

"Have you ever seen anything so beautiful?" she breathed.

"Tredan Bay has nothing on you, my love," Nicholas said, and when she turned to meet his gaze, he was grinning.

Blushing, she slid toward him again. She nestled back against his chest, noting the rays of sunlight streaming through the window. "You should've woken me. I'm sure you were bored."

He took her hand into his lap and smoothed his thumb over her knuckles. "I wouldn't have dared. You seemed so peaceful."

"I was. And I was tired."

"I gathered as much, from the pitch of your snores."

She leapt up and gasped. "I do not snore!"

He chuckled. "I know. I just wanted to see your reaction."

She pouted playfully. "You are very naughty for a prince."

"It is one of my most guarded secrets." He winked.

When the carriage arrived at the manor and they had unpacked, Emmaline and Nicholas walked down the long-treaded path, down a sea cliff, down to the white shores kissed by crystal waters.

Blown in the wind, the grass parted like a green sea as they waded through it. Seagulls sailed across the sky, and the waves roared as they crashed against the shore, like a beast succumbing to its fate.

The wind unfurled Emmaline's hair, her chestnut

brown locks tumbling in the crisp air. She closed her eyes and breathed in the salty aroma. Her chest heaved with pleasure. She'd spent many vacations with her family on beaches like this one. She and her sisters and brother had tumbled across the white sandy hills and skipped through the tide. The sun had set on that part of her life, but now, the sun was rising again. She could begin her life anew here. This place, with its shores of scattered shells and cornflower blue waters, was the start of her life with Nicholas, the beginning of her fairytale.

Nicholas ripped his hand away from hers. Emmaline opened her eyes in surprise. He laughed, running down the beach. "Catch me if you can!"

She giggled and cupped her hands around her lips. "You are such a child!"

He laughed again, zipping further away. His feet kicked up water as he ran through the tide and toward the sea cliffs keeping guard.

Emmaline shook her head, chuckling, then picked up her skirts and ran. The wind whipped at her eyes and made tears roll down her cheeks. Sea water sprayed onto her dress and into her mouth. She savored the salt on her tongue. Nicholas turned a corner and disappeared behind the pillars of rock.

Emmaline slowed down, the tide washing over her bare feet. Her heart roared like a train as she regained her breath. They were behaving like school children, playing a game of hide-and-seek and taunting each other. But she savored this youthful feeling, this feeling he gave her.

She turned cautiously around the corner, then saw a glimpse of Nicholas hiding behind another pillar. She covered her soft giggles with her hand and grinned slyly. Stepping lightly, she came up behind him and wrapped her arms around his middle.

He gasped and turned around. "Oh, you found me!"

She raised her brows ruefully. "You, sir, have just been bested by the reigning champion of hide-and-seek."

He grinned, tucking a strand of hair behind her ear. "I was not aware I was playing against such a professional."

"If I'd told you, you might have played better."

His eyes widened in false outrage. "Are you saying you cheated?"

She blushed, drunk with laughter. "Perhaps."

"Then you know the punishment for cheaters." He bent and caught her beneath her knees, cradling her in his arms. He stepped toward the water, grinning. "A good soaking."

Emmaline wrapped her arms around his neck, struggling to speak past her hysterical laughter and screams. "No! Nicholas, please!"

He kept walking, laughing all the way. When the water billowed around his knees, he stopped. She gripped his shoulders, her cheeks aching from her laughing. "Nicholas!" She could barely speak even his name now.

His arms came away from her body, and she fell.

Her skirts billowed like balloons as he dropped her into the water. It came up to her chest and dripped down her face.

Nicholas threw back his head as he laughed, his face glowing in the sun. She smiled at his tall figure standing in front of her. She wondered how the guests at Nicholas's birthday ball would react if they saw this side of him.

He sighed, pressing a hand to his chest. "All right, I'll help you up. I suppose you've learnt your lesson now." He extended his hand toward her.

She bit the inside of her cheek, grinning like an alley cat. "Yes, I have. Now it's time for you . . . to learn . . . *yours!*" She grabbed his hand and yanked.

He shouted as he fell in the water, his legs flailing. He surfaced, spewing water from his puckered lips. Emmaline exploded with laughter, the small waves swaying between them.

"You know, I'm starting to believe that you really were a mischievous child," he said.

She shrugged. "I'm afraid I never quite lost that part of my life."

"That's what I married you for." He winked.

She laughed. "Really?"

"No." His eyes softened like moonlight fading beneath dusky clouds. "But if I did list the reasons, I'm afraid I would never stop speaking." He swallowed, his Adam's apple bobbing beneath his chiseled jawline. He gazed at her, brushing a strand of wet hair from her eyes.

She gazed at his face. Drops of water rested on his lashes and fell down his face when he blinked. A dimple pulled at his cheek as he met her gaze. Had she ever seen eyes so blue? "Nicholas," she whispered. "I—"

He cupped her cheek in his wide hand. "Yes, I know."

The gentle rushing of the tide across the distant shore caressed her ears. His blue eyes, so blue. Not even the sea could compare. His eyes gave her the strength to do anything.

The sun emerged from its hiding place behind a cloud and bathed Nicholas's face in light. He smoothed his thumb over her cheekbone and came closer. Her breath hitched as she closed her eyes. His lips pressed against hers. Warmth spread through her in the chilling sea. She wrapped her hands around his arms and pulled him below the surface with her.

Emmaline lay suspended in a glittering world of endless blue, her skirts and hair drifting around her like lazy seaweed. She kept her lips pressed to his, kissing him slowly, deeply, gently, plunging deeper into the blue underworld with him, spinning with him into fathoms beyond. He weaved his fingers through her hair as tiny bubbles grazed her face. She closed her eyes, lost in this unknown sea but not caring to emerge for breath. She wasn't afraid of the depths anymore.

She gazed at Nicholas, heart quickening at the way he was looking at her. She pressed a hand against his chest as he held her around her middle.

Had she really been given this man for a husband? This man who gazed at her as one might gaze at an angel? This man who had tidied her ghosts away into a grave? This man who had given her a new life?

Nicholas pulled away, and they swam toward the surface. Her heart rang like a church bell when they surfaced, her lungs panting and her lips tingling with the taste of Nicholas's kiss. She'd never been so alive before in her life.

"Can we stay like this?" she whispered, inches from his face.

He touched her forehead with his own. "We'll stay like this forever if you wish."

"I wish."

Chapter Eighteen

"MOTHER, WE'RE HERE!" Nicholas shouted, lifting his suitcase in the air.

Emmaline giggled. "I don't think she'll hear you, Nicholas. This is a rather big palace."

He shrugged. "I know, but I've always wanted to say that."

She laughed again. "My husband—the boy who won't grow up."

He smiled and gazed down at her, noting the peony pink in her dimpled cheek. Was she really his? And was he really hers? "Say that again."

She raised a brow. "Say what?"

"The part where you called me your husband."

"Oh." A wide grin stretched her cheeks. She was even lovelier—if that was at all possible. The Tredan Bay sun had colored her face and enriched the shine of her rich brown hair. She raised a brow playfully, and he fell in love with her all over again. "*My husband*, don't you think it's time we go find your mother, rather than call for her and hope she hears us?"

He traced the outline of her cheek with his fingers. "Oh, you are wonderful." He glanced toward the stairs. "And yes, I suppose we should."

They scaled the staircase and walked through the halls. Servants hurried about, carrying objects and disappearing down corridors.

Emmaline held her shoulders back as she walked alongside him. Nicholas grinned to himself. He liked the way she walked: like a ballerina striding onto the stage, ready for her performance to begin.

"You look beautiful, you know." Nicholas gave his new wife a lopsided grin.

She glanced at him and blushed. "You give me more compliments than I deserve."

He took her hand, their fingers intertwining. "I could never do that." He looked down at her and caught her smiling.

They walked on and went into his mother's office, but she was not there.

"Where do you think she would be?" Emmaline

asked.

Nicholas pulled back his sleeve and studied his watch. "It's noon. Perhaps she's in the garden." They left the room and hurried into the gardens.

The sun fell from the clouds like beams of light. Blue birds bathed in the top tier of the bubbling fountain. The smell of snapdragons, dahlias, and cornflowers filled the air, as if someone had been spraying flowery perfume all morning.

Nicholas went down the stairs and found his mother sitting at a table covered with white linen and a vase of roses. A host of various delicacies lay scattered across the table, along with some of the finest china in the palace.

Mother looked lovely in her silvery green gown. She took a sip of her tea, watching the blue birds splash each other. She set her cup down and looked up, her eyes widening. "Oh, Nicholas, you're back!" She held her arms out.

Nicholas grinned, warmth flooding through him at her affection. *Thank You, God, for giving my mother back to me.* Just before the ball, his mother had come to him in private and told him she had made amends with Emmaline. She then had asked for forgiveness and a second chance. Nicholas would've given her a thousand chances, so long as she came back to him. In just a matter of weeks, his mother had returned, the bitter imposter gone for good.

Nicholas strode toward her and planted a kiss on her cheekbone. "It's good to be back, Mother." Though he did miss the enchantment Tredan Bay had held over him and his new wife. He almost wished he was there again, riding across the sea cliffs, watching Emmaline's hair dance in the wind.

"I've missed you. The palace wasn't the same without your laughter." Mother held his face in her hands, eyes glistening in the sunlight. She let him go and turned. "Hello, Emmaline."

Emmaline nodded gently. "Hello, Your Majesty."

Mother waved her hand. "Please, Emmaline, you might as well call me 'Mother' now. After all, we are family now, are we not?"

Emmaline smiled. "Of course, Your—I mean, Mother."

Mother beckoned them forward. "Sit down, both of you. I want to hear everything about your stay in Tredan Bay. It's been years since I last went, and I want to remember what it was like." She looked between the two of them as a servant filled two more cups with tea. "What did you do to entertain yourself while you were there?"

"First, we went to the beach," Nicholas said. "The waves were so powerful, the way they roared and tumbled along the shore."

Emmaline gripped the table, eyes wide with delight. "They sprayed the sea cliffs, too. I couldn't believe how high the waves could get."

Nicholas grinned as a memory overtook him. "Emmaline also let me teach her how to ride a horse. It wasn't difficult for her to learn." He jabbed Emmaline's side with his elbow in jest. "I dare say she knew how to all along!"

Emmaline smacked his arm playfully. "I told you before, I didn't know how."

He winked. "Well, anyway, she rode just as well as any experienced rider, I can tell you that. We galloped all across the sea cliffs. The ocean looked as if it never ends, as if it just keeps going."

Footsteps came up the cobblestone path, and a shadow fell upon the white tablecloth. "I hope I'm not interrupting anything, cousin," a man said.

Nicholas glanced up, trying to see past the bright sunlight obscuring his vision. He didn't recognize the man standing there, which was strange, since he'd called Mother "cousin." The broad-shouldered man loomed over the table like a tall tree. His hair matched his eyes, the darkest shade of brown Nicholas had ever seen. He straightened his handsome suit jacket and stepped closer to Mother's side.

"Of course not, Victor." Mother smiled. "My son and his new wife have just returned from their honeymoon, and they were telling me about their stay in Tredan Bay."

Victor glanced at Nicholas. "So, this is the boy you're always writing about." He reached across the table to shake Nicholas's hand, the corner of his mouth rising. "You're the image of your father, my boy."

Nicholas's heart lifted at the words. He'd always wanted to be like his father. Still, he hoped he carried Father's spirit within him more than he resembled him in looks. But he would take whatever honor he was given.

Rise

Nicholas's mother gazed lovingly at him. "I like to think so." Her face twisted as she began to cough. She turned her head, her shoulders shaking from the deep force of the cough. When she stopped coughing, she glanced up, grinning sheepishly. "Forgive me. I must have had something in my throat."

"It is quite floral out here," Victor said. "Perhaps the fragrance overpowered you."

Nicholas nodded. "Yes, of course."

Mother smiled and turned toward Victor. "This is Victor Hughes, Nicholas. He's my cousin on my father's side. We never knew each other until we were teenagers and ever since have written each other many letters. Yesterday was the first day we met again after all this time."

Nicholas raised a brow. "He's from Grandfather's side?"

Victor lowered his eyes and frowned. "Yes, I'm afraid to say your grandfather's brother spent far too much time at pubs and brothels. A prostitute—my mother—gave him a son. It wasn't long after that he drank himself to death."

Nicholas's mother smiled, putting her hand over her cousin's. "Thankfully, Victor is a much better man than his father was."

"I will take the compliment." Victor smirked. "After all, you are not entirely wrong!" He laughed.

Nicholas laughed with him, enjoying the man's strange, though hearty, laugh. He wondered why Victor hadn't visited during Nicholas's childhood. He and

Nicholas's mother clearly got along. Perhaps Victor's lack of visitation would be remedied during his stay, and he could learn all about this mysterious cousin of his mother's.

Emmaline sipped at her tea, ignoring her heart pummeling her chest. Surely she didn't know this man. Surely she was being silly. Where would she have met Victor Hughes? Where would she have come in contact with the queen's cousin? When she had been on the streets, covered in grime and starving? Certainly not!

"You're very lucky, my boy," Victor lifted his cup, smiling at Nicholas. "Your wife is as lovely as a goddess."

She didn't like him ogling her like that. She felt like a piece of meat lying in front of a ravenous man. She drew closer to Nicholas and caught his hand in her own, but smiled, not daring to expose her fear.

"Yes, she is." Nicholas grinned.

Victor sipped his tea as he slouched in his chair. "It's a shame that your honeymoon has come to an end." He set his cup down. "I'm told that they never last long enough. But all good things must come to an end, unfortunately." He smiled, though it seemed more like snarling. Was she losing her sanity? Or did she really know him?

"Yes, unfortunately," Nicholas agreed.

Emmaline spoke before realizing what she was doing. "So if you and Genevieve have not visited since you were young, what have you been busying yourself with?" She pressed her lips together, hoping she didn't sound intrusive. *Wait a moment—my husband is the crown prince of Tregaron. I can ask him anything I wish. And besides, I have to know who he is.*

Victor swung his arm over his chair, sitting sideways but still looking at her. "I was away on military missions, not unlike your dear husband. I was captain for quite some time but have been recuperating after acquiring some injuries. I have missed my ventures."

"He's a military hero," Genevieve chimed in, smiling proudly. "Decorated with many honors by Admiral Conroy himself."

Emmaline nodded. "I see."

"You do flatter me, cousin." Victor smiled. "Though it is somewhat deserved." He stood and straightened his suit jacket. "Well, I've got to be going. There are tasks I must attend to before supper is prepared." He glanced at Nicholas. "It was nice meeting you, my boy."

Nicholas nodded. "You as well."

Victor turned his gaze to Emmaline. "And of course, you too, my lady."

Emmaline swallowed the rising bile in her mouth. "A pleasure."

"Until supper, all." He turned away, his shadow following him as he left.

Emmaline watched him leave, unable to take her eyes away. Something wasn't right. Surely this feeling must have a source. And despite all her resolve to remain hopeful, to believe she was finally safe, Emmaline couldn't shake the feeling that a snake had entered the garden.

Chapter Nineteen

MOONLIGHT FILLED THE cathedral, its pure beams sanctifying the holy relics within this hallowed place. Ross sat on his knees before the crucifix, his head bowed and his heart galloping.

"God." He swallowed, surprised at the cracking of his voice. "I know that I am not very good at praying quite yet. My faith is still new. But I cannot help but ask you to guard this city of mine. I have heard rumors and whispers of someone moving in the shadows, ready to destroy my people. Guard them and protect them.

Take notice of them . . . and of me, and answer my prayer."

Ross couldn't remember a time in three years that he had trembled in fear, but he could not help it in this cathedral in the witness of God. Who was he that he could speak to God? He who had rejected Him countless times? He who had turned away from His voice? He didn't deserve to stand in this moonlit chamber or to bathe in the light breaking through the darkness.

But how could Ross not ask for help, given the circumstances?

He had to tell Emmaline. It was time for her to know. He had waited long enough, perhaps too long. But when? No one else could know besides her, at least not yet. He had to keep her safe, shield her from harm as long as he could. There was no telling if those in the shadows were already well-aware of the princess's true identity.

All thoughts of romance had slowly died since the wedding. Ross had prayed they would. But his friendship with Emmaline was still alive, and he would put his neck on the line to keep her safe.

Ross stayed on his knees, staring at the crucifix until his eyes burned from the candlelight. *Please, God. Place Your angels around my people.*

Ross waited, waited for a sign that his request had been heard: a draft of air falling over his shoulder, the room brightening—anything.

Nothing happened. He stood to his feet to leave the room. He had to leave the matter to God. Ross had prayed about it, and now he had to trust Him.

A girl stepped inside the doorway just as he left it. She turned toward him, a look of surprise falling over her ivory face. "Aren't you Captain Ross?"

Her red hair, flowing over her shoulders and falling around her face, caught his attention. "Yes." He gazed at her, trying to remember where he had seen these fiery locks before. "And you're Anna."

"Yes, I am." Her cheeks colored slightly. "You were in the cathedral?"

Her emerald eyes seemed to glint off the candlelight. "Yes. Yes, I was." *Why is she asking?*

Her smile grew, which seemed impossible given its already large size. "Oh, that's wonderful. Emmaline told us that we needed to pray for you."

"She did?"

Anna nodded. "Yes. And I have. Every night." She glanced down, blushing again.

Something swept through him. Who was he that such a gentle soul would pray for him? "Thank you."

"Of course." She stepped further into the cathedral, then turned around quickly. "It was a pleasure to officially meet you."

He liked her clipped, soft voice. "You as well."

She glanced at him once more, then practically skipped down the aisle. Ross watched her kneel at the altar before turning away. He walked down the halls, hypnotized by Anna Edwards' green eyes.

Emmaline moved her hair to one shoulder and brushed her curls. Nicholas had started a fire in the hearth. The flames flickered and crackled, glowing against the brick.

"It's odd for it to be chilly like this in August," Nicholas said while changing behind the dressing screen. She heard his shirt fall to the floor.

"Perhaps a storm is coming," Emmaline stepped toward the window, the moon casting a silvery glow on the garden below. The fountain twinkled with moonlight, spraying what seemed to be diamonds and not water. A shadow moved across the cobblestones. A long shadow.

She pressed her hand against the cold glass, straining for a glance. Her pulse jumped in her throat. Was it Victor? What was he doing, walking in the garden late at night? She held her breath, waiting to see who it was.

A golden-haired man walked down the garden path. Emmaline's mouth fell as she moved closer to the window and pressed both hands to the glass. *Ross?* What was he doing? And where was he going?

He put a cloak over his head and walked up the path, then he turned and looked straight at her window. She gasped, jumping behind the curtain. He couldn't know she was watching him. He might think her intrusive and distrustful.

Peeking around the curtain, she watched the guard at the gate open the entrance for Ross. He left the palace yard, disappearing into the fog of Lauderbury.

What could he possibly be doing so late at night? Was it some mission of his? Was he in search of a criminal? It was not his job to hunt down such ruffians, but she knew he would not care. He had tracked down the couple that had abused Minnie, hadn't he? Besides that, she had heard other guards retelling several stories of Ross's dangerous feats, of the many criminals he had encountered. What if this criminal was more dangerous than all the rest? What if he—

Hands gently squeezed her shoulders. Emmaline jumped.

Nicholas laughed. "Forgive me. I didn't mean to frighten you."

Emmaline breathed a sigh of relief, turning around. "Oh, it's all right, my love. I suppose I was faraway in my thoughts."

"Yes, I suppose you were."

She reached out and held Nicholas's shoulders. "I'd love to know how you've never managed to meet your mother's cousin. Especially since they seem to have such a good relationship."

He shrugged. "I don't know. She never talked about him—not that I remember, anyway. Perhaps she didn't want me to know about my great-uncle's behavior."

She chewed her lip. "You're going to think I'm airheaded, but something about him seems familiar to me."

Nicholas laughed. "Wouldn't that be odd, that you've

met him and I haven't?"

Emmaline chuckled. Nicholas was right. It would be odd. It was time to put all her ridiculous notions out of her mind. She pulled slightly away to look at him. "I like you in your nightwear. You look very dashing." She giggled.

He gave her a lopsided grin. "More dashing than my uniform?"

She laughed. "Perhaps."

He raised his brow. "Well then, perhaps the attire at our balls should be nightwear from now on. By order of Princess Emmaline."

She threw back her head and laughed, her whole body vibrating with the pulsing joy of it.

"I may look dashing in my night clothes, but you look unearthly in anything."

She felt her cheeks catch fire, and quickly slapped her hands against them to hide the ruby shade. "Except when I blush."

He pulled her hands away. "Especially when you blush." He kept his hands on her cheekbones, gazed into her eyes, and kissed her. All thoughts of Victor and Ross and mysteries vanished as the floor turned to vapor.

Nicholas pulled away and took her hand, leading her to bed. He climbed in after her and spread the blanket over them. He turned the lamp out, and the darkness swallowed the room and the joy that had thrived in the light.

Emmaline, in her childish fear, drew closer to

Nicholas and pressed her cheek to his iron-like chest. He wrapped his arm around her shoulders, and she closed her eyes, pretending she felt safe. Pretending she didn't hear voices in the dark.

Torches burned like tall stakes in the ground, each torch placed strategically to form a wide circle in the plain. The moon kept a watchful gaze over the cloaked crowd, but the stars hid behind the thick clouds of dusk.

Ross weeded his way through the throng of men and headed toward the front, where a man stood atop a wagon. The man's clothes revealed that he was middle-class, neither wealthy nor poor. In fact, most of the men gathered in the valley were dressed similarly. Only a few were decorated with patches and rags.

Ross glanced over his shoulder. More men trickled into the circle guarded by the torches. There were at least a hundred men here, if Ross counted right.

Ross made it to the front of the crowd but stayed behind the first row of men. He couldn't chance being recognized.

The man on the wagon had already begun speaking, but now Ross could hear the words coming from his coarse voice. "Gentlemen, we cannot go on like this! If we are not careful, these outsiders will take everything that belongs to us as citizens of Tregaron for themselves. We have to fight for our city!" The man's face was orange against the flames and his black eyes twinkled in the dim light.

"Fight for our city?" a man a few feet away scoffed. "The bloody war hasn't even stopped, and you want us to fight some more?"

A few others grumbled in agreement.

The man on the wagon glanced over the crowd, his jaw set. "I know we're tired of fighting, but this time, it promises to reap benefits for us all."

"What kind of benefits?" another man asked.

"The money kind."

Murmurs rose from the crowd. Ross studied them all. Didn't they have homes to go back to? Wives and children? They didn't look like men who would stand in the dark, surrounded by torches and meeting in secret. But they were.

"What we gotta do to get this money, Clives?" an older man with crossed arms asked the man standing on the wagon.

"I've got a man who says he'll pay everyone who agrees to follow his orders," Clives said. "I can't tell you his name because we don't want his name getting out for any traitors in our midst. But I can tell you he's more than able to drown each soul here in more gold than any man could dream of."

"Yeah, yeah, but what do we gotta do?"

Clives' upper lip drew back in a hungry snarl. "Kill the Konovians. Every last one of them."

Ross curled his hands into fists and forced away

the urge to kill every man here. His blood roared in his ears, but he took a deep breath in an effort to calm himself. He had to hear what else was said.

An outcry rose from the crowd.

"Kill the Konovians?"

"Women and children, too?"

"You mean, murder?"

"Well, he don't mean to rock 'em to sleep and sing 'em a lullaby!"

A few men turned and walked away.

Clives raised his hands in an effort to win back his audience's attention. "Gentlemen, I know it seems outrageous, but so does letting those outsiders take our homes and our food from our families! They don't belong here! For the past three years, they've been coming into our country, whole swarms of them, like cockroaches breeding under a rock! We must act now!"

A few of the men who had turned away stopped. Their arms were crossed as they shook their heads, but they stayed and listened.

"Yeah, so?" a scowling man shouted. "Why do we gotta kill 'em? Why can't we just run 'em out?"

"The Konovians are a degenerate race of people. They ain't civilized like us. They sell their children into slavery, and the children grow up and start thieving around. Some say they worship other gods. They aren't loyal to Tregaron, either. They're still bitter about what happened to their own country. Any moment, they could rise up against us all. Boss man tried to kill them before, but some of them escaped.

Rise

He was trying to do the world some good by getting rid of them, and now he wants to finish it, once and for all."

Ross chewed on his inner cheek and scowled. *Liar.* The Konovians were a peaceable people, and every one of them had become a citizen of Lauderbury. Every one of them was grateful for what little prosperity they were granted in a city that was not their own by birth. Every one of them worked hard and served God.

"That ain't right, taking vengeance into our hands," a man said. "That's God's job."

Clives glared at the man. "How is it any different from the Israelites killing all the pagans to have the Promised Land for themselves?" He raised his brows daringly. "Tell me that, my good man."

Ross glanced over the crowd. Several of the men were looking at one another, nodding. Something curled and snapped like a viper inside Ross.

"How much does it pay?" a man asked.

Every muscle in Ross's body screamed to rip his hood from his head, tear his sword from its sheath, and plow his blade through every single man standing around him. *God, give me strength.*

"One hundred pounds," Clives said. "One hundred pounds to each man standing here that swears his loyalty to our leader. One hundred pounds to put dinner on your tables, one hundred pounds to buy your wife a pretty dress, one hundred pounds to buy your children some toys and books and things. It's an offer you cannot refuse in times of war."

Silence filled the valley.

Clives scowled at the crowd. "Come on, men. You'd be fools to refuse this money! So we spill some Konovian blood—what does that matter? They're heathens, anyway! We gotta take our city back. They don't deserve to live here. Tregaron's our homeland. We cannot let anyone who refuses to abide by our morals live here with us. So I say, we get rid of them—once and for all!" He punched the air with his fist. "Who's with me?"

All the men raised their fists and roared. "Yeah!"

Like a pack of rats swarming together, the crowd stepped toward the wagon. Ross kept his head low.

"When do we get our money?" a middle-aged man asked.

"When the task is complete, my good man."

"And when will that happen?"

"We gotta wait for the boss man to tell us he's ready."

"How do we know this ain't some trick?" a clipped-voice man demanded. "That there ain't no money? I don't want to wait around for some no-name to get around to tell us when we can get the job done."

Clives crossed his arms. "Don't want to wait around for a hundred pounds? Don't be a fool, just be patient."

A few murmurs went up from the crowd, but Ross had heard enough. He stepped back slowly, making sure no one watched him leave. Once he'd gotten past the torches, he quickened his pace and hurried back toward the palace.

Why would some mysterious "boss man" want to kill the Konovians? They were not the heathens that Clives had described. And even if they had been, murder of the whole population was not a solution. Who was this man with no name? What kind of influence did he wield over the city?

Ross didn't know, but he knew he had to warn the Konovians.

Emmaline had to know. He'd kept it a secret for too long. But when was the right time?

***

Glass shattered. Emmaline jerked her head up and turned. She drew back and held her arm over her mouth, her chest pounding. The palace was on fire.

Flames blazed all around her. They crawled down the walls while smoke foamed at the top. It swallowed and devoured everything it touched. Its hungry roar throbbed in her ears.

Emmaline screamed, cowering backward. She turned to wake Nicholas, but he wasn't there. This wasn't her bed. And this wasn't their bedroom. This was a different place entirely. Snow blanketed the ground below her, and her back was pressed against a leafless tree. She was outside, watching the fire burst from the windows.

If this wasn't the palace, where was she?

She stood, her legs shaking like branches in a storm. Her skirts were ash-soaked and caked with soot. Sharp pain burned the side of her head. When she pulled her hand away, blood stained her fingertips. She gasped for breath.

She looked up at the top of the building, watching the smoke grow and grow. This was her family's house. Inside, their bodies burned while she stood outside in the cold, alive and watching the amber flames destroy everything she'd ever known.

Glass burst again and rained around her like diamonds. She screamed, covering her head with her arms. When she looked up, a man cloaked in shadow came toward her.

The blazes roared as a dark voice pierced her ears. "I might have failed once, but I will not fail again." The man disappeared.

Where did he go? Her heart panged hard, like a church bell caught in rough winds. She saw nothing, except fire, shadows, and spindly trees. *Where is he?*

Flames shot down from above and surrounded her in a circle. She screamed, the tawny tongues leaping toward her. She fell to her knees and covered her face. There was no way out. *Jesus, help me!*

In the licking flames, the voice returned. "I'm coming for you, Emmaline. *You will burn.*"

A scream.

Nicholas jerked off the covers and sprang to his

feet, reaching for his pistol at the bedside. The trigger clicked as Nicholas poised himself for an attack, every fiber of the soldier within him taut and ready.

The scream came again. Emmaline threw her arms against the pillows, shaking her head as her cries grew higher and louder. Nicholas disarmed the gun and dropped it. He leapt back into bed and crawled toward Emmaline. She had her hands pressed against her face now as she screamed over and over. The pitch of her shrieking went right through him.

"Emmy, wake up!" He grabbed her shoulders, lifting her into a sitting position. "Emmaline!"

Her eyes snapped open, round as saucers. She didn't meet his eyes but spoke rapidly, gasps of breath seizing her voice. "Fire—there was fire! It burnt the house. They were in there!"

He gripped her shoulders harder and looked into her face. He needed her to look into his eyes, to see that she was safe. "Who was in there?"

"He told me he wouldn't fail again—he said I would burn!"

"Who said that?"

"He's coming back for me! He's coming—"

"Emmaline!" He cupped her face with his hands, adrenaline seething through him.

She finally looked at him. Tears glimmered in her eyes, and her lips trembled. Her breath was hoarse as her face shattered. "Oh, Nicholas." She buried her head into his chest and shook with sobs.

He rubbed her back gently. "It was just a dream."

She pulled away slightly, tears dripping off her chin. "No, it wasn't. It was real. My family's house, it burned that night. Somehow, I escaped. I woke up in the snow and saw it burning."

"Who said that you would burn?" Rage pumped into his blood. Once he found out, he'd kill whoever had threatened Emmaline. He'd hang that man for all the scars he'd given her.

"It was a man in shadows. I don't know who he was. Fire was all around me. I was trapped. It felt so real, Nicholas." She crumbled into his chest again.

He pressed his cheek against her head and wrapped his arms around her. She fit against him like a hand in a glove. "You're safe now, Emmy. I swear to you, I won't let anything happen to you."

A spark popped against the grate. The bedside clock ticked, matching the crackles of the fire. Nicholas rocked Emmaline, cradling her in arms of safety. Her body soon relaxed against him as she began to breathe deeply. He laid her down gently and rested her head on her pillow. All the lines in her face had disappeared. She was at peace again. He sighed in relief. *Thank You, Jesus.*

He moved a hair from her forehead, her eyelashes stretching over her cheekbones. His heart fluttered in his chest. How could a woman have so much power over him, even when she didn't demand it from him? He didn't mind. He would've given her anything, as long as it made her happy.

Chapter Twenty

NICHOLAS TIGHTENED HIS tie, watching Emmaline shift in her sleep. The sun cast a glow over her face and her milky white nightgown. He'd let her sleep. Her night had been far from restful. He'd decided to visit his mother. It wasn't often they were alone together. Surely she would have these early morning hours to herself.

Glancing at Emmaline one last time, Nicholas left the room and shut the door quietly.

It was oddly silent in the palace. He'd lived here his entire life, and there was always some sort of noise coming from somewhere. But not today. Dust could have fallen from the ceiling and he would have heard it.

Hardly a servant was in sight. Nicholas glanced around as he passed through corridors. He saw a maid every now and then, but the rest of the servants seemed to have vanished entirely. *Where would they have all gone to?*

Whispers throbbed in the back of his mind. Something is wrong. Surely he would've passed someone already.

He walked to his mother's chambers. He'd find her and get to the bottom of this. Surely she would know why over half of her servants were missing.

Nicholas cupped his hand over the doorknob.

"Your Highness!" a man whispered loudly.

Nicholas turned, jerking his hand free from the doorknob as if it been on fire. Sir John Clark, one of his mother's long-time advisors, stood a few feet away. He'd aged a bit since Nicholas had seen him last. His hairline had crawled to the back of his head, and webs of wrinkles hung beneath his eyes.

"What is it, John?" Nicholas didn't like the tight look on the man's face.

John gulped in a breath. "I'm afraid your mother has fallen ill."

A stone dropped into Nicholas's stomach. Ill? Mother had always been strong. "What? How bad is she?"

John lowered his head and stepped closer. "She's very weak right now. It happened in the night. She began coughing severely, and Dr. Reid had a difficult time calming her lungs. We haven't been able to determine if it's contagious yet. The doctor hasn't yet discovered what ails her. But until we do discover what it is, you can't see her. As her heir, we cannot risk your health."

A thousand images flickered inside Nicholas, like the flames of candles in a cathedral. Mother had read him stories as a boy and held him in her arms when he'd been sick or afraid. She'd listened to his stories from his battle days. She'd always been a strong woman, and now she lay in her bed, weak and possibly dying. *My God, Mother could be dying!*

He stepped back toward the door, his heart pounding in his temple. "You don't understand. She's my mother. If something happens to her, and I haven't seen her—I have to see her!"

John ripped Nicholas's hand away from the knob, his brows drawn together. "You can't see her, Your Highness! You mustn't go in there until we know what ails her!"

Every fiber in Nicholas burned as hot blood raced through his veins. A memory. A young boy standing outside a door, waiting hour after hour, day and night for it to open.

A mother, a wife, pounding at the door, demanding to be let inside. Advisors shouting, "You are the queen! You cannot risk your health, Your Majesty!"

A feeling. A feeling of betrayal when the doors finally swung open, finally allowing a little boy and his mother inside, only to find a cold, dead father.

A freight train roared in Nicholas's ears, chugging faster and faster, gaining speed. No, that would not happen again. He'd die before it happened again.

The train flew off the tracks.

Nicholas tossed John aside as if he were nothing more than a sack of flour. John crashed into the wall with a cry of shock more than pain. In an instant, Nicholas had opened the door and stepped across the threshold when John's strong hands gripped his shoulders, pulling him back.

Nicholas stumbled into the hallway, John's actions unexpected. Nicholas's vision spun and clouded, but he regained his footing quickly as John shut the door. Heat flared behind Nicholas's eyes. He gripped John's shoulders, about to fling him aside, when suddenly, John shoved Nicholas backwards with an unexpected force.

"*Pull yourself together, boy!*" John bellowed, a fire in his grey irises.

Nicholas breathed hard, clenching the sides of his head with sweaty palms. He swore under his breath as sobs nearly choked him. He had to calm himself. Was this the behavior of the future king of Tregaron or of a hotheaded boy still grieving his father? His father would be strong and accept reality, rather than try to overthrow it. Nicholas must do the same.

John took calming breaths and straightened his suit. "I apologize for using such force against you, Your Highness, but you have the kingdom to think of, and your new wife. You must calm yourself and use your head."

Nicholas steadied his breath. John was right. He had to think of the kingdom and of Emmaline. If he became ill and died, what hope did they have?

Nicholas waved his hand over his hair, digging his fingers into the thick strands. His pulse vibrated in his throat. "Very well, John."

John's eyes drooped like a bay hound's. "I'm sorry, my boy. I wish there was something I could do."

Nicholas shook his head. He'd heard that line before. It sickened him. "I know."

John nodded. "Well, if you'll excuse me, I have to go see to the servants. I heard that most of them were holding a prayer meeting for the queen."

Nicholas's heart lifted at the news. "Thank them all for me."

"Of course, Your Highness." John walked away and disappeared down the hall.

Nicholas stared down into the abyss of the hall, his thoughts tossing and rolling over each other like waves in a storm. His head felt too heavy for his shoulders. He walked back toward his bedchamber.

He stopped at his bedchamber door, his hand poised to open the door. He couldn't do it. If he went in there, the perfect world Emmaline had just found would burst into flames. Had she not earned a reprieve? How could he wake her from her peaceful slumber so soon?

He pulled back his hand and sank to the floor next to the doorway, his head in his hands.

Dear God, why? Why my mother? So soon after we've mended things between us? Must my mother—

Trust me, My son. I will make everything right in its time.

Something soft touched his shoulder. "Nicholas?" The gentle voice nearly broke him.

He lifted his head. Emmaline towered above him. "Yes?" he answered.

Her wide eyes roved over his face as she frowned. "What's wrong?"

He bit his lip and swallowed back his emotions. "Mother has fallen ill."

Emmaline stared at him for a few moments, as if trying to grasp the severity of the situation. She sat beside him. "Is it serious?"

"No one is allowed to see her. They haven't discovered which illness it is yet, but it doesn't bode well." Nicholas glanced at her. "Emmaline, she's never ill."

She smoothed her thumb over his arm, the way he'd comforted her countless times. "Perhaps that means she will recover quickly, if she's so healthy." She tried to smile. As welcome as her smiles were, they brought little relief as his mother lay ill in the same room his father had died in.

"Are you all right?" she asked, the gold in her brown eyes shimmering.

He nodded, turning away. "Yes. Yes, of course I'm all right."

She caught his hand in hers, her grip gentle but firm. "Nicholas, your mother is sick. I would understand if you were upset or worried."

He shook off his head, trying to shake away her fears. "I'm fine, Emmaline, really."

"Nicholas." Her voice was sterner now.

He could no longer look away. He met her eyes, swallowing.

"Come here." She held her arms out and wrapped them around him. Their bodies closed together as he breathed in her violet scent. As she weaved her fingers through his hair, he closed his eyes.

A rush of memories pulled at him like rough winds. He had been a boy of nine years when he was out chasing frogs along the creek. He'd seen a daffodil growing a few feet away and knew that it belonged to his mother. He'd run back to give it to her. Though her lady's maids had been horrified at the sight of his muddied clothes, Mother had only laughed and accepted his gift. He remembered the way she'd smelled it, closing her eyes and smiling. She had never allowed her queenly duties nor societal expectations to pull her away from him. She was a mother first and a queen second.

Nicholas inhaled deeply. "I'm not all right, Emmaline."

"I know. But you will be."

Would he, when the first woman he'd loved might be dying? He wanted to believe Emmaline but couldn't. No matter how hard he tried, no matter how much he wanted to.

Emmaline barely heard the clink of teacups as she sat in the courtyard. The girls sat around the table with her, enjoying some refreshments as they spoke of the news about the queen. Emmaline could hardly believe the queen was sick. She seemed like such a strong woman, so her sudden ailment was strange.

"How is Nicholas faring, Emmaline?" Anna asked. The girls had tried to call her "my lady," but Emmaline had insisted that nothing had changed between the six of them.

Emmaline sighed, pinching the golden handle of the tiny teacup. "He's upset, more than he lets on, more than he wants me to know. But I can tell that he is worried." He would pretend to be brave, but she knew that inside her husband, there was a little boy that feared for his mother.

"Has she improved any?" Lydia gazed at her from across the table.

"No. In fact, Dr. Reid says that her cough has worsened. Three days have gone by, yet the fever still refuses to leave her." Emmaline bit her lip, blinking back tears. "I'm worried for her. Worried for Nicholas."

She was worried for Ross, too. She had meant to ask Ross where he had gone the night she'd seen him leave the palace yard, but the queen's sudden illness occupied all her time. She didn't want him to know she'd been watching him, but she also didn't want him to get hurt. If he was going out at night to hunt down rogues, he should at least have some of his men with him.

"Is Nicholas prepared to become king?" Julia asked innocently.

"Julia!" Eleanor hissed.

Emmaline shook her head. "No, it's all right. We haven't spoken about it yet. I know that he is, but I also know he is afraid. Who can blame him, after all?" *God, give him the strength he needs. Give me the strength that I need, too.*

"It's terribly sad," Diana looked into her cup dismally. "I can't imagine losing my mother."

Emmaline curled her hand in her lap, trying to pry the old memories of her mother's death away. The way her unmoving eyes had stared at Emmaline's family portrait. The way the blood had pooled around her and soaked the rug. The way that she had–

Footsteps came into the courtyard.

"Ah, Emmaline!" Victor came to the table, a newspaper tucked under his arm. "How are you holding up this week amidst the news?"

Emmaline didn't mean to be snooty, but she didn't like that he referred to her as if they were on a first-name basis. As if he were familiar with her. As if he knew her. She swallowed her bile. "I am well. It is my husband and mother-in-law I fear for."

Victor stared at her. His eyes reminded her of a hawk, the way he studied her like prey. "Yes, that is understandable. But I know my cousin. She is strong. She will recover, and she will return to her responsibilities as queen." He glanced over the table. "Enjoy your company, Emmaline, and your afternoon."

Emmaline forced a smile and then watched Victor leave.

"*That's* the queen's cousin?" Julia asked. The pink color in her cheeks spoke volumes.

"Quite the looker, isn't he?" Lydia grinned.

"He's so much younger than the queen, though," Diana pointed out. "He's at least fifteen years younger than her."

Emmaline folded her hands in her lap. "Nicholas and I met him when we returned a few days ago."

"You mean, Nicholas hadn't met him before?" Eleanor blinked. "His mother's cousin?"

Emmaline shrugged. "Apparently. He told us that he was the illegitimate son of the queen's uncle, King Fredrich's brother. His mother was a prostitute."

Julia gasped, her eyes twinkling in jest. "Scandalous!" She bit into a lemon scone.

"Though his past doesn't seem to have affected his present," Lydia said. "I heard that he's a military hero, and that he earned several honors when he was just starting out. He seems to be a respectable gentleman."

"You think so?" Emmaline asked.

"Do you not?" Anna turned wide green eyes on her.

Emmaline sighed as she remembered the apprehension she felt every time she was in Victor Hughes's presence. "I don't know. I've hardly met him, so I suppose it's unfair to come to such a sudden conclusion about him. He is the queen's cousin after all, illegitimate or not. He deserves my respect."

"Your Highness!" a male voice called.

Emmaline turned in her seat and then stood to her feet when she saw the servant was panting. Something was wrong. "What is it?"

His eyes held hers, and his terror became her own. "It's the queen."

Nicholas pressed his cheek against his mother's arm, holding her hand in an effort to keep her on this side of heaven. Every few moments, she would have a coughing fit, and he would be afraid that would be the end of it.

He wasn't alone in the room. Dr. Reid dampened a cloth while a servant took away what little Mother had eaten. Mother's face was red and sticky with sweat. He had never seen her looking so unkempt before in his life. She had always worn an elaborate hairstyle and one of her best gowns.

He was glad he'd been allowed to see her. Thankfully, she wasn't contagious and could not infect him. But he so wished she'd never fallen ill at all.

Mother's hand tightened in his. "Nicholas, my boy, are you ... prepared ... to become king?"

Long claws seemed to rip his chest open. He wasn't prepared to lose her, he knew that much. But he was prepared to become king, to take her place in providing the kingdom with safety and provision and to strive to be the ruler she had been. He took in a painful breath. "Yes. I am."

Mother nodded. "Good." She sat up slightly as she coughed violently.

Nicholas ran his hand over her cheek, trying to soothe her. "I am prepared, Mother, but you must try to recover. Your reign isn't over."

Mother shook her head. "Yes, it is, Nicholas. It's... your turn... now."

A rushed knock came at the door. When the servant opened it, Emmaline stood in the doorway for a moment, then ran to the bedside, kneeling beside Nicholas.

"Is that you, Emmaline?" Mother asked.

Emmaline swallowed, tears sparkling in her eyes. She smiled. "Yes, it is, Mother."

Mother reached out for Emmaline's hand. Emmaline took it, lifting it to her cheekbone and pressing it to her skin. Mother smiled. "My son's sweet bride. I was... a fool... to not see what... he saw in you." She sat up again, her chest trembling with coughing. Nicholas wanted to give her his lungs so that she would stop coughing so much. He couldn't stand to hear his mother struggling for breath. It was driving him mad.

Dr. Reid came to Mother's side and put the cold cloth on her head. Mother soon calmed down and laid back against the mattress.

"Please, don't apologize," Emmaline said. "There's no need."

Mother shook her head again. "No. I... have to.

Forgive me ... for ... everything. I was ... cruel ... and cold. You didn't ... deserve that." She took a deep breath. "I was ... afraid ... that my son ... would be hurt ... like I am. I lost ... the love of my life ... and it nearly ... killed me. I was afraid ... the same ... would happen ... to my son." Tears rolled down her chin and mingled with the sweat shimmering on her face. "But I realize ... now ... that love ... is worth dying for. I can't ... rob my son ... of the joy ... that I felt when ... his father ... was with me." She looked deeply into Emmaline's eyes. "Promise me ... that you will give my son ... the life he deserves. Give him ... beautiful children. Give him ... all your love."

For months, Nicholas had prayed that his mother's gentle heart would be returned to her. And when the ice within her had finally melted, time had flown by. And now she lay before him sick, disheveled, and breathless. He savored each word and blessing she spoke over him and Emmaline. He savored each breath she took. He savored the touch of her hand in his.

Tears fell down Emmaline's cheeks now, so quickly it could have put the tide to shame. "I promise."

"I want ... both of you ... to promise me ... that you will ... seek God in all that ... you do. Protect this kingdom, nurture ... your children, and ... love each other."

They both nodded.

"Of course, Mother." Nicholas forced a broken smile as he tucked a strand of hair behind his mother's ear.

Mother smiled again, and then sprang up and coughed. She was like that for several moments. When it was over, Dr. Reid cast a glance at Nicholas and Emmaline. Nicholas's world shattered in that one glance.

Emmaline turned to Nicholas, kissed his cheek, and then whispered in his ear. "I'll be outside." She stood to her feet and left the room.

Nicholas glanced at his mother and her paling skin. She was fading fast.

"One of . . . my fondest memories . . . with you, my son . . . is you lying in my bed. You were sick . . . and I . . . insisted . . . that you be . . . put in with me." Mother waved her hand over the mattress. Tears sprang in her eyes and her voice cracked with each word. "And now . . . you watch me . . . dying . . . in my own bed."

Something fat and wet slipped down Nicholas's face. He swiped it away. He had to be brave, at least until she was gone. He leaned against the bed and pressed his head against her arm. "I'll always remember you that way, Mother. How you held me close."

"And now . . . you . . . hold me . . . close." He could hear her smile. She took a deep breath. "But . . . it is time . . . for new things. I have . . . had my time . . . and now . . . it is yours." She took another breath. Her eyes were hazy, like fog drifting over the surface of the sea. "Lead with justice. Lead with . . . integrity. Lead with wisdom. Lead . . . with kindness. Lead with love." Her chest fell deeper and deeper.

She stared at the canopy stretching above her, her eyes and chest unmoving. Nicholas gripped her hand, wishing he could pull her back, but she did not return.

Nicholas cupped her face in his hands. The lines of pain faded from her forehead. "Mother." He pressed his head against hers, willing her to move again. "Mother." Tears streamed down his cheeks and onto hers.

She did not move.

A familiar ache filled him, growing and growing, until every fiber in his body roared with the pain of the ache, cried with the memory of the ache. He buried his face in his mother's side, breathing in her scent as if it were oxygen.

When he left the room, Emmaline stood there, her back toward him. She turned at the sound of the door opening, and seeing him there, came swiftly to his side. He was glad she had been there to catch him, glad that he could crash against her. He would have collapsed without her.

Chapter Twenty-One

FALL ARRIVED EARLY, bringing with it crisp breezes that swept the amber leaves from every tree. The sky rarely unfurled its grey covers to reveal its blue face. Songbirds sang mournful ballads. For a month, the palace staff dressed in nothing but black. The girls told Emmaline that every family in the kingdom wore black, too. It was as if the whole country, and not just its human inhabitants, mourned the passing of its queen.

The funeral had been long and agonizing. The sky

had been so dark, it seemed the sun had ceased to exist. Rain fell from the sky like rushed tears, pelting the ground with despair and fury. No one but the priest spoke. And the worst of it was when Emmaline had watched Nicholas holding back his tears. He finally crashed into her in the seclusion of their bedchamber, his head pressed against her chest as he sobbed. She held him tight, wishing she could hold him tighter, wishing she could take his pain and throw it in the deepest sea.

Emmaline hadn't expected the fairytale to die so soon after marrying Nicholas. He had his good moments and his bad moments. She could tell when he preferred to be quiet and when he wanted to talk about his mother. One early morning, when the sun itself had barely awakened, they sat at the window. Emmaline enclosed her hand in his, hoping to comfort him, knowing from experience it was impossible.

"She used to read to me when I was little," Nicholas had told her. "I loved Charles Dickens the most. Sometimes she would even animate her voice. She was quite good at it. It kept me entertained for at least an hour before bed."

Emmaline was glad that she had the opportunity to help him as he had helped her when she'd been broken and bruised. She often awoke early in the mornings, watching the sunlight filter over her sleeping husband's face. She would pray for strength for him and hold his limp hand against her face. *Please, God. He'll be king soon. He needs Your comfort and strength.*

Help him.

Now the day of the coronation had arrived. The girls had dressed Emmaline in purple, a color they loved to dress her in, and hung jewels around her neck and from her ears.

Emmaline and Nicholas rode in the carriage on their way to the abbey. The horses' hooves clapped against the cobblestone, seeming to join in with Emmaline's anxious heart. Children ran alongside the carriage, cheering and waving. Some people sang songs while others shouted exclamations of joyous expectations for their soon-to-be king and queen.

Emmaline brushed down her skirts, her corset squeezing her lungs. Her hair felt too tight, and a few pins poked her. She wasn't used to wearing her hair up. She wasn't used to any of it. Could she really be queen? Could she really live up to all Nicholas's mother had been? Could she make these people happy? Could she keep them safe?

"Your fear is driving you mad, isn't it?" Nicholas asked.

She glanced at him, willing a smile that didn't come. "Yes."

He took her hand and caressed her knuckles with his free hand. "The only thing keeping me from insanity is knowing that ultimately, it's not up to me. It's up to God. I wouldn't be here without Him, and neither would you, so we simply have to keep trusting in Him."

She could smile then. "I love you."

Rise

Sea waves seemed to crash and billow and play in his eyes. "I love you."

Emmaline watched as Nicholas grew nearer, and closed her eyes when she felt his breath on her face. Their lips touched, and she held his cheek in her hand. This was it. The world they had once known was coming to an end. They were journeying to a new world, a new beginning. They'd be the king and queen there, together, for a reign as long as God allowed.

They were still kissing when the horses' hooves stopped clapping and the carriage came to a halt. Nicholas pulled away, squeezing her hand. He was anxious, she could tell. She squeezed back before the carriage door opened.

"This way, Your Highnesses," the driver said.

It's time.

Jewels. They glittered around Emmaline's neck and sparkled on the scepter in her hand. The crown the priest placed on her head was heavy. *God, give me the strength to carry this crown. Let me be deserving of it. Mold me into the queen that this kingdom needs.*

Nicholas sat in the throne next to hers, wearing his own crown. The crown weighed arduously, making her neck and shoulders ache already. The weight appeared to be nothing for Nicholas. He was born for this life, born to rule, born to become king. She was just a girl, wearing the jewels of queens before her.

St. Sidus Abbey shimmered in the bright rays of the sun spraying through the mosaics. The black and white marble floors glistened in the candlelight. The room was heavy with the scent of flowers and peppermint and melting wax.

Hundreds of eyes stared back at her, watching in silent anticipation. Emmaline could feel her heart thumping in her throat. She stared at the mosaic on the wall in front of her. The mosaic depicted Jesus ascending to heaven, the light of heaven crowning His head as the disciples watched from below.

"As she holds the holy properties," the priest announced, "and is crowned in this holy place, I present to you... Queen Emmaline!"

The crowd cheered, applauding and shouting and calling out blessings.

"Long live King Nicholas! Long live Queen Emmaline!"

"May God give them heirs to take the throne after them!"

"May God grant them peace and prosperity!"

Emmaline glanced at Nicholas, her eyes glassy and burning with tears. Chills pulsed through her whole body, as if a sudden breeze had overtaken her. Nicholas smiled back at her, swallowing his own tears. He rose from his throne, and she joined him. The cheers and applause roared even louder.

Emmaline held her head high, the diamonds on the chandeliers nearly blinding her. Where was that orphan girl, hiding in the streets and running from her past? Had she ever actually existed? It had been so long since Emmaline had seen her, it was as if she'd never been real at all.

Now she was a queen, drowning in purple satins and glimmering jewels. She was the wife of a king and was quickly gaining the love of her new subjects. In all her days wandering long roads, she never would have dreamed of a palace. In all her days of almost dying, she never would have dreamed of rising again. But she would. She would rise again and again.

The clouds hanging over Lauderbury were heavy and dark. The sky grumbled and growled as the clouds gathered together, as if preparing for war. A slight breeze pulled at Victor's suit jacket. The sun was nowhere in sight. Just the way he liked it.

He'd been walking for hours, up and down the cobblestone streets. He was far beyond what was known as "Rich Man's Avenue," or, in other words, the finer parts of the city. Rats dodged carriages and horses, squeaking as they escaped from one dark alley to another. Drunks slung glass bottles into each other's heads, the shattering almost drowned out by cursing and jeers for the fight to escalate.

A woman whistled at him from the doorway of a brothel. He turned and drank her in from top to bottom. Fire grew inside him as she winked at him. **Not tonight**, a voice warned. **When you're through with this, you can have dozens like her.** He turned away and kept walking.

The voice had been his strength and stay for the past twenty years of his life, but more so in the last three years. His captain had taught him black magic when he was a young, inexperienced soldier. Captain Polov had seen Victor's potential and knew he was destined for success. And he knew just how he could help Victor capture that success for himself. He'd given Victor a ring of black onyx stone, promising that if Victor obeyed the magic's whims, the magic would give Victor the glory he wanted, the glory that was stolen from him.

For the first year, Victor had learned to trust the magic more and more. He had to admit, he had been reluctant to believe Polov's promises at first. But the magic proved it was more than capable of fulfilling Victor's desires. First, he used it on measly subjects, victims of his boyish wrath. Then the targets became bigger and bigger. The more magic he used, the more he craved vengeance against all who had ever held power over him. And one night, his scavenging for meager meals came to an end. He finally feasted on what was only the first course. The ring had spoken to him like a voice. Together, he and the ring had gotten the job done. If he played his cards right, he would feast again until he'd had his fill. The ring was wise in all its commands to Victor.

Well, at least partially. It was not until recently that Victor had learned the ring had not caught one technicality that had proven to be disastrous. It was probably that God that everyone worshipped in those cathedrals that had muffled the magic's power that night. Now Victor had to clean up the ring's mess.

Heat shot across his finger, sizzling the blood beneath his skin. Victor swore under his breath.

Obviously, the ring did not appreciate such disloyal thoughts.

But of course, the ring had more than made up for that one mistake. With it, Victor already had so much and so many in his possession that he could almost see his plan coming into being. At last.

Children ran past Victor, splashing the murky puddles and spraying their tattered clothing. He was getting closer.

Undergarments and shirts hung from laundry lines and billowed in the quickening breeze. Babies cooed and cried in prams outside, their mothers inside cooking what smelled like cabbage. A group of young men sat at a makeshift table of barrels, arm-wrestling one another. Young girls wore crowns of decaying flowers in their hair and danced to a make-believe orchestra. Old men with long beards sat outside with pipes, watching him walk along the street.

Heat filled his blood as he curled his fists. Victor kept his head down and kept walking.

Over a hill of cobblestone, a building began to crest. It was short and made of brick. The shattered windows smiled back at him like someone with missing teeth. The doors squeaked as he stepped inside and straightened his suit jacket.

Victor breathed in the scent of beer, tobacco, and

sweat. A group of old men played cards and slapped coins onto the table beside him. Young men sat at the bar singing incoherently as the barman filled their glasses with amber liquid.

Victor craned his neck, searching the shadows for some lonely soul drinking by himself. In the back corner was a man hunched over his glass, the dim light from the tiny window grazing his pale face. Victor grinned. He'd found his man.

Victor sat across from the man at the table. The man's suit jacket was patched, and his hair fell over his forehead like an oily, black wave. Stubble peppered his angular jawbone, and dry blood stained his bony knuckles. Victor had to bite back the laugh bubbling inside him. This man was almost too perfect.

"What do you want?" the man sniffled without looking up.

"I have a proposition for you."

The man's gaze raised then. His green eyes glinted with annoyance. "What sort of proposition would a man like you have with a man like me?"

Victor leaned back, making himself comfortable. "First, I need to know your name."

The man scowled. "Suppose I'm not interested in this proposition of yours?"

"Then I would call you a fool and say that you weren't getting any money."

The lines of rising anger left the man's face. "Money? How much?"

Victor wagged his finger as if he were a professor

reprimanding a schoolboy. "No name, no money."

"It's Harry. Harry Little."

Victor grinned. "Good. Very good."

Harry gripped his cup tightly. "I told you my name. Now tell me about the money."

"Patience, Mr. Little. Now, judging you merely on your appearance, I would say that you need the money very badly. Your knuckles are also bloody, so that must mean you're a very hard worker."

"I am. Have to be, place like this and being a father. I got four kids and a wife to feed. Can't afford to be lazy when you're poor. Don't get no help from nobody, either. Except for one man. But that was long ago, and everything's worse off now."

The aroma of tobacco and ale wafted in Victor's nose and filled him with warmth. "Would sixty pounds hold you and your family over for a while?"

A smile broke across Harry's face, like the sun breaking out from behind the clouds. "Sixty pounds! I would say so." His smile faded slightly. "What would I have to do?"

Victor glanced across the saloon. The old men were still playing their card game, and the young men were still singing half-heartedly from the bar. Victor turned back and leaned closer to Harry. "Kill the new queen."

Harry's face was alabaster white, and his eyes grew twice their size. "What do you take me for? A fool? How could I do that? A husband, a father, a working man, and you want me to risk my neck for money? Ain't worth it. Ain't worth it, mister." Harry rose from the table, his chair legs screeching and scraping the floor.

Victor snatched Harry's wrist and pulled. Harry fell back into the chair, his eyes dazed until they focused on Victor.

Now that Victor had touched Harry, he could get him where he wanted him. The ring would work its magic. All Victor had to do was lace his words with enough appeal to fool this half-brained Konovian.

Victor leaned in close and kept his voice low. "Listen to me, Mr. Little. Who is worth more to you: the queen or your family? Wouldn't you do anything to provide for them? Winter is coming quickly. Do you really want to watch them starve to death this winter while the young queen dines on the finest fowl in her marble palace? She doesn't care about you or your children or any family like yours. Tell me who deserves to live: your beautiful children, or a queen who doesn't care?"

Victor leaned back and released his sharp hold on Harry's wrist. He watched Harry's eyes rotate back and forth. Color came into his pasty cheeks. The scowl returned to his face as his jawline hardened. Victor's words had hit their mark.

Harry glared into Victor's eyes. "Sixty pounds, you say?"

"Sixty pounds to feed your innocent children, Mr. Little."

Harry glanced down at his trembling fingers

drumming the table.

Impatience slithered through Victor. He was ready to strike the man if he didn't give him an answer, but he swallowed the venom rising in his throat. "Her life, for a price."

Harry was silent for a moment more, then met Victor's gaze, a new darkness in his eyes. "I'll do it."

Exultation filled Victor's lungs. He stood to his feet and gave Harry's shoulder a jubilant slap. "Good man, Mr. Little, good man." He pulled the pouch out from his pocket and set it in front of Harry. "Your children's destiny is now in your hands."

Victor stepped toward the bar and set down another pouch. "Drinks for everyone," he told the barman. All the men roared with joy and clapped their hands.

Victor stepped outside, tightening his suit jacket against the brisk cold. He took a couple steps, then glanced at the streets and spit. He hoped those cursed Konovians choked on their drinks.

He glanced down at his hand. The faint sunlight captured the shine of the onyx stone. This ring would serve him well again and again, until every fortress that stood in his way crumbled to the ground and fell at his feet.

Chapter Twenty-Two

"I WANT THOSE two horses leading the king and queen's carriage," Ross commanded. He pointed at Thomas. "Bring me my horse and saddle."

Thomas hurried off across the stable yard. Ross remembered being new and wanting to please the captain. Of course, that was before Ross found out what a snake the captain had been. Then he'd quickly realized that it wasn't the captain's favor he needed, but the queen's. He missed her quick wit. Still, Nicholas was just like his mother, making wise decisions for

Rise

the good of his subjects. Even if she was dead, the queen lived on in her son's spirit and reign.

Thomas led Ross's horse Felix across the stable yard, the stallion's black coat gleaming in the sunlight. "Thank you, Thomas." Ross took the stirrups from the boy.

Thomas nodded, then skirted away.

Once Felix was saddled, Ross walked him toward the carriage being prepared for Emmaline and Nicholas. Today, the king and queen would go on a carriage ride, a parade for the people. It was a good day for a parade. A little breezy, but good weather, nonetheless. He'd heard many of the servants say that all of Lauderbury had been looking forward to this, setting aside their daily work for a few hours to watch the king and his wife ride through the city.

He was glad Emmaline and Nicholas were in such good standing with the people, though he was not surprised by it. After four years of bullets blasting through sinners and saints alike, the people needed the inspiration that came with young faces.

The whole palace had been buzzing with excitement about the parade for the past two weeks. All the servants would send the king and queen off, and then welcome them back when the parade was over. Ross didn't think there was an unsmiling face in the palace—except for Victor Hughes' face. He was feeling unwell, apparently, and would stay behind to rest.

Ross wasn't sure what to make of the queen's cousin. He liked luxury, that was for sure. Not even

Nicholas, with all the riches of Tregaron, dressed in suits as fine as Victor's. He also wore a ring more exquisite than most of Emmaline's own jewelry. Ross had never seen a man wear such a ring: big and almost square-shaped, holding a large onyx stone. Victor also seemed to enjoy conversation—probably because his speech and mannerisms were so eloquent.

Ross supposed he would learn more about the queen's cousin in the coming months. Emmaline had told him, not altogether happily, that Nicholas had invited him to stay for Christmas, which was still a few months away. Despite the somewhat strangeness of the man, Victor did give the young king wise advice and told him stories of his father that were a comfort to him. While not a usual Tregaron man, Victor seemed to be a gentleman.

He positioned Felix beside the carriage. But there was still something odd about Victor. Though a gentleman, something about his mannerisms roused Ross's suspicions, chilled his usually warm blood. And why did he arrive now, right after Nicholas and Emmaline were married? He had been absent from the family for years. Was it no coincidence that—

A head smacked his chest.

Ross grunted and stumbled backward from the force. A burst of red hair filled his vision.

"Oh, please forgive me," a familiar, light voice cried. The red-headed girl bent down.

"Anna." He couldn't hide the surprise in his voice. He'd hardly seen her since he'd spoken with her at the chapel. He bent down and helped her gather the flowers scattered across the grass.

Anna met his gaze, surprise filling her eyes. "Captain! I didn't see you there. I was distracted picking flowers for Emmaline so she could throw them to the crowds." She stood to her feet.

"No harm done. Really." He stood to his full height. "I'm pleased to see you again." He grinned, his heart warming at her thoughtfulness.

She gazed at him for a moment, smiling shyly. "Yes. Me, too."

A flower rested in her hair, weaving its way through her curls. It must have flown into her hair when she dropped her bouquet. He stepped forward slightly and pulled the tiny pink-petaled flower from her hair. He held it out for her to take.

Her cheeks grew pink, and she glanced down, biting her lip. Timidly, she took the flower from his hand. "Thank you."

Her delicate fingers were cold, yet they sent heat up his arm and into his neck. Somehow, he managed to smile.

Anna cast her green gaze onto the palace. "Well, I have to find Emmaline and give these to her."

"I'll see you soon, then."

She smiled. "Yes." She turned and hurried off.

He watched her go. *She could turn any season to spring with that smile.*

"Ready, Emmaline?" Nicholas straightened his jacket as he stood in front of the mirror.

"Almost," she called from behind the dressing table.

He laughed. "When I was a boy, I hadn't any idea what my father meant by saying that waiting for a woman to get ready was like waiting for winter to end. Now I do."

She peeked around the side, a playful scowl on her face. "*Men* don't have to wear corsets." She stuck her tongue out, then disappeared behind the dressing table, giggling. Like him, she preferred to dress herself, rather than depend on her maids for this task.

"True." He grinned.

Finally, Emmaline emerged from behind the dressing table, her hair brushed to one side and her head down. She turned around, her back facing Nicholas. "Can you fasten the last few buttons? I can't reach them."

"Of course." He stepped toward her and buttoned her bodice. His fingers brushed her skin as he gazed at her ivory neck and the long brown curls spilling over her shoulder.

She turned around, her gaze soft on him. He leaned forward and kissed her, long and warm, until a knock came on the door.

"Your Majesties, the captain is ready."

Nicholas moved away. "We're coming!" he called. He turned and grabbed Emmaline's coat from the wardrobe. He helped her into it and then hurried out of the bedchamber.

Anna came around the corridor, her cheeks pink and her smile giddy. "Oh, Emmaline! There you are." She held out a bouquet of wildflowers. "I wanted to give you these. I thought you could throw them into the street for the people as you pass by."

Emmaline gasped in delight. "What a wonderful idea. Thank you, Anna." She took the flowers from the girl and embraced her.

Once released from Emmaline's grasp, Anna backed away. "Have a good time, both of you."

Nicholas nodded. "Thank you, Anna."

Emmaline shared a smile with her friend before turning away and leaving with Nicholas.

The breeze was swift across Nicholas's face as he and Emmaline came outside to the stable yard. Emmaline took his hand, her eyes bright with excitement. She'd been looking forward to this parade for some time, so it was no surprise how quickly she walked down the staircase. Nicholas could barely keep up.

Ross stood in front of the open carriage, the door already opened. "You're both looking well, Your Majesties," he said.

"Thank you, Ross." Emmaline grinned.

Nicholas helped Emmaline into the carriage and sat beside her. A servant handed them a blanket, and Nicholas covered Emmaline with it until she was stuffed tighter than a turkey.

"Nicholas, leave some for yourself," she protested.

"I don't want to take it all!"

"As your husband, it's my duty to prove chivalry isn't dead." He grinned at her.

She shook her head. "Far be it from me to claim that it is when I have you."

"Ready, Your Majesties?" Ross asked.

Emmaline nodded so quickly that Nicholas was afraid her head would loosen from her shoulders.

Ross turned and mounted his stallion. He led the way, and the driver urged the horses on their carriage into a trot. Three guards rode behind the carriage.

Emmaline took Nicholas's hand from under the blanket and turned to him with the biggest smile he'd ever seen. "This is so exciting!"

He laughed. She was excited about the parade, but he could hardly wait to watch her excitement. He slid in closer towards her, wrapping his arm around hers as their fingers weaved around each other.

Ross led them out of the stable yard and through the gate. Soon, the crowds on either side of the street came into view. The people cheered like they had the day of his coronation. He waved at them with his free arm as Emmaline threw Anna's flowers. Some people tossed roses into the street, and a few landed in the carriage. Emmaline caught one thrown by a young boy and kissed the pink petals. The boy gasped, tugging his mother's sleeve and pointing at Emmaline, obviously thrilled that Emmaline had caught the rose.

"So, is this parade everything you'd hoped?" Nicholas asked, continuing to wave to his subjects.

She nodded. "So many subjects came to see us."

He grinned in jest. "Surely you must realize that they all really came to see their king's beautiful wife."

She blushed, giggling. "You flatter me."

He raised his brows, feigning seriousness. "I speak truth." He pointed at a throng of subjects talking amongst themselves. "Look? They're talking about you. They're saying, 'Would you look at our new queen?' 'She's so lovely.' 'How in the world did King Nicholas win her affection? She must be half-blind!'"

Emmaline laughed, pressing a hand to her mouth. "Oh, Nicholas."

He grinned at the melodious ringing of her chuckling. His fingers found their way to hers as he turned his gaze to the crowd. Children danced and spun colorful ribbons through the air. Their parents called out blessings on Nicholas and Emmaline. Warmth filled his chest.

He remembered doing this with his mother and father as a boy. Everyone had always looked so happy to see them. He hoped to carry on the tradition with his and Emmaline's own children.

Movement caught his eye. A man in a black coat and a flat cap weaved through the crowds, never looking up from the ground. Nicholas's heart thumped.

"I'm sure many of the young women are jealous of me." Emmaline smirked. "After all, you're very handsome. Any girl could see that."

Nicholas barely heard her as he kept his gaze on the crowd. He couldn't see the man anymore. It was as if he'd been swallowed by the throngs of cheering subjects. Perhaps he had been a figment of Nicholas's imagination. Nicholas turned toward her and forced a grin. "Uh . . . thank you."

She smiled before turning to wave at children calling her name.

Nicholas searched the crowd again, just to make sure the man was still gone. He stopped on a pair of dark eyes scowling back at him. The man held something. Metal. Glistening metal.

A gun. Pointed at the carriage.

Nicholas jerked his hand free of Emmaline's and shoved her to the floor of the carriage. She cried out as she smacked the wood, the wildflowers scattered around her.

A familiar roar filled the air, and the burning sensation that he still felt in his leg shot through his chest. The horses screamed, and the crowds joined them, running into the street, running from the gunshot.

Emmaline shot up from the floor as he struggled to breathe. She screamed, touching the wound. Her face was pale, and her eyes were wild. "*Nicholas!*"

He grabbed her shoulders to force her back down on the floor, grinding his teeth in pain. "Emmaline, get down! It's not safe up here!" He didn't like shouting at her, but he had no choice.

She didn't listen. She clambered up on the seat, ripping the blanket from the floor and pressing it against his wound. He grimaced in pain. Emmaline gasped deeply over and over, pitiful sobs bursting

Rise

from her at intervals.

"Emmaline, get down!" His head pounded as the world rolled around, hazy and grey. He fell back against the seat, the blood draining from his shoulder and onto the blanket.

"I can't!" She sobbed. "I have to help you!"

Ross was shouting. "After him!"

The guards behind the carriage took off toward the man with the gun.

"Get to the castle!" Ross bellowed.

Emmaline grabbed his shoulder, her grip hard as she pressed the blanket to the wound. He grimaced and tried to focus on her face. "Emmaline, get down. Get down. Please."

She shushed him, her tears pouring against his shirt. He wanted to tell her all would be well. He wanted to tell her he would make it. He wanted to comfort her, to scare away the ghosts that were certainly haunting her now. But how could he, when even he wasn't sure he'd survive?

Ghosts screamed and shrieked in Emmaline's ears and dragged their icy nails down her back. The horses squealed as they flew down the streets. Nicholas's blood stained the blanket and her hand. His face was white as ivory as he stared up at the sky, panting. The world spun, spun, spun, and Emmaline was quickly falling into the past.

Nicholas's face was James's face. Was Papa's face.

Was Mama's face. Was her sisters' faces. So many faces. So many faces.

She whispered prayers under her breath, unsure of what she was saying. *God, please. Please, let him live. Let him live. Let him live.*

Ross leapt off Felix's back when they were in the stable yard. Emmaline could barely breathe, barely stand. Her legs shook as if she stood on quaking ground. Two of the guards took Nicholas and carried him into the palace. Emmaline ripped her skirts from the ground and ran after them. Her throat was hot and raw. She hadn't realized she'd been screaming until she heard herself.

Jesus! Jesus! You can't take him from me! Please, don't take him from me.

Ross ran off to find Dr. Reid. The two guards flashed through the hallways toward Emmaline and Nicholas's bedchamber. They dove into the doorway and toward the bed, laying Nicholas across it.

Ross and Dr. Reid stormed through the doorway. The doctor's face was grey and panicked as he rushed to the bedside. He glanced at Nicholas's ruby red chest, and then looked from Emmaline to Ross.

"Get her out of here." Dr. Reid's words came out slow and seemed to echo.

Emmaline did not want to leave. She tried to shove Ross away, barely able to see him through the watery surface of her tears. She pleaded and reached for Nicholas. She had to be next to him. She had to let him know she was near. Why wouldn't Ross allow her to

Rise

stay?

Ross grabbed her around the middle and carried her out. Emmaline pounded Ross's shoulders, but he closed the door firmly and stood in front of it.

Emmaline reached for the doorknob, but Ross moved and blocked her way. "I have to go in! I have to go in!"

How could Ross do this? How could Ross bar her from entering her own bedchamber? She was the queen! That was her husband in there, bleeding to death and lying unconscious! How dare he keep her away from her husband? Didn't he know Nicholas could—? Didn't he know that she wanted to be with Nicholas if he—?

"Let me in, Ross! I am your queen. You have no right to keep me from my bedchamber." She yanked at his shoulder to shove him out of the way, but she could not move him.

Ross cast a stony gaze on her, his curls disheveled. "You're right. As your subject, I have no right to keep you out of your bedchamber." He paused. "But as your friend, I think I am bound to keep you from going in there."

She balled her hands into fists, heat rising in her face. "You don't understand. Don't you know that that is my husband in there? Don't you remember that I have seen this before? Don't you realize that he could—?" She dared not finish that sentence. She grabbed at his arm, pulling and tugging and jerking at it. "Let me pass."

He did not remove his gaze.

"MOVE!"

He still did not move.

Sobs shook her and weakened her. She fell to her knees. "Move. Please, Ross. You have to let me in. He needs me. Nicholas needs me. Move. Please."

"I can't." His voice sounded unusual. Broken.

She glanced up and met his gaze. His own eyes shimmered with tears.

Emmaline pressed her hand over her mouth, her whole world shattered glass. *Dear God, this can't be happening again.*

Ross knelt down, still blocking the door, and held out his arms. A sob ripped from her throat as he held her tight. She stayed like that for a long time.

The door opened after several moments. Emmaline's neck ached from the speed at which it jerked up. The guards stood there. "What news?" She barely recognized her small voice as she stood.

"Dr. Reid says it will be some time before he can say anything. Apologies, Your Majesty." The guard nodded at her before leaving with the other.

Emmaline watched them leave. Chandeliers crashed to the floor in her memory. She could still hear the roar of the gunshots. The screams of the crowd. The screams of her sisters. Why did death haunt her every step? Why did it hunt the blood of everyone she loved? Why did she break everything she touched?

Emmaline hid her trembling mouth beneath her hand. Ross touched her shoulder as tears escaped her burning eyes. "Emmaline. He's going to be all right."

She looked at him but quickly looked away. She couldn't meet his soft gaze without crying. "I can't lose him, Ross. Not when I've lost everything else."

"You won't lose him."

Emmaline held herself and took steady breaths. If she wanted to survive this, she had to believe. The world was crumbling, but her fortress was strong and sure. *God, I believe. Help my unbelief.*

Ross couldn't imagine that torture could be any worse than watching Emmaline cry with such despair. Though all thoughts of romance toward her had died, he wanted to hold her again, to give her some feeling of safety again. Just when her world had finally stopped burning, someone had lit another match.

Dark thoughts came unbidden toward the man who had shot the king. Ross and Nicholas were good friends. Not only that, but Emmaline's world would crash if she lost someone else.

Ross rubbed his eyes. *God, please. Let Dr. Reid be your instrument of healing for Nicholas. Do not let the enemy have victory through his death.*

Running footsteps came up the hall. "Oh, Emmaline, we've just heard!" Lydia embraced Emmaline. "Are you all right?"

"Of course, she isn't!" Diana retorted.

Lydia glared at Diana. "She knows what I mean."

As the other girls flocked around Emmaline, Anna

stepped toward Ross. Her eyes were pink from crying, and a frown replaced her usual smile. "Any news of the king, Captain?" she whispered.

Ross shook his head. "No. Only that the doctor said it will be a while."

Anna bit her pink lip. "I do hope he makes it. One of the guards told us that Nicholas was protecting Emmaline from the assassin."

Hot and cold washed over Ross. "Protecting her?"

Anna nodded. "Yes. He said that Nicholas shoved her to the floor of the carriage."

It was as if Anna had punched him in the middle and made him lose his breath. Had the bullet been intended for Emmaline? What if Nicholas hadn't noticed the gunman? Ross hadn't seen the man until after the damage had been done. Ross had been in front, leading the parade. He should have been more careful. Now the king was bleeding in the room behind him, and Emmaline's ghosts were returning.

Someone wanted to kill Emmaline. Had someone from her past returned to finish the job? He remembered the rumors he'd heard filling the shadows of the city. Were these two points connected?

Ross glanced in Emmaline's direction, but she was not there. He caught a glimpse of her running down the hall and around a corner.

If the assassination attempt had been directed at her, it was time to tell her the truth of her past.

Rise

Victor's footsteps pounded down the hall. He gripped his suit jacket, imagining he was choking that Harry Little. What an idiot! What a fool! He'd given the man one job, and he couldn't do it! Victor had awakened with the smell of Emmaline's blood in his nose, and instead, Harry had given him the king's blood. Victor didn't want the king! He wanted the queen. He wanted her dead. He wanted her blood.

The ring had helped him kill dozens of girls like her before, in a dozen different, delicious ways. Not one of them had appreciated that he'd spent all his earnings as a youthful barman on them. One night, they'd welcomed him with open arms. The next, their new customer had kicked him around like a stray cat. The customers had grown more and more violent. One night, when a large man had Victor pinned between the floor and his knee, Captain Polov had come to his rescue. Victor had left that night with Polov, bleeding and bruised and bitter.

Polov had promised him that the ring would satisfy Victor's desires. At first, Victor had thought the man was a lunatic—until Polov had grabbed one of his men and the man had suddenly started choking. As Victor had watched with increasing terror, the choking man had collapsed on the ground, convulsing in the dirt until he became still. With a single touch, Polov had killed the man. And with a single touch, Victor could have the same power.

Victor devoured all he could during the black magic lessons Polov gave him. Then, when the time came, he'd had his revenge on any woman who had dared betray him. He had given one girl, a bishop's daughter, a fate worse than death: a life without love. She had deserved it after stabbing him in the back. It would not happen again. He liked his women to be under his control.

But this girl—Emmaline—defied him with her very existence. No matter how many attempts he made against her life, something kept him and his ring from satisfying their thirst for her blood. Something was protecting her. Someone.

Victor spat on the marble floor. God would not win. His ring would make sure of it.

Fire spread through his body. If they didn't hang Harry before dawn, Victor would do it himself. He'd get his fill of blood at least. He'd kill Harry, and he'd kill Emmaline himself if he had to.

Wait...

Victor stopped in the hall, realization awakening inside him.

What if this is all for the better? This little mistake of Harry Little's might work in my favor. I can still have the queen and all her people.

He grinned to himself before heading to the Tregaron prisons. Yes, this little mistake of Harry Little's would work wonderfully in Victor's favor.

He remembered when his captain had taught him how to play chess. He'd been taught that the queen was the most important piece in the game, the piece that determined everything. Victor's plan would be no different. With Queen Emmaline, the rest of the pieces—and the kingdom—would fall right into his hands.

Emmaline wandered down the halls, her steps slow and aimless. Trembling, she wrapped her arms around herself. Her thoughts were one continuous prayer with mismatched words strewn together like pieces of fabric in a quilt.

Amidst the prayers, her mind flashed to moments with Nicholas. The waves lapping around their bodies, the salt on his skin and lips, his blue, blue eyes gazing at her like a lost sailor who had found dry land.

His hands lifting her veil and resting on her cheeks as he kissed her for the first time as her husband.

Rose petals scattered around her feet as she walked in the gardens. The hopeful joy in his eyes as he dropped to one knee and offered her a star to put on her finger.

His arms around her the day he'd helped her put her family's ghosts to rest.

The way he'd twirled her to the swelling orchestra music the night of his birthday. His lips brushing her knuckles as he'd kissed her hand.

His smile across the table as he defended her against his mother in front of her wealthy friends. The way he'd come after her when she'd been frightened by the shattered bowl. His story-telling as they shared supper in the kitchen.

His infectious laughter as he chased her across

the glittering snow. His warmth as he pulled her from the icy pond and into his arms.

Nicholas leaning against the doorframe, listening to her play the piano as her back was turned. The way he had first looked at her.

Oh, God. How will I bear it if I lose him?

Emmaline stood in the middle of the hallway, legs shaking as if she were standing on a minefield. She put a hand against the wall and the other across her middle, struggling to breathe.

She glanced up. She was in the coat of arms hall. She'd never been in here before, but she'd heard the girls talking about it. Coats of arms hung along the walls, including Tregaron's coat of arms and the coats of arms from ally kingdoms.

Emmaline gathered her strength and wandered down the room. Anything to distract her.

The coats of arms varied in colors and designs and cluttered the walls. Her footsteps clicked against the marble floors as she descended further along the hall.

A purple coat of arms caught her eye. A cross stretched across the fabric while a bear stood in front of the cross, his teeth bared and his claws ready to strike. Silver stars were strewn across the coat of arms.

Stars. Stars. Where had she seen these stars before? Why did stars follow her everywhere she went? Why were stars, of all things, her guiding light?

A description on a golden plaque rested above the coat of arms: *The Royal Coat of Arms from the Kingdom of*

Konovia.

Konovia. Memories swam through her mind until she was caught in their torrent.

Applause filled a grand ballroom. A grand orchestra paused its symphonies. Emmaline stood at the top of a staircase, watching her sisters make their descent, their skirts swishing.

A man called out with a loud voice, "Announcing Her Royal Highness, Emmaline Marie, Princess of Konovia!"

Emmaline stumbled back and covered her mouth with her hand.

Those were her stars. This was her coat of arms. Her family's coat of arms. She'd seen it a dozen times at parades with her family, at the balls her father had held, at the ceremonies she had attended. It was her country's pride, and the key to her forgotten past.

Konovia. It all came back to her, in a dizzying whirlwind of memories. She stumbled back further, against the opposite wall. She was the princess of Konovia. Her parents had ruled the kingdom with grace and kindness. They, along with their ancestors, had been loyal allies to the rulers of Tregaron.

Emmaline had grown up in a palace. She'd learned to dance at balls and skipped through marble halls with her sisters. Her father had gone away for weeks at a time, forging peace treaties and alliances with neighboring countries. The palace guards had treated little James like their own brother and taught him how to use a sword. The crowds had cheered as her family rode by in carriages in parades. She remembered.

She remembered it all now.

No. It can't be true. Surely it isn't.

But the coat of arms was there, reminding her of everything she had known and everything she had lost.

She'd once been a part of the Konovian royal family. And now, she was the only one left.

Emmaline snatched her skirt and ran from the hall. Her breath ripped out of her body, her body flashing hot and cold. Her legs pumped as her feet flew across the floor. Running was what she did best. Running from the past. Running from the pain. Running from the truth.

They'd killed off her family, those men who seemed to have come from the darkest shadows. They'd tried to kill her. But she'd awakened with dried blood on the side of her head, the place she'd struck it on the fireplace. Fire had devoured the halls as Emmaline had made her escape through the palace. Paintings and furniture had shattered and fallen to the ground. Smoke had stolen her vision and breath. She'd thrown a vase through a window and then leapt outside into the snow. She'd run as fast as she could through the forest, her head roaring with pain. Then she'd collapsed and fallen unconscious.

Her memories had returned, but they ripped through her like a storm of bullets. Her chest roared with pain, forcing her to stop running.

She looked up. She was in the ballroom. She hadn't even known where she was going. Just far away. She'd spent the last three years running from the past, and just when she thought she could finally stop, her demons had come back.

She craned her neck, spinning around slowly as she took in her surroundings. Her childhood had been spent in a ballroom like this one. She and her sisters had worn lavish gowns and twinkling crowns. Swelling orchestras had played Swan Lake as candlelight from the chandeliers had shimmered on the iridescent floors. Papa had danced with all his daughters in a circle, his laughter hearty and rich.

Oh, God. How could I forget all that? How can this be? All this time, I thought I was nothing when I was a king's daughter.

Her whole body trembled as she held herself. Beautiful Konovia. How could she forget it? Its rolling hills, its majestic mountains, its shimmering lakes and rivers, and its flower-filled pastures? Her subjects, her family, and her ancestors?

Someone had wanted to destroy all that. Heat rushed through her veins. But why? Why attack a peaceful kingdom like Konovia? Her father would never have started a war with anyone. He'd won many battles protecting other innocent kingdoms, but he would never antagonize someone. Her father had been a good king, a just king, a peaceful king. And they'd slaughtered him like a pig.

Who had done it? Who was the monster who'd sent everything she'd ever known down in flames? Who was the monster who'd caused her to forget who she was and where she came from? Who was the monster who'd taken her family away and left her with the scars of that night?

Tears burned behind Emmaline's eyes as she held herself tighter. She rubbed her lips together in an effort to keep from crying.

"You remember everything now, don't you?" Ross asked behind her.

Her heart fell into her stomach like a boulder dropping into a river. Remember everything? She turned to face him. "What are you talking about?"

He stepped closer, his eyes steady on her. "You've remembered that you're the princess of Konovia, haven't you?"

Emmaline's pulse quivered in her throat. How did he know that? But did it really matter how he knew? She wasn't that princess anymore, and she never would be again.

She forced a smile. "I don't know what you mean. I'm simply here to collect my thoughts." She swallowed. "If you'll excuse me, I want to be alone." She stepped around him and toward the grand staircase.

"Your name," Ross said, his words reverberating around the room and hitting her in the chest. "It was the Grand Duchess Emmaline Marie of Konovia."

She didn't face him. She couldn't. Her body was solid ice. That name hadn't been spoken in years, and now the sound of it ripped her open. "Not anymore. That girl is dead."

Ross's footsteps came behind her, but she did not

turn around. "No, she survived. By some miracle of God, she's alive." The footsteps stopped. "I've known who you were ever since we met."

Finally, she whipped around as heat roared through her. "How do you know? How can you be certain?"

"Because I'm Konovian." He exhaled before continuing. "I went to the parades and saw you and your sisters and your brother walking behind your parents. I watched you being blessed by the priest. I watched you doing the Konovian dances to honor our history."

She closed her eyes. "Don't. Don't do that."

"It's you. I know it's you. I've always known."

Emmaline stared into his eyes, rolling her hands into fists. He had known who she was and didn't tell her? He had kept the truth of her past from her all this time? Heat flooded her cheeks. "Then why didn't you say something? Why did you bring me here to remember everything? The memories have buried me alive. Why didn't you tell me?"

He took her hand, and for the first time, looked afraid. "I wanted to, Emmaline, but it was never the right time. I had to wait until I was certain you were safe."

She looked into his eyes, brown and stony, and couldn't face him anymore. "I have to go. I can't do this right now." She had to get away from him. She did not want to say something she would regret. She did not want to face the past when her future was bleeding to death.

"Emmaline, wait!"

She turned, tears burning her eyes and throat. "Ross, I can't do this right now. Please."

Ross didn't release his gaze on her. "You're afraid. I know. But you can't be. Not now, not ever. Not with that crown on your head."

She stared back at him, her nails digging into her palms. "Who are you to tell me who to be? After you kept my identity a secret from me all this time?" Disobedient tears trickled down her face, one after the other.

Ross crossed the distance between them and grabbed her hand, but he was not as gentle as before. "It was not the right time yet. You must believe me. I would never do anything to intentionally harm you. I know you are frightened, but you cannot allow that to cloud your judgement. You must be strong."

How many times would her heart shatter in just a matter of moments? "How can I be strong, Ross? My husband may die the same way my family did."

His grip softened, and so did his gaze. "I know you're frightened, but you must remember that Nicholas is in good hands—God's and Dr. Reid's. And you are not alone this time. I am here, a survivor like you."

She wanted to believe him, but the icy words screaming in her ears refused to allow it. She couldn't forget the blood draining from Nicholas's chest.

"You have to face your past," Ross said softly. "You have to, Emmaline. There's a shadow descending on your kingdom, and you have to be the one to destroy it."

She pulled away from him. "What do you mean?"

"A small population of Konovians live in the city. Some of the Konovian men of high repute have heard rumors that someone wants to get rid of them."

Her breath trembled and expelled itself from her lips. "Why?"

"The same reason that they destroyed the kingdom three years ago. And now they want to finish the job. And if they're going to finish the job, they'll recognize you and kill you. I have seen these people meeting and plotting to kill the Konovians. There are at least one hundred men in the city that I know of who have agreed to murder our people." Ross sighed. "I'm not trying to frighten you, Emmaline, but just because you and I are the only ones who know about your lineage doesn't mean you can ignore the needs of you people so that you stay safe. God gave you that crown for a reason, and perhaps this is it. Perhaps you are meant to rescue your people."

Emmaline walked into the center of the ballroom, her back toward Ross. She stepped across the reflection of a chandelier shimmering in the floor. She'd been raised in a palace like this one. A glittering palace, with marble halls and exotic rugs that stretched across the floors. She'd been born a princess, a daughter of a king. The people of Konovia had sung her name in parades and thrown flowers at her feet as she passed by. Her name was in their prayers every night. Her people had been loyal to her, so how could she be any less loyal to them? How could she abandon them when the same shadow that had stolen her family would come to steal theirs?

Yet how could she face the wolves again? How could she come so near to death again? If someone was plotting the deaths of the Konovians, Ross was right—it wouldn't be long before they discovered Emmaline's secret and plotted her death, too. Emmaline knew all too well that even the strongest castles do not make good fortresses. Her father's had fallen, and so could Nicholas's. She was not safe simply because she was in the castle. Yet Ross wanted her to step out of her hiding place and defend the Konovians at the risk of her own life?

She turned to face him and shook her head. "I can't, Ross. I am not brave enough."

"Yes, you are." His jaw flexed as sparks danced in his eyes. "You survived for three years on your own. You lived on the streets. Emmaline, when I found you, you were trying to defend yourself from those two brutes. You made peace with your family's deaths. You are braver than you know. Braver than you want to believe. And you have to believe."

Emmaline chewed her lip. Was she brave? Was she really? Was she the queen her people needed? How could she abandon them because she was afraid? How could she hide from the shadows that had followed her for so long and that now descended upon her people?

Something stirred within her. Bravery was a

choice. And it was a choice that she must make, a choice that would determine if she and her people would live or die.

It was time to face the past. It was better for her to jump in front of the wolf pack than to stand behind and allow her whole kingdom to be devoured by them. She had to honor her family and all her ancestors by saving their people. She was their queen. Perhaps this was the moment for which she'd been crowned.

"You'd have to keep it a secret, Emmaline," Ross said. "We do not know who is behind the plot, so we do not know who to trust. Don't tell anyone who you are, even the king."

Emmaline bit her lip again. How could she keep a secret from Nicholas? Wouldn't that put their marriage on shaking ground? How could she crack her marriage's foundation and expect it to go unnoticed? But she had to. Her people's lives depended on it. Her own life depended on it, too. In the past three years, she'd always known that somewhere, in the dark alleyways and in the shadows, the man who had tried to kill her was waiting for her. Waiting to finish her off.

This was her chance. The past had been written for her in her family's blood. And now God had the pen again. He'd had it ever since the assassination of her family, and now the story He'd been writing was unfolding in front of her. It was time to live out the pages He had written for her. It was time to use the crown she'd been given and use it to protect her people. It was time to rise and take her place as queen.

She raised her chin, defying the fear inside. "I'll do it."

Chapter Twenty-Three

CANNONS ROARED IN Nicholas's head as he opened his eyes. The room around him blurred until he blinked several times and righted his vision. His eyes weighed heavy. He wanted to close them again and slip back to sleep.

"Your Majesty?" A man's voice.

"Yes?" Nicholas's own voice sounded gravelly and hoarse.

"Are you feeling well?"

"What?" Why was the man asking him that? Why

wouldn't he be?

A gunshot screamed in his mind. Memories filled him. He had been riding in a parade, with the crowds cheering all around. A man had shot a gun. Nicholas had shielded Emmaline—*Emmaline!* Was she all right? The sleepiness disappeared as adrenaline saturated his veins.

"Emmaline, where's Emmaline?" Nicholas tried to sit up, but the man grabbed his shoulders and pressed him back onto the mattress. The sudden movement sent a searing pain into his chest.

Dr. Reid's face came into view. "You can't move, Your Majesty. You might injure yourself further."

"I need to see Emmaline. Where is she?" He furrowed his brows as he forced his voice to sound more commanding.

"Your wife is safe, Your Majesty. I promise."

"And where is the gunman? Has he been arrested?" If he was still out there, he was still a threat. And if he was still out there, Nicholas would hunt him down himself.

Dr. Reid's peaceful face reflected a calm Nicholas could not feel, not after hearing Emmaline's screams. Not after feeling the burn of the bullet. Not after the whirling ride back to the palace. Not after seeing the dark scowl in the gunman's eyes.

"Yes, Your Majesty. He has been arrested. He's—"

The door swung open. "Nicholas!" the familiar, silvery voice called. Emmaline ran to the bed and collapsed at his side. "You're alive." She wrapped her arms around his neck and pressed her face against his throat. Her breath was warm on his skin. The adrenaline faded as relief that she was unharmed filled him.

Her head rose, and he saw all the emotions he was feeling in her face. She was so beautiful, even with slightly swollen eyes. How long had it been since he'd lifted her wedding veil and sealed their life together with a kiss?

"I thought you were going to die today," she whispered.

He reached toward her with his hand and caressed her arm. "No, my love. I was simply trying to prove to you that chivalry is not dead." He winked.

She smiled and then pressed her lips against his. The adrenaline returned. His whole body burned with every kiss she gave him. This one was no different.

A knock came on the open door, and the sound of footsteps appeared. "I hope I'm not interrupting anything, Your Majesties." Victor stepped toward the bedside. "But I have just been to speak with the man who shot you."

"They caught him?" Emmaline asked, surprise and relief mingling in her voice.

Victor smiled warmly at Emmaline. "Yes, Your Majesty, they did. I would expect nothing less than success from the king's royal guard."

"What did the gunman say?" Nicholas asked. He tried not to harbor hatred toward the man who had nearly taken his life away.

Lines webbed Victor's forehead. "He told us his name was Henry Little. He also revealed his place of residence, so the guards have gone to question his wife and anyone they suspect of being loyal to him." He sighed. "Mr. Little also told me—through some force, I must admit—that you were not his target, Your Majesty."

Nicholas's heart sprang into his throat. "I wasn't?"

"No." Victor shook his head. "It was the queen."

Emmaline's hands turned cold around Nicholas's neck. His skin turned to fire. "Why would he want to kill her?" He tried to shut out the dark thoughts coming to his mind, but several snapped their venomous heads at him.

"For now, it seems Mr. Little was envious. His family is very poor, and he felt that you were flaunting your wealth. He wanted to kill the queen as revenge, but you ruined his plans."

"Thanks be to God," Nicholas added, and Emmaline attempted a smile.

"I'm afraid that is all the talk the king needs for now, Mr. Hughes," Dr. Reid said. "If he wants to get better for the sake of his kingdom and his wife, he must rest."

Victor gave a curt nod. "I agree completely, Doctor." He bent at the waist toward Nicholas. "Get some rest, Your Majesty. You will need it."

Once Victor had left the room, Emmaline turned to Nicholas. She had been surprisingly quiet while Victor had spoken. He supposed she was frightened. He brushed her cheek with his knuckles. "I won't let anyone hurt you, Emmaline."

Rise

She nodded, but fear still shimmered in her tired eyes. "I know." She stroked his hair from his forehead, leaned down, and warmed his skin with her lips. "I love you." She stood and left the room, closing the door quietly.

Nicholas tried to sleep but couldn't. Surely there was more to the story. Why would someone suddenly become angry with him and try to kill Emmaline? Had Henry Little been working alone, or did more people envy Nicholas, too?

He did not know, but he prayed that the fears wrestling him were wrong.

Emmaline bent in the chapel, her knees cold against the floor and her neck aching. She hadn't known the crown would be so heavy. The foundation of everything she thought she'd known these past three years was crumbling.

How could she keep her past a secret from Nicholas? Wasn't her duty to be first and foremost a wife to the man she loved?

"Seek ye first the kingdom of God."

No. It was her duty to look after the oppressed, to protect her people, to be their queen. This was why she sat on the throne and wore the crown.

Emmaline's chest tightened like a corset. Her breath was less than steady as she bowed her face toward the floor. "God, I need You. The Konovians need You. I choose to believe that You made me queen for this moment, for this time. I choose to believe that You want me to save them. Give me strength. Carry me when I am weak. Make me brave. Protect me so that I can save my people."

Victor had said the gunman's family was poor, and Julia had said the gunman had hung himself only hours after Victor had interrogated him. Emmaline felt sorry for the man, but she knew choices came with a cost.

Still, Emmaline remembered shivering at night with nothing but thin clothing to keep warm. She remembered living with a belly so empty that almost anything looked appetizing. The man might have done wrong in trying to kill her, but his family had not. They needed her help, especially now that he had left them with no livelihood.

Emmaline rose to her feet and went down to the kitchen. Edna was chopping vegetables when she turned and saw Emmaline standing there. She curtsied, then looked up and smiled. "Your Majesty, it is a pleasure to see you again. What might I help you with?"

"I want to help the gunman's family. Can you prepare a meal for them?"

Edna's grey eyes glimmered with tears. "Oh, if we could all be a saint like you, Your Majesty. I will certainly do that. I'll make them a meal fit for a king."

Emmaline thanked her, and then ran off to find a maid. With the maid, she gathered some soap, blankets, freshly stuffed pillows, and clothing that Nicholas and Queen Genevieve had worn as children. She also brought a few of her own dresses for the man's wife.

She had a servant put the supplies into a modest carriage, one that she could ride in without giving away her royal identity.

Once that was finished, Emmaline went in search of Robert Blaine, one of Ross's more senior guards. He had been at the prison for Henry Little's interrogation. Now that it was evening and the changing of the guards had occurred, he would be serving at the palace.

She found him outside, giving orders to younger guards. "Mr. Blaine?" she called.

Robert turned, brows raising in surprise to see her standing there. "Your Majesty." He bowed before standing to his full height again. "How can I serve you?"

She clasped her hands together. "Did Henry Little say where he lived before his execution?" She could not ask Ross for Henry's address because he had not attended the interrogation. Instead, he had been busy lining the palace entrances with his best guards, preventing any other threats from harming them. And besides, even if Ross did know Henry's address, he would never have allowed Emmaline to go.

He frowned suspiciously at her. "If you don't mind my questioning, why would you want to know that?"

"I want to give his family supplies. Do you know where he lived?"

"I do, Your Majesty, but I think it is too dangerous for you to visit his home."

Emmaline shook her head. "The driver will accompany me there, Mr. Blaine. And no followers of Henry's cause were found when guards scouted his district. It will be perfectly safe."

"But, Your Majesty—"

"I would like to know where he lived, Mr. Blaine." Her voice sounded surprisingly commanding. She liked the way it sounded, liked the way it felt.

Robert sighed. "He lived in the Konovian district."

Emmaline paled. The Konovian district? One of her own people had tried to kill her? Had shot her husband? Were they so hopeless that they'd commit murder?

Surely one man could not define a whole nation. It would not be fair to give up on her people simply because one of them had tried to kill her.

She bit her lip and nodded gratefully at Robert. "Thank you, Mr. Blaine." She hurried back into the palace to finish her mission.

As she entered the kitchen again, the smell of roasted chicken filled Emmaline with pleasure. Edna handed her a basket and sent her on her way with a smile.

Emmaline hurried to the carriage, told the driver where she wanted to go, and stepped inside. The reins slapped the air, and the horses trotted across the palace yard. She watched as the city grew gradually bleaker. The beautiful houses soon turned into worn-down apartments, with laundry hanging overhead. She remembered this street. She'd spent many nights

Rise

in the alleys, shivering in the brisk cold and watching for things moving in the shadows.

Nicholas had said his father had taken care of the poor while his mother had overseen foreign issues. But after his father had died, and the war had begun, crime had ravaged the streets and military affairs had taken all his mother's attention. Now that he was king, Nicholas had told Emmaline he planned to clean up these streets and that he would provide better housing and living conditions for these people. Emmaline was glad he cared so much for the poor and hoped that no one would have to endure the streets again.

The carriage passed a sign, which bore the words "Konovian District" written sloppily in red paint. The driver stopped the carriage.

Emmaline raised her hood over her head and stepped out. An old woman stood outside her house, scrubbing a piece of clothing against a washboard.

Emmaline stepped toward her. "Excuse me, ma'am, but do you know where a family called the Littles are?"

The old woman didn't turn from her chore, and Emmaline was glad. She didn't want to reveal her identity to everyone in the district. "Only three doors down, miss."

The house three doors down was the worst Emmaline had seen. One window was boarded up to keep out the chill at night. Scratches and bruises marred the front door, and the knob hung loosely from its place. A baby and a kettle wailed from inside.

Emmaline stepped up to the door and knocked. She took a deep breath and prayed quickly for strength.

The door yanked open, and a pretty woman with tired eyes and a disheveled braid appeared. "Yes? Do I know you?" she snapped.

Emmaline bit her lip, surprised by the woman's mood. But she could not blame the woman. Her day had been just as horrendous as Emmaline's.

"I'm afraid not," Emmaline answered. She raised her head and met the woman's gaze.

The woman gasped and stepped back from the doorway. "Oh, Your Majesty!"

Emmaline lifted a finger to her lips, hoping to keep her presence a secret. "I've brought some things for you and your children. Please, don't be afraid."

The woman blinked rapidly and took a deep breath. "Come in, please, Your Majesty. My house is yours, although it isn't much, I'm afraid."

Emmaline stepped into the steamy house, the floorboards creaking beneath her feet. The kettle was still screaming, and so were the children running around a small table. Broken and torn toys were strewn across the floor. A baby sat in a pram, its cheeks wet and red from crying. Once they noticed Emmaline, the two children stopped running and froze right where they were.

The woman ran to the kettle and silenced its whistling. "Please excuse the mess, Your Majesty. The guards were here asking questions of me all day, and

I've just been able to return to my chores."

Emmaline looked around. This was the wife of the man who had almost killed Nicholas, who had wanted to kill her. This is where the man lived, here in this broken-down house, with his wailing children and the groaning floor and his tired wife.

Emmaline pulled on a smile. "It's perfectly all right." She set the baskets down on the table and brought out the contents.

When the woman turned, she gasped and hurried to Emmaline's side. "What's all this?"

"Clothing for you and your children. I've also had a meal prepared for all of you." Emmaline bit her lip, a twinge of emotion grappling her. "I'll make sure a servant is hired to bring meals here every day, at least until you get on your feet again."

The woman covered her mouth with her hand, her eyes bubbling with tears. "Why would you do this? After what my husband did to yours?"

Emmaline looked around at the low ceiling and the boarded-up window. "Because your children deserve better than this. And because you need someone's help."

A tearful chuckle sprang from the woman's throat. "You have no idea how much." She gazed at Emmaline for a moment. "Am I allowed to hug you, Your Majesty?"

Emmaline nodded, biting back emotion. The woman closed the distance between them and wrapped her arms around her.

The musky smell and the roughness of the

woman's clothes filled Emmaline with memories. Not long ago, Emmaline herself had worn rags and not silk. She knew what it was like to shiver in hollow houses like this and go hungry when nothing salvageable could be found. She had been rescued from it, and now it was time for someone else to experience the same redemption she'd found.

The woman pulled away, drying her tears. "Thank you, Your Majesty. You're an angel from heaven above."

Emmaline blushed, shaking her head. "I wouldn't go that far." She glanced up at the woman. "Might I have your name and your children's names so I can pray for you?"

The woman chuckled sadly. "My name is Sarah, and my children's names are Freddy, Eliza, and Augie." She sniffled. "We'll be keeping you and your husband in our prayers, as well, Your Majesty."

Emmaline smiled warmly at Sarah, already feeling a connection with her.

When the meal had been eaten and the children had been bathed and dressed in their new clothing, Emmaline and Sarah sat at the table. The children played quietly in the corner while the baby slept.

"If you don't mind my asking, Sarah," Emmaline said, "do you know why your husband would do what he did? I keep trying to picture him with you all, and I can't imagine him to be a cruel, wicked man."

Sarah sniffled, her hair hanging in her eyes. She pushed it away with long, thin fingers. "He wasn't. I don't know what possessed Harry to shoot your husband."

Emmaline raised a brow. "Harry? I thought your husband's name was Henry."

Sarah smiled sadly. "It was Henry. But he commonly went by Harry. He said that name fit him better." Tears shimmered in her eyes as she gazed at Emmaline. "The Harry I fell in love with would never have done what he did. I am sorry for all the heartache it's caused you."

"It's not your doing."

Sarah shook her head. "No, I should have spoken to Harry. I saw him falling into gambling and drinking. He wasn't the man he used to be anymore, not since he lost his job and Freddy got sick. Then last Saturday, he came home drunker than he'd ever been, and he had a pouch of gold. Said a man gave it to him. He wouldn't tell me how or why. A few hours before the parade, a man came to see him and spoke to him outside. Never seen the man before. He was a handsome man with dark eyes. They spoke for a few minutes, then Harry had to leave. I let him go, and he never came home." She swallowed, curling her fingers against the wooden table.

"Did you catch the man's name?" Emmaline asked, hoping to solve more of the mystery around the Konovian rumors and Nicholas's shooting.

Sarah pressed her fingers to her head. "Oh, I don't know. I've been so worried about the house and the kids and Harry that my head is muddled." She moaned, and then gasped. "Victor! Victor Hughes! That was the name."

Something coiled in Emmaline's middle as the house seemed to shake. The blood and warmth drained from her face as her heart thundered in her chest and ears. "Victor Hughes? You're certain?"

She nodded. "Yes, Your Majesty. That was the name."

Emmaline's suspicions had been right. No wonder she had been afraid around the man. Victor was behind Nicholas's shooting. Did that mean he was behind the Konovian rumors, too? Why had he wanted her dead? Was he this rebellion's leader, or simply part of the movement? Did he know she was Konovian?

She had to get back to the palace. She had to tell Ross. Emmaline leapt up from her chair and nearly stumbled over the hem of her skirt.

"Your Majesty, are you all right?" Sarah asked.

Emmaline nodded quickly, the movement making her dizzy. "I must leave."

"Don't go!" Eliza begged.

"Hush!" Sarah said softly. "Don't be rude." She turned to Emmaline. "God bless you for your kindness, Your Majesty."

Emmaline managed a smile. "Of course. Thank you for your time." She turned, went out the door, and ran to the carriage. "To the palace," she ordered the driver. "And quickly, please."

The horses squealed as they galloped across the street. Emmaline could barely believe what Sarah had said. Victor Hughes. He was the man in the shadows.

Rise

And if Emmaline had anything to say about it, he was about to be yanked out of the shadows and dragged into the light where everyone could see him for what he was.

Chapter Twenty-Four

"ROSS!" EMMALINE RAN across the stable yard as the sunlight died and faded into red. "Ross!" She called his name but could not find him. Perhaps he was making his evening rounds in the palace, positioning his guards in every corridor to protect the palace as it slept. Little did Ross know, the enemy had already made his way into their fortress.

Emmaline swept up her skirts and ran inside. Her heart screamed in her ears. Victor Hughes was the culprit. He was the one who had hired Harry Little. But why, if he was connected to the plot against the Konovians, had he hired a Konovian man to do his dirty work?

Emmaline scurried up the staircases, each of the levels whirling by. She hadn't run so fast in quite a long time, especially under all these layers of clothing.

She searched up and down the halls and peeked inside every doorway she passed, but she saw no sign of Ross. She was running out of breath.

Ross would be furious when he found out it was Victor, and so would Nicholas when she told him. Would Nicholas be angry with her for keeping a secret from him? She hoped he would understand. She couldn't help that her crown came at a cost.

Emmaline slowed down, her legs shaking and her breath shallow. She walked briskly down another hall.

"He hung himself, the poor fool." A deep voice laughed.

Emmaline recognized the voice as Victor's. She stopped at the closed door and pressed her ear against it, listening. She heard glasses clinking and liquid pouring.

"But this wasn't part of your plan, Hughes," a new, higher-pitched voice said. "You wanted the queen dead."

Shivers ran down Emmaline's spine as her stomach cramped. A man who wanted her dead was in her own home, under the guise of the late queen's gentlemanly cousin? Emmaline resisted the urge to run and hide. She had to keep listening.

A glass slammed down. "I know what I wanted, Clives!" Victor shouted. "But I have a new plan. A better one."

"And what about the Konovian man? Why did you hire him if you want to kill the Konovians?"

"Because I'm going to turn it all around on those pathetic people." More liquid poured. "Once I convince the king, the Konovians will be in my hands, and I'll be able to do whatever I wish with them."

Heat nearly overpowered Emmaline, but she swallowed the rising anger.

"And just how are you going to convince the king? He's clever like his mother. He won't fall for just anything, Hughes."

"Haven't you ever played chess, Clives? Don't you know that the queen determines the whole game?"

The other man chuckled. "Ah, yes, I see now."

"I'll use the king's pretty little wife to get what I want. He's so concerned about protecting her that he'll do anything to keep her safe. I'll have him eating out of my hand when I tell him a group of Konovians hate his wife. He'll be all too willing to stop them. And once I have his approval, I'll finish what I started with Emmaline three years ago."

Emmaline blinked, listening harder. *Three years ago? What?*

Victor went on. "I knew I should have made sure she was dead and cut her bloody heart out after she fell on the fireplace that night."

Emmaline's hands flew to her mouth. *Victor.* He was the man who had been in that room. He had ripped bullets through her sisters. He had caught her throat and thrown her against the wall. She remembered his voice now, the deep voice that had cursed in that room. It was as if his hand was squeezing her throat then, his fingernails digging into her skin. Emmaline slammed her eyes shut, forcing herself to stay at the door and listen.

"But why did you wait all this time to finish the Konovians off?" the man asked. "Don't you realize how many Konovian babies have been born in the last three years?"

"I was tracking down others who made the mistake of crossing me. Some of them had found clever hiding places—but not clever enough." Victor paused. "And besides, I might not have ever found the princess again if she hadn't come to the palace. Even if I'd destroyed all her subjects, my mission wouldn't have been truly complete."

"True."

Someone stood up.

"Luckily, it seems fate itself has handed her to me," Victor said.

Footsteps neared the door.

Emmaline gasped softly and dashed around the corner. She flew down the staircases again, her lungs struggling to keep up with her feet.

Victor. The man who had made ghosts of her family. The man who set fire to her home. The man whose snarling came alive in her dreams, whose tall figure appeared in the shadows. The man who wanted the Konovians dead. The man who wanted her dead.

He was living in luxury, dining in a royal palace and wearing silk suits, while her family's ashes joined the breeze and dusted what was left of Konovia. He was alive and well, and her family was dead and gone. Emmaline could barely see through the tears scalding her skin as they fell down her cheeks. How dare he murder her family and then pose as a friend? Under her roof, her own roof! He ate her food, he drank her wine, he slept in her chambers, he—

He may be following her.

In her hurry to leave the door, she hadn't checked to see if Victor or the other man had noticed her. She glanced over her shoulder. No man in sight. No one was—

She rammed into something tall and firm. A body.

Emmaline screamed and then covered her mouth with her hands.

Ross's face filled her vision.

She nearly fainted with relief. "Oh, Ross, it's you."

His gaze was confused as he looked down at her. "Emmaline, what's the matter?"

Emmaline gulped down tears, but they still burned in her eyes like embers. "Victor. It was Victor. He's the one . . . behind it all. Victor."

Ross grabbed her arms, his grip tense. "Wait. What are you saying?"

"In here." She took one of his hands and led him to the ivory quarters, a small, private room in the back of the palace. She closed the door and took a few calming breaths that hardly worked. "I went to visit the family of the man who shot Nicholas."

Ross looked ready to protest, but Emmaline held a hand up. "I know it was a risk to my safety, but it was something I felt I had to do. And if I hadn't, I wouldn't know as much as I do now. Victor was the one who hired Harry Little."

"Who?"

"The man who shot Nicholas."

Ross's eyes widened as he stumbled backward a bit. "Harry Little? You mean—the gunman is Harry Little?"

Emmaline blinked. "Yes." Why was he acting so strange?

"My men told me his name was *Henry* Little, not *Harry*."

"His wife told me he preferred to go by Harry." She turned her head to the side. "Do you know him?"

Ross looked down, his jawline flexing as his features tensed. "I've only met him briefly. Him and his family. He got into a fight with the apothecary for stealing medicine for his ill son. The apothecary wouldn't let him have the medicine on credit. Harry said it was because he was Konovian." Ross stared at the wall, silent for several moments. Then he went on. "I bought the medicine and went to his house that day. I told him he didn't need punishment." He glanced at Emmaline briefly. "You should have seen his face. He was badly beaten." He looked away again. "And his family was poor. So I let him go. I let him go. And I prayed every day since for him."

Emmaline bit back tears. "Oh, Ross." *How low he*

must be feeling! To have prayed for someone and find out they turned off on the wrong path. To have hoped for someone's future, only to find that they had destroyed it with their own hands.

Ross smoothed his hand over his face. "I should've realized Henry Little and Harry Little were the same man. I was so distracted that I didn't make the connection." He shook his head. "Perhaps if I had gone to see him, if I had shared salvation with him, perhaps he ..."

"Don't think like that, Ross, please," Emmaline said. "You are not to blame. Little is a common surname. And you have been far too busy getting Nicholas help and ensuring the palace's safety."

Ross scoffed. "It's too late for that now, isn't it?"

She met his gaze. "Victor had us all fooled. And now we know who he really is." She frowned. "I'm just sorry that the gunman was someone you knew."

Ross shook his head. "No matter. He made his choice. I know I did everything I could." He finally looked at her again. "So, what else did you find out?"

Emmaline took a deep breath. "Nicholas wasn't Harry's target—I was. Apparently, my death was part of a former, foiled plan of Victor's, but I just heard him saying to a man called Clives that he has a new plan."

Sparks of rage flickered in Ross's eyes. "Clives? He's in the palace? That's the man who was rallying the men of Tregaron to join the plot against the Konovians."

Emmaline remembered watching Ross leaving the palace yard a couple months ago. *So that's what he was doing that night.*

He turned back to her and crossed his arms. "What is this new plan?"

Emmaline swallowed, barely believing the words she spoke were true. It sounded like another nightmare of hers. "Harry was a Konovian, so Victor's going to turn it all around on the Konovian people." She caught her breath. "He said he's going to use me as a pawn to convince Nicholas that he must protect me from the Konovians."

"Right, then." Ross's jawline hardened with tension as he gazed at her. "There's something else, though, a reason for your tears."

Emmaline took a deep breath, letting it fill her lungs. She had never felt this angry before, as if she might burst into flames at any moment. She forced the words out. "Victor's also the man that killed my family."

"What?" Ross's eyes flashed.

"He was there that night. He killed my sisters and threw me against the fireplace." Emmaline looked up at her friend. "Ross, he's here."

Ross balled his hands into fists, shook his head, and grunted. "The man who took our country away from us. The man who burned my home to smithereens and killed my family. Living in the same place as I am." He tightened his fists and then kicked at the rug.

Emmaline's eyes swam with tears. Her friend had been hurt just as she had. It was time to fight back. She swallowed her emotion. "He has Nicholas completely fooled. We must tell him, warn him."

Ross whipped around, shaking his head. "No, Emmaline, we must keep it a secret."

Emmaline couldn't believe her ears. Hadn't Ross heard a thing she said? "But why?"

"Because Victor said that he would convince the king. As much as I hate the idea of the king being under the influence of a devil like Victor, it would do more harm to tell him and risk our secret being unveiled. As long as Victor believes he can get away with it, we can watch him working in the shadows and pull him into the light when he's least expecting it."

Emmaline's gaze roved over the marble floor, Victor's muffled, snarling voice echoing in her ears. *"I knew I should have made sure she was dead and cut her bloody heart out after she fell on the fireplace that night."*

Ross was right. Victor was too dangerous to risk the secret getting out. She did not want her husband listening to the lies of a snake, but it would be wiser to use the element of surprise to catch the snake and cut off its head in one fell swoop.

Emmaline took a deep breath, letting it fill her lungs and loosen her limbs. "I will do as you say." She glanced at him, her voice dropping to a whisper. "This is terrifying, Ross."

Ross took a breath. "I know. But we can stop him. If God favors our mission, Victor won't be able to escape."

Rise

Emmaline nodded. Ross was right. If God was fighting alongside them, there was no way Victor could run from the shadows he'd filled her life with. *God, please be with us.*

Ross strode through the palace, on his way to the palace yard to run his men through a round of drills. The kingdom was on shaky ground, and he did not want his men to be unprepared if the walls began to crumble.

Though only a few knew of the plot against the Konovians, the whole country had been in a stage of unrest ever since the king had been shot. He did not blame anyone. After all, with a man like Nicholas as king, who but an evil man would want to kill him? Only now had the people begun to calm, but he knew that the worst part of the storm was on the horizon. It was not finished yet.

He still couldn't believe that Victor was behind it all. He could hardly wait until that man was out of the palace. He wasn't keen on sharing his home with a bloodthirsty wolf, a wolf that had already feasted on the carcasses of his family, his friends, and his country. Ross wouldn't be happy until his howling was silenced forever.

A girl appeared at the end of the hall, her skirts swishing left and right. Tiny red strands of hair swept her face. *Anna.*

"Captain, is that you?" she called.

He grinned. "Yes, it is." It had been days since he had seen her. Of course, they were both busy, she with her duties to Emmaline and he with his duties as captain. Still, it had been far too long since her smile refreshed his soul. He strode toward her, noting the pink in her freckled cheeks. "What have you been up to of late, Miss Edwards?"

She clutched a set of books to her chest, smiling gaily. "Oh, just waiting on Emmaline." She frowned before going on. "The queen, I mean. She's suddenly very interested in reading about Tregaron's history, so I went to the library to get her some books."

"Interested in reading, is she?" Ross's chest expanded at the news. He'd always known Emmaline would be a devoted queen, that she would work hard and do all she could to protect her people. It was wise of her to learn as much as she could about this country—and all its skeletons—that she had inherited.

Anna's freckles danced across her nose as her face crinkled with a smile. *She really is lovely.* "Yes, she is. When she's not checking up on Nicholas or attending her duties in the palace, that is." She clutched the books tight across her chest.

"I'm glad that she has each of you to help her. I know she enjoys having you live in the palace with her." *As do I.*

Her cheeks turned pink as peonies as she inhaled. "Well, if you'll excuse me, Captain, I must be getting back."

He nodded. "Of course. Until we meet again."

She smiled. "Until we meet again." She gave him one last look and hurried off.

He grinned to himself, admiring the way her curls bounced and flew behind her. She had the loveliest red hair he had ever seen, the way it caught the light and glowed around her face. The way it hung down her back and over her shoulders. He would have recognized her even if she was one in a crowd of hundreds. *Is it wrong to hope, Lord?*

Footsteps came behind him, whispering against the marble floors. "Ah, Captain!"

Ross closed his eyes and clenched his teeth together. *Not Hughes.* He turned around and nearly groaned at the sight of Victor standing there, his white grin contrasting with his black suit. Ross fisted his hands but forced his fury away. He had to remain calm. If this predator sensed his emotions, Ross would easily become prey between Victor's claws.

Victor strode toward him, still smiling. "I don't believe I've properly acquainted myself with you yet."

Ross forced a smile. *Oh, you've acquainted yourself with me quite well, Mr. Hughes. And my family and my country. Yes, you've acquainted yourself very well.*

Ross lifted his chin. "We are both men devoted to our work, Mr. Hughes. It is very likely that we have not crossed paths because of our diligence to our . . . *agendas*, don't you think?" He hoped he didn't sound as sardonic as he felt.

Victor winked. "Quite true, Captain, quite true."

He nodded his head, as if considering. "And I've also seen you busying yourself by talking to that red-haired girl." He winked at him. "Quite a looker, isn't she, lad?"

Ross bit his inner cheek. He didn't like that Victor had seen him with Anna. Had he been watching them? What would he do now that he knew Ross was linked to Anna? "And what of it?" Ross's tone was terser than he would have liked.

Victor shrugged. "Nothing, of course, Captain. But I must say, I would keep a watchful eye on her." His dark eyes glistened like the moonlight behind the clouds of dusk.

Ross stared at him, studying his face, wishing he could knock the man's fangs out. "And why is that?" He could no longer hide the dislike in his voice, and he no longer cared, either.

"Well, you are the captain of the royal guard. Surely you see how much danger the kingdom has been under of late. And since you have such a close relationship with the king and queen, I would not doubt it if someone tried to hurt those who are close to you."

What a bloody—

Ross grabbed the collar of Victor's suit and shoved him into the wall. He was certain his body was emitting so much heat, he would turn Victor to ash. And he would love nothing more. "Tell me, Mr. Hughes, who this person is who wishes to do this."

Victor's eyes carved gashes into Ross. "I'm simply

warning you, Captain. I wouldn't want someone to crush your little flower." He glanced down at Ross's clenched fists, still gripping his collar. He touched Ross's arm, as if daring him to fight back. "Now release me, or I'll tell the king of your violence toward me."

Ross glared at him and jerked his hands away. He stepped back, his fingernails stabbing into his palms. He couldn't believe his foolishness. He'd let his anger erupt, and now Victor knew that Ross recognized him for the devil he was.

Grinning, Victor straightened his suit jacket. He nodded curtly at Ross. "It's been a pleasure, Captain." He turned and walked away.

Ross's nostrils flared as Victor slipped past the corner. He shook his head, trying to shake off the effects of his anger. The audacity, the nerve of that snake! If Victor went after Anna—

Lord, protect Anna. Keep her away from Victor.

Do not be afraid, My son. If I can shut the mouths of lions, I can shut this wolf's mouth, too.

Victor adjusted his collar as he walked down the hall and toward the king's chamber. He didn't want Nicholas to grow suspicious of the bruises Ross had given him.

Though his throat had paid a price, testing Ross's temper had proved favorable. Victor's men had said they'd seen Ross sneaking out of the palace under the cover of night. Victor had not liked the sound of that. What if he was secretly gathering with the Konovians in defiance of the plot against them? The young captain was clever, and Victor had worried Ross knew what lay beneath Victor's mask. Now that Ross had threatened him, Victor knew for certain. How had he found out? And had he told the queen? She still behaved the same way around him, so perhaps not.

Still, it didn't matter if Ross had sniffed him out. Victor would silence that hound before he bayed.

Victor greeted the guard standing at the king's door. "I request an audience with the king."

The guard disappeared inside. When he returned, he nodded in approval. "The king will see you now."

Victor stepped inside and straightened his suit jacket. The young king was sitting up in his bed, the sunlight flowing over his mattress and radiating the healthy glow in his cheeks. It wouldn't be there for long.

"You're looking well, Your Majesty," Victor said.

Nicholas smiled at him. "Thank you, Victor. I'm feeling much better."

Victor smiled back. It was obvious the boy trusted him. And why wouldn't he? The boy's own mother, even with her hound-like nose, had trusted him and never once smelled a whiff of anything suspicious about her darling cousin. And if Victor played his cards right, neither would Nicholas.

"I'm very glad to see you sitting up. Your health reflects the health of this kingdom."

"I couldn't agree more." Nicholas looked down, took something from beside him, and held it out to Victor.

Victor stepped toward the bed and took it. It was a newspaper, detailing the prayer vigils held for the king. Victor had to swallow the bile rising in his throat before speaking. "The kingdom's loyalty is quite impressive, Your Majesty. Not many kingdoms can boast of such devotion to their king."

Nicholas shook his head. "It is undeserved. I could never be the ruler my parents were."

And you won't have the time to prove yourself wrong. Victor held his hands behind his back. "Oh, no, Your Majesty. I can see you're doing quite nicely." He paused before going on. "And while your mother was an excellent ruler, your father is the one who most impressed me. After all, compared to our late queen, he was in the shadows. Yet he chose to serve his kingdom rather than use his lack of noticeable position as an excuse for laziness."

Nicholas smiled, a twinkling in his eye, the kind of twinkling one sees in a boy who has a special love for his father. "I've always thought the same thing." He shook his head. "Still, I'm not sure I can ever live up to his example."

Victor chuckled. "Oh, dear boy. I'm sure if you try hard enough, you can."

"Well, I thank you for your praise." Nicholas turned to him, his eyebrows slightly raised. "Is there something you came in here for? Something you wanted to speak to me about?"

Victor cleared his throat, keeping his voice calm and steady. "Yes, I'm afraid there was. And unfortunately, it is not good news."

Nicholas frowned. "Go on."

"I have been to the prison again, to speak with the executioner. He told me that the man who shot you—who tried to kill the queen—said something in a fit of rage. He shouted, 'Long live the Konovians!'"

Nicholas raised his eyebrows, his jaw tight. "Konovians? I remember them, but I was only eighteen when their kingdom was destroyed. Parliament would not listen to me when I told them we needed to find the culprit."

Victor forced away the grin that begged to overtake his face. Little did the king know that the culprit was in the same room as him.

"Mother had still been grieving Father's death, but I thought she had done well in gathering her strength and helping the Konovians." He bit his lip in thought. "Of course, their living conditions have dwindled as the war has gone on." He leaned forward in his bed. "What connection is there between these two situations?"

"Unfortunately, there was more to the motivation the man had for his actions than I originally stated. The Konovian kingdom was destroyed three years ago, and many of its people now live in the poverty-stricken areas of Lauderbury. As someone who was close to your mother—may she rest in peace—I try to stay informed on the many rumors that run through the kingdom. With Tregaron being such a close ally of Konovia, I have heard that many Konovians were dissatisfied with what Tregaron did to help them after the brutal attack on their homeland. So they want revenge on you, and the man who shot you thought the best way to avenge his country would be to attack your wife. Apparently, he wasn't alone in his beliefs, either. He has several followers. During the past three years, they've been growing like cockroaches breeding under a rock. I would not be surprised if one of them tried it again, Your Majesty."

"But Ross told me that no followers had been found." Nicholas frowned, puzzled.

Victor shook his head. "Oh, no, Your Majesty. He certainly had followers. I'm afraid they're quite a clever race. Your guards didn't find anything simply because the truth was buried too deep."

Nicholas's eyes flashed. Victor bit back a grin. He was getting the king's attention, all thanks to Emmaline. Who knew that thorn in his side would prove to be so useful? With one mention of any harm coming to her, Nicholas exploded with fury. This would be an easy game for Victor to play.

"So, how many followers did Mr. Little have?" Nicholas asked.

"At least a hundred." Victor glanced casually at the floor, admiring the shine of his leather shoes. "It seems Mr. Little was a leader of sorts for this band of renegade Konovians. And this was not his first time of acting out. A few months ago, Captain Ross had to break up a fight between him and an apothecary. Mr. Little said he was angry with how Konovians were treated in Lauderbury. He was trying to steal medicine for his son."

Nicholas bowed his head, frowning. "I see."

"Forgive me, Your Majesty, but something like this did not occur when your parents ruled. While your dear mother paid heed to the foreign matters, it was your father who served the poor. No one wanted for anything in his day." Victor let his words hang in the air, let the young king bear their full, crushing weight. If Victor kept these mind games up, Nicholas would become the weak king Victor accused him of being.

Nicholas gazed out the window for several moments. "You're right," he said softly.

Victor grinned while the king's gaze was drawn elsewhere. *I've got him.*

Victor went on quickly. "I do not believe they are a formidable foe, however. They will be no match for your army of guards, Your Majesty, I can assure you."

Nicholas shook his head, expelling angry breath. His tone was short and rough. "I'm not so sure, Victor. No one saw their attack coming the day that I was shot. How can you stand there and be so certain that the Konovians pose no real threat?"

Victor's blood boiled so hot, he had to curl his hand into a fist to return his blood to a dormant state. Who did this boy think he was, daring to talk to him this way? Victor wanted nothing more than to take the fireplace tongs from the corner of the room and teach that boy a lesson. He held back. It wasn't yet time. His mission was not complete. He'd soon have his revenge. He'd soon teach this boy that he wouldn't speak to him that way. He'd crush that spirit of his and grind it into dust.

Nicholas sighed, resting his head in his hand. "I shouldn't have raised my voice. Forgive me. I'm simply worried about Emmaline. She already has enough ghosts in her life, and I'm afraid that this will bring the ghosts back to haunt her again. And I can't let any harm come to the kingdom. Forgive me, Victor."

Victor's lips stretched upward. "Of course, Your Majesty. I took no offense. After all, not every man has the patience of your father."

A dark, torn look webbed the young king's face. The ring had done its work. Just a few little words from Victor, and the king had drunk the poison.

Nicholas shook his head and picked up the journal beside him, scribbling something down. "Something has to be done about these Konovians. We cannot let them succeed."

Victor held his breath, studying the shine of his leather shoes again. Then he raised his head. "I could take care of it, Your Majesty." His heart beat like a thousand drums as anticipation trickled through him.

Nicholas jerked his head up. "What?"

"I could take care of it for you. After all, you're

still recuperating from your wounds and you have enough to deal with, with the danger your wife is in and the protection you must provide for her. One hundred rebellious Konovian hearts will not be too difficult for me, Your Majesty. I will put an end to their treachery so that you, your wife, and the kingdom can live in peace."

Nicholas held his chin between his fingers, gazing at his bedcovers. "Are you sure, Victor? After all, you are a guest in my palace, and not one of my attendants."

"I am quite sure, Your Majesty. Please, allow me this one task, to repay you, your wife, and your late mother for the kind hospitality you've given me."

Nicholas rubbed his chin before nodding. "Right, then. It is your task to complete. What will you do with them?"

Victor had to urge the smile off his face once again. "My men and I will find the identities of the leaders of those who conspire against you, and once we find their names, we will round them up and lock them away in your dungeon. They will await trial there. I believe execution befits such a crime as attempting to murder the queen, don't you?"

Nicholas frowned. "I suppose." He stabbed a finger toward his desk. "Get a piece of parchment and write a contract. I will relay it to you, and then I'll give you my signet ring to sign it and make it binding." His finger still waved in the air. "The parchment and quills are in the third drawer."

Victor stepped toward the desk and opened the drawer, forcing down the laugh bubbling in his throat. He couldn't believe how relatively easy this was turning out to be. He had the king—and the Konovians—right where he wanted them.

Victor sat at Nicholas's desk and barely heard the king as he relayed to Victor what he wanted the contract to say. Instead, Victor wrote something entirely different. When he was finished, he stepped toward Nicholas's bedside. Nicholas slipped the ring from his finger and placed it in Victor's palm. It was gold and slightly heavy. Victor pushed it over his finger and dipped it in wax. Once the contract was marked with the signet ring, Victor rolled up the decree and tied it.

"Thank you for taking care of this for me," Nicholas said. "It is most appreciated."

Victor smiled. "No, thank you, Your Majesty, for allowing me to assist you."

Nicholas slid a hand through his hair and laid back against his pillows. "Forgive me, Victor, but I must rest now."

Victor nodded. "Of course, Your Majesty." He turned his heel toward the door.

"Victor?" Nicholas asked.

He turned. "Yes?"

"Thank you for helping me to protect Emmaline." He exhaled in relief.

Victor swallowed a chuckle and grinned instead. "It is my pleasure, Your Majesty."

The corner of the boy's mouth turned upward, and

his eyes brightened. He was a man but youth still shined in his face. He was nothing but a boy, a boy buckling beneath the weight of God and country. He wasn't much older than Emmaline's father had been when he'd decided the fate of Victor's father. And just like Emmaline's father, Nicholas's kingship would come to a quick end.

Victor turned back toward the door and left the room. His shoes clicked on the marble floors. Not another sound could be heard in the halls.

"What will you do with them?" Nicholas had asked.

A grin like butter slipped across Victor's face, filling him with rushes of delight. *What will I do with them, "Your Majesty?" First, all the Konovians will be mine. My men will go to their houses after midnight and kill them all. The women, the children, the crisp old men, and the fathers. Every last one of them will be dead, their presence purged from the earth. None of them will survive like last time. Not even the babies. Their bloodline will disappear within hours. They won't ever see it coming their way. And when I am done with the people, their queen is mine.*

"Anna, aren't these your favorite?" Ross gestured toward a large patch of white-petaled flowers. They were in the meadow together, taking a walk and picking the last flowers before winter swept them away. The forest, green and tall, loomed around them like a barricade.

Anna looked up from gathering a bundle of lilacs.

She smiled, her hair glowing in the sun. "Yes, daisies. They're so lovely, don't you think?"

He grinned and plucked one from the ground. He stepped toward Anna and put it in her loose curls. "Not as lovely as you." Against his better judgement, he let his hand rest against her cheek. Was he making her uncomfortable? Nothing could be further from his mind. Yet he could not pull his hand away from her warm skin.

She closed her eyes and placed her hand over his. She didn't seem to mind his touch at all. Was that the sun warming his insides, or was she, this green-eyed, gentle soul who loved every flower God had ever created?

Anna's eyes snapped open. She spun away from him, her skirts whirling in the wind as she skipped toward the forest. She giggled as her bare feet trampled over the swaying blades of grass.

"Where are you going?" Ross shouted, laughing.

"Flowers. There's flowers in the forest!"

"In the forest?" Ross raised a brow. That seemed odd, since the forest surrounding them was quite dark and seemed to swallow the sunlight flowers would need to survive.

"Come on!" She spun again, laughing, and then ran off.

He laughed again at her glee. "Well, wait for me!" He hurried after her.

But she had already disappeared, her laughter ringing in the distance.

Ross raced through the trees but could not make her out in the brush. Where had she gone? Surely, she was not as fast as she seemed.

"Anna?" he called. She was quite light on her feet. He'd have to tell her that when he caught up with her. She'd get a smile out of that.

A shrill scream shot through the forest and up his back. "*Ross! Ross!*"

"Anna!" He flew through the forest, looking left and right, desperate to find her. She was in trouble. Where was she? What had found her? What if he was too late? "Anna! Where are you?"

"*Ross!*" She was crying, shrieking his name.

Oh, God, no. Not her. Not that girl. Oh, God, no. No, God, no.

His legs. They weren't moving. He looked down, but no, there was no quagmire, no sinkhole. He grunted, pulling them to move. But his feet would just not leave the ground. It was as if his lower half had suddenly turned to marble.

"Ross, help me!"

"I'm coming, Anna!" But he couldn't. He threw himself, jerked himself, grabbed his thighs, and wrenched his legs from the earth, yet they would not move. Could not move.

"*Ross!*"

"I'm coming! I'm coming, Anna!"

But he wasn't coming. Couldn't be coming. And her screams faded farther and farther and farther...

Ross sprang up in bed, out of breath from the struggle, sweat trickling down his chest. His vision spun as he struggled to keep his head upward. *Dear God, it was a dream.* He ran a hand across his face, trying to calm his racing heart. Still, Anna's desperate cries rang like echoes in his ears. Why had he dreamed something so horrible?

Emmaline had had a terrorizing dream shortly after Victor's arrival, even after she had lost the haunted look in her eyes and stopped jumping at every sound. Was Victor the cause behind these dreams? Was he causing these dreams to happen somehow? Ross had heard of those who used black magic, but Victor surely did not practice it.

But what else could be the cause?

And what kind of danger had Anna been in? Was it a warning from that snake? Victor had spoken of her earlier. Was she a target just to wound Ross? He didn't know, but he wouldn't have peace from her tormenting cries in his head until he knew she was safe.

Ross threw the covers off his legs and yanked a shirt over his shoulders. He opened the door and crept into the palace halls, illuminated only by the moonlight. Once he made it to the door leading to Emmaline's maids' bedchamber, he pressed his ear against the door, listening for a scuffle, a cry, any sound of struggle.

Nothing.

He sank to the icy floor and leaned against the wall.

He'd stay awake all night and make certain no one got through that door to hurt anyone inside. He would die before anyone could even dare to lay a hand on her.

Chapter Twenty-Five

THE PALACE WAS dark. So dark. Not once had Emmaline walked through the halls so silently. She was the queen, yet she felt like an intruder in her own home. No one could see her or hear her. If they did, she would be caught, and it would all be over.

The floor creaked beneath her as if it were rotten wood and not smooth marble. As a child, she'd always had an overactive imagination. Her mother had often rushed into Emmaline's bedchamber to turn on the lamp and assure her that the shadows were merely her dolls leaning against the furniture.

Even now, Emmaline had to calm herself as the shadows stretched across the palace walls. Yet it was not the long hallways cloaked in darkness that frightened her tonight. It was the mission that lay before her. It was the man who had threatened her life yet again.

She eyed the door of his room as she turned down a hallway. Emmaline knew Victor would have eyes watching for him, waiting for any sign of resistance to his plan. He could not know that she knew about his plot, or that she and Ross were going to meet the Konovians tonight to reassure them of rescue. So earlier this evening, she'd told the girls she was going to visit a maidservant who was recovering from a difficult birth.

"That's kind of you, Emmaline," Eleanor had said while brushing Emmaline's hair. "But in light of recent events, please promise us you'll be careful."

"Of course I will," Emmaline had replied. She knew how to protect herself from the shadows. It was the only way she'd stayed alive for the past three years.

Julia had poured Emmaline more tea, a remedy for Emmaline's nerves. "It's a good thing Anna's visiting a friend tonight. I don't think she'd like to hear of you going out at night."

Emmaline didn't really like it, either, but what choice had she? The Konovians could not meet in daylight, and she was a much easier target for assassins when they could see her.

When Emmaline had told Nicholas of her pretend plans for tonight, he'd frowned and shook his head.

"Are you sure that's safe, Emmy? After the assassination attempt at the parade?" His brows had lowered anxiously. "I don't want you to get hurt."

Emmaline had only smiled and stood at the foot of the bed. "I'll be perfectly fine, Nicholas. Ross will be with me, and no one will notice us in the dark because most of our subjects are asleep." She'd moved to his side and took his hand. "You mustn't worry about me."

His blue eyes roved over her face as if he were thinking. "Why can't you take another guard with you, at the very least?"

"I don't want to startle the new mother. I'm taking Ross with me because he is a friend of the husband." She'd kneaded the skin of his knuckles with her thumb. "And need I remind you that Ross is very capable of protecting me?"

Nicholas had finally smiled then. "No, there's no need to remind me." The smile had faded a little. "But please, be careful."

She'd pressed her lips to his forehead, and then to his mouth. "I will be." She'd turned away and walked toward the door.

"I'll wait up for you," he'd called softly. She'd smiled in response and closed the door.

She was glad to see Nicholas looking so much better. His wound had almost completely healed. There wasn't a night that went by that she didn't thank God for sparing her husband, and she couldn't imagine a night that would.

Still, she had noticed a slight change in him. He seemed to hang on every word Victor spoke, and he had become so self-critical. No decision he made was ever good enough, even though her heart swelled with pride for her husband. Victor was playing mind games with Nicholas, and Nicholas was not even aware of it.

What if Nicholas became angry with her when he found out she'd allowed him to trust Victor? Did she really want to risk losing his trust? His love, even?

His love is not such a fragile thing, but the remnant of Konovian lives that remain are fragile. She'd taken the crown and scepter. She'd pledged allegiance to God to uphold the kingdom, and she'd pledged her life to the kingdom to serve her people. She could not allow her people to come to such an end. She could not allow them to join the ashes of their Konovian brothers and sisters. She was a survivor, and she'd lead the rest of the survivors against Victor if she had to.

And besides, she would not have to keep the secret for much longer. In just two weeks, the lords and the dukes of the land would be coming to stay at the palace for a week to discuss new policies with Nicholas. It would be the perfect opportunity to warn the lords, the dukes, and Nicholas about Victor's intentions. But she could not tell Nicholas before. With

Victor's influence over Nicholas, Victor could change her husband's loyalties from the kingdom and to himself. Nicholas needed to be among men who had the kingdom's best interests at heart. And Emmaline needed the patience to wait until the end of Victor's reign of terror.

God, give me strength. Help me to remember that sometimes doing the right thing can feel like the wrong thing. I need you, God. You placed the crown upon my head again. Let me be worthy of it, and worthy of being called Konovian.

Emmaline came to the bottom of the stairs, glancing from the right to the left. Ross had told her he would be on the first floor of the palace, waiting for her so they could leave for the city tonight. But she didn't see him. It wasn't like him to forget something as important as this.

She stepped further into the room, turning toward the left. Something hard came down on her shoulder. A hand.

Emmaline whirled around, and someone pressed his finger to her lips. The moonlight spilled through the long hall of windows and caught the golden hue of Ross's hair.

Emmaline sighed in relief. "Are you ready?" she whispered.

He nodded and stepped out of the shadows. He led the way through the halls leading to the servants' gate.

Emmaline gripped the button of her cloak tightly. What would it be like to see other Konovians again?

Rise

Of course, she'd been around Ross, and she'd met the Littles, but what would it be like to see so many Konovians in one place again? She'd seen thousands of them in parades and hundreds of them at balls. She hadn't known it, but her heart had missed their company. It had been three years since she'd been among her people, three years since she'd been their princess. And now, she was their queen.

Ross and Emmaline came to the servants' gate. "State your purpose," one of the guards standing there ordered.

"Her Majesty and I are visiting a servant," Ross said. "We shall return in an hour."

The guard lifted a brow. "At this dark hour?"

Emmaline swallowed. Would this guard discover they were lying?

"We are doing it under the cover of night." A scowl twisted Ross's face. "Are you really going to stand here and question your captain, or are you going to let him and your queen pass?"

The guard turned scarlet and stepped aside.

Emmaline sighed in relief. She followed Ross into the courtyard, wrapping her cloak tighter around her body to shield herself from the crisp air. She glanced at Ross. She'd never seen him look so utterly exhausted. Was the weight of everything crushing him?

"Ross, are you well?" she asked, her voice low. "You seem tired."

"I am. I kept watch at your maids' door last night."

She blinked. Had there been a threat he had not

warned her about? Surely Ross would have, knowing him. "Whatever for?"

He didn't look at her. He seemed to search for the right words. "I . . . had a suspicion about Anna's safety."

Her heart skipped a beat. "Suspicion? What kind of suspicion? Is she in trouble?"

"It was nothing," he said quickly. "Nothing to worry over."

As they left the courtyard and entered the city, she quickened her steps to catch up to him. "Nothing to worry over? As both Anna's queen and friend, I need to know, Ross."

He scratched the back of his neck. "I . . . had a nightmare. About Anna. In the dream, she was in trouble, and I wanted to make sure she was safe."

Anna? Why had he dreamed of her? "What kind of trouble was she in?"

His breath puffed like fog around his face. "I don't know. I couldn't see it. I couldn't get to her. Something was keeping me from finding her." He inhaled. "Nothing happened last night, but I had to be certain she was safe."

Emmaline bit her lip, her cheeks warming despite the chill hanging over the city. "Ross, do you have feelings for Anna?"

Ross stopped in his tracks, still avoiding her gaze. "I am not certain the captain of the guard should confide to the queen such private matters."

She raised a brow playfully. "But what about a

friend to another friend?"

He turned to her, half-smiling. "I suppose I do, then."

Emmaline grinned. "You couldn't have chosen a finer girl, Ross."

He glanced at the cobblestone, still smiling. "I know." He turned back around and resumed his pace through the city.

Emmaline held herself and rubbed her gloved hands over her arms. She dodged puddles reflecting the torch light of the streetlamps. The flames danced behind the glass, like the flames in the nightmare she'd had a few weeks ago.

"Ross," she said softly, glancing up at him. "Don't you think it's strange that both you and I have had nightmares since Victor's arrival? After all, my nightmares stopped when I married Nicholas, and now they've returned."

Ross's jaw twitched. "Yes, I thought that was strange, too. I think he's practicing black magic."

Emmaline screeched to a halt, her cape sweeping backward. "Black magic?"

Ross spun around, eyes wide. "Shh!" He lifted a finger to his lips and glanced around, looking for anyone in the shadows.

Emmaline bit her lip, her cheeks stinging with shame. She shouldn't have spoken so loudly, but she could not help her shock.

Ross turned back to her. "Forgive me, but no one can know we're here."

She shook her head. "No, forgive me. But do you

really believe that about Victor?"

He motioned for her to keep going and kept in step with her. "Yes. I do. It makes sense, Emmaline. How could one man do all that he has done without some otherworldly force helping him? He has destroyed a whole country and countless lives. And now we're having dreams after he's arrived? It can't be a coincidence."

Emmaline's breath puffed around her face as chills spiked up her back. She'd forgotten most of her memories around her family's assassination, but ever since the parade shooting, her memories had been slowly returning. And now, Ross's words stirred more from the dark corners of her mind.

"Ross, I've remembered something."

"Remembered what?"

She swallowed, her lungs heavy. "About a month before my family's assassination, my father told us about a man who was empowered by black magic. This man was killing various people in countries surrounding Konovia. There were rumors that the source of this man's power was the ring he wore."

Ross turned to her, his eyes wide. "Victor wears a ring. It's onyx stone."

Emmaline bit her lip, exchanging an anxious glance with Ross.

"This means we're not just going against one man and his followers," Ross said. "We're going against the very powers of hell."

Emmaline swallowed, her stomach churning.

Rise

"That's true, Ross, but those same powers were defeated by one Man, the very Man we follow." The words she spoke shook the chill from her shoulders and stood her upright.

The corner of Ross's mouth went up. "You're right."

She turned her attention to the mission ahead of her. "How many Konovians will be at the tavern?"

"Dozens, counting the families. Word has travelled that you will be in attendance."

"Do they really believe that I am–"

"Their lost princess? That you will have to see for yourself. I'm afraid I can't speak for the whole population."

Emmaline strangled the button between her fingertips. Ross was right. There was no way of knowing how many people believed she was the lost princess. She would have to find out for herself.

"We have all heard the rumors against us Konovians! We have all heard the grumblings that those stuffy businessmen have against us! They don't want to have anything to do with us."

Emmaline clutched Ross's hand as he led her through the thick mass of people in the tiny ale house. She pressed her lips together and swallowed in an effort to keep down the nausea. She'd never been in an ale house, and the smell of ale and sweat was awful. Candles burned on shelves, tabletops, and windowsills, the waxy smoke adding to the odor.

There had to be more than fifty people in this tiny building. Bearded men with patches for clothes, women with heavy eyes and faded dresses, children clinging to their mother's chests and hips. Some people sat around the seven round tables, but most of them stood against the leaning walls. A baby wailed in the corner, and its mother hushed it to sleep as the speaker continued.

"They don't care about our wives or our children," the man boomed. He was broad in form with a mass of red hair on his head and face. His eyes were alight with anger, and his face was carved with sharp lines. "There are even rumors that they want to kill us all!"

The cries of women rose as the men grumbled and cursed. The baby wailed louder.

Emmaline stood behind Ross's tall form, her heart pulsing in her throat. Tears and smoke burned her eyes. The man was right, but Emmaline could not understand it. Who would want to kill such a hopeless people?

They are not hopeless, My daughter, a soft voice whispered. ***I have given you to them as their queen. I will move mountains through you, and your people will not die.***

Emmaline swallowed, listening as the Konovians erupted.

"I say we get rid of them before they get rid of us!" a man called.

"Yeah!"

"Go to their 'omes and teach 'em a lesson or two."

"Make 'em pay for all they've done!"

"And what good would that do?" Ross's voice broke through the jeering.

Silence fell upon the crowd like a holy presence. Even the baby stopped wailing.

Ross stepped through the mass. He took a lone chair and stood atop it. The candlelight bathed him in a golden hue, and everyone in the room watched him, waiting for him to speak. "What good would taking revenge against our enemies in the aristocracy do?" he asked, eyes sharp.

"It would give us the bloody justice we deserve!" a scowling man shouted.

Three men behind him punched the air with their fists and cheered.

"How would that make us any better than they are?" Ross's steely gaze silenced the naysayers. "Would this thirst for revenge please God? Do you think God would give us victory or the provision we once had when He sees what we have done?"

No one spoke.

Ross went on. "No, He would not. And He would be justified in doing so. We cannot carve our own paths through the sea. We must wait for God to move."

"It's been three years since our 'ome was destroyed, Captain," a woman called. "Exactly how much longer are we 'posed to wait?"

Another cheer shot through the room. Emmaline bit her lip. She didn't blame her people for questioning

God's timing. She only hoped they would listen.

Ross cast his gaze over the crowd. He stood so tall over them, like a giant. "The time is now, brothers and sisters. While we have waited, God has brought our redemption to us."

Chills shot up Emmaline's back and spread over her body. Her eyes burned, but she could no longer tell if it was from the smoke of the candles or tears.

"What are ya talking 'bout, Cap'n?" An old man scrunched his nose in confusion.

"Long ago, our Konovian queen gave her husband five children: Kathleen, Charlotte, Rose, Emmaline, and James. When the palace was attacked three years ago, we were left without hope that one of their children could rise up and take back the Konovian throne. For three years, we believed our royal family had all been assassinated."

The man with the crossed arms stared at Ross. "You sayin' that they ain't all dead?"

Ross cast his gaze on Emmaline, and another shiver went through her.

"Yes," Ross said.

The crowd murmured in shock.

"They left us one daughter, a princess who'd rise as queen."

"Well, where is she, then?" the man with the crossed arms sneered. "Where's this 'lost princess,' this 'redemption' of ours, huh?"

"She is here."

Ross's words hit her so quickly, she nearly tumbled.

The people's murmurs grew louder. She wasn't even sure she had a heartbeat anymore, it was pounding so hard.

"Our queen gave our king four daughters, but only the youngest survived. And God has raised her up again as Tregaron's queen."

A gasp rose from the room, as well as several whispers.

Emmaline bit her lip. *Lord, give me strength.* She dropped the hood of her cloak as she stepped through the crowd. She felt the eyes of everyone on her, and she'd never felt so naked before. Ross motioned to her, and she stood on another chair.

"It's her!" someone whispered loudly.

"Why, it is!"

"I thought she was dead!"

"She's grown up so much now."

"She looks just like her mother."

"Where's she been for three years?"

"Well, she made it out all right. Livin' in the bloody palace now."

The whispers quickly turned to grumbling and the grumbling to shouts, curses, cries of outrage as the people argued over their opinions of her.

Emmaline's breath came rapidly. What if they ran her and Ross out of the alehouse? What if they rejected her, her own people?

No. She wouldn't let fear get ahold of her. She had a mission to fulfill, and she wouldn't let anything stand in her way.

"Let me speak!" she shouted. Hot blood coursed through her veins and melted her fear.

Everyone turned to meet her gaze and fell silent.

She swallowed and straightened her shoulders. "The night of the assassination, my family and I were all enjoying ourselves. My mother was playing the piano, and my siblings and I were dancing. The soldiers came in and disrupted us. They shot my brother first, then my mother and father. My sisters and I hid, but a man found us. He thought we were all dead, but I had survived his blow to my head. When I awakened, I discovered my home was burning. In fact, the whole kingdom was burning. I escaped with a head injury and little memory of who I was. I wandered cities and villages and streets for three years. I eventually found my way to Lauderbury where I was rescued by Captain Ross and brought to the palace. There I married the king. The day my husband was shot, I remembered everything. I remembered that I was once your princess.

"I soon discovered that the same man who had killed my sisters, who had thought he'd killed me, was the queen's cousin. His name is Victor Hughes, and he is plotting to destroy the remnant of Konovia. You all know how capable he is. Using black magic, he has tricked my husband into believing that a group of Konovians plotted against my life and tried to kill me. Now, Victor has persuaded Nicholas to go after this non-existent group of Konovians, but Victor really intends to destroy all of us. He wants your wives, your

Rise

husbands, and your children.

"God has placed me in the palace so that I can protect my people from Victor and his followers. Ross and I will reveal him as the villain he is. This time, Victor will not succeed." Tears formed in her throat and burned her eyes again. Her voice shook. "I will pray for you, just as I trust you will pray for me. God is with us all. He will rescue us."

All eyes were on her. The man in front of the crowd had uncrossed his arms. The women wiped their eyes, and some of the men smiled at her. Children gazed at her, hope glittering in their eyes.

Emmaline's chest expanded. These were her people, the ones who sang songs to her and her family during parades, the ones who prayed for her every night, the ones who told their children stories about her ancestors. They were all so beautiful, standing before her, even with dirt on their cheeks and rags on their clothes.

God, help me save them. Preserve your people. Let your justice rain down on them. Show them your provision yet again.

Emmaline felt Ross's gaze on her, and she glanced at him. He grinned at her, much like an older brother would grin proudly at his little sister. He turned to the crowd and punched the air with his fist. "The Grand Duchess Emmaline Marie has come back to us. And with God's help, she will rise again!"

Every voice in the room roared with passion.

"Long live the queen!"

"Long live Queen Emmaline!"

Emmaline closed her eyes and breathed in this moment, bathing in the love reverberating in this small alehouse.

Ross strode beside Emmaline as they walked down the street toward the palace. Her face was hidden beneath her cloak, but he could still sense her smile. The people had peppered her with questions, and their children had showered her with embraces. Ross was certain his chest couldn't bear the full weight of the pride he felt for her. She'd handled herself so perfectly. He knew she would make her family very proud.

A thick, misty fog blanketed the ground, but Ross could still see that the palace and its gates were close. In just a few moments, Emmaline would be back inside, safe and sound. He was glad. Fall had quickly departed, and now winter had arrived, bringing with her frosty nights. The queen shouldn't be outside in this cold.

"I feel so happy, Ross," Emmaline chirped. "They were all so wonderful to be around."

"I'm sure they could say the same about you." He smiled down at her.

"I feel as if I've been asleep for the past three years, and now, I'm slowly awakening. I'm becoming the girl I once was again." She spun around, laughing.

"Emmaline?" a girl called. "Is that you?"

Rise

Emmaline stopped spinning and stopped where she stood. "Anna?"

Ross turned around, his heart soaring into his stomach and landing painfully. They'd been caught, and now the plan was at risk. And what was she doing here at night, alone and unguarded?

Anna stepped toward them, her red, moon-kissed hair unmistakable. "What are you two doing out here at this hour?"

Ross's gaze didn't leave Anna's. "Emmaline asked me to take her to see a maidservant who's just given birth. She hasn't been doing well."

Anna's eyes widened. "Do you mean Catherine?"

Emmaline smiled. "Yes, Catherine! Poor girl."

Anna shook her head. "Not anymore, thankfully. Catherine is doing much better now. I've just come from there." Ross didn't miss the suspicious look she threw his way.

Emmaline glanced at Ross again, all traces of her smile gone now. Ross's heartbeat drummed in his ears and nearly deafened him.

"Are you sure it was Catherine?" Anna asked. "It wasn't another maidservant?" Clearly, she didn't want to accuse them of lying.

Emmaline stepped forward and took Anna's hands. "Listen to me, Anna. No one can know why we were really out here. Come back with us to the palace, and we'll explain every—"

Crack! A barrel behind Emmaline exploded. *Crack, crack, crack!* A barrage of bullets peppered the barrels.

Anna screamed, covering her head with her hands and ducking low with Emmaline. Ross whipped around. Three men cowered behind the shadowy corners of the alleys, firing their muskets repeatedly.

"Run!" Ross grabbed the girls' arms and jerked them to their feet. "Go, go, go!"

"*Ross!*" Emmaline shouted, her eyes wild and her face pale.

He tightened his grip on her arm. "Go, now! I'm right behind you!" He shoved them down the street.

The girls stumbled forward, holding hands as they raced toward the palace. Emmaline looked over her shoulder at Ross before being tugged forward by Anna.

Ross dived behind a stack of crates. Splinters from the barrels flew around him like falling stars as he fumbled for his pistol. As he cocked the hammer, a chunk of wood plunged into his hand. He winced but raised his pistol and fired. One of the men fell to the ground while two more sped through the fog toward him. Ross sprang to his feet, his bloody fingers fumbling for the trigger as he aimed and fired again. The bullet pierced one of the men's chests while the remaining man fired. A brick behind Ross's ear exploded.

Ross turned and ran in the direction that the girls had went. He could not leave them unguarded without a weapon. He skidded round a corner as another bullet cracked and sped through the back of his coat collar.

The girls were still running up the street but not quickly enough for Ross. Emmaline twisted her head toward him.

"Go up the alley!" he shouted, catching up with them. His heart beat with the sound of war. "Come on—hurry!"

Ross couldn't believe his foolishness. He should have been more careful. What if something happened to the queen? What if something happened to Anna? It would be his fault that two innocent girls were hurt—or worse. For three years, he'd blamed himself for his family's deaths, for not protecting them. He wouldn't let that happen again.

Emmaline and Anna splashed through murky puddles, spraying his clothes and boots with the dirty water. Some of the water joined his hand wound and made the cut hiss with heat. He ignored it, following the girls as they wove around crates and beneath naked clotheslines.

Exactly how many men had Victor hired? How many were still chasing after them? How hard would they fight? Did they truly want to kill them tonight, or did they only intend to scare them off the path? Surely Victor would wait to go after the queen.

As they rounded the alley's corner, a gun roared. Anna screamed as she fell and clutched her shoulder.

"Anna!" Emmaline shrieked, dropping to her knees beside her.

Ross stared down at Anna's broken expression and

the blood leaking through her lilac sleeve. *Anna. They shot Anna.* The fire of a thousand suns poured into his veins. He spun around and fired his pistol just as the assassin cocked his musket. The man screamed as the bullet shattered his chest, and he fell behind the crates. His own musket misfired, but the shot went wide, skidding off the wall beside Ross. Ross leapt to the side, dodging it.

Emmaline's short, sobbing breaths came in gasps now as tears dripped down her cheeks. She pressed a blood-stained hanky against Anna's shoulder. "Ross, help me!"

Ross's mind spun in a thousand circles, but he kept his gun ready as he leaned down toward Anna. "Put your arms around my neck!"

Anna's green eyes spilled over with tears as she nodded. She raised her arms and cried out as he lifted her against his chest. She let her wounded arm dangle in the air.

"We have to go!" Emmaline cried. "We have to help her!"

Anna whimpered against him. Each pitiful cry boiled his blood even hotter. He pressed her closer to him. "It's just a shoulder wound. We have to get to the palace. Lead the way."

Emmaline bit her lip and then ran off.

Ross kept his eyes out for more shooters. He put his gun back in its holster so he could carry Anna, but if anyone else came out of the shadows, he'd be ready to whip it out. He strode as quickly as he could. He

Rise

hated causing Anna more pain by jostling her around, but if he didn't move fast, they would either get shot or she would bleed out. *God, please, guide us through this darkness. Put your angels around us. Let there be no more shooters. Let Anna's wound stop bleeding. Protect Emmaline.*

They hurried through the servants' gate. Fog swallowed the palace grounds, but Emmaline dove head-first into the earth-bound clouds. Ross joined her and hurried over the gardens. The guards standing at the gate sprang into action, following Emmaline toward the servants' entrance.

Ross tightened his grip around Anna's back. The aroma of the winter flowers joined the odor of Anna's ruby blood trickling down her arm.

"Look, Anna," he whispered gently. "Flowers."

She nodded, but her eyes were glazed over. The smile that had greeted him in the chapel that night was nowhere in sight, and her red hair was disheveled over her shoulders. His nightmare about Anna had come true, as well as Victor's threats. He quickened his step.

"Go get Dr. Reid!" Emmaline ordered the two guards once they were inside the palace.

Instantly, the guards disappeared around the corner. Soon after, they returned with Dr. Reid. "What happened?" he asked.

"Shot. Shoulder wound," Ross said quickly.

Dr. Reid motioned for Ross to follow him to the nearest bedchamber. Ross laid Anna across the bed and sat on the floor next to her. Emmaline joined him, grasping Anna's hand tightly.

"Is it going to hurt?" Anna asked, her breath coming rapidly.

Ross brushed a strand of hair from her damp forehead. "Yes, but I'm here."

Anna inhaled and turned her gaze toward the ceiling. Ross took her hand in his own and waved his thumb over her skin. Each motion quickened his heart.

Emmaline suddenly snatched his hand away, staring at the splinters in his skin. "Ross, you're injured too!"

Ross took his hand back. "It's not bad, Emmaline. Anna must be taken care of first."

Emmaline jerked her head to the side and released a sharp sob. "It's my fault, Ross. If we hadn't been there, Anna wouldn't have been hurt." She put her hand over her mouth.

Footsteps thundered as Nicholas nearly tumbled into the room, his hair disheveled and his eyes wide. "Emmaline, what on earth happened?" His gaze roamed the room, taking in the events, and then he rushed to Emmaline's side. He grasped her face in his hands. "Emmaline?"

She collapsed in his arms, sobbing. "It's my fault. It's all my fault."

Nicholas waved his hand over her head but cast a worried glance at Ross. Ross sighed, his fury bubbling as Anna's whimpering grew.

Victor would pay for what he had done. And Ross could hardly wait.

Rise

Nicholas dampened a cloth in the washbowl, his whole body tense. Emmaline cried softly behind him, her head lowered as she sat on her knees before their bedchamber fireplace. Nicholas couldn't take the sound of her sadness. It was worse than when Dr. Anderson had taken the bullet out of his leg with no chloroform left to give him. What on earth had happened tonight?

Nicholas squeezed the cloth and turned toward Emmaline. Shards of glass flew into his chest as he watched her pressing her lips together, tears running down her face like raindrops. He knelt beside her. She stifled a sob as he waved the cloth over her tear-stained face. He swallowed, wishing he could wash away the pain of tonight, wishing he could wash away the shadows of whatever she was afraid of, wishing he could wash away the grime of her blood-stained past.

"Emmaline, you don't have to stop crying for me. I'm here. Let it all out."

He hadn't seen her so lost since that nightmare she'd had a few months ago. Her lashes were soaked, and her eyes were pink underneath. "It's my fault that Anna was shot. It's my fault that she's hurt."

He cupped her cheek in his hand. "No, it's not. You can't blame yourself, Emmy."

She shook her head, not meeting his gaze. "No, you don't understand!" A sob escaped from her throat.

He sighed, the shards of glass cutting deeper. No. He didn't understand. And he never would. He'd been through much heartache, and while he'd been greatly wounded, his scars weren't as large as Emmaline's.

He brushed his hands over her shoulders. "I want to understand, Emmaline. Let me understand, please."

She gazed at the fire, a faraway look on her face.

"What happened tonight?"

Tears glimmered in her eyes as she shook her head. "No, I can't tell you."

Lava seeped through his veins, but he extinguished it immediately. There was no reason to be frustrated with her, and frustration would not solve their problems. But he still couldn't help but wonder why she couldn't tell him. What secrets did she have that she couldn't share?

You must wait for her, Nicholas. You must wait until she is ready.

He took a deep breath and released his desire to have his own way. "Right then. You can tell me when you're ready."

Finally, she looked at him fully in the face. Her face broke, and she threw her arms around his neck, nestling herself against his body. He cradled her in his arms as she sobbed in his ear.

"You're safe now, Emmaline," he whispered. "You're safe."

And he'd always make sure that she was, even if it killed him.

Rise

Bagpipes and gunfire roared in the cacophony of battle. Nicholas glanced at Tom, his faithful companion since he'd enlisted. He looked just as terrified as Nicholas felt. Their fellow brothers-in-arms climbed up the trembling ladders and out of the trenches, the constant booming shaking the muddy ground.

Screams added to the noise as men were shot down. Nicholas jumped back as a man fell from the air and onto the ground. Nicholas dropped to his knees, but the man's throat had been ripped open by a bullet.

Tom growled bitterly under his breath, his eyes alight with tears.

"Steady, Tommy," Nicholas slapped a hand against Tom's back. "We'll get through this."

Tom nodded, biting back the tears and watching the climbing soldiers. It was almost their turn to climb.

A woman giggled.

Nicholas whipped around, looking for the source of the sound. There couldn't be a woman here, much less a giggling one. His mind was finally going after the months of bloodied corpses, roaring gunnery, and constant fear.

"Did you hear that?" Nicholas asked, still looking around against his better judgement.

"Hear what?" Tom said. He looked around. "There's nothing but noise."

Nicholas waited a moment but heard nothing. He shook his head, trying to shake away the sound. "It was nothing. It's just my head."

"Keep going, men!" the general bellowed.

Only a few more rows and Nicholas and Tom would be over the top.

"Nicholas," a woman's voice whispered.

He ignored the voice, pushing it away. It was almost time. Only two more men.

"Nicholas. I know you can hear me."

There wasn't a woman here. It was just his imagination.

"Nicholas, why do you ignore me? Don't you love me anymore?"

The last man had climbed to the top. He had to focus, or he was going to get himself killed before he fired a single shot. He gripped the sides of the ladder and stepped through its rungs.

"Nicholas, it's me!"

Nicholas couldn't ignore the siren call any longer. He looked to his left. A girl wearing a lovely white dress stood there, her chestnut hair flowing all around her.

Emmaline.

Why was she here, and not safe at the palace? How had she gotten here? What was she doing here in this hell?

She locked eyes with him, smiling. Didn't she know where she was?

A soldier ran through the trench. "*GAS!*"

Dear God, no.

An explosion of fog consumed the trenches, snaking toward Emmaline.

"Emmaline!" Nicholas turned around on the ladder, getting ready to jump down. He didn't care if they shot him for turning around. He had to get her away. But there were too many men surrounding the ladder, blocking his way. "Move!"

The fog descended toward Emmaline. Her smile disappeared as terror took its place. *"Nicholas!"*

"Emmaline!"

"Nicholas!" Emmaline cried.

Nicholas sprang up, finding his bed was beneath him instead of quaking, rain-soaked ground. *Only a dream. It was only a dream.*

Emmaline stroked his cheek, her eyes wide with fear. "Nicholas, whatever's the matter?"

"A dream," he panted. "It was just a dream." He wiped his face, groaning. It had felt so real. The gunfire. The trembling ground. The misty gas. Tom's presence. Emmaline's screams.

Emmaline forced him to meet her gaze. "What happened?"

He blinked, trying to get rid of the images flickering in his head. "I was in the trenches with Tom, getting ready to go over the top. I heard your voice. You were there, Emmaline, and there was a gas attack." He bit his inner cheek, his heart still thundering. "I couldn't get to you."

She embraced him, nestling her head against his chest. "I'm here, Nicholas, safe and sound. I'm not on the battlefield, and no one can hurt me. Not when I have you."

He held her tighter as if he were afraid she would slip away if he let go. "I haven't protected you like I should have, Emmy. You've been in danger so much lately. Forgive me." When would he become the husband his father had been? When would Victor's words become untrue?

Emmaline pulled away from him, frowning. "Nicholas, what are you saying? Have you forgotten the way you took the bullet for me? The way you scared my ghosts away? The way you pulled me from the pond?" She cupped his cheek in her hand. "You keep me safe." She met his gaze for a few moments before sighing sleepily. "Lie back and calm yourself. I'm here."

Nicholas sank beneath the covers again, holding Emmaline against him and wrapping his arm around her shoulder. Her breathing soon became heavy, but his eyes wouldn't peel away from the bed canopy.

If he lost Emmaline, he'd lose everything of worth. She had tried to reassure him, but he knew he was nothing like his father. His mother's life had never been in jeopardy, but Emmaline's had been twice now.

It was time to become the ruler his father had been. If he didn't, it would be too late for both Tregaron and his wife.

Chapter Twenty-Six

"I TOLD YOU, Your Majesty," Victor said. "Those Konovians want nothing more than to separate you from your wife." He rubbed his chin, frowning deeply.

Nicholas wanted to punch something as he sat on his throne, his chin resting on his fist. So that's what had happened last night. Those bloody Konovian renegades had sniffed out Emmaline and Ross during their outing, had hunted them down like prey.

What made them so angry with her? What had Emmaline ever done? Why didn't any of the other Konovians feel the same way as these others who wanted to kill her? Would these renegades draw more to their side and against Nicholas's wife?

He shouldn't have let Emmaline go last night. She was not safe under the cover of night, even with Ross by her side. He wanted her to have freedom, but there were too many people who wanted her dead. And if she had been killed, it would have been entirely his fault. He had to keep her here until the danger was over.

She had cried herself to sleep in his arms. She had insisted that it was all her fault that Anna had been hurt. He hadn't understood what she'd meant, but he'd listened to her anyway. He'd held her tightly, dried her tears, and brushed his fingers through her hair.

He had to do something about those Konovian men. He had to punish them.

"Why haven't you done something about those Konovians yet, Victor? You told me you would take care of them." Nicholas felt the heat burning from his gaze.

Victor swallowed and glanced at him. "I did tell you that, Your Majesty, but I must wait until the time is right."

Unquenchable heat tore through him. "And when will the time be right, Victor? When my wife is dead?" He pounded his fist on the arm of the chair.

Anger is a foothold for the devil, a soft voice whispered.

Nicholas sighed and rubbed his temples. "Forgive me, Victor. Just do something about those Konovian men."

Victor nodded, his hands clasped behind his back. "I understand, Your Majesty. But you must understand that I have been working very hard to discover the names of the leaders of these Konovian rebels. It has taken some time, as they have been difficult to find. But I am happy to announce that I have found all of them now, and your wife will be safe by the fifteenth of January."

Nicholas raised his brows, annoyed. "The fifteenth of January? That's weeks away!" He was beginning to wish he hadn't put Victor in charge of this situation, but he couldn't go back now. He'd given Victor his signet ring.

"Yes, I know, Your Majesty." Victor held up a hand. "But I have heard word that the rebel leaders will be gathering in January to scheme against your wife. If my men attack then, we will have the element of surprise and will be able to capture all of them." Victor glanced casually at his nails. "I have done my best with the task I was given. After all, it was not my decision to let my wife leave the palace when she is obviously under great threats. Your father would be shocked at such a mistake."

How could he accuse the king that way, whether he was a relation or not? Nicholas opened his mouth to protest but closed his mouth. Victor was right. Nicholas should have insisted that Emmaline stay at home and let some of her lady's maids attend to the new mother. His father would not have made such a mistake. Nicholas rubbed his temple, trying to shove the accusing, ghostly voices away.

Nicholas sighed again. "I suppose you're right, Victor. Thank God for Captain Ross. If it wasn't for his presence last night, I don't know what would have happened."

"Yes, of course. Thank God for Ross," Victor muttered.

Nicholas propped his chin on his fist again. Ross was a good man and an even better friend of his, yet he had never been recognized for his great deeds. While Nicholas and his mother had basked in the glory that comes with being royalty, Ross had lived in the shadows, unseen and unheard. It had been two months since Ross saved his life from the parade attack, and it was high time that Nicholas honored him for his accomplishment.

Nicholas turned to Victor. "Victor, I need your help with something."

Victor's eyes were wide with expectancy. "Yes, of course, Your Majesty."

"I want to have a day to celebrate Captain Ross. A holiday."

Victor blinked. "But everyone has such a day, Your Majesty." His uncertain expression stretched to a smile. "I believe such days are known as birthdays."

Rise

He chuckled.

Nicholas chuckled, too, waving his hands. "No, no. I want a holiday entirely dedicated to him. The whole kingdom will celebrate and honor him for all he has done for me and my wife."

Victor's smile departed from his face again. "Oh, I see, my king. A whole holiday just for Captain Ross? Are you sure the kingdom can bear the expense?"

Why was he so reluctant to celebrate Ross? Nicholas waved his hand again and shook his head. "I'm well aware of our current financial limitations, but it doesn't have to be extravagant. I want to make a point to celebrate the people that deserve it. I will discuss it later with you and my other advisors, but I want you to begin to think of ways we can celebrate Captain Ross on his holiday." He stepped down from his throne. "Now, I must go and see my wife and tell her the news."

Nicholas left the throne room with a certain lightness in his step. Mother had always been fond of Ross, and he knew that Father would approve of celebrating the captain of the guard with such a holiday. Father had always given the servants, whatever their rank, their due reward. He knew Emmaline would like the idea, too. He could hardly wait to tell her.

Victor stood alone in the throne room, scarcely believing what he'd just heard. It took every ounce of strength to stop himself from chasing down the king and strangling him as he waltzed away to tell his pathetic little wife about his news.

A holiday just for Captain Ross? The Konovian? A man descended from the people that Victor hated with the fire of hell? And the king wanted him to plan a celebration for this man? Next, the king would have him plan a tea party for the queen and her lady's maids.

Victor was sick and tired of these royals telling him what to do. It was their fault he thirsted for blood. He could not help his fury. He'd been subject to their power since he was five years old, when Emmaline's father, King Alexander, had stuck his nose into Tregaron's business. King Alexander had only been a prince—a boy—when he'd visited Tregaron's parliament with his father. A foreigner, he'd had no business telling Parliament what he thought should be done about Victor's father, Tregaron's wayward Prince Christopher. It was Alexander's words that had satisfied Parliament, his words that had made Christopher lift the noose around his neck. And Victor was ready to put an end to their rule, just as they had put an end to his father's.

Victor had wanted Emmaline, Ross, and Anna dead last night. But none of the men he'd hired had been able to fulfill his desires. Apparently, he wasn't good at hiring men to do his dirty work, but at least he wasn't so easily fooled into believing lies as his victims were. All it took was a few offensive words from Victor's tongue, and Nicholas had ingested the poison. Now that the king was under his control, it wouldn't be long before he could wring his tail around the boy's neck and feast.

But not everything was going according to plan. With Ross still alive, he would continue to fight against Victor's scheme. And while Ross was a worthy foe, Victor would not be defeated. Not again. And certainly not by a Konovian.

He was glad that he'd been able to locate every last Konovian dog living in this kingdom. Now that he knew where they'd all been hiding for the past three years, his men could hunt them down in the safety of their homes. And it would all happen on the anniversary of the last time he'd attacked their people. The day it all should have been finished. The day their blood should have been his. The day he should have had complete victory.

He just had to wait until January.

In the meantime, Victor had to keep his disguise intact. He'd plan a party for Ross, all right. Perhaps he could order a guillotine from France and let the guest of honor give it a go. Victor wouldn't be satisfied until he'd guzzled every last drop of Konovian blood.

Ross stepped into Anna's bedchamber, his senses drowned in the fragrance of the plentiful bouquets decorating the room. When the palace staff had heard that Anna had been wounded in the shooting and that she adored flowers, everyone had brought their best bunches to encourage her well-being. The bouquet he had brought her—her favorite, daisies—sat next to her in a marble vase.

She was sitting up and reading a book, the morning sun streaming in and lighting up her freckled nose. His heart shifted in his chest as the aroma of flowers hypnotized him.

Emmaline, standing next to him, smiled. "I see you're doing much better now." Tears glittered in her eyes.

Ross wished that Emmaline wouldn't take so much responsibility for what had happened to Anna. She wasn't the one preying on innocents—Victor was.

Anna beamed. "I am. The doctor said the bullet passed through, and that it had just missed an artery. He says that I will mend well."

Ross curled his hand into a fist as the moments of the night before crashed through his mind. The roaring of the guns, Anna's screams, her blood streaming down her arm, Emmaline's cries, his rushing heart. But God had shielded them. It could have been much worse. If someone had been waiting in the fog for them, Emmaline could have been killed. If the bullet had not missed Anna's artery, she could have—

"Thanks be to God," Emmaline said, wiping a tear away.

"Yes, of course." Anna nodded her head.

"I can only imagine what might have happened

Rise

had He not been there." Ross gazed at Anna, his head heavy with images of what might have been. But here she was, safe and alive. A miracle.

Anna met his gaze. "I can only imagine what might have happened had you not been there, either." A smiled graced her lips. "You saved my life, Ross."

Sparks rippled through his skin and electrified him. He glanced down, trying to hide his grin. "It was nothing, really." He glanced from Anna to Emmaline, who was beaming knowingly. He bit his inner cheek and looked back down.

"Still, though, I'm still not certain exactly what happened last night. Why you two were out together so late, I mean." Anna pressed her lips together.

Ross shot Emmaline a look, and she nodded. "That's one of the reasons we came to see you," he said softly. "Emmaline and I have decided that you deserve to know the details of last night." He gripped the railing at the foot of the bed. "But you must promise you won't utter a word of it to anyone outside of this room."

Anna's green eyes flickered with concern, but she nodded. "Of course."

"There is a plot against the Konovian people. I have known about it for a while now, but Emmaline only found out a few weeks ago, after Nicholas was shot. Both Emmaline and I are Konovian. Both of our families were killed. Mine died during the destruction of the country, but Emmaline's family was assassinated, and she nearly was, too."

Anna blinked, paling. "But why would her family be chosen for assassination if all the other families were killed in the fires and cannons?"

Ross glanced at Emmaline, her skin now ivory. Emmaline inhaled. "Because my family ruled the country. My father and mother were the king and queen. I was their youngest daughter."

Anna gripped the covers lying across her, her eyes even wider. "So you are . . . the Konovian princess? The one rumored to be alive?"

Ross frowned. How would Anna know that? That was a secret the last remnant of Konovians kept, a hope that they had buried deep within themselves so no one could destroy it like they had destroyed their home. How would Anna have heard of the rumors that Emmaline had survived the assassination?

Emmaline nodded. "Yes."

"How did you know about the rumors concerning the lost princess?" Ross asked.

Anna looked down, then lifted her gaze toward them. She took a deep breath, fear flashing in her eyes. "I am half-Konovian."

Emmaline jerked her head toward Ross. He swallowed, the fibers of his skin tingling. Anna was Konovian, too? Had the gunmen known that? It would make sense. If they had been aiming for Emmaline or Ross, surely they would have succeeded. They had obviously been experienced in their line of work.

Anna bit her lip, staring at the bouquets filling her bedside tables, as if the flowers gave her the strength to go on. Her voice trembled. "I did not find out until I was thirteen. I was looking for a book in my mother's room when I found her diary. She had written about her first love and how they had fought when she'd told him she was going to marry a wealthy Konovian instead of him. She said that she would never forgive herself for losing Victor's love."

Shock ripped through Ross as his breath left him. Anna's mother had been in love with Victor Hughes, the very man that lay in the dark corners of every Konovian's mind? The wolf who had feasted on their families' carcasses and had returned for more?

Emmaline's hand flew to her mouth. "Your mother was in love with Victor Hughes?"

Anna nodded, but she raised her brows, obviously not understanding why they were so shocked. "Yes. She said in her diary that it had been a mistake to marry my father. I'd never understood why my mother didn't love me or my father until that day. I would have read more, but she found me and locked me in my room. I tried to learn all I could about my father's heritage, so I asked him questions. He told me about the royal family, about the good things the king was doing for his subjects, and about how all the people loved them. I wanted to visit his country so much, to see this land he'd told me about." She swallowed. "When I was fifteen, my father told me the news of the destruction. He said there were rumors that the youngest princess had survived, but I never believed them ... until now."

Ross closed his eyes and pressed his lips together, heat bubbling inside him. Yet another life Victor had ruined. Perhaps if Victor had not been angry about Anna's mother choosing a Konovian over him, Anna would have been given the mother's love she desired.

"I've spoken to Victor since he came to live at the palace," Anna said. "He seems very kind. He told me that he had forgiven my mother and that I look just like her with my red hair." Anna smiled childishly.

That animal. Daring to speak to Anna, pretending to be a gentleman, all the while hiding hatred for her within him—plotting her death!

Ross shook his head and curled his fingers tighter around the railing. "Anna, Victor Hughes is the one behind it all. He's the one who wants the Konovians dead, the one who tried to kill Emmaline at the parade, the one who destroyed our country and assassinated the royal family. He's fooled the king into believing he is nothing more than the late queen's doting cousin, but he's a devil."

Anna paled, her eyes round and her lips parted. "No. Surely not—are you certain?"

Emmaline's breath hitched. "Yes, we are. I did not know it until I visited the family of the man who shot Nicholas. His wife told me that she had seen Victor speaking to her husband and giving him money. When I returned to tell Ross, I overheard Victor telling another man about his plot, how he had killed my family, and how he was going to use me to finish what he started three years ago." She stepped forward, sat next to

Anna, and took her hand. "I remember him now, the way he hurled the couch across the room, how he grabbed me, how he threw me against the fireplace. It was him. Victor."

Anna stared at Emmaline, her eyes glassy as if she were shattered by what Emmaline had recounted. There seemed to be no doubt in Anna now. It was as if the iciness of Emmaline's past had spread to Anna just by holding the queen's hand.

Ross sighed. He would never have dreamed Anna would get tangled up in this. But it was not her fault. As half-Konovian, she'd been born to this life, this life of running and hiding from the howling wolves. Even if Anna hadn't been Konovian, Victor had caught onto Ross's connection to her, and that alone would have motivated him to hunt her down, if only to wound Ross. Her nationality only made Victor hungrier for her, made her life more at risk.

But now Ross and Emmaline knew the truth about Anna. Now they could protect her. And if Ross had anything to say about it, Victor wouldn't lay one claw on her.

"Anna, I don't believe that you getting hurt was an accident." He looked her straight in the eyes, and she met his gaze, swallowing. "I believe you were one of their targets. Victor told them who you were. He's after us. He's after all of us. And he'll take advantage of any opportunity he gets to kill us."

She glanced from Emmaline to Ross, brows raised. "So, what do we do, if we're the only ones who know and if he has the king fooled? Surely he has the upper hand."

Emmaline smiled ruefully. "Perhaps he thought he had the upper hand at one time, but he was wrong. His identity won't be a secret for long. In just two weeks, the lords and dukes of the land will arrive at the palace for council with Nicholas. That is when I will reveal his identity. I cannot tell Nicholas yet because of Victor's influence over him. Ross and I have prayed, and we are certain all will go accordingly. Victor cannot fool or best God, after all."

Anna pressed her fingers to her lips and grinned. "Silly me, I forgot."

"We'll all protect each other," Ross said. "Victor may have won the battle, but the war is just beginning."

And Ross would die before he waved the white flag in surrender.

Emmaline's shoes clicked across her bedchamber floor as she walked in circles. Her hands were behind her back, and her mind was a raging battlefield, her thoughts flying around like released arrows.

Victor wanted the Konovians dead, just as he'd wanted three years ago. But why? Why was he so thirsty for their blood, so ravenous for their flesh? She hardly knew anything about his background, save for the fact that his mother had borne him in prostitution. That could not have been a healthy habitat for him to grow in. No wonder he now howled at the moon, calling other wolves to his side to hunt down innocent prey. And she knew that Anna's mother had rejected him so that she could marry someone that he deemed low-born. But she still did not understand why he thought so little of the Konovians. She could understand his anger at the rejection, but would he have resorted to annihilation if Anna's mother had rejected him for a man who wasn't Konovian? Something that she had not yet discovered, the reason for his hatred, was lying in wait beneath the surface.

She may not know why he wanted to destroy her people, but Emmaline did know she wouldn't go down without a fight. She had long spent a sleepless night wondering why she had survived her family's assassination, wondering how she had survived both blows to the head and the fire that had consumed her home. She had once heard a priest tell the story of how Saul had tried to kill David with a spear and how God had rescued him twice. David had been destined to become king over God's children and to rescue them from many foes. Had God rescued her from certain death for the same reason? Had He made her queen for this very moment?

Victor would not quench his thirst on her people's blood. She would not live through that horror again. She would not allow Victor to dishonor God by destroying His creation. Already he had hurt Anna, and even Ross just a few nights ago. Both of them were healing well, but Emmaline had had enough. The cries of her family and her people became an anthem in her head, an anthem she would shout until the battle was finally won.

She had to work quickly. Ross's sources had told him they'd heard that Victor planned to attack them in January next year, on the same day he first tried to annihilate them. Emmaline hadn't been surprised by the news. Victor was certainly cruel enough.

Christmas was in just four weeks. Even now, snow fell like cotton from the silver sky. She and Nicholas had not given a ball yet since becoming king and queen, and it was time for just such a ball—a Christmas ball. The lords and the dukes and their wives were coming in two weeks, just in time to celebrate Christmas. Why not have a ball while they were here? The meal would be spectacular, and the music would come from the best orchestra in the kingdom. And of course, she would invite Victor. He would be delighted to be invited to such a lavish event. The proud peacock would be so honored, he would not guess that the queen had only invited him to pluck his feathers.

Yes, it was perfect. She would trick him and expose him, and his wickedness would finally come to an end. His sins would be no more, and the ghosts he'd made of her family and her people would finally sleep.

The plans had been made, and now Emmaline had to convince Nicholas that a ball was in his best interests. Tregaron could not bear much expense. Though the war had just ended a few weeks ago, it would take some time for the kingdom to get back on its feet. Still, she knew that Nicholas would do whatever she asked of him, and that once the real reason for the ball came out, he would not mind the expense at all.

Emmaline stopped her pacing and stepped toward her wardrobe. She would dress as the queen she was, and she would wear the dress Nicholas liked the most on her: a seafoam blue gown with a wide neckline, a long train, and blue flowers flowing down the skirt. Once she was dressed, she called the girls inside to help her finish preparing.

Emmaline said silent prayers as Julia wrapped strands of pearls around her neck. She pleaded for inner peace as Eleanor pinned up her hair. She begged for strength as Diana painted her face. She whispered cries for courage as Lydia placed the crown on her head.

When the girls stepped away from her, Emmaline went to her mirror. A queen stared back at her in the glass, but Emmaline knew the girl inside trembled. The girl inside felt as if she might heave. The girl inside felt as if she might fall to the floor in fear and exhaustion. But the queen staring back at her motioned her to rise.

And she did.

"Germany will pay for the hell they put us through!" Mr. Dudley shouted.

"I agree they must be punished, Dudley, but we

cannot stir up the hornet's nest again." Mr. Cohen balled his hands into fists but did not shout. "If we are too harsh, they will sting us again." His eyes widened with fear. "Only next time, I fear it will be much worse."

Nicholas rubbed his forehead as he sat in his throne room, listening to two of his advisors quarrel over what should be done about Germany's war crimes. Dudley and Cohen had always had a certain sourness to their relationship, with Cohen being a Messianic Jew and Dudley being a Darwin-worshipping atheist. Both of them gave sound advice, but it was during arguments between the two of them that Nicholas was glad that he took his final advice from the Holy Word.

Dudley was right. Germany had to be punished for all they had done. The thousands of bodies of Nicholas's brothers cried out to him for justice, and his own body burned with anger over what had been done to them.

Still, Cohen was right, too. Though punishment was necessary, no one should assign all blame to Germany. There had been other causes for the war, and it would be unjust to place all the guilt on one country. If the punishment was too severe, Germany would turn on them again, and they would not stop until they had their revenge.

Dudley and Cohen's shouting grew so loud, Nicholas could not understand what they were saying. He was certain their shouting would shake the room and bring the gold-encased pillars and the domed ceiling crashing to the floor. Nicholas stood to his feet. *"Gentlemen!"*

They both fell silent. Dudley's eyes were wild with fury but softened within moments, as if he'd realized he was scowling at the king. Cohen's face was red with shame as he gazed at the floor.

Nicholas cleared his throat in an effort to calm himself. "Respectable advisors would not put on such a show before their king, gentlemen." He stared hard at both of them until he knew his words had sunk in. "Now, I don't believe shouting about it will solve any problems the kingdom has with Germany. Besides, it is not for us as a nation alone to decide. Many countries had a stake in this war, and so they have a stake in deciding how justice will be served. The war only ended a few weeks ago. Might we have some peace for now until things with Germany are settled?" He raised his eyebrows.

Cohen hung his head while Dudley scowled, staring out the long, gold-trimmed window to his left. Nicholas was certain he saw Dudley's lip trembling. A bolt of pain sliced through Nicholas's chest. He felt sorry that the man was so angry over the loss of his son in battle. Nicholas had been the same way himself for a few months after returning from battle, and he knew what a lonely life it was. Thankfully, Nicholas had never lost God as Dudley apparently had.

"My apologies, Your Majesty," Cohen said softly. "My behavior was out of line."

"Likewise, my king," Dudley muttered, not looking at him.

Nicholas nodded. "Your apologies are accepted, gentlemen." He sat back down.

A figure emerged several feet away at the entrance to the throne room. He could barely see the woman's face, but he knew who she was from her dress and from the way she held herself. Nicholas stood to his feet again, a jolt of energy bubbling through him. "Emmaline?"

He was surprised to see her here. She had been recovering from the attack for the last few days and had barely left their bedchamber. She had seemed lost in deep thought. Now, here she was, his favorite blue gown flowing around her and her crown glittering upon her head. Was there something wrong?

"What is *she* doing here?" Dudley snapped.

"To ask something of her husband, I suppose," Cohen shrugged, looking almost as surprised to see Emmaline as Nicholas was.

Emmaline came forward, her long train trailing behind her like the sea. She looked past his advisors and met his gaze. His former frustration with his advisors melted away as he studied the stars in her eyes. Nicholas's heart squeezed in his chest and nearly choked him. He hoped something was not amiss. She hardly ever visited him here, especially when she knew he was entertaining advisors.

"What is it, my love? Is everything all right?" he asked.

She smiled. "Yes, of course. I have come to ask your permission for something."

His chest swelled with relief. "Name it, and it will be done for you. Name anything at all."

She bowed her head and then met his gaze again. "Well, we have not yet held a ball since becoming king and queen. Christmas is also fast approaching, and I believe that the best way to celebrate the holiday and the end of the war is to host a ball, the first of many to come in our reign."

Nicholas nearly laughed at himself. *A ball? She only came to ask for a ball?* He'd been worrying for nothing. He sat back down.

"What a wonderful idea, Your Majesty." Cohen beamed at Emmaline.

"Pish-posh, Cohen, it's a nonsense idea," Dudley grumbled. "Our country has just come back from war. Now is not the time for balls and other such foolishness."

Nicholas ignored him. "I love the idea, Emmaline. A Christmas ball would be a wonderful celebration. Who would you invite?"

"Since the lords and the dukes and their wives will be arriving in two weeks, I thought we might have the ball then. I also want to invite Victor Hughes, your mother's cousin. I want this to be a lavish, elegant ball, a statement of the prosperity we will bring to the kingdom."

"What prosperity, Your Majesty, are you speaking of?" Dudley scowled deeply at Emmaline, balling his fists and practically baring his teeth. "The prosperity we enjoyed before the war? That prosperity is long gone! We have just barely survived a war, and now you would throw a 'lavish, elegant ball'? I've never heard of such foolishness!"

If Dudley did not stop speaking to Emmaline that way, Nicholas would punch his teeth out of his mouth. Nicholas gripped the arm of the throne to hold himself back from the man. "Dudley," he warned.

Emmaline turned to Dudley, her eyes hard and her chin raised. "I am aware, Mr. Dudley, that the prosperity we once had is gone, but this is only temporary. Do not lack faith in my husband's reign or in God Himself. Our kingdom will be prosperous again, and the best way to remind our people of that is with this ball."

Nicholas grinned, his chest swelling. He'd married a strong woman capable of speaking for herself, and he wished he had her eloquence.

Dudley glared at Emmaline so deeply, it was as if he'd forgotten Nicholas was in the room. "Go back to your embroidery," he sneered.

Cohen gasped, his bushy eyebrows jumping like startled deer. Emmaline's eyes flashed with pain, and her cheeks reddened as if Dudley had just slapped her.

Nicholas slammed his fist down onto the arm of the throne. He stood but did not permit his feet to move for fear he would rush toward Dudley and strangle him. "How dare you speak to my wife that way! She is your queen, and I am your king! I will not have anyone who disrespects my wife serve in my palace. Get out, and never return!"

Dudley's eyes were wide with shock. "And just how do you propose to run the kingdom without me? Advisors like Cohen will run this kingdom into the ground!"

Nicholas chuckled angrily. "Believe me, Dudley, finding an advisor to replace you will be far easier than you attempting to live your life without God."

Dudley's eyes darkened like a stormy sky. He straightened his suit jacket, huffed, and stomped out of the room. Nicholas was glad when he disappeared from view.

Nicholas's breath shook with fury, but he calmed when he saw Emmaline's look of gratitude. No doubt she had spent the last three years being spoken to in a fashion equal to or worse than Dudley's. He would not permit that to happen again, not while she was queen, not while she was his wife.

He hurried down the raised dais and grasped her hands. "Are you all right?"

A flash of uncertainty passed through her eyes like a falling star, but she quickly recovered and nodded. "Yes, thank you."

"I apologize for the way he spoke to you. I don't know what came over him." Nicholas was sorry he'd ever made Dudley his advisor. If he hadn't, Emmaline wouldn't have suffered such abuse.

"Don't worry yourself, Nicholas. He's gone now."

She smiled at him.

All fury left him with the gentle happiness overtaking her face. He let his eyes glaze over her and take her in. He caressed her cheekbone with his thumb. "You look magnificent. What made you dress in such a way? I thought you were feeling unwell."

Her eyes glittered. "I had a queenly request to make, so I dressed the part."

"I see. And you look the part, most definitely."

Cohen cleared his throat and shifted his feet. "So, my king, will there be a ball?"

Nicholas glanced from Cohen to Emmaline and smiled. "Yes, there will be a ball. A 'lavish, elegant ball,' fit for a king, a queen, and their entire kingdom."

Chapter Twenty-Seven

NICHOLAS GRINNED AS the early morning sunlight fell over Emmaline's face. How was she able to completely captivate him even while she lay sleeping next to him? Would he ever know how he had won her love?

She still had not told him what had happened four nights ago when she and Ross had gone to check on the new mother. But even before then, he had noticed her behavior changed somewhat after he'd been nearly killed. He was worried about her. She wasn't eating much at all of late, even when the cook prepared her favorite dishes at his request. She wasn't waking up before him, either, as she used to do. He had asked her what was wrong when she left her plate halfway full, but she simply shook her head and said nothing was amiss. What could be so heavy on her that it would cause such things? What could be so heavy that she did not trust his hands to bear the weight of it?

He would keep waiting. She was worth waiting for, after all.

Nicholas brushed a hair from her lashes, and her eyelids fluttered. A moan rose from her throat as she stretched.

"Good morning, my love," he whispered.

She smiled, and the beauty of her lips nearly choked him. "Did I sleep in again?"

"Not really. I haven't gotten up yet, either."

One brow shot up. "What have you been doing then?"

"Art study. Someone put this masterpiece in bed next to me, so what else could I do but take in her every color and shade?"

She blushed, giggling softly. "Oh, you." She reached and closed her hand over his face.

He leaned down and kissed her, his pulse jumping at her touch. He pulled away a few moments later, reluctant to get out of bed.

"Right, love. It's time to get the day started." He threw off the covers and crawled out of bed. He grabbed his clothes for the day and went behind the dressing closet.

Rise

When he came back around, Emmaline was still sitting on the edge of the bed, rubbing her temple. The nerves in his body quickened. "Emmy, are you all right?"

She ripped her hand away from her head and nodded. "Yes, of course." She cleared her throat. "So, what do you have to do today?" Slowly, she got out of bed and went to the washing bowl.

He knelt and plucked a tie from his drawer. "I am hoping that Victor has better news for me today. I want to put an end to these Konovian threats, once and for all." And once he got rid of this problem, perhaps Emmaline would feel safe enough to tell him what was going on.

Nicholas went to the mirror and fastened his tie. He glanced over his shoulder in the reflection, watching Emmaline washing her face, her shoulders hunched over.

"I see." Emmaline said. "And you're sure it's the Konovians that are behind everything?"

"With certainty. Victor and I have created an irreversible contract that will deal with this group of renegade Konovians by whatever means Victor deems necessary. He promises your fears will be over after January fifteenth."

Emmaline pressed her hand to her forehead again. She took a step backward and started to tip over.

Dear God, she's going to faint.

Nicholas spun around, rushed to her side, and

swept her in his arms. He laid her across the bed, his skin turning to ice. Her eyes were closed. He shook her body over and over. "Emmaline. Emmaline!"

Her eyes would not open.

He ran to the bedchamber door and nearly fell to his knees in thankfulness that a servant happened to be passing. "You—fetch Dr. Reid! Tell him the queen has fainted. Hurry!"

The wide-eyed servant nodded and ran off.

Nicholas shut the door just as Emmaline moaned. He ran back toward the bed and to her side. "Emmaline, thank God. You're awake."

She rubbed her temples. "Did I faint?"

"Yes. Emmaline, are you sick?"

"No, I was just so dizzy." She closed her eyes. "And I'm so tired."

Something was wrong. She had been perfectly healthy for as long as he had known her. Now she was fainting and wasn't eating or sleeping?

Lord God, let it be nothing. Please, help my wife with whatever it is. Help her to bear it. Help me to bear it.

A knock came at the door.

"Come in!"

Dr. Reid stepped inside, his eyes wide and his shirt half-unbuttoned. Apparently he had been in the midst of getting ready, too. He crossed the room and came around the bed.

"Good morning, Your Majesty. I hear you fainted." He put his bag on the floor and looked at Emmaline through his gold-rimmed spectacles.

"So it seems," she said.

"Were you dizzy?"

"Yes, very badly. It's better now, though."

Dr. Reid looked at him. "Did she hit her head when she fell?"

Nicholas shook his head. "No, I caught her before she fell. I saw it happening." He took a deep breath. "She hasn't been eating or sleeping, either."

Dr. Reid frowned, glancing from Nicholas to Emmaline. "Oh, I see." He opened his bag and fiddled with some of the tools in it. "I apologize, Your Majesty, but I'd like to speak to your wife alone."

"But—"

"It will not take long. Just step outside the door for a few moments."

Nicholas sighed and stood to his feet. He was sick of these traditions. He was sick of being locked out of rooms while the ones he loved suffered without him by his side. First his father, then his mother, and now Emmaline? Still, he obeyed, not wanting to excite Emmaline any more. He closed the door slowly, his hand hovering over the knob.

Several moments went by as Nicholas paced. Would Dr. Reid wait to open the door until Nicholas had carved a hole in the floor with his incessant steps? A cold sweat trickled down his back. Why hadn't Dr. Reid opened the door yet? Why hadn't he come out of the bedchamber to tell him that Emmaline was all right, that all his worrying was for nothing?

He wouldn't know until Dr. Reid opened the door.

He glanced at the knob, expecting it to move. Nothing. He sighed and kept on pacing.

He stared at the ceiling, painted with cherubs flying over God in the clouds. *God, why does this keep happening? Why do I keep getting locked out of rooms I should be in? Why am I always prevented from protecting the ones I love when they need me most?*

I need your trust. I will teach you the lesson again and again if I must. You are locked out, but I am not. I am with her, just as I am with you. Trust.

Nicholas sighed, his breath wavering. He ran a hand through his hair. Trust? That's what this was about?

He glanced at the golden knob and then at the ivory door. Doors didn't stop God. He was in there with Emmaline, just as He had been with her in that room with the assassin that night. He was with Nicholas, just as He had been with him on the battlefield as enemy fire sprayed all around him. God was with them both, and they had both seen it for themselves.

The door was closed, but God was in the room.

Emmaline sat up from her bed and held onto the banister, barely swimming above the fear threatening to drown her. Why had she fainted? Was the anxiety of everything truly pressing her down that much?

She'd never carried a burden like this. Surely that had to be it.

Dr. Reid put some things away in his medical bag and closed it with a strong *clasp!*

"I'd say you're a little more than two months gone, Your Majesty," he said.

"Two months gone?" Her thoughts spun around. Surely he couldn't mean—

Dr. Reid turned to her with a smile. "With child, Your Majesty."

The words seemed to echo around the room, surrounding her until they all landed on her with a resounding *crash!* A child? With child? Inside her, growing, living, thriving? A baby? Two months gone? She had noticed some signs but had been so busy with her ball-planning, so fearful of the impending annihilation that she hadn't realized—

"You'll be three months along in two weeks. The perfect Christmas present for the new king and queen, I think." Dr. Reid winked.

Emmaline wanted to gasp, but no sound came out. A child. With child. Inside *her*, growing, living, thriving. A baby. Two months gone. For so long, she'd carried her family's deaths with her, and now, she was continuing their legacy and creating new life. She wanted to shout it from the rooftops. She wanted to tell Nicholas. She wanted to tell everyone!

A sudden thought sliced through her like winter gusts.

No. Not everyone. Victor could not know. If he'd

wanted to kill her before, he'd most certainly want to kill her now. He wanted her whole family line gone forever, and this child would ruin his chances. He'd kill her to end the line, possibly even before he killed the rest of the Konovians. Victor could not know. No one would know, save for Nicholas, and perhaps Ross so that he could protect her from Victor's watchful eyes. She had to tell Nicholas it was a secret, too. With him so influenced by Victor, she could not risk Nicholas revealing her news.

But even those cloudy thoughts couldn't remove the sunlight of the moment. She smiled, laughing. A real baby, growing inside her! She wanted to run to the mirror and watch the child grow as she grew with it.

"Can we bring Nicholas inside now?" she asked Dr. Reid, certain her giddiness reminded the gray-haired man of an elated child.

He laughed. "Of course, Your Majesty." He opened the door and stepped outside. The doctor's voice was muffled, but even with Emmaline's heart thundering in her ears, she could still make out his words. "You can go inside to your wife, my king."

The door opened, and Nicholas entered. His eyes did not leave hers as she sat on the bed. Her pulse hummed in her ears and beat in her throat.

Nicholas shut the door and walked slowly toward the bed. "What news?"

She extended her arms toward him, and he quickly closed the distance between them, taking her hands and falling on his knees before her. "Is it serious?" His voice rose with panic.

She smiled, taking in the man in front of her, the man who had pledged his life to her. She'd never seen another man with a jawline like his. His eyes were the bluest blue. His black curls were disheveled and fell over his forehead in gentle swoops. His arms, the arms that had held her when she'd awakened from a nightmare, were so strong. They were the same arms where he'd cradle their child. Her heart sang an unknown melody, a melody that burned her eyes with the sheer joy of it.

"I must confess," she breathed. "It will change our lives forever."

"What do you mean?" His voice sounded strangled.

She removed one of her hands from his and caressed his dimple. "It will be the most wonderful adventure. And you, you will be so wonderful." Her voice broke as tears spilled down her cheeks.

Nicholas opened his mouth to speak, but tears twinkled in his eyes instead.

She grappled for her breath and swallowed. "Nicholas, we're having a child."

Something broke in Nicholas's eyes. He smiled through his tear-stained gaze on her. "Oh, Emmaline!" He sprang from where he'd knelt and wrapped his arms around her. Tears spilled onto her shoulder where he'd buried his head.

Even when he pulled away, he still held her shoulders tightly. "Emmy, I thought you were—" His smile fell as his eyebrows creased. "But why did you faint?"

She shook her head, her cheeks aching from smiling so much. "I have heard that is sometimes common in pregnancies. I suppose with the recent attack, I became overburdened. But the doctor mentioned nothing wrong with my health. All is well, my love."

Nicholas gazed at her with a look of admiration. "Yes, all is very well." He took her hand and kissed her knuckles.

She stroked his disheveled hair with trembling fingertips. "Just look at us, Nicholas. Our pasts are scarred with death, but just look at us. We're creating new life, you and I."

He smiled. "You've given me one of the greatest gifts a person can give to another."

"As have you." She smiled warmly down at him.

He rubbed his thumbs over her knuckles and kissed them again. Tears spilled over her lashes and down her cheeks. *God, thank You for this wonderful love, for this wonderful gift.*

When Nicholas looked up at her again, she gripped his hands tightly. "I want to keep this a secret for now," she said. "It is the season of our Savior, and I do not wish to take any of the attention away from Him. We will announce the news in the new year."

He smiled at her. "If you wish, my love. For now, we will keep this gift a secret."

Yes, it would be a secret. And while Victor lay awake at night, dreaming of the day when every last

Rise

Konovian would vanish from the earth, her child–the seed of her murdered family–would be growing, crushing his dreams, and fulfilling all of hers.

"I heard about the celebration being held in your honor." Anna smiled up at Ross. They were both walking in the garden on this unusually warm winter day. Anna had felt up to it, but Ross had made her swear she would tell him if she began to feel weak. Her arm was in a sling, but she still walked with the same grace that befitted a queen's maid of honor.

Ross cleared his throat and glanced down at the garden path. "Oh, yes, that."

Anna giggled, and he was certain no angel's voice could sound purer. "Something tells me you're not entirely in love with the idea."

He grinned. "Not really. I'm not one for being in the public eye."

"Neither am I. I've always been shy. My night with the king several months ago was one of the most difficult nights of my life."

Ross was glad Nicholas had not selected Anna to become his wife. The king had had a wide array of flowers from which to choose, but the very best had been saved for Ross. And he wouldn't want it any other way.

Ross glanced at Anna. The smile had faded from her face like the sun drifting behind the clouds. "I've been wanting to ask... why did you come here?"

She looked up at him, fear shooting across her face. "Oh." Her face tightened as if she were pretending that nothing was amiss, pretending she weren't afraid. "My mother sent me here."

She'd said before that she and her mother didn't have a good relationship, but he didn't know much else. Perhaps she needed to talk about it with someone. He didn't want to press too hard and crush her, so he trod lightly. "Do you miss her?"

She frowned, her steps slowing. "A little. I'm afraid she doesn't miss me very much."

"Why do you think that?"

"Oh, I don't think. *I know.* We've never been close. She was raised in a strict household, and her parents pressed her into marrying my father for his money. She always regretted rejecting Victor for my father. My parents argued quite a lot when I was young, and then he began to go on trips a few times a year. One would think his absence might make things better, but she simply turned her anger on me."

The spark of her words lighted his anger, and Ross burned with it. "She beat you?"

She paled. "No. She never beat me. But I didn't have a childhood. She sent me to boarding school, and in the summers, she taught me how to be a lady. She picked out all my clothes, my hairstyles, my activities. She even picked out my friends–although they weren't my friends. They were perfect ladies until my mother left the room. They would break vases or tear curtains and then blame me for it. They didn't like me because they thought my love of the outdoors was strange. My mother believed I was acting out because I wanted attention, but she punished me by locking me in my bedchamber."

A cold draft blew right through Ross. He knew it was impossible, but he wished he would have been there to keep so much pain from happening. Just because her mother had never beaten her didn't mean that Anna didn't have scars. Words were often sharper than any blade. "Did she never find out that it wasn't you destroying the vases and the curtains?"

Anna shook her head. "No. The lessons grew more and more strict. She didn't let me decide what I wanted. She wanted me to marry someone rich. She wanted me to have the same kind of life that she had. I couldn't let that happen. So I ran away. I stayed away for three days, out in the meadows and fields."

"How did you survive?" His voice couldn't hide his surprise. Surely her etiquette lessons hadn't taught her how to survive in the outdoors.

For the first time in several moments, Anna smiled. "I didn't survive. That was the first three days in my life that I had actually lived. I was free. Free from my mother, free from her anger, free from her wishes, free from everything. I tore my dress, I tore my stockings, and my hair was disheveled, but I didn't care. I was free. I'd been locked away from the sun for so long, and I never wanted to go back." Her smile disappeared. "But I did go back. My mother's servants found me and brought me back to her. She screamed at me and told me she was going to send me away again. This time, she was sending me to the palace."

Ross couldn't believe that Anna was related to this woman. But he was glad her mother had sent her to the palace. If she had not, they would not have met, and Anna would still be trapped like a caged songbird. "Didn't your father try to stop her?"

She bit her lip, her eyes twinkling. "My father died from an attack of the heart two years ago." She swiped at her tears.

He brushed his hand over her arm. "I'm sorry. And I'm sorry that your mother was so horrible to you."

Anna glanced up at him. "It's not your doing."

"Nor yours." He met her emerald gaze for several moments and wondered if it was her pretty eyes or the sun that was making him so warm.

She shrugged. "I know it's maddening to believe, but some part of me wants to please her so much. But I don't know how. Nicholas has already married Emmaline, and they are a far better match together than he and I ever could have been." Tears glimmered in her eyes. "I fear I'll never please her, Ross."

He couldn't believe her softness. She'd been through tragedy just like him, but she hadn't allowed herself to become a pillar of marble, hardened and bitter. Many of her petals had been ripped away by hateful people, but she harbored no ill will against them. Her heart was still lovely. His heart sank. *Oh, God. Why couldn't I have been more like her?*

Rise

And yet, would she have been happier had she ended up with Nicholas? Would she have rather had a life of elegance and pomp, chandeliers and crystals and castles, all to impress her mother? Would she have rather married Nicholas than Ross? He couldn't give her the life Nicholas could have. Ross lived in the palace, but he was no king. With his dangerous line of work, he was not even sure he could grow old with her. Marrying a man like him would only further taint her mother's view of her, and that wouldn't help Anna.

Yet if her mother could not see Anna for the wonder she was, was she worth trying to please? Shouldn't Anna carve out her own path? He didn't want to fool himself, but he believed she cared for him. She did not want to marry Nicholas out of her own desire. She only had wanted to marry him at first to respect her mother's wishes. And Ross was glad. He'd never been lucky in the game of love, but he may have finally won a girl with springtime in her smiles.

Ross shook his head. "Don't do that to yourself. You've been through enough. All your life, your mother tried to mold you into who she wanted you to be. But if you try to please her anymore, you won't be you any longer. And I think the Anna standing next to me is wonderful as she is." He cupped her face in his hand.

She stared at him in that fairy-like gaze of hers. "Do you think so?"

He smiled. "Yes, I do." His heart raced like a steam engine running off course. Her lips were so pink as the sun set her red curls on fire.

"Captain Ross!" a young boy cried.

Ross jerked away, annoyed at the servant boy's interruption. Anna was blushing like roses. He turned toward the boy. "Yes, what is it?"

"It's the queen. She's requested your presence in the royal library."

Ross glanced apologetically at Anna, but she shook her head. "Go on, it's all right."

He gave her a stern look. "Remember your promise to me."

She smiled. "I know. I won't overdo it."

"I'll hold you to it." He gave her one last look before stepping away.

The servant boy kept pace with Ross. "And I must tell you one more thing, Captain."

"Yes?"

"The queen fainted earlier this morning."

Panic ripped through Ross like an array of bullets. "What?"

"She's well now, but no one knows why it happened."

Ross left the servant there and rushed toward the palace. Why had she fainted? He quickened his pace and entered the palace.

He sped down the hall and trotted up the staircase. Ross knew the weight of the plot against the Konovians must be terrible upon such a young woman that had already endured so much in life, but he had not known to what extent. He had to make certain nothing was amiss and that nothing serious had caused her to have such an episode.

Emmaline's back was toward him when he entered the library. She was dressed normally, and her hair was fixed, so she was well enough to groom herself. Perhaps it wasn't such bad news.

He stepped toward her. "I got your message, Emmaline."

She turned, and a certain joy sparkled in her eyes. He'd never seen that before, except for when she spoke of Nicholas. "I'm glad you came, Ross."

"I heard what happened this morning and wanted to make certain nothing was amiss. Are you well? Is there something you need to tell me?"

She smiled. "I called you because I wanted to make certain you remembered to assign the guards around the ballroom for the night of the ball. I know how overwhelming your schedule can become."

He exhaled, relieved. "Oh, yes. I remembered. I organized everything so that my strongest men can watch each exit. No mischief will be happening at the ball, I can assure you."

"Thank you, Ross." Her smile dipped into a frown.

Something was wrong. "Emmaline, is there something else?"

She met his gaze, looked to the side, and then looked at him again. "Yes, but you can't tell anyone. It has to be a secret, Ross." Panic and fear flashed in her eyes.

His chest tightened. "All right, then. What is it?"

"I'm with child."

He blinked, looking down at her with parted lips. She was—What? Surely he hadn't heard her right. But he knew he had. He smiled. "Oh, Emmaline, congratulations! Does Nicholas know?"

She smiled but only for a moment. "Yes, but—"

"What's wrong?" Was something wrong with her health? The child's health?

"I'm afraid of Victor finding out. I've told Nicholas I want to keep it a secret until the new year, but Victor's eyes watch so closely. If he finds out my family's bloodline is continuing, he'll—" She sucked in a breath.

Heat like a roaring fire rushed into his cheeks. He wouldn't let that happen. He would die before Victor put a hand on her. "Don't worry, Emmaline. Victor won't find out. Your secret is safe with me."

Her face softened. "Thank you, Ross. I knew I could count on you." She glanced over Ross's shoulder at the door. "Well, I must visit the kitchen staff and see how they're preparing."

He nodded. "Of course."

He smiled as he watched her leave the library. A child for Nicholas and Emmaline. His heart swelled with joy for them.

And if Victor even thought of hurting Emmaline or her child, Ross would make Victor wish he'd never been born.

Emmaline stood in front of her mirror dressed in her

Rise

nightgown, glancing over her body and smoothing her hand over her slightly swollen middle. Her pulse thrummed in her throat so quickly she was sure it was visible. A cold sweat trickled down her back. Two weeks had passed. Tomorrow night was the night of the ball, the night when all her guests would gather together in shimmering evening wear, the night when she would reveal Victor for who he really was.

She'd carried herself with grace and poise with her guests all week. She'd made conversation and laughed at every joke. Even though her stomach churned at the sight of food. Even though all she wanted was to hide. Even though she was certain she would burst with every secret she kept inside.

If Emmaline failed tomorrow, the last of the Konovians would be destroyed, just like Victor wanted. If she failed, Victor would kill her and end the life of her child before it ever saw the light of the sun. If she failed, Nicholas would never know the truth about her.

But if she did not fail, the Konovians would be free to live without threat of death by merciless enemies. Her child would be born and would learn all the Konovian stories, dances, and songs. Nicholas would know the truth, and he would love her for all that she was.

She could not fail. So many lives depended on her. Her shoulders ached with the weight of it all, the burden she carried. *Jesus, protect me. Protect this life You've put inside me. Protect the lives of my people.*

Look down on me and be gracious. Give me Your strength, and I will be victorious.

Footsteps came behind her. Nicholas embraced her from behind, wearing his nightshirt and a boyish grin. "Can't sleep?"

She smiled, her pulse slowing at his touch. "No."

"I'm afraid lack of sleep is common for women in your condition." He looked into the mirror, sliding his hand down her middle and keeping it there.

She closed her eyes and clasped her hand over his. She'd finally returned to the life she once knew as a girl, a life of warmth, safety, and love. Now, the ghosts were awake again, begging her to prevent others from joining them in death. The wolves had returned, licking their teeth, hungry to consume her and the life she now had. And everything depended on one night. One night in which she spoke boldly against a man who had her husband's trust, a man who had shattered her childhood, a man who wanted to break her until she was in shards.

And now she was with child. She had grown in the past two weeks, but not enough to be noticeable with all the layers she wore every day. Still, she would not feel safe until Victor was behind bars.

She tightened her closed eyes and her grip on Nicholas's hand.

"Emmaline, are you all right?" Nicholas asked.

"Yes," she breathed. She looked at his reflection in the mirror. "I've never thrown a ball before. And I'm so anxious about it all."

Rise

"Everything will be perfect." He twirled one of her curls around his finger. "The servants seem very excited about helping you to prepare it tomorrow. From what I've heard, you've done a marvelous job of planning everything."

I only hope I have. She waved her thumb over Nicholas's knuckle. "Tell me everything will be all right. Please."

He stepped in front of her. He held her face in his hands, his eyes like calming seas. "I promise, everything will be all right." He closed the remaining distance between them and pressed his lips to hers. Falling stars shot up and down through her, her whole body flashing hot and cold.

He pulled away and pressed his forehead to hers. "Do you believe me now?"

His breath was warm on her cold face. Her heart galloped like a thousand thoroughbreds, but something small and quiet washed over her. ***I am with you.*** "Yes."

Nicholas moved away but caught her limp hand. "Come on, then. I'll hold you until you sleep. Tomorrow's a big day, and I don't want my beautiful wife to fall asleep on my shoulder as we dine with our guests." He grinned in jest.

Emmaline laughed, following him into bed. She lay against his chest and listened to the melody of his heartbeat, the moonlight illuminating the frost crystalized on the window. She stared at the ceiling of their canopy bed and whispered silent prayers.

Be with me, God.

And the small, quiet voice returned.
I always am.

Chapter Twenty-Eight

THE ORCHESTRA THUNDERED with Tchaikovsky's *The Nutcracker*, the notes falling around the room like snowflakes. The ballroom, decorated with wreaths, garlands, and fir trees and alight with massive chandeliers, burst with shades of ruby, emerald, and gold. At least a dozen couples waltzed on the dance floor, while dozens of others gathered around, talking gaily and trying the hors d'oeuvres from the offered trays of servants.

Emmaline smoothed down her silvery-blue gown, resisting the urge to pull at her pearl necklace. She tried to concentrate on the waltzing guests, but her gaze kept flickering upwards to the golden clock. *Only ten more minutes until supper.*

Victor had arrived twenty minutes before, dressed sharply in a black tux. He smiled smugly at several young girls, the daughters of noblemen. Some of them giggled in response, and Emmaline had to force down the bile rising in her throat. If only they knew he was a monster in disguise.

Ross stood at the beverage table, drinking punch and scowling darkly at the back of Victor's head as Victor laughed with several noblemen. He looked ready to throw his glass at Victor's head. Emmaline was glad Ross was here. Between him and Nicholas, she knew she would come to no harm if Victor became violent.

What if he did become violent? She knew what it was like to be held in his grip, to feel his fingers squeezing her throat until she couldn't breathe. The man had thrown an entire couch across the room without difficulty, and he'd felt no apprehension about shooting down three innocent girls. When she ripped off his mask tonight, would the beast beneath attack her again?

Nicholas stepped in front of her, expelling her anxious thoughts. "I've brought you some punch," he said, holding two glasses filled with ruby liquid. "I'm told it's cranberry." He bent toward her and spoke softly. "You can have that, can't you?"

Emmaline laughed, grateful for the way he was

Rise

able to unknowingly soothe her. "Yes, I can. And thank you." She took the glass from him and sipped at it. The tart sweetness danced over her tongue.

He stood by her, taking in the scene around them. "I told you everything would be perfect." He winked.

"And so it is." The words she would speak played over and over in her mind. She was ready to speak those words, to finish this once and for all.

"Ah, Your Majesties!" a familiar voice called. Emmaline's heart fell into her stomach, and she was sure the child inside her squeezed it. Victor walked toward them, flashing a smile.

Emmaline uttered a quick prayer to herself. *God, give me victory over this man. Stop this devil from making life a living hell for his victims. Issue your justice swiftly so I do not have to stand in his presence any longer.*

Victor met her gaze. "I was delighted to receive your invitation to the ball. I must say, it's been quite a long time since I've attended one, much less a ball as grand as this one." He practically guzzled his drink.

"It would not have been a ball without you, Victor." Nicholas clapped him on the shoulder. "You deserved an invitation after everything you've done for me since my mother's death."

Emmaline swallowed her disgust. She could hardly wait for the truth to be revealed so her husband would see this snake for what he really was.

Victor gave a curt nod. "That's high praise, Your Majesty. Thank you." He took another sip and then turned to Emmaline again, glancing her over. "I must say, my queen, you look exceptionally beautiful tonight."

Her stomach curled. She was grateful she had picked a dress with a fuller skirt. While her condition was still not obvious with so many layers of undergarments, she had not wanted to take any chances. Still, Emmaline was surprised at the relative ease she felt as she forced a smile. "Thank you, Mr. Hughes. You are too kind." She swallowed her nausea.

The orchestra stopped as the butler clapped his hands. "Attention, ladies and gentlemen, supper will be served in just a moment. You may be seated as the servants bring out the meal."

An appreciative chatter rose from the guests, and everyone flocked to the long table waiting on the far right of the room. Nicholas sat at the head of the table with Emmaline on his right and Victor on his left. Ross stood in the corner nearest to them.

Spoons clattered against the china bowls as the guests ate their steaming soup. Servants cheerfully made their way around the table, filling each guest's cup and bowl. The hearty laughter of several gentlemen rose from the eastern side of the table, while the ladies leaned in as close as social etiquette allowed, whispering the latest news to one another. The rubies, sapphires, and emeralds the ladies wore shimmered in the candlelight. Everyone seemed caught in their own world, drinking from their glasses and sharing smiles across the table.

Emmaline pressed a hand to her middle from

behind the table, a slight cold sweat trickling above her lip. She did not feel like eating, but what choice had she? The time had not yet come, and she had to keep pretending so Victor would not notice something was awry.

Emmaline took a sip of her soup, the warmth filling her veins. Nicholas told Victor a story he'd told her about his friend Harry, and they both laughed as if they were brothers. Victor had him so fooled. How dare Victor trick her husband like this?

The first course was soon finished, and the bowls were whisked away and replaced with the main course: two enormous roasted geese, aged cheeses, potatoes, cranberry sauce, and steamed puddings. Emmaline ate slowly, not wanting to make herself sicker than she already was. She barely tasted the food and did not know how she would survive until dessert.

Finally, the servants bustled away with the remains of the main course while others brought out the desserts: sweet puddings, figgy pudding, and three different types of cake. As the servants scurried around the table refilling the cups again, the Duke of Bendricks, a stout man decorated with war medals, rose from his seat, clinking his cup politely. All eyes turned to him.

"I simply wanted to thank our beautiful hostess, Her Majesty the Queen, for allowing us to dine so elegantly in her palace. She has welcomed us into her home and her heart."

As the duke spoke, Nicholas took her hand from beneath the table and held it. Emmaline smiled as she listened to the duke.

The duke raised his glass. "Let us raise our glasses for our most gracious hostess, Queen Emmaline!"

"Hear, hear!" The resounding cry rose around the table as each glass sprang into the air.

"God bless their reign!" a lord called.

"May their union be as sweet as this punch!" another said. Many chuckled.

"May their palace be filled with many children!" a woman cried.

Nicholas squeezed her hand, and she squeezed back.

Victor rose from his seat. "And may God Himself grant them unmeasurable glory on their reign."

A chill sprinkled over Emmaline's shoulders. He did not mean those words. Even in this moment, he was probably imagining the day when he would sacrifice the Konovians on the altar to himself, forever purifying his world of their presence.

Nicholas beamed and stood to his feet. "Thank you all for your kind words. The queen and I were more than happy to celebrate our Savior's birth with you during your stay. As I look across the table, I am filled with certainty that our great kingdom will be filled with its former glory, despite all the war has taken from us."

Applause roared from the table. Emmaline's heart echoed in her ears. It was her turn to speak.

Rise

Emmaline looked across the table. Victor gazed at Nicholas, smiling smugly.

Her stomach curled. This was it. This was the moment when she would yank Victor from the shadows and expose him for who he was. No longer would he be able to hide his fangs or claws. The blood staining his hands and the ghosts he had made would finally have justice. It was time to speak.

Emmaline glanced at Ross, and he put his hand on his sword hilt. Emmaline swallowed, her heart fluttering clumsily like a baby bird learning to fly. She clutched her skirts in her hand and said a quick, silent prayer for strength.

Nicholas sat down in his seat again, nodding at her as if he were giving her the opportunity to speak. She forced a smile and rose to her feet. She was nearly certain that an earthquake was happening, but she knew it was only her legs trembling beneath her.

"Speech! Speech!" many guests called.

Emmaline chuckled, resisting the urge to play with her fingers. "I am honored by all the kind words and blessings you have spoken over me and the king. As he has said, we are more than happy to welcome you all into the palace for a time of celebration. It has been a delightful night, one that I hope to repeat every year."

She swallowed and rolled her shoulders back. "Christmas was always my favorite time of year to spend with my family. I've missed them dearly ever since they were tragically killed." *Calm yourself.* "I have never told any of you where I was born. That is because I was afraid. But I cannot afford to let that stop me any longer, and neither can my people. My home was destroyed by a gang of wicked men. They killed my family and burned my house. The same man who led the attack against my people is hunting us down again. He has used black magic to trick the king into going along with his plan, and he has concealed his real intentions from the king. He wants to destroy us completely. He wants me and my people dead."

She glanced at Victor, whose smile had turned into a dark scowl.

"But why?" Nicholas snarled. "Why would he want to kill you?" His nostrils flared, but his face was ashen.

She swept her gaze across the table, starting with Nicholas and moving to the guests before finally landing on Victor. His eyes were sharp like daggers, but she did not bleed. "Because I am the Grand Duchess Emmaline Marie, princess of Konovia."

The guests exclaimed in shock. Whispers peppered Emmaline's eardrums.

Nicholas stared in shock at Emmaline, his brows raised and his mouth open.

She looked over the vast crowd of wide-eyed gazes again. "The man hunting me and my people killed my family. I am the only remaining heir of King Alexander."

Nicholas leapt to his feet, his blue eyes unusually dark. "Who is this man?"

Rise

Emmaline stabbed a finger across the table. "Victor Hughes."

Unanimous gasps rose around the table. Dishes clattered as Victor lunged across the table. He plunged a knife at Emmaline's throat. Screams filled the room as Emmaline jerked back. Nicholas grabbed Victor's shoulders and pulled him to the floor.

Emmaline's breath came in short bursts. "Nicholas!" She hurried around the corner of the table, but Ross caught her arm and kept her from going any further.

"Stay there!" he ordered before running toward the action.

Emmaline drew in a hasty breath, praying Victor's knife wouldn't be sticking out of Nicholas's body. She glanced down at the two men wrestling on the floor, Nicholas on top of Victor. The knife lay several feet away, glinting in the candlelight. Ross lunged toward Nicholas, but Nicholas fought off his

grip and pinned Victor to the floor. Victor shouted incoherently and tried to hit Nicholas, but Nicholas sent him back down with a blow to the face.

"Guards!" Ross bellowed. "Take this man away!" He lunged toward Nicholas again, who was still pummeling Victor, and grabbed his arms. "Come, Your Majesty. The guards will handle him."

Nicholas's head jerked up, his eyes wild and his face scarlet. With a growl, he sprang to his feet, wiped his lip, and scowled at Victor as the guards yanked him to his feet.

With a dark expression of his own, Ross shackled

Victor's hands with a ready pair of cuffs. Victor cursed, wrestling Ross's grip until Ross restrained him.

Emmaline rushed to Nicholas's side and took his arm, afraid he would go after Victor again. The heat emitting from Nicholas's body burned Emmaline's hands.

"You traitor!" Nicholas roared. He leapt forward, but Emmaline had a tight grip on his arm and held him back. "My mother loved you, and I trusted you! I allowed you to come into my home, *and you plotted to kill my wife!* You will rot in prison until I decide your fate. And believe me, Mr. Hughes, it shall be a just fate for all the blood you have on your hands!"

Victor's eyes shot darts at Nicholas, his hair disheveled and blood leaking from his nose and lip. "You stupid boy!" He spit toward Nicholas, and blood trickled down his shirt. "It is you who gave me your signet ring, and you who sealed the fate of the Konovians. Their blood is on your hands."

Nicholas lurched forward again, and Emmaline tightened her hold on him.

Ross held up a hand. "Steady, Your Majesty!"

"Take him away!" Nicholas snarled.

Victor struggled against the guards as they dragged him along the floor. "You won't win that easily!" he screamed. "You cannot save them! The Konovians will be vanquished—forever!"

The ballroom doors slammed. Emmaline jumped at the thundering noise, her whole body trembling like a crumbling fortress.

As the guests whispered around the table, Nicholas turned to Emmaline, his scowl melting into a soft, anxious gaze. He must have seen a weakness in her eyes because he grabbed her mid-section and held her upright. "Are you all right?" Sweat glistened on his forehead as he gazed down at her.

She gulped a few breaths and gripped his forearms. "Yes."

His brows creased as sadness shot across his eyes. "It's all my fault. Victor is right. I gave him my signet ring because I trusted him. I let him get into my head. And now, he has put a plan into action to kill your people. I was so foolish, Emmaline. Forgive me, please."

Emmaline caressed his arm. "Nicholas, don't blame yourself. It is not your fault. There is nothing for me to forgive. He had everyone fooled."

"Not you." He grinned sadly.

The whisper of his boots on that moonless night three years ago echoed inside her. She bit her lip. "I'll never forget his face."

Nicholas caressed her cheek, his jawline flexing. "He's gone now. He's not coming back, and he won't hurt you. I promise." He looked her over before enveloping her in his arms. He held her for several moments.

As Emmaline stood there pressed against his chest, drowning in his warmth, she gazed at the ceiling. She could breathe again. The monster was gone, and the darkness had fled. *Thank You, God.* She wished she could say more, but "thank you" was all she could manage. *Thank You, thank You, thank You.*

As the guests whispered at the table, Nicholas held Emmaline tightly as if he were afraid she would fade away. He had made a grave mistake. How could he have let Victor trick him? Why hadn't he realized before? Victor had been behind it all: the assassination attempt on Emmaline during the parade and the night attack just weeks ago.

If Emmaline had not spoken out, Nicholas would still not know of Victor's plot. The Konovians would all be dead in a matter of weeks, and Victor would have killed Emmaline—and now their unborn child.

Victor's words echoed in Nicholas's mind. *"It is you who gave me your signet ring, and you who sealed the fate of the Konovians. Their blood is on your hands."*

So when Victor had sworn to exact justice on the Konovian renegades, he had lied. He had tricked Nicholas. He had written a completely different contract, and Nicholas had ignorantly given that devil his signet ring. On the day Victor had promised the blood of the men who had plotted against Emmaline's life, he had really promised that the Konovians' blood would be shed.

But not anymore.

Victor would pay. He was in God's hands now, and Nicholas knew God would not allow such a wicked man to go unpunished. Victor had chosen his path, and now he would pay for his choice.

Nicholas pulled away from Emmaline, marveling at her bravery. She must have been so frightened, carrying that secret and keeping it from him for the sake of her life and the Konovians' lives. No wonder she had fainted and acted so oddly.

He smoothed his thumb over her full brow, watching tears twinkle in her dark eyes. "You are wonderful," he whispered.

She smiled, a tear falling down her cheek. He wiped it away.

He turned to the guests gathered at the table, who were still wide-eyed and whispering. "I apologize for that "little" scene, ladies and gentlemen. As the queen stated, I had no idea about this plot, and I deeply regret the mistakes I made that led to it. I will be working with my captain of the guard and my closest advisors, as well as the queen herself, to figure out a way to preserve the lives of every single Konovian." He turned to his wife, noting the color that had returned to her face. "But for tonight, let us continue to honor our hostess for her extraordinary bravery."

One by one, the lords and ladies and the dukes and duchesses all rose to their feet, clapping and cheering. Emmaline covered her mouth, her face stretched with a hidden smile.

As they walked back to the table, Emmaline bent and picked something up from the floor. She held it in her hands, turning it around to examine it, and then threw it back down. She stomped it with her foot, her brows drawn together and her teeth clenched.

Nicholas stared down at the remains of a golden ring. "What was that?"

"Victor's last hope."

Chapter Twenty-Nine

EMMALINE LAY IN bed, staring up at the silk canopy stretching over her. After weeks of scarcely sleeping, she had finally gone a night without awakening in a fit of fear and anxiety. Though today was the day when Victor's men would attack the Konovian region of the city, Emmaline knew God had sent His armies to surround her people's homes and protect them. He had given her victory the night of the ball, so why would He not silence the howls of the wolves today?

The sun had not been up for long, but Nicholas

was already awake and out of bed, leaning over the wash bowl and scrubbing his face. Emmaline pressed her knuckles to her lips and smiled as she watched him.

Nicholas had done so well in helping her find a way to rescue the Konovians. Since he had given Victor his signet ring, they could not abolish the contract but could only work around it. He had ordered Ross to have his finest soldiers keep track of Victor's men, and then he, Emmaline, and Ross had created a plan. On the day of the attack, Ross would hide out in the Konovian region and wait for their enemies. Then, Ross, the royal guard, and all the able-bodied Konovian men would strike back at Victor's party when they arrived.

"The Konovians will easily overpower Victor's men," Ross had promised, much to Emmaline's relief. "Victor only has about a hundred men ready to do his bidding."

As for Victor, he had spent the last several weeks in the dungeon. Though Emmaline hungered for justice, they could not begin Victor's trials yet because that would notify his followers that he had been arrested. If they caught wind of Victor's capture, his men would flee like rats and remain free to hurt the Konovians. So, the trials could only begin after the day of the attack. Emmaline and her people could hardly wait to see this beast finally slayed.

Last week, she had secretly visited the Konovian region with Ross again, but this time with Nicholas,

Anna, and a few guards. She had bolstered the Konovians to prepare them for the impending day. Many of the women had shed a tear or two, and others had told her she was just like her father. She had cried into Nicholas's shoulder all the way home. She hadn't known she was anything like her father. She'd hoped, yes, but she'd never believed she was like him—a wise, strong ruler who protected his people. She missed him. She missed all of them.

Emmaline yawned and stretched her legs before sitting up. It was time to get ready. She may not be wielding a sword or firing a gun, but she did have a battle to fight today—on her knees.

She grabbed a dress from her wardrobe and hurried behind the dressing table. The nightgown fell to her feet, and her heart skipped a beat as she looked over her growing body. Six weeks had passed since the Christmas ball, and now she was four months gone. Her mid-section was now obviously swollen no matter what she wore, and the news of the coming child had spread like a wildfire within the palace walls. But though the staff was jubilant about the news, they'd been sworn to secrecy concerning anything taking place within the palace. Emmaline was glad her secret was still safe, since Victor's men were still roaming free in the city.

When the girls had found out, they had all squealed with delight, behaving more like young girls receiving invitations to a ball and less like lady's maids. Emmaline had simply laughed.

"We'll be just like aunts!" Julia had cried, wrapping her arms tightly around Emmaline.

"Julia, not so tight!" Eleanor had scolded. "You'll squeeze poor Emmaline to death!"

Emmaline hadn't minded at all and had squeezed Julia tighter.

Emmaline gazed at her belly and brushed her hand over it. She'd never felt so beautiful or full in her life, save for her wedding day. With one last look, she quickly dressed and then stepped out from the dressing table.

Nicholas was combing his hair in front of the mirror but turned toward her. He smiled warmly as he glanced over her body. "You're looking well." He closed the distance between them and kissed her on the mouth.

She smiled when he pulled away. Ever since the night of the ball, Nicholas had been peppering her with questions about her Konovian upbringing. She'd told him all about her family, her kingdom and its people, and their traditions. She'd recounted tales from her childhood and described the buildings that had once graced the land. She had even taught him a few Konovian dances as the moonlight glowed across their bedchamber floor.

In all those lonely nights on the streets, when she was left with nothing but scraps of her past, she'd never believed she could regain most of her memories back. But ever since she'd found Konovia's coat of arms, the memories had been washing back across the shore of her memory. Every piece of the past was precious to her, and she was grateful they had all been returned to her.

Emmaline picked up her brush and ran it through her long waves. "I feel less afraid today than I was the day of the ball," she confessed.

Nicholas stood next to her in the mirror and tightened his tie. "I think that's because you've placed it all in God's hands."

"I knew it was in God's hands before, but perhaps even more so now that my part is complete." She pinned back her hair. She'd given the girls the day off so that they could pray for the Konovians.

"And you played it beautifully." He took a step back from the mirror and turned toward her. He frowned, unusual lines marring his forehead. "I'm only sorry I was the cause of all this." He took a breath and glanced down. "I put you all in danger—you, Ross, your people, our child." He shook his head, scowling.

Emmaline cupped the back of his head and forced him to meet her face. "Nicholas, it wasn't you. It was Victor." Her thumb smoothed his skin as she tried to smooth his fears away.

His eyes searched hers, and the corners of his mouth sprung up. "I love you."

She embraced him, burying her face in his chest. "And I love you."

After a few moments passed, he waved his hand over her back. "Well, I'm afraid I have to go and meet with the advisors now. Where will you be today?"

"The solar. I want to pray up there." It would be quite a few steps, but she enjoyed the walk and the solar's view.

He grinned but furrowed his brows seriously. "All right, but be careful. Take it easy. Promise me."

"I will, I promise."

He leaned forward and kissed her cheek, and then fully and warmly on the lips. Sparks shot through her as her chest lightened. "I'll come up there when it's all over," he said against her ear.

She nodded as he stepped back. He left the room and closed the door.

Emmaline enveloped her middle with her hands, studying her reflection in the mirror. She bit her lip, grinning. There was no hiding it now.

Just last year at this time, she'd been running from the ghosts and wolves of her past, dreaming of the life she'd once had, longing for love, and wondering where she'd come from. Now, she was safe from the screaming ghosts and the howling wolves, living in a glittering marble palace, loved by the most wonderful man in the world, and united with her own people again. What had she done to earn such favor from God?

Turning from the mirror, she walked out of her bedchamber and toward the solar.

Ross couldn't remember seeing a lovelier set of green

Rise

eyes than Anna's. They shone like emeralds, even now when they shimmered with tears as she watched him prepare for battle. She'd been worried sick ever since she found out he would be fighting Victor's followers. She'd heard the news after Nicholas had finally stopped trying to convince Ross to let him fight. Ross appreciated his friend's offer, but this was the Konovians' battle to win.

Anna stepped closer to him. "Ross, promise me you'll be careful," she said.

He hated seeing her so upset, but her voice was a welcome sound. After spending hours and hours with her, he'd grown accustomed to hearing her soft voice.

He tightened the last straps of the saddle. "I will, Anna. I promise. How could I not be, when I've got you to return to?" He looked over his shoulder and grinned at her.

She smiled and shook her head. "Listen to you, charming me when I'm worried out of my wits."

Ross sighed and stepped toward her. He took her hands in his own and looked her in the eyes. He couldn't leave her before reassuring her. He couldn't leave her before stopping her trembling. "Do you remember how we met?"

Anna nodded, blushing. "Yes. We ran into each other in the chapel."

"And we were both there to do what?"

She raised her brows. "Pray, of course."

"Perhaps that is what you should do if you are so worried about me."

She smiled again. "Perhaps you're right."

A figure appeared in the corner of Ross's eye. "Captain, the men are ready!"

Ross turned to the guard and nodded. "As am I. Tell them to mount their horses. I'll be there in a moment." He glanced back at Anna.

A shade of white crept over her face as her lips trembled. "Come back to me, Ross," she whispered.

He didn't want her to be so afraid. He wouldn't allow fear to trample his flower.

He brushed his hand over the side of her face and held her gaze. "I will." He pressed his forehead against hers and took in the scent of her skin. He pressed his lips against hers, and the winter winds howling within him turned to spring.

When he pulled away, her eyes were wide, and a shade of pink crept into her cheeks. Clearly, she hadn't expected that. Perhaps she was not ready for that yet. His pulse raced and then quickened even more when she grinned at him. So she hadn't minded it after all.

He smiled and then mounted his horse. "I'll find you when I come back."

She opened her mouth to speak but simply beamed. He reluctantly turned away and urged his horse into a gallop. He had a battle to fight. And he'd fight to the death for the lovely red-haired girl who smelled like spring.

Nicholas sat on his throne, his fist rested beneath his jaw as he silently prayed. Running footsteps pounded into the throne room. Nicholas's eyes snapped open, and he jumped to his feet.

A young boy panted and bent over in front of Nicholas's throne. Blood stuck to the side of the boy's head, but the wound did not look serious. Beads of sweat made trails through the soot covering his skin.

"What news?" Nicholas asked urgently.

"The battle . . . is over." The boy huffed. "The Konovians . . . won."

All the advisors standing with Nicholas cheered, slapped each other on the back, and shook hands. Nicholas's heart swelled as his burden lifted from his shoulders. God had allowed him to mend his mistake and rescue his wife's people.

"And what of Victor's men?" Nicholas's blood heated as he spoke. Whatever men weren't killed would be trialed, jailed, and executed for their crimes. They would pay for attempting to cause division in his kingdom and for nearly destroying the last remnant of an innocent people.

"All but twenty have been killed, Your Majesty." The boy bowed low to the ground. "My people thank you for rescuing us."

Nicholas shook his head and held a hand up. "I accept your gratitude, but you must accept my apology for nearly destroying you all." He swallowed painfully.

The boy didn't raise his head. "The king was innocent and needs no forgiveness."

Tears welled in Nicholas's eyes, and he smiled. "Thank you, young man." He took in a deep breath and remembered the girl waiting for him in the solar. Doubtless she was bent over her Bible, whispering silent prayers for her people. "I must inform the queen now." Nicholas hurried off and walked quickly down the halls.

Because of God's mercy, Emmaline was reunited with her people. Their child would grow up and learn the ways of its people. And Emmaline could rest in the peace God had given her after so many years of fear and anxiousness.

Ross appeared around the corner, perspiring just like the young boy had been. Soot covered his golden curls, and dried blood stained the side of his forehead. He raised a hand in a friendly gesture toward Nicholas, breathing hard.

Nicholas pointed at Ross's head, gesturing toward the wound. "Is it serious?"

Ross frowned, as if puzzled, and touched the spot. He glanced down at his fingers and shook his head. "No harm done, Majesty. It's just a scratch."

Relieved, Nicholas smiled. "I've just heard the news. Thank you for leading the charge."

Ross grinned back. "It was my duty and privilege, Majesty."

Nicholas's chest warmed in gratitude. Not all kings were given such loyal servants and staff. Not everyone would choose to help someone who had almost destroyed a whole nation, whether it was accidental or not. The battle may have been won, but would Nicholas ever forgive himself?

Ross's smile faded as his expression became unusually soft. "If I may say so, Your Majesty, I wish you would not take the blame upon yourself. Hughes was a snake, and you did not see him any more than any of us did. You were simply trying to do what was best for your kingdom. So please, do not entertain any more guilty thoughts."

The corner of Nicholas's mouth jerked upward. "Thank you, Captain. I suppose you're right." He glanced at the hall behind him. "I better be going. Emmaline will want to hear the news."

Ross nodded. "As will Anna." He held his hand up before spinning on his heel and hurrying away.

Nicholas dashed toward the solar, his feet echoing off the marble floors.

The battle was over, and God had allowed him to redeem himself from the part he'd played in Victor's plot. Emotion swelled in him, and his eyes burned.

Thank You, merciful God, for protecting my wife and her people. You have rescued her from her enemies when I was too blind to see the wolves surrounding her.

I already defeated her true adversary centuries ago with My blood, My son. And this jackal is helpless against My saving power and might.

He quickened his pace until he practically flew through the halls. He panted as his muscles pulsed in his legs, like a wild mustang galloping across the seashore.

It was time to relieve his wife. She'd waited for rescue for far too long, and he wouldn't waste another moment now that salvation had arrived.

Emmaline sat at the solar's window as an army of dark clouds advanced across the blue battlefield. Thunder roared like battle drums. War waged in the sky.

The Konovians' battle had been raging for quite some time now, as evidenced by the faint explosions ripping through the streets. She could see debris soaring to the sky and smoke rising in the distance.

It wasn't fair that Emmaline was tucked safely in the tower, like a bird perched on top of the tree. While bullets ripped through her people's homes, Emmaline sat in silence. As the cannons roared in her people's ears, a hearth roared against Emmaline's face. As her people struggled to stay alive, she was high in her tower, unreachable to any who might try to hurt her.

Still, she knew her place was not among the warfare. She was their queen, and she could not be their godly ruler if she were dead. And besides, she was with child, and the thought of manning a cannon almost made her laugh.

But the voices condemning her would not silence, and neither would the voices frightening her. She hated herself for feeling so afraid. God had surely held the seas back until now. Why would He release them now when her people were so close to reaching the shore? Why would He not win this final battle for them?

Stop thinking like that, she told herself. *You've seen God's hand move before, and you'll see it move again.*

Her worn Bible lay on her lap, open to the fifty-sixth psalm. She whispered the words to herself, praying the words over her people. "'Be merciful unto me, O God: for man would swallow me up; He fighting daily oppresseth me. Mine enemies would daily swallow me up: For they be many that fight against me, O Thou Most High.'"

She bent her head over the pages, begging silently for mercy. "'What time I am afraid, I will trust in thee. In God I will praise His Word, in God I have put my trust; I will not fear what flesh can do unto me.'"

She closed her eyes. *God, what can mere mortals do to my people with You fighting this battle? The weapons may not be in Your hands, but my people are. Put Your angels around them. Protect them from harm. Give them—*

A sudden movement in her middle made Emmaline jump. Her heart quickened as joy and fear rushed through her. She placed her hand over her abdomen for a moment, waiting. Another movement came, like the fluttering of wings. She gasped.

She'd never felt something so strange and yet so wonderful in her life. It was proof, proof that life was within her, growing and thriving, proof that life could emerge from death.

Nicholas had to know. He would be overjoyed to find out. She closed the Bible firmly and rose from her window seat.

"Emmaline!" a man called.

She spun around. Nicholas crossed the threshold, his arms ready to embrace her. Chills sliced up her back. What news did he bring? Did he want to embrace her to comfort her or to share his joy?

She could not wait to find out and closed the distance between them. "What news?" What was that look in his eyes? Fear? Ecstasy? Relief?

He met her gaze, his own glittering with tears. "The Konovians won."

Her legs swayed as her vision spun. Nicholas caught her and held her tight. She nearly choked on the tears swelling in her throat. She'd heard the words but could scarcely believe them. The Konovians won. The Konovians *won.* After years of hiding in the shadows, the Konovians were free again. No longer did they have to run at the sound of gunfire. No longer would the smell of blood twist their stomachs. No longer did they have to fear death's toll.

Could it be true? Had God won yet another battle on their behalf?

"It's over," he whispered. His warm breath tingled against her skin, and relief washed over her like salt-kissed waves. "It's over."

Vengeance is Mine. I will defeat all your enemies before you. You and your children will live in the land peacefully, cradled beneath My wings.

Rise

Emmaline released a sharp cry as she sobbed. Now the battle was over, Victor could face the punishment that he deserved. Her family's ghosts could finally have their justice.

Tears splashed against her cheeks. *Oh, God, when does Your goodness end for sinners like me? When does it end? Do You deal with everyone as You have dealt with me? You have rescued me, my husband, and my child from death's doorstep. You have saved my people from the hands of their attackers. You have answered my prayers, even when I doubted.*

"Oh, Nicholas, I was so afraid." She swiped tears away. "When I saw you, I thought you would say—"

He leaned forward, kissing her and silencing her fears. She kissed him back and pressed into his chest.

He released her, his breath heavy on her hair. "Where's that courage you have so much of?"

She smiled. "Perhaps we should share the news with the palace."

"Good idea." He began to lead her away from the balcony.

Emmaline started to follow but stopped where she stood. The same entanglement of fear and joy came over her as another fluttering sensation rose in her belly.

Nicholas turned back, glancing over her. "What is it? Is something wrong?"

She bit her lip, laughter bubbling up her throat. She took his hand and placed it against her abdomen. He stepped closer, his brows knitting together in confusion. Another movement made its presence known, and Nicholas gasped. "I felt it!"

Emmaline smiled. "It feels real now, doesn't it?"

He glanced down at her, and the earth shook beneath her. "Impossibly real." He leaned forward and kissed her, strong and hard, as his hand came under her back. His touch lifted her to the stars.

He released her and smiled like a schoolboy.

She swung his arm gently and smiled. "Come, Your Majesty. Mustn't keep the palace staff waiting."

"Quite right, my queen. Quite right." He led her away, and the fear that had filled her moments before turned to faith.

Emmaline bit her lip as she walked behind Nicholas. Hadn't that been what God had done during these past several months—transforming her pain into His goodness? She had lived through a nightmare in a palace, yet God had placed her in another palace and made her feel safe again. She had been afraid to love again, but God had mended her heart over countless weeks. Her family had been destroyed, and God had given her a new one. Her enemy had returned to take her life, and God had taken his instead. Her journey had begun in darkness, but God had filled her night sky with stars, one-by-one, until the night sky had become a glittering array of twinkling lights. There wasn't darkness anymore, not with so many stars shining above her.

And their light would never fade.

Chapter Thirty

THE DRUMS BEAT like a heartbeat slowly rising in speed. Thick clouds darkened the sky, darkened the prison courtyard. A crow screeched, black wings fluttering in anticipation.

Emmaline and Nicholas stood on the tower, hand-in-hand. No one in the courtyard spoke. The drums pounded, pounded, pounded.

A man hooded in black dragged another man, disheveled and scowling, into the courtyard. Emmaline swallowed, the same chills she felt every time she saw

Victor blowing through her.

The executioner pushed Victor up the staircase of the gallows. Victor shouted curses upon his audience, creating a cacophony with the drums.

Nicholas's hand tightened in hers, and a deep frown darkened his face. Emmaline knew her husband was just as glad to see this man face justice as she was. During one of his many trials, Victor had confessed to poisoning Nicholas's mother.

"I killed her because her father stole the throne from my father!" Victor had shouted, pounding the table. "She didn't deserve the throne any more than my father deserved to be thrown into the streets."

Nicholas had rose from his chair, ready to strangle Victor there in the courtroom. "My mother trusted you, you devil!"

"Order, order!" the judge had bellowed.

Emmaline had tried to calm Nicholas, but she could understand his rage. All that time, he'd thought his mother had fallen ill when her life had been stolen from her. And Victor had fooled them all.

The drums grew louder as her unborn child shifted. She pressed a hand to her abdomen, wishing she could calm her husband and child. Wishing she could calm herself.

She'd never forget the look on Victor's face when he'd realized she was with child. He had shaken off the courtroom guards restraining him and flown toward her. He'd bared his teeth, his eyes wild. Nicholas had leapt between them and punched him across the face.

As the guards had yanked him back, Victor had shouted at her. "You and your child are pig spawn. I will go to my grave cursing your father's ghost. He had no right to sway the decision of Parliament. He had no right to force abdication on my father! It's his fault that my father hung himself. It's his fault my mother raised me in a brothel. Your family is a curse!" He had sworn at her as the guards had dragged him from the room.

Emmaline had scarcely believed Victor had blamed her father for everything. Victor's father had been a drunk who had caroused with harlots. He hadn't deserved the throne, and her father had been wise enough to see that. And what's more, the historical records said her father hadn't intentionally swayed Parliament's decision. He had been visiting Tregaron with his father at the time, and he'd simply had a casual conversation with one of the members of Parliament. He'd done nothing to deserve murder.

The drums roared now, the noise escalating higher and higher. The executioner pulled the noose over Victor's head. The chains around his wrists and ankles clattered. Emmaline held her breath, her neck tense.

The drums suddenly stopped, and her heartbeat took their place in her ears.

Ross stepped forward, holding a parchment of paper in his hand. "Victor Hughes, you are charged with treason and murder in the first degree against

His Majesty the King Alexander and Her Majesty the Queen Sophia, and against their children, Their Royal Highnesses Kathleen, Charlotte, Rose, and James. You are charged with murder in the first degree against the late queen of Tregaron, Her Majesty the Queen Genevieve. You are charged with treason and attempted murder in the first degree against His Majesty the King Nicholas and Her Majesty the Queen Emmaline. Finally, you are charged with attempted murder in the first degree against the Konovian people. You have been sentenced to hang by the neck until dead." He scowled and stepped back. "May God have mercy on your soul."

The executioner, his face hidden from view, stepped toward the lever.

Against her better judgement, Emmaline met Victor's gaze. Even from here, she could feel the power of his glare, feel it burning through her body. She raised her chin, refusing to cower beneath his gaze.

The executioner closed his hand over the lever.

Emmaline turned away and closed her eyes. Nicholas wrapped her in his arms and spoke softly to her. She could not watch. She had seen death in action far too many times already, even if this man was responsible for her scars.

The lever squealed.

The trap-door swung open.

A *thunk*.

Hot tears burned Emmaline's cheeks as Nicholas

rubbed her back. "He's gone." His fingers played in the loose curls falling down the back of her neck. "He's gone."

Emmaline breathed in his scent, breathed in the scent of a world without Victor. Could such a world exist? Could she live safely here?

She pulled her face free from Nicholas's shoulder. Victor's body hung from the noose, his head hanging awkwardly over his chest.

Emmaline inhaled. He really was gone. She really was free. And the new world around her was pleasant to her lungs.

Ross's heart beat fiercely like a battle drum, but for the first time in his life, the sensation was not a warning of someone's impending doom. Rather, the battle drum declared that new life was finally beginning for the Konovians, for Emmaline, and even for himself. It played a thumping song of triumph, like a song of David that Ross's mother had read to him as a young boy.

It had been nearly five months since the battle between the Konovians and Victor's followers. The battle had been long and hard, hot and fast. The Konovian village had acquired much damage to its houses, but surprisingly, no lives had been lost. The men he'd fought with had barely taken a scratch home for their wives to nurse. Meanwhile, most of Victor's followers were dead, and the few who had survived were severely injured and awaiting trial.

Ross had traded blows with many enemies as ferocious as lions, but this time when the lions had come prowling for their prey, their mouths had been shut. It was as if God's armies had surrounded them that day, carrying their spiritual swords and shields, fighting on their side.

The panging of the noon church bell aligned with his quickened heartbeat as Ross sat in the garden. Spring budded all around him. Bees buzzed in the tulips and daffodils while blue birds danced in the air above him. His fingers tapped nervously on his leg as he waited for Anna. *When is she coming?*

When he'd returned from the battle, she had been the only person he'd wanted to see. He'd thought of her constantly during the fight. When a cannonball had struck the ground where he'd stood and dirt had blown in his face, he'd thought of her red hair floating in the wind, blowing her flowery scent on his face. As his stallion had screamed and charged at the enemy, he'd remembered the way she'd kissed him before he'd left on his horse. She was his battle cry and his courage.

After the slashing of the enemy's swords had been silenced, Ross had returned to the palace, eager to tell Anna the good news. He'd found her standing at the bottom of the staircase, waiting for him. Her green eyes had ignited all the emotion he had suppressed during the battle. By God's grace, he had survived and come back to her. With a laugh, he'd swung her into his arms as she'd squealed and giggled, sending melodious notes to his ears. She'd kissed him first that time, warm and soft, melting against his chest as she'd held him close.

For the past two months, they hadn't seen each other as much. They usually spent their free time strolling in the garden, or, if it was raining, talking in the library. But she'd been quite busy of late, attending to Emmaline's needs. Emmaline hated losing her independence, but no one in the palace would heed her stubborn protests—especially Nicholas, who was adamant about his pregnant wife's needs.

But today, Emmaline had managed to convince Anna to see Ross. He had been hoping to find the right time to see Anna, and now Emmaline had given him the perfect opportunity.

Ross grinned, shaking his head. Though she was great with child, Emmaline had put her foot down and demanded that Nicholas allow her to help the Konovians. Ever since the battle had been won, more and more Konovians had left Tregaron to return to their homeland to restore it to its former glory and honor the dead. Because of the Konovian exodus, Emmaline and Nicholas had created a decree that would make Konovia a territory of the Tregaron Empire so that both she and Nicholas could rule over her people with a fair hand. Ross had always known that Emmaline would be a more than capable queen. She was born for this role.

"I saw your note, Ross."

Ross jumped and turned toward the girl behind him.

Anna laughed. "Did I frighten you?"

Ross chuckled. "Yes." He stood to his feet. He had to calm himself. He didn't want her getting ideas before it was time. He couldn't understand why his insides were in knots today of all days, after he had faced so many perils in his life. Surely this moment in his life shouldn't be all that terrifying.

She came toward him, her purple skirts fluttering. "I thought brave captains like you didn't get frightened."

"Oh, we do. Believe me." He glanced over her and admired her as one admires a flower. Her red hair was ablaze in the bright sun. "You look lovely today."

She lowered her gaze, blushing. "Thank you." She looked back up and brushed the spot over his right brow. "And your scar is most becoming." She smiled. "I knew it would be."

He smiled back and took her hand, leading her to the bench. "Here, sit down." He released her hand as she sat in front of him. He stayed standing, too anxious to sit.

The smile faded from her face. "Ross, is there something you need to tell me? You seem worried. Is something amiss?"

He counted the freckles dancing across her nose. How could there be anything amiss when she was with him? "Anna, I—I . . ." Words failed him as they had never failed him before. "I know that your mother wanted you to be with someone of stature, but I can't help wondering if that's what you want."

She bit her lip and lowered her head. "I know what my mother wants, but I know I don't want to spend my whole life trying to please her. I've wasted far too much time seeking her love already." Her eyes twinkled as she looked at him. "I want to marry for love."

He smiled, relieved to hear her words. "And I want to watch the flowers grow with you."

The smile dropped from her face as tears filled her eyes, like a glistening emerald sea. "Oh, Ross." She took a deep, shaky breath.

His heart squeezed inside him as he kneeled before her. Tighter and tighter, his heart twisted. Dampness spread on his forehead, but he had never felt so elated. His fingers trembled and fumbled as he pulled out a box from his pocket and opened it. The ruby enclosed in a gold band twinkled in the sunbeams.

Anna's mouth fell open. "Oh, Ross! It's beautiful!"

Tears burned his eyes. After years of loneliness, he had found someone who understood what it was like to live among the ruins of a broken life. Something hard swelled in his throat. "Anna Edwards, will you give me the honor of becoming my wife?"

She smiled at him, tears of her own trickling down her face. "Yes, of course I will." A sob choked her soft voice.

He slid the ring down her finger. Without a

second thought, Ross lifted her from the bench and swung her around, laughing the way he had when he was a child. That was it. He'd figured it out—she was his elixir. She awakened him to the youth of heart he'd once possessed. She pulled at the ghosts of his past as if they were nothing more than cobwebs. And the spirit of his mother's son came back to life.

He set her on the ground and kissed her, warmly, sweetly, tenderly, making sure she felt every ounce of love she'd been denied during her childhood.

Oh, God, You were being good to me when You denied me Emmaline's heart, weren't You? You took the queen from me but saved this flower for me. And oh, wasn't she sweet?

Emmaline closed her eyes and slipped her feet out of her shoes, wiggling her toes through the grass. The sensation tickled her skin and sent pulsing sensations of pleasure through her. In response, the baby kicked a foot into her abdomen. Emmaline smiled at the movement within her, raising her chin and bathing in the warmth of the sun.

It was such a lovely spring day. This morning, she had spoken to Nicholas's advisors about her plan for the Konovians. She and Nicholas had decided on an amount of money to give to the Konovians to help them get started in rebuilding the country. Ever since it had been decided that Konovia would become a part of the Commonwealth, even more Konovian families had traveled back to their native land. Ross had issued several guards to accompany the families to guard them from wild animals and to help them rebuild their homes. More and more Konovians were leaving Tregaron every day, and Emmaline could hardly wait until they were all reunited.

The baby kicked again, and Emmaline gasped, chuckling. It would not be long until the Konovians' number grew by one.

She had watched in awe as she had grown over the past months. She had been too young to remember her mother carrying her younger brother, and she had scarcely been around any other pregnant women. She had not known her body could shape and grow the way it had. She had not known what it was like to carry such a wonderful treasure within her. She had not known that she, with a past so marred by death, could give life.

She was so swollen now that she felt as if she might tip forward as she walked. Sometimes she could hardly believe how big she had gotten. The girls hardly let her go anywhere on her own, but she was grateful she had successfully snuck away from them long enough to drink in this glorious sunlight and think. It was good to be out here. It was as if she could breathe more freely.

She had been glad to hear the news of Ross and Anna's engagement. She loved them both equally, but she was especially happy for Ross after everything he had done for her. She couldn't imagine a better girl for

Ross to marry, and she would enjoy seeing him experience the same happiness that she had.

Men's chuckling came from the distance. Nicholas and a dozen of his advisors were standing on the lawn, playing croquet. Nicholas cheered as his ball made it through. Emmaline smiled, placing her hand on her middle. Nicholas had thought it wise to develop friendships with his advisors. He didn't want men like Victor or Dudley back into his circle. Emmaline thought it was wise, too, and she enjoyed seeing him so happy.

Though she didn't want him to see *her* right now. If he knew she was out here on her own, he'd march her right back into the palace. She knew he was only trying to take care of her and their child, but she couldn't spend another moment inside those walls. She needed to be out here in the warmth.

It had been a long nine months. She had spent many nights in bed next to Nicholas, listening to him as he talked about everything he wanted to do once the baby came. They had discussed many names long into the night. Sometimes it seemed as if making a treaty with a bear would be easier than choosing a name for their child.

A cloud swept the sun from view, and Emmaline grimaced as the ache returned to her back. Pain in her abdomen and back had come and gone all day. When it had happened a few days ago, Dr. Reid had said her body was merely preparing for childbirth. She closed her eyes again, trying to ignore the ache.

Her family would have been happy to see her life turn out so wonderfully. Her parents would have rejoiced over the birth of a grandchild, and her sisters would have loved becoming aunts. Her brother would have promised to teach the child how to climb trees, just as they had done as children.

Even during the hard days when Emmaline knew her mother wouldn't be with her during the birth and her sisters wouldn't dote over her sleeping infant, she knew God was with her. The last year and a half had proved just that.

He had been so good to her. Healing her scars. Giving her love. Keeping her safe. Defeating her enemies. Bringing friends to her side. Growing a child within her. What had she done to deserve such goodness? Who was she that she would be so blessed? How had she—

Pain gripped her abdomen. Emmaline tried to gasp but could not take in enough air. She stiffened, afraid moving would make it worse. She blinked and tried to breathe. Her heart galloped against her breastbone. Had she moved on from preparation? Was this the moment that she had been waiting for?

Oh, dear Lord. Already?

Terror and ecstasy seized her. Was this the moment her body had been growing and shaping for, the moment her child would enter the world God had made, the moment when her life would change forever?

Perhaps she was wrong and getting excited for

nothing. How foolish would she look if she waddled over to her husband to tell him the child was coming and then turned out to be wrong? The very picture made her want to giggle behind her hand.

Another pain took her captive again. This was her moment. This was her time. And it was time to give life.

Emmaline leaned on the statue of an angel for support as the pain rolled through her. "Nicholas!" she called. The pain stole her breath. He could not hear her. But though the pain climbed, it would not subdue her. "*Nicholas!*"

Nicholas and his advisors turned. Nicholas's smile dropped as he saw her leaning against the statue. He dropped his mallet and rushed across the lawn toward her.

He cupped her face in his hands and panted, his eyes round. "What's the matter, my love?"

She gulped in a breath. "It's getting worse."

He blinked, paling. "Are you—?"

"Yes."

He smiled, laughing. "Oh, Emmaline!" He embraced her, and she clung to him, gripping his shoulders, her knuckles tense as the pain climbed. She forced a smile, though her breath swept away faster and faster, though her mind was spinning and spinning.

He leapt away from her as if she were on fire. "Let's get you inside. The baby can't very well be born in the garden." He swept her into his arms, and she wrapped her arms around his neck. He turned to his

Rise

advisors and waved. "Sorry, gents. We'll have to wrap up the game another day. The child is coming."

The men cheered and clapped as they made their way up the stairs, slowly but surely.

The pain rushed and rushed as he carried her through the palace. Nicholas held her tightly and spoke softly to her. She prayed silently. *Oh, dear Lord. Help me. Help me, Lord, help me.*

They came to a stop. Emmaline tightened her grip as she lifted her eyes and gazed at the staircase spiraling upwards in front of them. She bit her lip, her skin turning to ice. How was she going to do this? How was she going to give birth without Nicholas by her side?

Nicholas smiled, even as his eyes flickered anxiously. "'When you go through deep waters, I will be with you. When you go through rivers of difficulty, you will not drown. When you walk through the fire of oppression, you will not be burned up; the flames will not consume you.'" He waved his thumb over her leg as he cradled her.

She smiled, her eyes burning as tears gathered in her throat. "I love you."

He leaned forward and kissed her forehead, then began the mount up the staircase.

Even amidst the fear, she could not help but smile as the child within her pressed against her middle. Death's day was done. Now was the time to give life.

Nicholas paced the hall outside his bedchamber, his hands behind his back, his heart strangled in his chest. He glanced at the door, waiting for it to open, praying to hear the midwife say he could enter. But he heard nothing.

Perhaps that was a good thing. If he could not hear Emmaline crying out, perhaps she wasn't in much pain. Still, his heart ran at a pace that his lungs could not keep up with. Sweat dampened his back, his forehead, and his palms.

He dropped to the floor and put his hands against his head. Women had been doing this since creation, and Emmaline was strong. But now that the time had come, it felt as if Nicholas's world was quaking.

He couldn't forget the look of fear in Emmaline's eyes as he'd left the room. She had been happily awaiting the child's coming, but he understood that she was afraid now that the moment had arrived. It was all new to her, and she had no comrade to do battle with her. He shouldn't have left her. She had never left him, so why he had so easily given in to the midwife's insistence?

He ran trembling fingers through his hair, biting the inside of his cheek. He didn't understand why he couldn't be in the bedchamber to help Emmaline. He knew there was little he could do, but he could hold her hand as she had when he'd been shot. He could encourage her as she had when he'd mourned over his mother's death. He could remind her to breathe, could try to ease her pain, could wipe away her tears.

But the midwife—and tradition, the old fool—had insisted that he stay outside the bedchamber.

Hadn't he been outside the bedchamber enough? Though he knew that God was in the room, he still didn't feel peace.

A muffled cry came through the door. Nicholas sprang to his feet. His hand dangled over the knob, uncertain of what he should do. Perhaps there was some reason unbeknownst to him that forbade him from the room.

Another cry. Louder. It turned his skin to ice.

Dash tradition! She needed him in there. She was his wife, and that was his child! He swung the door open and stormed into the room.

Emmaline's maids flocked around him as soon as he entered, like seagulls surrounding beached prey on the shore.

"Your Majesty, you must leave," Eleanor pleaded. "The midwife has everything under control."

"I know you're worried, Your Majesty, but Emmaline is safe," Lydia insisted.

From the bedchamber suite, Emmaline's cries crested higher and higher. Nicholas's nerves buzzed until he felt as if he might go mad.

Nicholas shook his head. He did not care if the midwife had everything under control. His wife needed him just as he had needed her. "I must be with her." He burst through them, despite their incessant squawking.

Nicholas dashed toward the bed, finding Emmaline

huffing with a tight look on her face. She was so flat in the bed, the mattress practically consumed her.

"Breathe, Your Majesty! You can do this!" the midwife cried. Her wimple caught the evening light and mimicked angel wings.

Emmaline unleashed a roaring groan that ended in exhausted sobs.

The midwife sighed heavily and then turned and saw him. Her brows jumped in surprise. "Your Majesty! What are you doing in here?"

He ignored her question, more concerned with Emmaline's condition. "Why hasn't the baby come yet? She's been like this since yesterday afternoon."

She opened and closed her mouth, as if uncertain that she should answer him. "I am not sure, Your Majesty. She has been pushing for a long time. Her waters broke last night, and if the baby is not born soon, it will not bode well."

Nicholas had seen this before. Three months into his military campaign, Nicholas and his platoon had discovered a French village smoldering in flames from a German attack. A laboring young woman with a tight expression on her face had been among the survivors. She had pushed and pushed, but the baby had refused to come. Tom had brought out a rag and motioned for her to tug the cloth on one side while he tugged on the other. Tom's trick had helped the girl to bear down, and the baby had been born only minutes after.

Nicholas would not allow his wife and child to be

in this kind of danger, especially with so much torment for Emmaline. He snatched the cloth from the wash basin and hurried toward the bed.

"What are you doing, Your Majesty?" the midwife cried.

"Helping my wife." He leapt on the end of the bed and crawled on his hands and knees to Emmaline's side.

Sweat glistened on her forehead as she looked at him. Her eyes spun, and a deep flush burned her cheeks. "Nicholas . . ." she breathed.

He smoothed the damp curls from her forehead. "This will all be over soon, my love. Just do what I say." He handed her the cloth. "Tug on this side, and I'll tug the other. Bear down when you're tugging. All right?"

She nodded, clenching her lips as another wave of pain crashed over her.

He crawled back toward the end of the bed.

"This is not necessary, Your Majesty." The midwife frowned. "I have forceps in my bag."

"Believe me, this will work." He glanced at Emmaline. "Bear down, Emmaline!"

He gripped the cloth, tugging against Emmaline's even tighter grip. Heat radiated off her body. She jerked upwards, her groan spiraling into a cry as she bore down. The fibers in his fingers burned as he yanked at the cloth. Emmaline gasped for breath.

"Pull, Emmaline, pull!"

"The head's crowning!" the midwife cheered after

a few moments.

Emmaline swung her head back, the cords in her neck pulsing through her skin. She pulled the cloth closer and closer toward her. He fought her grip, ready for it to be over. Ready for her pain to end. Ready for her cries to cease. Ready to meet his child.

"The head is born!" the midwife cried.

Tears stung Nicholas's eyes. He glanced down and saw a patch of dark hair on a tiny head. Dear God, it was real. He was really a father.

"One last push, Your Majesty!"

"Come on, Emmy!"

Nicholas jerked the cloth toward him. He could barely see past his misty eyes. Emmaline wrenched the cloth back toward her face. Her swollen abdomen rose higher and higher until it fell. Her groans finally ceased.

Nicholas's gaze dropped down. There, in between his wife's raised knees, was his child. Mewling like a kitten, roving its head around, baptized in blood and water. A girl, no less. His heart burst as he glanced at her glorious face.

"Splendid job, Your Majesty!" the midwife cheered. "Well done!"

Emmaline sank into the mattress, covering her mouth with her hand as she sobbed.

Hot, plentiful tears gathered in Nicholas's eyes and drenched his chin. "Oh, wonderful God. Merciful God." He couldn't keep the emotion from his voice.

There she was. A long, fleshy, pink baby with ten

fingers and ten toes. Her long lashes were sprinkled with water. The evening sunlight crested around her and bathed her in an unearthly glow. She cried loudly, her perfect lips trembling. That was his child. The fruit of his and Emmaline's love. His daughter.

He scooped her up, and she silenced her cries immediately. She nestled her head against his chest. Love overpowered and consumed him until he was certain it would break him.

The midwife took the baby from him to clean her and wrap her. Nicholas scrambled to Emmaline's side with trembling limbs and a whirling mind. She was still crying as she gazed at him.

"Oh, you clever girl," Nicholas whispered. "Do you know what you've just done?"

"Is the baby all right?" Her lips were parted as she panted.

"All right? Emmaline, if I had known I was going to be visited by an angel, I would have become a holier man."

She smiled, eyes glassy. "What is it? A boy or a girl?"

He grinned so deeply, he was sure he would shatter his face. "A girl, and she's just as glorious as her mother is."

Emmaline's lip trembled. "A little girl." She looked toward the midwife, who leaned over a table and dipped a cloth into the water basin. She glanced back toward him and stroked his cheekbone. "You wonderful man. You helped me."

The sunlight poured on Emmaline's face and enriched her curls. She was so lovely, so wonderful, so marvelous. How she had withstood all that pain was beyond him. He caught her cheek in his palm. "I love you."

Fresh tears glistened in her eyes. "And I you."

The midwife came to the bedside. "Here she is, Your Majesties. A daughter."

Emmaline reached and took her baby in her arms. She gasped as she lay their daughter upon her breast. "Oh, God." She slammed her eyes shut as tears rolled down her cheeks. "She's perfect."

Nicholas glanced down at his daughter's pink face again. He had never seen such a tiny nose or pair of lips. *God, she's so beautiful. Surely she belongs to a better man than I. Surely I don't deserve her.*

The baby yawned and raised her fists to her face, and Nicholas felt every fortress he'd ever built tumble down. He smoothed his knuckle down his daughter's cheek.

His daughter. His *daughter*. When would he believe she was his? When would he believe that he had a daughter?

"Oh, Nicholas, she's so beautiful," Emmaline breathed. She stroked the baby's hair. "I've no idea what I'm doing," she whispered. "I'm afraid I'll break her."

"You carried her for nine months, my love, and she is perfect." He pushed a hair back from her face and tucked it behind her ear. "*You're* perfect." He leaned forward and pressed his lips against hers.

Standing at the altar on their wedding day, watching her come to him in a cloud of white, Nicholas hadn't thought it possible to love her any more than he already had. But over the past several months, as she had grown and grown with their child within her, he'd been proven wrong. He'd fallen in love with the shape of her. And as he kissed her here in their bedchamber, he knew he'd spend his whole life falling in love with her. And he couldn't think of a better way to live.

Emmaline glanced down at her daughter sleeping in her arms, her tiny eyelashes casting shadows over her round and pink cheeks. Even after two months had passed, Emmaline still found herself occasionally doubting that this child, with her constant grin and her father's blue eyes, was really hers. That she had really nurtured this new being within her body for nine months, that this infant had slipped from her body. Surely it was a dream. Surely she and Nicholas were being visited by an angel that would return home soon. But every morning that Emmaline awoke to feed her child proved otherwise. This angel was here to stay.

A saintly presence had fallen over the castle ever since Clara had been born, the same kind of saintly presence that had fallen over the castle at Christmas. During those long months of growing and aching and dreaming, Emmaline hadn't known just how much a baby could change everything. She hadn't known how much love she was capable of feeling until she'd held her wrinkly daughter against her chest for the first time.

Before Clara was born, she had thought it was impossible to love Nicholas any more than she already did, but she was wrong. There had been many nights that Nicholas had rocked Clara to sleep. He looked especially handsome wearing his oversized undershirt in the evenings, holding their child and singing softly to her. Emmaline had whispered tearful words of gratitude to God the first time she'd awakened to her husband's lullabies.

The girls—now Clara's honorary aunts—would dote on her every chance they got, especially Eleanor and Anna. Julia teased Anna that she would be next to have a child, with her and Ross's wedding in just a few weeks. Anna had only blushed, but Emmaline had never seen her so happy. Anna made Ross smile in a way Emmaline had never seen before. She was glad for both her and Ross. She knew they would make a handsome pair.

The carriage bumped along the street. Emmaline held Clara closer so that the constant moving would not awaken her. She was being christened today, and Emmaline did not want her crying during the ceremony.

Emmaline smiled. Clara looked especially beautiful today. During the final months of her pregnancy, the Konovian women had secretly gathered together and sewed a christening gown for her child. About a week after the birth, they had come to the palace and requested a personal audience with the queen. Emmaline had struggled to control her emotions when they'd presented her with the long dress of ivory lace embroidered with yellow peonies, the flower of Konovia.

"She looks like her mother," Nicholas said, nestling against Emmaline's side.

"I think she has your eyes, though, don't you?" Emmaline glanced at him.

"Well, you can't give me all the credit. I'm told that all of my mother's personal maidservants insisted that I had my father's eyes."

Emmaline played with the ribbon of Clara's bonnet tied beneath her plump chin. "Do you suppose they'll be with us today?"

"Our families?" Nicholas said softly.

"Yes." She bit the inside of her cheek, trying to ignore the sting in her chest. She had healed over the past year, but the wound was still there. It always would be until she saw them again. She knew Nicholas felt the same. "Clara never met any of them."

"I think they're always here with us, but perhaps even more so on days like today." He smiled gently at her. "And what's more, God is with us and with Clara. And no one can ever take Him away."

Tears burned behind Emmaline's eyes as she leaned into Nicholas's chest. "How did I get so lucky?"

Nicholas tipped her chin up and gazed into her eyes. "I ask myself the same question every day." He leaned forward and kissed her.

Emmaline closed her eyes and savored the touch of his lips and the sparks he sent shimmering through her. Never would she have thought the boy watching her playing piano would vow his life to her and become the father of her child. Never would she have imagined her life would mend as well as it did. Never would she have believed it could all be true, that God could care so much for her.

Clara awakened as Emmaline and Nicholas climbed the staircase into the abbey. She yawned, sucking in her lower lip, and then grinned up at Emmaline.

"Just in time," Nicholas joked. "She might have been frightened had she awakened when the priest sprinkles the water over her head."

Emmaline laughed, shaking her head.

They walked together down the long aisle between the crowded pews, Clara gnawing on her fist the whole way. Emmaline greeted her guests with a smile. Ross and Anna, chosen to become Clara's godparents, stood proudly at the altar with the priest. The priest read from the Scriptures and focused on the story of John the Baptist jumping for joy in Elizabeth's womb after he'd heard the cry of Mary.

"Children are a gift from the Lord, and, as the Scriptures state, have the capacity to love and worship God our Father even from the womb itself. We as a nation will pray for the young princess's health, but even more so, we will pray for her faith to be as strong as the faith of her father and mother."

Emmaline nodded. She would indeed pray for her

Clara every night. She had often seen her own parents bowed low on their hands and knees, uttering her and her siblings' names as they pleaded to God. She and Nicholas would do the same.

"Your Majesties, is it your will that your child should be baptized in the faith of the Church which we have professed in you?" the priest asked, looking at them with raised eyebrows.

Emmaline glanced at Nicholas and melted at the smile on his face. "Yes," they said in unison.

When the time came for Clara to be christened, Emmaline held her baby over the baptismal font. The priest splashed the water over Clara's head three times. "Clara Genevieve Marian, I baptize you in the name of the Father, the Son, and the Holy Spirit."

Emmaline bit her lip and urged the tears away at the uttering of her child's name. Surely her child was destined for greatness with such a name. She was called Clara because of the light that God had shone in Emmaline's darkness. She was called Genevieve after her grandmother and because Emmaline wanted her daughter to be a woman of the people, as the name implied. She was called Marian, too, because she was not only born of her parents' love but also of God's grace.

Emmaline glanced at Nicholas, whose eyes were glistening with tears. Her heart expanded so much, she was afraid it would burst in her body. Never had he been so beautiful.

"May this child become as famous as Moses,

through whom God parted the Red Sea to make a way for His people. May this child become as gracious as Ruth, who sacrificed her honor for others and was honored by God in return. May this child become as strong as Daniel, who did not compromise his faith even in the face of lions."

Emmaline closed her eyes. *Oh, God, let the words of this priest be true. Clara is not my child—she is Yours. You are her Father, and You will protect her and raise her up as You did for me. Let her grow healthy and strong. Let her become all You desire her to become.*

"May she be filled with the Spirit when the time comes," the priest said. "May she choose the right path for herself and walk in righteousness. May she always have unending joy"—Clara squealed in delight—"as she appears to already have." The priest grinned as many of the guests chuckled. "May she never lose heart and always have faith."

Emmaline smiled, glancing from her husband to her child. She and Nicholas would grow their daughter's faith by telling her their story. The story of how God had brought an orphan girl into the palace and into the prince's heart. The story of how He had removed her crown of ashes and given her a crown of stars instead. How God had called her to rise.

Acknowledgements

I BEGAN WORKING on *Rise* two years ago during a writing workshop at Liberty University. Because this novel took two years to create, there are quite a few people for me to thank.

First, I must begin with God because I wouldn't be a writer without Him. God, You put this storytelling dream in my heart when I was eleven years old. I couldn't stop making up stories in my head, so You led me to make them up on paper, too. You have also blessed me so much through *Rise*. During this writing journey, you've given me friendships, joy, and knowledge, beautiful gifts that I never expected to receive simply by writing a story. Thank You, Jesus, for your amazing love.

I also want to thank my parents. I wouldn't be a writer without them, either. Mom and Dad, you taught me how to pursue my dreams. For the past twelve years, you've known that my ultimate goal was to become a writer, and you've always supported me. I know that this dream is difficult to attain, but you have been patient with me. You also raised me to love Jesus, and that was so important for God's calling on my life. I'd also like to thank Dad for telling me I should read the book of Esther. I'm not sure you remember that since it was a long time ago, but I have the memory of an elephant, so thank you. It was life-changing. In addition, I'd like to thank Mom for giving up her teaching dreams to stay home and teach me. You fueled my love of Anastasia and Esther and taught me how to be a skillful reader and writer. You have been intentional and thoughtful in your encouragement, and you have taught me how to be a strong young woman of God. I love you both.

Thank you to my siblings. You three have taught me what it means to be human and what it means to belong in a family. We're all grown up now and are pursuing our own dreams, and I'm so proud of all of you. Thank you for encouraging me on my writing journey.

I would also like to thank my friends Addy and Hannah, who read *Rise* in its raw beginnings. You both

Rise

have encouraged me so much, and I am so grateful for the praise and constructive criticism you've given me. I am also very grateful to call you both my friends. You make my life so much better.

My creative writing professor was also brilliant. Thank you, Ruth Ronk, for helping me become the writer God wants me to be. You were so encouraging to me when *Rise* was in its zygotic phase.

I'd like to thank my graphic designer, Elena, who designed this beautiful cover and captured the story so well in your cover design. Thank you!

Thank you to everyone who followed my Instagram account and so kindly interacted with my posts. Your encouragement and excitement for *Rise* means so much to me.

I'd also like to thank my sweet shih-Tzu, Truffles. Sadly, you are no longer here, but you are always remembered. During the past two years of writing *Rise*, I could count on you to snuggle on my lap and keep me company in my room. I will always treasure our writing time together. Your love for me gave me the strength to keep going, and I can't wait to see you again.

I want to thank Queen Esther and Anastasia Romanov. I live in an age where godly influencers are scarce, so you both gave me women I could look up to. I can't wait to meet you both in eternity.

Last but not least, I want to thank you, the reader. Thank you for picking up this book. For over ten years, I have dreamed of someone like you reading my stories. Thank you for making that dream come true.

About the Author

GRACE IRWIN IS a Christian historical romance and fantasy author. She graduated summa cum laude from Liberty University where she earned her Bachelor of Science in English and Writing. As a storyteller, her mission is to draw her readers to faith in Jesus. She lives in coastal North Carolina with her parents and siblings. When she's not creating stories and crafting characters, she's listening to music, shell-hunting with her sister, spending time with friends and family, watching romantic or adventurous films, or dreaming about her next trip to Disney World.

Made in United States
Cleveland, OH
03 April 2025